ELLA

'Uri Geller was the last person I expected to turn into a first-rate novelist. Yet that is exactly what he has done. *Ella* has a sharpness of observation and insight into character that reveal the true novelist . . . it is the most exhilarating novel I have read in years' COLIN WILSON

ELLA

Uri Geller

HEADLINE
FEATURE

First published in Great Britain in 1998
by HEADLINE BOOK PUBLISHING

A HEADLINE FEATURE edition

10 9 8 7 6 5 4 3 2 1

All characters in this publication are fictitious and any
resemblance to real persons, living or dead, is purely coincidental.

A catalogue record for this book is available
from the British Library

ISBN 0 7472 7643 9 (softback)
ISBN 0 7472 2127 8 (hardback)

Typeset by Avon Dataset Ltd, Bidford-on-Avon, Warks

Printed and bound in Great Britain by
Mackays of Chatham PLC, Chatham, Kent

HEADLINE BOOK PUBLISHING
A division of Hodder Headline PLC
338 Euston Road
London NW1 3BH

DEDICATION

To all sick children around the world – may this story come true soon.

Part of the proceeds of *Ella* will go to the Bristol Children's Hospital and to the Great Ormond Street Hospital For Children.

ACKNOWLEDGEMENTS

My very special thanks to Nicola and Christopher Stevens for their magnificent support and assistance with the researching and editing of this book.

My thanks to Dan Computers for their fantastic and reliable technology.

My thanks also to Lanier for their unstoppable fax machines and copiers.

PART ONE

CHAPTER ONE

Ella said, 'Stop fighting,' but nobody listened.

It was her birthday, and the table was set with her birthday tea. Ella and her brother were not supposed to talk at the table, not unless they were spoken to. Her parents were talking, but they weren't talking to her. When Ella worked up the courage to say, 'Stop fighting,' she was not brave enough to say it very loudly. Nobody paid any attention.

Her father kept mashing his fork into a slice of birthday cake. 'I ain't discussing it no more,' he was telling Ella's mother, over and over.

Juliette nodded, and nodded, and stared at her slice of the cake without ever eating it. 'I'm not asking to discuss it. I know very well the score.' She tried hard not to copy the Bristol slang her husband used. She tried hardest when she was angry. Juliette would not say, 'I ain't'. She said, 'I'm not,' in a tremulous French accent. 'I'm not asking to discuss it.'

Ella's brother, Frank, said nothing. He had already eaten his slice, and was waiting silently for the chance of another. Frank knew he wasn't supposed to say much.

It was a good cake. Ella's Auntie Sylvie had baked it in the shape of a heart, and dressed it in frills of pink icing, with fourteen pink candles arranged in a small heart at the Centre. Auntie Sylvie had not been there to see Ella blow out the candles and pierce the brittle pink shell with a bread knife, because Ella's father had lain down the law: 'I ain't having her coming and sitting down, all coo-ey coo-ey and luvvy duvvy, when I'm trying to have my tea. Make me throw it all up again.'

'Of course, you don't ever have to see my sister,' Juliette said. 'It is your house. Of course we have only the guests you wish. All I am saying, Ella is so fond of Sylvie.'

'I don't care who Ella's fond of. What I'm telling you is this: you have your sister Sylvie round here if you wants. Just don't think I'm going to be here at the same time.'

That debate had been at breakfast. When Ella came home from school at half past four, Auntie Sylvie had brought the cake round and gone again. Auntie Sylvie wanted to see her brother-in-law even less than he wanted to see her.

The argument at tea was about something else entirely. It started as Juliette was lighting the candles.

'Come on, Ella, hurry up and get them blown out,' her father told her.

'It is my fault,' answered her mother. 'Always I am so clumsy with matches.' She shook out another and scrabbled with the box to light the next. 'But why are you in such a rush to eat the cake? Do you decide you like my sister's cooking now? There, Ella, that's the last one now. Before you blow, we have to sing to you.'

'Oh, for pity's sake!' Ken Wallis started to stand up, checked his watch and sat down again.

'Happy birthday to you,' sang Ella's mother, and Frank chimed in. 'Happy birthday, oh of course, it's Wednesday,' Juliette added innocently.

'Happy birthday to you,' sang Frank, squinting at their father from the corner of his eye. Ken was not singing.

'Wednesday, who is it Wednesday?' murmured Juliette. 'Marcia Wednesday, of course.'

'Happy birthday dear Ella, happy-birthday-to-you,' rushed Frank's little voice.

'Are you going to blow those out?' Her father's voice implied Ella could expect a wallop if she didn't do as she was told, sharpish.

'Marcia likes you to be at her house by seven, doesn't she? Well done, Ella, all out in one breath. But does she not forgive you to be a tiny bit late, if it is your daughter's birthday? Cut the cake now, darling.'

'I ain't discussing it now. You knows that. Children present.'

'I am not asking to discuss it. I know very well the score. Give the first slice to your father, Ella.'

'I ain't discussing it no more,' insisted Ken.

'I am not asking.'

'Stop fighting,' said Ella, her chin pressed against the lace neck of her birthday dress. Her parents ignored her.

'I'm here, ain't I?' said her father. 'What more do you want?'

'I want you to do what is the best thing, of course you know best.' Juliette spoke painstakingly, her hand picking at the tablecloth the whole time. She had never learned to think in English – she had not known one word of the language fourteen years and nine months ago. She had simply thumbed a ride away from her father's house in Orleanais and ended up driving with Ken and his friends, to Britain, to Bristol, in a VW Kombi camper van.

Her thoughts were always in French, and she had to translate carefully. 'Naturally it is Wednesday.'

'Yeah. Wednesday! And?'

'Like you are saying. Marcia Wednesday.'

'I never mentioned Marcia. It was you what mentioned Marcia.'

'Of course,' his wife said instantly. 'I am wrong. I said it. I am sorry.'

'I never brought it up. That was you what says it in front of the kids.'

Ella had not met Marcia. She didn't remember hearing the name before. Marcia would never come to the house, or sit in church with them. Still, Ella knew who Marcia was. There had been Marcias all her life. Ken would go out of the house about seven o'clock with a sports bag over his shoulder, and his chair would be empty at breakfast the next morning. Wednesday nights and Sunday nights.

'Of course Sunday night is different,' said Juliette. 'Not Marcia. Aileen? I hope I am right. I am so bad with names.'

Ken leant towards her. His broad shoulders were heavy with menace. 'Ai-*lish*,' he corrected her with a cruel smile. 'Her name's Ailish.' His weight loomed over the table. This word Ailish, this was going to be the last word on the subject. He wasn't discussing it further.

Juliette nodded. Pick, pick, went her raw nails on the white cotton tablecloth.

'Ella!' Ken Wallis sat back and glared at his daughter. 'Your mother told you to blow those candles out.'

One thin pink stalk was burning on the cake.

'I did,' said Ella.

Her father regarded her with contempt. 'What's that then?'

Ella stood up and snuffed it. The flame flared back.

'It is a joke candle?' Juliette asked anxiously. She never understood jokes.

'You been spending your pocket money on stupid jokes, Frank?' demanded his father. Frank sat rigid, his head quivering from side to side. The candle was not a joke.

Ella was still standing. She blew the flame out again. The wick smouldered for a second before burning once more.

Ken spat on his fingers and pinched the flame, pulling the fragile stalk from its holder and crushing it in his palm. 'Out,' he said.

Juliette and Ella kept their eyes down. Frank broke the silence – 'Dad, can I have another slice of cake?'

'Is your room tidy? Go on, then'

Before Frank could even wipe his knife, the cake landed icing-down by Juliette's chair. It hit the floor with a thump that shook the table.

'Ella! What do you think you're doing?' Her father seized her by the lace collar and pulled her out of the chair.

'Oh my God look at the mess,' shrieked Juliette.

'I don't believe you just did that!' Ken bellowed.

'I didn't,' answered Ella, hanging terrified from his fist. She knew better than to struggle when her father had a grip on her.

'Don't lie to me! I saw you do it.'

'I didn't touch it,' she pleaded.

'Don't,' and he was shaking her hard, 'don't you lie to me, my girl, don't you try, don't you make it worse.'

'My God, the stain will never come out.'

'Don't you blaspheme, woman,' he warned his wife. The sponge and the jam filling were ground into the polyester pile as though the cake had been trampled by boots. 'Ella's going to get the stain out. Aren't you, my girl?'

'Yes, Dad. Yes.'

'Dad,' implored Frank, daring to hang on his father's other arm. 'Ella didn't touch it.'

'Well, who threw it then? It weren't you what threw it?'

'No, honestly. It just fell.'

'Don't you stick up for her Frank, she ain't worth it. That cake was in the middle of the table. She just deliberately chucked it on the floor.'

'I didn't, honest Dad honest.'

'I SAW YOU!'

But he hadn't seen her. In one instant the cake had been suspended, upside-down, at the edge of the table and then an invisible hand had driven it down on the floor, so hard that bits of cream and jam spattered the walls.

'I ought to make you eat it. On your hands and knees. Every bit of it.' Ella barely had one toe on the floor, and her father's face was hot against her lips and nose. 'Are you going to keep lying to me?'

'No.'

'Did you throw that cake?'

'Yes.'

'Why?'

'Don't know.'

'Get it cleared up.' He shoved her away. Pointing at Frank, he added, 'Don't you help her. And if there's one crumb when I get back . . . just one.' He slammed the door, and then the front door banged. Ella, kneeling beside her mother's chair, began to scrape the pink lumps onto a plate.

Ella was small for her age. Her silver-blonde hair hung all the way down her back. Across her forehead it was cropped harshly, like a helmet around her white face. Her father had started to insist she tie it up at the back, or else have it shorn to neck-length. It was indecent to walk around with hair that long. Just vanity. She wasn't a child any longer, he declared, and vanity in a woman was an evil.

Ella didn't think she was evil, but she did wash her hair every night, and brushed it morning and night. The monotonous movement of her hand against the flowing silk of her hair helped shut out all her feelings.

She sat on the edge of her bed on her birthday, when every speck of cake had been polished out of the carpet. Frank was asleep in the next room. Her mother was downstairs – Ella could hear the blurred echo of the *Nine o'Clock News*.

With only a thin chink of light from her bedroom door, Ella brushed and brushed her hair until her arm ached. She liked the tug of each tress at her scalp and the watery touch as each length slid over the back of her hand.

The crack of light from the landing shone on her wall. She had painted a picture of an angel during school art class, and cut around it, and Blu-tacked it to the wallpaper. The angel had blond hair, which flowed out into blond wings. The wings were half folded, and the tips reached to the angel's sandals. Ella thought the Archangel Gabriel must have looked like this when he appeared to Mary.

She had not told this to her father, when he saw the angel on her wall. 'What's that?' he demanded, during one of his spot-checks for tidiness in her bedroom.

'I made it at school.'

'Is that what they teaches you? Blaspheming? D'you know what's the Second Commandment?'

'Thou shalt not make thee no graven image.'

'*Any* graven image. God speaks proper English, not like you.'

'Sorry, Dad. It's just a painting, 'cos the wall looked bare.' She always spoke so softly to her father, he could barely hear her. 'All my friends, they got posters up, but I knows you don't like that.'

'Any graven image,' repeated Ken, 'or any likeness of any thing that is in Heaven above.'

'Yes.'

'You knew that, and you went ahead and made a picture.' He shook his head and left the room. But he hadn't told her to take it down.

An angel came to Ella in her dream. Tonight, the birthday night, was not the first time she had dreamed it, but it frightened her more than ever tonight. The dream had been returning for weeks now, always beginning under the water. She was fighting towards a point of light, bubbles streaming from her lips and nose, with a whirling rush in her ears. Ella kicked and struggled, but a strong hand was clamped to her ankle. Its fingers were clawing her to the bone. She reached up and up for the light, and another hand caught her wrist. It was a small hand, weak, like a child's, and it tugged desperately at her arm. Against the merciless grip of the hand at her ankle, this feeble rescuer was pitiful and powerless.

She always managed to get her lips to the surface in this dream, and gulp down a breath sprayed with droplets of icy water. The droplets choked her and she opened her mouth again, and this time what rushed in was much more water than air. Ella had never swum even in the sea, was barely able to paddle a width of the warm, chlorinated baths at the leisure centre, but the water flooding into her lungs now tasted terrifyingly real. It was saturated with mud and flecked with debris, and just above her eyes it was pitted and rippled as though heavy rain was hosing down on the surface.

She twisted down through the dark water, scrabbling at the remorseless fingers that clamped her leg. And she kept fighting to the light at the surface, but the surface got further and further away, until her lips could no longer break into the air and when she heaved another breath it was all water.

Ella's dream began to drift now – she did not leave the water but the sensations became less intense. Her leg numbed. Her arm drifted above her but she could not tell if she were reaching for the pitiful, childlike hand of her helpless rescuer. The water in her lungs ceased to be cold – or perhaps her lungs ceased to be warm. The light still lingered above her.

She felt the tickle of her hair as it washed around her face.

The light grew brighter. It throbbed, and the throbbing built to a steady pulse. With each pulse she saw more clearly that the light was in fact three lights. Three lights, spinning around each other.

They flared like a halogen halo through the film of water, and behind them where grey clouds had been was sunlit blue sky. The lights were straining down for her. There was safety inside them. If they could only touch her, touch her only for an instant.

The lights, like a flame hissing through water, reached her face. For one moment, she saw an angel in the blue sky. The angel's silver hair flowed almost to its feet, and its hands were clasped straight before it. She wanted to believe the angel was pleading for her to go with it, but she could not make out its face against the blindingly intense glow. And then she was conscious of nothing but the lights.

That was the end of the dream.

*   *   *

She always woke up with a void behind her ribs, as if she had forgotten to breathe properly.

This time, when Ella woke up, she was floating several feet above her bed.

CHAPTER TWO

For a few seconds Ella was still drowning in the water of her dream. Her eyes were open and she was staring through the lights as the hand reached for help. Then her arm banged against the wall and she froze. The bedcovers had slipped off, she was lying face up and she could feel the worn cotton of her night dress draped around her. She could not feel the mattress or the pillow.

Her hair hung down heavily. It was the only weight she could feel in her whole body.

She reached down and patted the space behind her. Her body was not touching the bed.

Ella turned her head sideways. She was on a level with the shelf for her piggy-bank and the black velvet bull from a schoolfriend's Majorcan holiday. She looked up – she didn't think to twist and look down. She was barely an arm's length from the ceiling. Floating.

All around her, like the gentle wash of water, she could feel a clear current, buoying her up.

She was not asleep. She knew she had woken up. Her dream had ended the way it always did, with the intense, spinning lights. This was not a new part of the dream.

She heard the blood pulsing in her neck and head, like a distant piston. Alive, said every pulse. Alive, awake, alive.

Perhaps she was being visited by an angel. Perhaps the angel was invisible, and holding her in its arms. That was why she felt calm and unafraid.

She peered past her feet to see the painted angel on the wall.

All that hung there was a wisp of black paper.

Ella gave a little shriek, as though she had been jabbed with the tip of a blade. The moment she made the sound, she was no longer floating.

She did not fall. There was no transition between air and bed. There was no impact as she landed, no bounce as the bedsprings pushed her up. One instant she was above the bed – the next she was upon it. The bedclothes were on the floor and her body was cradled in the hollow of the mattress, and her head was muffled by the bulky pillow, just as it would have been if she had lain perfectly still for an hour.

Gripping the edge of the bed, Ella braced her muscles and pushed herself as hard against the mattress as she could. She did not want to float again.

She had no doubts. When she woke up, her body had been carried above the bed. Her skin retained a physical memory of the sensation. If she had lain and thought about it, she would have started to wonder, and then convinced herself it was a mistake. A dream, after all. Or just one of those odd feelings.

But Ella never lay and thought about things. She felt things powerfully. She just couldn't think about them very clearly.

She did not try to be rational. There was a simple fact – when she woke up, she felt herself to be floating. She didn't understand, but all her life people had told her that she didn't understand.

Hanging on to the bed was starting to make her muscles ache. It had been a safe feeling, to be afloat. Why didn't she want to float again?

Because her angel was gone.

Ella sat up. The chink of light from the landing showed clearly – where her angel had been, there was a dark smudge. She went to touch it. One charred wing still hung from a scrap of Blu-tac. Wisps of ash were scattered on the worktop below.

Ella called out, 'Mum!' Her watch was downstairs, but she could hear the TV so it couldn't be late.

No reply.

Ella rubbed the ash and her hand turned black.

She screamed out, 'Mum! Mum! Mummy!'

No reply.

She ran to the lightswitch and it didn't work. Panic drove her heart harder. 'Mum! Mum!' She pulled open her door, lunged to the top of the stairs and left a black handprint on the banister post.

Her mother's face appeared at the sitting-room doorway. 'What have you done?'

'My angel's gone, it's all burned.'

'What are you yelling for?' She came to the foot of the stairs, her dry face weary. The rims of her eyes were inflamed, and the line of pencil she drew round them each morning had been washed onto her cheeks.

Ella forgot the angel. 'Mum, you've been crying.' She started to go down to her.

'Get up those stairs. There's nothing the matter with me. I'll come up.'

Frank, a boy of seven with Brillo-pad hair and crumpled pyjamas, stumbled out to ask what the problem was.

'Ella's had one of her dreams again, that's all. Back to bed darling.'

'It's not a dream, my angel's all burned. Look!'

'What is that on your hand? My God, even when I send you to bed, you turn my house into a pig-sty. Frank, if you're not back in your room by the time I climb these stairs . . . Ella, Ella, what is it you have been doing?'

Ella's black hand clasped Juliette's arm – 'My God, be careful, my cardigan' – and dragged her into the bedroom.

'What is it, how am I to see without the light on?'

'The bulb ain't working.' But when Juliette's hand touched the switch, the light came on.

'Now calm down.' Both her crisp, brittle hands rested on her daughter's shoulders.

'Look,' insisted Ella. 'It's all burned.' Then she asked in alarm, 'Did Dad burn it?'

'Daddy is not here. Remember? On Wednesday he likes to go out . . .'

'And it weren't you or Frank?'

'Ella, you have done this yourself.'

'No!'

'Of course it is not Frank. He is not so childish. And I have been downstairs.' Juliette brought her face down close, chiding her, and Ella smelled her mother's cloudy, bitter breath. Gin and tonic.

'It weren't me.'

'Then it is your lamp.' Juliette pointed at an angle-poise reading light, three feet away at the desk-top's edge. 'You are always leaving it on, it gets hot. I told you. It wastes electricity, your father doesn't like that. And now you maybe burn down the house.'

'There weren't no lights on.'

'It is no good trying to cover up for yourself. Go back to sleep or I will tell your father.'

'I don't want to go back to sleep,' pleaded Ella.

'You are only doing this to make me more tired.'

'Mum, can I come downstairs with you for a bit?'

'Ella, I am too tired to be arguing. You have had a nice birthday – if you want to spoil it that is up to you.'

'I don't want to go back to sleep.' She was clinging to Juliette's fingers, to stop her from going.

'Mr McNulty says you have to be working harder in his class. Then maybe you will want to go to bed and sleep properly like a good girl. Now let go, I am tired if you are not.'

'Don't Mum, stay. I'm scared.'

'What of are you scared? Dreams! Say your prayers and trust in Jesus. Dreams can't hurt you.'

'Mum, I was floating.'

'What do you mean? Let go, Ella.'

'I did have a dream, but when I woke up I was floating.'

Juliette tugged her hand free. 'You are a stupid, baby girl,' she said, 'and you deserve your nightmares.'

From the night of her fourteenth birthday, Ella no longer seemed to have control over her life. Where she went, things happened. The things had no meaning and no pattern. They could not be properly explained, or interpreted. At first, they could not even be connected with Ella.

At four o'clock in the morning after her birthday, all the lights at 66 Nelson Road came on. All of them, even the lamps which were unplugged and the strip light in the bathroom with the blown starter. They were switched off or they went out on their own, one by one, before five o'clock.

Before anyone was up for breakfast, Juliette's bottle of Beefeater and an empty tonic bottle were taken from their careful hidey-hole under the stairs and smashed. Juliette did not accuse her children as she hurried to sweep up the glass. She could not admit she had hidden a gin bottle in the under-stairs cupboard, but she believed Ella had broken it, out of spite.

The telephone rang constantly for fifteen minutes, even when it was picked up.

Ella's watch was stopped at eleven past eleven. When she tried to wind it on, she saw the hands had curled upwards and were jammed against the glass.

Twice, when Frank picked up a bread knife, the house shook with a boom that seemed to well from the foundations. The second time, Juliette went to the window and peered up at the grey sky. 'It is Concorde,' she declared, though the rainclouds hid everything. 'It is not supposed to fly so fast and so low over our houses.'

The kitchen was filled with an electronic whine, almost too high to be heard. It was loudest when water was running. Juliette said the taps were picking up next-door's radio.

Frank's sports bag was zipped shut, and resisted every effort to open it. This was the only thing which Juliette admitted was odd that morning. 'I do not understand it, it is jammed but I cannot see where. I am so stupid at zips, your father he could mend it just like that in an instant. Here, you try, you're a boy, you are better at these things. I cannot see where it is sticking, can you? Ella, keep your head away, you are in my light.'

The bag opened when Ella touched it.

When Ella closed the front door behind her, the radio-cassette in her room came on full blast. And for the rest of the day the house was normal.

But at school it was much worse.

CHAPTER THREE

Juliette was thinking, 'Little cow,' as she picked slivers of glass from the edge of the carpet where the vacuum would not reach. It was not just the wasted gin – she had not left as much in the bottle as she thought – but the stress. Every fragment had to be disposed of before Ken came home and spotted it. His eyes, like radar, picked up everything she didn't want him to see. It was as though he knew what to look for.

Of course, it was Ella who smashed the bottles. Juliette knew that, even if she wasn't going to say anything to Madam's face. It wasn't Frank. He wouldn't have known the bottles were there anyway. He was still very young. No, it was Ella, though how she got back up those stairs before she was spotted, Juliette couldn't guess.

Mean, spiteful, little cow.

Still, that wasn't the only bottle. Ella had found one hidey-hole, but she didn't know them all . . . Suddenly in need of reassurance, Juliette checked the chimney breast behind the gas fire and the bottom of the washing bin. Both bottles were safe.

She fetched a beaker from the dishwasher. It was only twenty past nine, but Juliette had been treated to a hard morning already. All that chaos before the kids went to school, and then the vacuuming. And if Ella thought she could rule her mother by creeping around in the small hours and switching on lights or smashing people's personal possessions, she had to be shown she was wrong. Juliette was very justified in having a drink.

She hardly drank at all anyway. Only Sundays and Wednesdays, when Ken was off with his cheap women – Juliette didn't mince words when she was talking to herself. And Mondays and Thursdays, before he got back. The other days, she didn't drink at all. Only if other people were drinking. She wasn't saying she was teetotal, that would be a lie, but really she drank so little it made no difference. Only those days when Ken was demeaning himself. Then she had to have something, she deserved to have a drink, two drinks if she wanted, to keep her spirits up. It was his fault.

Juliette always took the blame for anything that happened when Ken was around. For what she did when she was on her own, she blamed him.

She poured a wide taste of Beefeater into the beaker, then added a splash more in place of the tonic water. She was leaning on the wall alongside the stairs, by the phone, twisting a curl of her straw hair. She ought to phone Sylvie. Just to say thank you for the cake. Before Sylvie phoned her. It had to be done, though she wasn't in the mood. Juliette didn't have the strength to hear that Sylvie was *so-o* pleased Ella had a nice day. *So-o* happy she liked the cake, *so-o* glad because she had been *so-o* sure the cake mix was too soggy. And wasn't it *so-o* wonderful to be fourteen?

Juliette couldn't remember anything wonderful about being fourteen. Her father beating her unconscious when he found out she'd slept with Marco Bouchere. Her stepmother being brought home in a wheelchair after both her legs were smashed by a hit-and-run driver in a Citroën truck. Marco's sister, Simone Bouchere, disappearing, and three months of newspapermen and prayers before her decayed body was uncovered by a heatwave which dried out the quarry pit. All of that was being fourteen.

Ella didn't know she was born. Both her parents at home, plenty of money coming in, good school. That girl didn't know she was born.

Like Sylvie. The pretty little sister. Sylvie had been fourteen when Ken and his mates smuggled Juliette onto a car ferry at Le Havre. Now look at pretty little sister. Twenty-nine, had two husbands she hadn't been able to keep, had a baby she couldn't keep either. And always sounding *so-o* upbeat, because it was *so-o* important to stay positive.

Could Juliette stomach Sylvie's baby-girl squeak, telling her she was *so-o* lucky to have her lovey-lovey-lovely family?

She took an eye-stinging swig from the beaker. Yes, she could stomach that. It was better than waiting till Sylvie rang up, all sulky, declaring her *silly* pink cake must have been a disaster, and she was *so-o* sorry.

Ella was having a bad morning too. Every morning at school was bad for Ella, but this one was worse than usual.

She was old enough to know all that stuff at breakfast was weird, and weird stuff didn't happen to other people she knew. When she was a child, she hadn't taken so much notice – and anyway, weird stuff hadn't happened so much. Every now and then, something disappeared, or flew around. No one usually noticed.

The past few hours, though, had just been non-stop. The cake – she hadn't touched it. She only owned up to stop her dad giving her a kicking. And floating in bed, and her angel somehow getting burned up by her dream.

Her mother had an excuse for all the weird stuff before breakfast – it was sonic booms, it was Frank mucking around, it was the telephone company getting their lines crossed.

Ella was always relieved when her mother ignored the weird stuff. She preferred being ignored by Juliette to getting a major row from Ken. Like when he freaked out about the birthday cake. If it had just been her mother, the mess would have been scraped up without any comment.

Juliette only got her hair off when you got in her way, like if she was trying to watch TV and you started talking to her. Then she could really get heavy. But not like Ken. He could lose it if you just happened to walk in front of him. The only safe thing to do with Ken was keep right out of his way unless he was expecting you to be there, like meal times or when he sprang one of his 'tidy checks' – inspecting the children's bedrooms for neatness. And then it was best to just be there and not say anything.

Ken thought his daughter was basically dim-witted, definitely below average. She hardly spoke, and when she did say something it was usually inaudible. But then even her friends didn't regard her as bright. Everyone said she was a bit thick. Her best friend Holly stuck up for her: 'She's got lush hair,' Holly always pointed out, when people were getting at Ella.

Her morning had started off badly. Around ten o'clock it got worse. She was doodling when she should have been reading. 'This isn't drawing class, Ella,' announced Mr McNulty.

Ella glanced up and then back at her desk. She had been completely absorbed in drawing an angel on a book cover, carefully shading in every feather on its wings, and she had not even known she was doing it.

Everyone turned to look at her.

Ella hated that most. She'd endure anything rather than have all the class staring at her.

The only person not looking was Mr McNulty. He had turned to face the board, presenting the thirty-seven pupils in Year Nine English B-Group with the back of a sweaty nylon shirt and his fat, shiny trouser seat.

Year Nine English B-Group waited. The longer Mr McNulty paused, the worse it would be.

During ten seconds of silence Ella tried to cover up the drawing and find the right page in her work book.

'I have my back to you, Ella.'

She did not reply.

'Ella Wallis!' Mr McNulty put his fingertips to his temples. 'Is there anybody there? Are you receiving me on Planet Ella?'

Year Nine English B-Group spluttered with laughter. McNutty was obviously in the mood for some fun this morning. He got like this sometimes. Towards the end of term, usually. No one except Mr McNulty thought this McNuttiness was really funny, but everyone laughed because everyone was grateful they weren't in the firing line.

'Ella, I am going to astound you with a feat of mental power. I am aware that you were drawing because I saw your pen moving. You could not have been writing because your lips were not moving. But I was unable to see *what* you were drawing because your right arm was crooked around your book.

'With an extreme exertion of grey matter the Great McNulty, ladies and gentlemen, will look into the mind of Ella Wallis *TELEPATH-ICALLY*. The drawing is . . . an animal!'

'Yes Mr McNulty,' said Ella. It was a lie, but everyone else was joining in the joke and she was too scared to fight back.

'It is . . . a pet! And the pet . . . the image is a little blurred . . . but then this is Ella Wallis's brain we are talking about . . . the pet is a cat!'

'Yes Mr McNulty.'

Mr McNulty turned round. He bared big, yellow teeth at Year Nine. 'You may applaud.' They did.

'How was that achieved, that terrific feat of telepathy? Who believes I read Ella's mind? Hands up!'

About half the class claimed to believe McNutty had psychic powers.

'And who thinks I had seen the drawing?' The other half raised their arms. 'From this distance? When she was hunched like this over the picture? Impossible. But . . . BUT! I'll tell you this now, and you better not forget it, no matter what hypnotists and conjurors on the television try to make you believe – *there is no such thing as telepathy*. I did not read Ella's mind. What I did read was . . . Ella's homework!'

Mr McNulty reached into his desk drawer and fished out a wad of paper. 'Monday's essays, all marked, no one scores over seventy-five per cent . . . again. Top scorer was Richard, so Richard, your prize is – you get to hand all these round.' He reached over to give the wad to the boy – he was enjoying his little bout of McNuttiness today.

'You were asked to list A Few Of My Favourite Things, with reasons. I suggested eleven would be an appropriate number.' He scrawled '11' on the board. 'It's a good thing this isn't maths class, because hardly anyone could count to eleven. Ella Wallis can, I grant her this, she can count to eleven. I was so impressed that I memorised

Ella's eleven favourite things. In reverse order, they are (Ella, you'll correct me if I get these wrong . . . which I won't), Number Eleven: Frogs. Number Ten: Dolphins. Nine: Wild rabbits. Eight: Parrots. Seven: Tropical fish, except sharks. Six: Giraffes. Five: Birds in the garden, like robins. Four: Foxes. Three: Pet birds, especially Aunt Sylvia's budgie Tutu. Two: Dogs. All dogs, apparently. And Number One: Ella Wallis's very favourite thing, a cat called Rambo.'

Not many people were laughing now. This was too much. Ella was staring down, her face hidden by her silvery hair.

Mr McNulty was too elated by his own amusingness to stop talking now. 'What do we notice about Ella's Favourite Things? Richard? Anyone?'

'They're all animals, Mr McNulty.'

'Exactly. Not a lot of variety there, is there? I'd've liked to have seen a little more *imagination*, Miss Wallis. Such as, "One of my favourite things is doodling when I should be paying attention in Mr McNulty's class." Message understood, Ella?'

There was a silence as Ella's small voice steeled itself to say, 'Yes Mr McNulty,' without quavering.

Perhaps the fact that no one wanted to stare at Ella now was the clue, for Mr McNulty seemed to realise he had taken the joke a little far. He tried to reel himself in. 'There is a serious lesson there. Next term I shall explain how I was able to recite Ella's homework without looking at it – our memories are very powerful tools if we train them properly. Everybody in this class has got a huge brainpower potential, if you train it properly. We only use ten per cent of our brain – Albert Einstein said that. But telepathy is just a con-trick. Everyone clear on that?'

For an instant Ella caught a whiff of Lewis McNulty's mind. She was not trying to prove him wrong – she had not even looked up yet, but suddenly she was aware of his thoughts in her head, like a waft of body odour or a spray of spittle on her face.

It happened, sometimes. She was always sensitive to what people were about to say. She saw images of what other people were seeing and heard the words they were trying to suppress. Their emotions sometimes ran through her like a shiver. It was not as if she felt the same way – but one or two drops of the essence of other people's lives would trickle into her mind.

She didn't think of it as telepathy. She didn't think of it at all – it was natural to her, like hearing the words when other people spoke.

Mr McNulty's mind tasted of bitter things, like boredom. Frustration at being surrounded by so much youth, and an ache for his own, ebbed-out youth. Loneliness. Fear of ridicule. These flavours lasted only for a couple of seconds and then dripped away.

Ella wanted the lesson to be over very much. She gripped her book and wished she could be slamming the door of the classroom behind her.

There was an explosion of glass in the corridor outside, making the thirty-seven pupils of Year Nine English B-Group shriek.

CHAPTER FOUR

Holly said, 'I thought it was a bomb.' Her Bristol accent, like Ella's, made everything sound like a question. 'I thought it was, like, the IRA? I thought we was all going to die!' Holly giggled.

Holly and Ella and Flora Sedgewick were standing in front of the Bristol Transport Through The Ages display in the lecture theatre at St John's Lane Secondary, Bedminster. The first lesson of the afternoon was geography, the last geography period of the Christmas term. As a special treat, Mrs Hyde would be showing some slides she had taken in the course of twenty-five years, showing the changing face of life in Norway. So they were waiting in the lecture theatre, the only room in the school with a slide projector, for Mrs Hyde.

'Mr Evans said it couldn't happen natural,' said Holly. Mr Evans was the janitor. 'He said someone must've thrown a stone, but no one did, right? Anyway, one stone couldn't have broken all that glass.'

All through lunch break, she had talked of nothing but how the panes had blasted out of the classroom door during English and sprayed razor shards all around. Holly Mayor had been right by the door when it shattered, and she still could not quite believe she had not been hurt.

Ella and Flora were staying faithfully close to Holly, because the shock had made her excited and tearful. She needed looking after. Holly and Flora Sedgewick were always inseparable, but Holly, a small girl with dark eyes, was Ella's best friend too.

'No one threw nothing,' asserted Flora. 'And the door was closed. I know Mr McNulty said we left it open, but it weren't. So it weren't the wind.'

'Maybe it was like an earthquake,' suggested Holly.

'Yeah, that'd make sense,' said Flora, delighted to have a solution none of the teachers had considered. 'And I did kind of feel the room, like, vibrating, before it happened.'

'Did you? Did you feel it, Ella?'

'Ella weren't looking,' Flora answered for her. Ella had already pleaded complete ignorance about the exploding glass. She said she was daydreaming when it happened. The other girls knew what she meant – she was too upset by Mr McNulty's tirade.

'It must've been an earthquake,' decided Holly.

'It's been a really weird day,' offered Ella.

'I didn't think you got earthquakes in this country,' agreed Flora.

'All the lights came on in our house in the middle of the night. And my tape recorder, just switched itself on full blast and there weren't no one near it.'

'That's *really spooky*,' said Holly, gripping her arm.

Ella stood, looking intently at the transport display, wondering whether to tell how she had levitated.

'That's like a spirit or something,' said Flora.

'Don't. You'll give her the creeps.'

Ella stared at a photo of Bristol city centre before the blitz, when trams ran outside the Hippodrome. At the front of the display was a blueprint of The Matthew, the ship in which John Cabot sailed from Bristol to discover Newfoundland. There were two pictures of Concorde, being tested on the BAe runway at Filton. And at the Centre of the table, labelled Do Not Touch, was a 1/8 Airfix model of a Bristol Motors sports car, painstakingly constructed and painted by Mr Evans.

'What I was daydreaming,' admitted Ella, 'when the glass smashed, I was imagining I was slamming the door.'

'Spooky,' repeated Holly, without much interest. She liked the earthquake theory.

'Sorry I'm late.' Mrs Hyde rolled back the sliding door of the lecture theatre and raised her voice. 'Seats please everybody, we've got a lot to get through. Stop looking at that, please, Ella.'

They sat down to be shown slides of Trondheim in the 1970s, and there was no more time for Ella to talk about the strange events of the morning. If she had been able to explain, her friends might have believed her later on.

The janitor, Mr Evans, went straight to the headmaster, and the head went to Mrs Hyde, and Mrs Hyde called all the Year Nine pupils back into the lecture theatre before any of them could slip through the school gates. It was ten to four and the buses were waiting.

'Quickly, quickly,' the head was shouting as the children were herded in. 'I know you've all got transport waiting, but because of the stupidity of one person among you, you're all going to have to suffer. Barbara,' he added more quietly to Mrs Hyde, 'perhaps you could nip out and ask the bus drivers to be patient a moment.'

The head was a reedy man, with a high voice and long fingers which he waggled in front of him constantly, as if he were about to play the piano.

'Sit down – those who can't find a seat quickly, stand at the back. I very much regret . . .' he paused to build up for the final word, 'somebody here is a *thief*.'

Mr Evans stood in front of the Transport Display. His white side-burns bristled with disgust.

'Immediately after Mrs Hyde's geography lesson this afternoon, Mr Evans came to lock up the theatre. He was quite shocked to discover that something had been removed from our Transport Display. A model sports car which Mr Evans had himself made – is not there.' The head gestured dramatically to the table. Do Not Touch, read the label standing emptily at the Centre. 'I am assured everything was as it should be when Mrs Hyde left the room. Therefore, it is obvious one of you has taken this car.

'Would anyone like to own up to taking it now?' Silence. 'I can promise you, it will be easier to stand up now than be caught out later. And you will be caught. Very well. Mr Evans was particularly generous in allowing us to use his valuable model in our display, and we have betrayed that trust. This theft brings shame upon the whole school, and you will all suffer. Everybody, swap your bag or your satchel with the person next to you. Quickly, now, and look very carefully for this car. And never mind about trying to protect a so-called friend, because no true friend would damage the self-respect of the school.'

Ella handed her sports-bag to Holly, but Holly swapped bags with Flora Sedgewick, so it was Flora who squealed and leapt up.

'Mr Pritchard, is this it?'

She pulled the red plastic car from Ella's bag. The windscreen caught and broke on the bag's zip. Mr Evans hurried over and gathered it like a wounded bird in his hands. One wing was splintered and the wheel was buckled underneath it. Mr Evans's face showed no surprise. 'Ruined,' he remarked, but he carried it carefully back to the table.

'Whose bag is that, Flora?'

Flora pretended she didn't know. She did not want to look eager to betray Ella.

'Whose bag!'

'Ella's, Mr Pritchard.'

Ella's face was so drained of blood that, in the dim light of the theatre, she appeared like a ghost. Her bag had contained nothing but books and clothes five minutes earlier. 'You put it in there,' she protested at Flora.

'Did not!' hissed Flora, with such venom that people edged away in their seats.

'Ella Wallis, down here please.' The head let every eye follow in silence as Ella stumbled through the chairs. 'All right, get going, the rest of you. Flora, would you wait a moment too please. Did I say you, Holly Mayor? Outside, then.' Mr Pritchard stared down at Ella and Flora as the rest of the scowling class shuffled out behind them. He was easily twelve inches taller than the two girls.

'Why did you take the car, Ella?'

'I never. It weren't me,' she whispered in despair.

'Now how did I know you were going to say that? Flora, did you put this car in the bag?'

'I never,' Flora proclaimed fiercely. 'She had it, stuffed under her trainers.'

'All right Flora, you can go too.'

He waited until the last pupil had slid the door shut. The two men were standing only a few inches from Ella, as she gripped the handles of her bag.

The head bent forward suddenly and all the pompous kindliness in his voice vanished. 'I don't like little girls who turn into little thieves.' His skeletal fingers caught her hair above the ear and pulled her face close to his chest. 'What made you take it?'

'Never touched it,' gasped Ella.

'You're a nasty little liar. A nasty, dirty, lying little girl!' He tugged hard on her hair, forcing her to look up into his face. 'Aren't you?'

'I never. I didn't even want it.'

'Stop snivelling. What are you going to do to say sorry to Mr Evans?' His other hand hovered above her face, anxious to slap her but restraining itself. 'Do you think he's going to accept an apology from a nasty little lying girl?'

'Don't hit me!'

'I wish I could put her over my knee,' the janitor snarled.

She felt the violence tingling in their arms and legs, felt it so vividly she could hardly tell what the men were saying and what they were holding back.

'Dirty! Little! Thief!'

She heard the sliding door rumble and, as Mrs Hyde returned, Ella was jerked upright. Sobbing, she clutched the burning skin of her scalp where the head's hand had held her.

'We have our little thief, Mrs Hyde.' His voice was controlled again, filled with gentler disgust.

'Ella?' asked the geography teacher. 'Whatever did you want with that silly car?'

* * *

'What I cannot see the point of,' said her father, as Ella stood to attention in the middle of the sitting room and he circled her, 'is why? What for? What you want it for?'

'I never took it.'

'I almost believes you. If I didn't know you tells lies just for a laugh, I'd think you was telling the truth. Did you want to give it to Frank? I won't have you stealing nothing, even for presents.'

'Honest, Dad, honest. I ain't lying. I'd tell you if I took it.'

'Someone put it in your bag then. That's the only other answer. Ain't it? So who was it?'

'I don't know.'

'Did you give your bag to anyone else?'

'I didn't even open my bag since dinner.'

'But you knew about the car? Before it got stolen?'

'I was looking at it when we was waiting for Mrs Hyde,' Ella admitted.

She wanted to run, fling herself in a corner, but her father's broad chest hemmed her in. Her eyes were on a level with the dusty, grey hair curling out of his open shirt collar. His abrasive aftershave filled her nose. For the third time that day Ella shook in silence, waiting for a middle-aged man to attack her.

Ken's hands suddenly went to the belt of his trousers. 'You know what I thinks it is?' he asked, slipping the pin from the buckle. 'I think you likes all the attention. Don't you? You likes having all your mates looking at you. Well they don't admire you. Don't you think anyone'll respect you 'cos you thieve things. And you'll make God hate you.'

She couldn't listen. She could only watch as the thick black blade of belt with the silver cross on its buckle was bent double in her father's hands.

'I'll show you what it's like to get your father's attention. You know what they does in some heathen countries. They cuts a thief's hands off. It's the hands what sinned against God.' He seized both her wrists in his left hand. 'If thy right hand offend thee, Jesus said, cut it off and cast it from thee. Is that Scriptures? Is it?'

'Please Dad. I never nicked it.'

'You mean you wishes you ain't. And I'm going to make you wish it some more. Don't you snivel, don't you make it worse for yourself.'

Ken Wallis raised his right arm and smote his daughter's open palms with the belt. The arm of the silver cross bit into the flesh of Ella's thumb. The stinging leather was like a white-hot wire across her fingers.

He hit her again, and the doubled tongues of leather slapped together with a whipcrack.

He hit her again and the silver buckle exploded.

CHAPTER FIVE

With a bang like a gunshot the metal shattered as it touched Ella's bruised hands.

Ken held the ripped end of his belt in front of his face in amazement. He was still gripping Ella's wrists, tightly enough to stop the blood-flow. All that remained of the buckle was the pin, dangling. His eyes hunted the floor for the silver cross.

'Where'd that go?' he demanded.

'Dad. Let me go.'

He shoved her arms away. 'Get to your room.'

As Ella reached the door her father was on his knees, patting the carpet for the broken buckle. She pushed past her mother and Frank in the hall and ran to curl in a ball with her back jammed against her bedroom door. Her throbbing hands were clamped between her calf muscles. She sobbed, trying to muffle the noise between her shoulders so they would not hear her downstairs.

After twenty minutes hunched like that, staring sometimes at the purple welts darkening across the heels of her hands, Ella heard her brother's voice.

'Elly? Elly?'

She didn't answer immediately.

'You all right Elly? Dad didn't hurt you, did he?'

'I'm all right,' she whispered back.

'Frank! What is it you are up to?'

That was their mother's voice.

'I'm going to the toilet, Mum.'

'Your father told you, not to go in and talk to Ella.'

'I ain't, Mum.'

Ella heard his footsteps as he ran to flush the toilet and make good his lie. Ten seconds later a scrap of folded paper appeared under the door and Frank's small feet shook the floor as he banged down the stairs.

A round face with two dots for eyes and a banana for a smile was scribbled on the notepaper. She knew what he meant. 'Don't worry, be happy.' It was Frank's favourite chant. He hated Ella to be low.

Just like Frank. Being down was simply a waste of time to him. When Ella was down, his answer was to nick thirty pence from Juliette's purse and get his sister a Mars bar from the corner shop. That worked, usually. When there was a family crisis, and high spirits were out of place – like most days – Frank had to sit still and keep quiet. It drove him up the wall. He was only seven, but sometimes Ella saw him clutching his Brillo pad curls in both fists, wrenching them, mad with keeping silent. When Juliette was morose, he caught her hands and danced in circles, trying to swing her round. He needed to yell and belt about, twelve hours a day, and if it wore his mother out just watching him, that was too bad.

When their parents were rowing, and Frank sat grim and motionless, Ella could hear the energy building up inside him. Actually hear it, a grating buzz like interference close to a power generator. That's what Frank was: a generator. Ken said you could run a lightbulb off that boy, and he might not have been wrong.

Sometimes, if she closed her eyes and focused her mind, Ella could see what her brother was seeing. She did it sometimes when she missed him – when they were at their different schools, or when Frank had been sent off to Scouts' camp. Just to know where he was. She had a technique for this: she imagined a television screen. The television was running a sequence which played back whatever Frank's eyes saw. If he was in class, the screen displayed the face of the teacher, the books on his table, the backs of other children's heads. If he was doing sports, the television tracked the ball, and monitored Frank's shouts.

Once, when Juliette was getting panicky because Frank was late home and he wasn't at any of the usual friends' houses, Ella stared into the screen in her head, and saw water and heard yells echoing. She started to panic herself, until she realised her brother was in a swimming bath. He had gone to the pool with the Year Six team – Frank was getting good at swimming and could join in training sessions with the older children. Juliette refused to believe her daughter, and would not even phone the baths to check – but when Frank came home wet, Juliette blamed Ella. 'You knew,' she accused her, 'he had told you. I think you like it, to see me get in a state.'

Frank was not punished. He was threatened with punishment often, but the threats were empty. He had learned to look worried and pay no attention. To Ella, on the other hand, punishment came often and without warning. Sometimes, like today, Frank would come and whisper half an apology when Ella had taken a hiding. He knew he didn't get his fair share – he was not anxious for it, either, but he got no pleasure when she was hurt.

Ella clutched the scribbled, smiling face as fiercely as if she were clutching the hand which had drawn it. She loved her little brother. She mothered him when he was a baby, cuddled him and petted him, dressed him, cleaned him. Protected him as he got older. Told lies to help him, and fought back when anyone said a word against him. She loved him, and he knew it.

If he was aware of a telepathic link with his sister, he ignored it. No seven year old expects to understand his big sister.

Her bedroom was dark now, but Ella did not stand up to switch on the lamp. She did not want to waste her father's electricity bill on something as unnecessary as light for her room.

She was wretched, coiled by the door. She could smell the grime in the greasy carpet and the raw chipboard in the door.

Her back ached from the draught coming in around the hinges, but she did not move for a long time. She deserved to be uncomfortable. Her father knew it – he had deliberately beaten her hands until they ached. Her headmaster knew it – she had not forgotten the scalding tug on her scalp when he wrapped a long hank of her hair around his hand. She had been humiliated, by adults, by grown-ups who were superior to her. Of course she deserved it.

Ella could hear the clink of cutlery downstairs. Her family was eating, but she was not permitted to join them.

She knew it was her own fault.

She could not remember how the model car had got into her bag. She knew she had been looking at it. She knew she had not touched it. Her hands felt clean of that. They would remember the contact with the plastic, if she had picked up the car and slipped it under her trainers.

She must have willed it into the bag. Willed it without wanting it. She couldn't imagine why. Perhaps because she knew the car was valuable – that was, she had been told it was valuable, though she couldn't see how. She did not know who would want it, except Mr Evans, or who would buy it.

There seemed to be some sort of memory connected to the car, but she could not find it or put words to it. Something in her head, just beyond the reach of recollection. It was the same with the door and the smashed glass – she knew she had been daydreaming about slamming that door, but there seemed to be a greater memory than that. Like a name she knew, but could not bring to mind. Ella felt she must have been asleep, or daydreaming, just for an instant, when the glass exploded and when the model disappeared.

She sucked her bruised thumb. The vapour of boiled potatoes

mingled with the scents in her room – she was hungry, and she wanted to have whatever her family was eating.

When her mother tapped on the door and said wearily, 'Your father wants you to eat your dinner,' Ella did not dare answer. She heard the plate clunked down and her mother's footsteps receding.

It was boiled potatoes, with sausages and gravy. All of it cold and hard. Ella sat guilty on the edge of the bed, eating a congealed dinner she did not deserve.

She felt a fraud when her stomach was full. She felt better for it, and she ought not to feel better. Feeling better was like cheating, one more crime in a wretched day.

Her father had wanted her to eat the meal – she supposed he was forgiving her, but Ella did not see how he could. She hadn't said sorry. She did not know what to be sorry for. It was all her fault, but she did not know how to prevent it from happening again.

'Saying sorry,' Ken always told her and Frank, 'means making sure you don't keep on doing it. Sorry means it won't never happen again.'

God would not forgive her either until she said sorry. That's what prayers were for, saying sorry. She knew that.

She was making it all worse, having that meal inside her. She should not have let herself eat it. It was wrong. Maybe she could not do anything to stop herself from stealing that model, but she could have denied herself the dinner.

The sausages and potatoes weighed solidly on her stomach. She wanted to vomit them onto her bedclothes.

She couldn't do that. Her mother would be livid.

Ella crouched nauseously at the foot of her bed. When she had summoned the courage, she turned the door handle and peeped out. Everyone was downstairs. She edged along the landing, desperate no one should hear her. In the bathroom she shut the bolt with painful silence and then stared into the toilet bowl. She thought of the congealed gravy.

With one heave it all came up. The next heave was an empty reflex, and the third, more of a cough, just brought slimy dribble dripping from her chin.

She wiped the bowl with toilet tissue and flushed, then rinsed her face. Every trace of the meal was gone. She had done what Ken wanted and eaten it, but now she was hungry again. Hungry and uncomfortable.

For the first time that day Ella felt she had done something right.

*   *   *

In the darkness of his lover's bedroom, Ken Wallis heard something go bump.

He sat up and reached out a hand for Ailish's wide body. She was gone. The covers were turned back and his hand patted the crumpled sheet.

'Aili? That you, girl?' He called to her like she was a dog. Funny – he thought he was wide awake, but he had not felt her slip out of bed.

'All right, lover?' she called out. 'I banged my toe on this damn door. What you doing awake, then?'

'What you doing, crashing round in the dark?' he countered.

'Looking for my ciggies, lover. Hang on.' She flicked the lightswitch in the next room and Ken could see her, naked as she prodded sofa cushions and scrambled under the coffee table to find her Marlboros. She was a big woman, lardy and dimpled. As she bent over, he thought that his wife, Juliette, could squeeze both her scrawny thighs into one leg of Ailish's jeans.

She was a lot older than Juliette. She was at least ten years older than Ken. Pushing fifty. So what? She was still a very attractive woman. Woman enough for him and that, Ken thought with satisfaction, was saying a lot.

'You're a gorgeous sight, girl.'

'Cheeky.' Ailish turned out the light and perched her broad behind on the end of the bed. 'Is my Kenny still feeling naughty?' She lit her cigarette with the flare of an oily Zippo. When the flame was out, the only light in the room came from the dull embers of a Marlboro. 'So what's keeping you awake then?'

'Something on my mind, girl.'

'You going to tell me you can't come see me no more?' Ailish did not sound too anxious about it. These things happened, all the time. 'Your wife getting stroppy?'

'That cow can get as stroppy as she likes. She ain't going to tell Ken Wallis what to do. I'll still be coming here, every Sunday. Don't you worry.'

'I weren't worrying!'

They laughed.

Ailish liked to know what was going on with her men friends. She always kept asking till they told her. 'So what is it? What's keeping you awake?'

She sounded concerned, but Ken knew it was just nosiness. He told her anyway – he needed to talk it over with someone who didn't care about it, someone who wasn't family, someone who had never met his daughter. Someone who was, basically, a stranger.

'My oldest child, Ella. She's been behaving a bit odd. Downright weird, sometimes.'

'How old is she?'

'Fourteen this week.'

'All fourteen year olds behave odd, Kenny. She got a boyfriend?'

'Not so I knows of. She's too much of a baby.'

'Fourteen ain't a baby, Kenny. Not in a girl.'

'She's a bit backward, tell you the truth. Too much of her mother's side in her. She ain't grown-up at all. Sometimes I wonders if she ain't never going to grow up.'

'She will do,' said Ailish confidently. 'All of a sudden she'll be asking to marry some boy, and she'll go off and you'll be a grandad 'fore you knows it.'

'Maybe. I wouldn't say "no", that's for sure. Won't be sorry to see the back of her. Nothing but a nuisance, she's always been. Nothing to make you proud of her – she ain't pretty, she ain't good, she ain't godly. She just kind of hangs around. Not like her brother. Frank, now he's a good lad. All mischief. Always up to something, like what a boy should be. Course, if it weren't for Ella coming along, I wouldn't never have had to marry her mother.'

'Ain't fair to hold that against her. You never had to marry her, just 'cause of a kid. Look at me. My dad didn't marry my mum.'

'That ain't godly,' said Ken, fiercely. 'That's an abomination against the Lord. Course,' he added, after a pause, 'it weren't your fault.'

'Nice of you to say so.'

'She's always been an odd girl. Sits in her bedroom, hours on end. Got the radio on so quiet she can't hear it. Draws things. Pictures in her homework books, when she should be writing. Know what she's drawing? Angels. It's always angels. Angels with big wings, flying all over the place. Maybe it's blasphemous. Sometimes I wonders if she ain't got the devil trying to creep into her soul.'

'Why? What does she do that's so wicked?'

'There's things . . . sometimes I think she can read my mind.'

'Thought you said she was a bit backwards.'

'So she is. But you can be sitting there, thinking to yourself – "I wants to see the telly pages," or, "I wants a sandwich" – and she goes off and gets it for you. When you ain't said a word.'

'That don't sound wicked, it sounds clever to me.'

'She ain't clever. Not one bit.'

'Helpful then.'

'Ella's helpful enough,' her father conceded.

'So what's the problem?'

'There ain't one. I don't know what made me talk about it.'

What was the point? How could Ken make Ailish understand, when he did not have the faintest idea himself?

He watched the glittering cigarette embers being ground out in a glass ashtray. It was completely dark again. He reached out an arm to pull Ailish back into bed.

CHAPTER SIX

No one spoke to Ella when she walked back into class. They stepped back as she passed and turned their backs. It was Tuesday – only ten days to go till Christmas. Chains of coloured paper were strung across the ceilings, and stars and camels were sprayed in glitter across the windows. But there was not much good will towards Ella.

Flora Sedgewick was slouched by Mr McNulty's empty desk, with her hands in the back pockets of her Calvin Klein jeans. She looked steadily at Ella.

'Hi,' Ella said uncertainly.

Flora's stare never flickered.

Ella edged past one of the boys who stood, ignoring her, barring her way. She wanted to get to her desk.

'Watch your valuables,' remarked Flora. 'Watch out, there's a thief about.'

Ella ignored it. Flora and one of the boys were clutching each other, giggling. Ella sat down and dumped her bag in front of her, like a sandbag.

'Oi, I can't find my money,' shouted Flora. 'Ella, have you nicked my purse? Oh no, here it is. I thought Ella Wallis had nicked it,' she announced.

'I never nicked nothing,' growled Ella, clutching the bag tighter.

'Don't think Mr Pritchard said that yesterday,' said Flora. 'What was it he said now?' she asked her boyfriend, who was on the verge of collapsing from sniggers.

'Theft is a crime against man and God,' declared another of the lads, in a fair copy of the headmaster's sententious delivery. 'The thief murders civilised society.'

Ella did not know what that meant, except that they were talking about her. She had missed two days' school, kept at home until Mr Pritchard had exacted a promise from Ken Wallis that the janitor would be reimbursed for his damaged model. She had missed the Monday assembly, when every pupil from Year Seven up endured a half-hour's lecture on honesty, and integrity, and dirty little thieves.

'What's in your bag now, Ella?' demanded Paul Cary. Paul was an oily boy, barely taller than Ella but twice her weight. He swept the bag off her desk and plunged his head into it.

Ella leapt up to grab it, but Paul's fat hand clung on without effort. He pulled her fountain pen out. 'Anyone had their pen stolen?' he asked, shrilly.

'Me,' someone yelled. Paul flicked the stainless steel Parker in an arc across the classroom, so that the top flew off and ink sprayed out.

'You geek, Cary!' One boy was smearing ink off his white shirt.

Paul ignored him and tipped the bag out, scattering books. The tiny pins and cogs of a technical drawing kit spilt over the floor.

'Give it back,' hissed Ella. She was tugging with all her weight. Paul shrugged and let go, letting her tumble backwards. He turned away.

Ella bruised her leg against a desk, caught herself and lurched forwards at Paul Cary, swinging the empty bag. It caught the back of his head with a slap.

The impact was almost nothing, but he skidded on one of the scattered cogs. Paul fell with a little shriek and a compass needle in his backside.

Shouting and giggling, thirty pupils crowded around to see him sprawled on the floor. Ella was crouched, head bowed, thrusting books back into her bag. Paul Cary scrambled to his feet, clutching his buttock and swearing. His face was bulging, blood vessels pulsing around his eyes. He lashed out wildly with his foot, missing Ella by several inches but, when nobody tried to stop him from kicking her, he caught his balance and prepared to take better aim.

'Do what!!' The teacher's deep bellow silenced everything. The pupils stopped in mid-movement. Paul Cary, his right foot drawn back to deliver a kick at Ella's head, stayed frozen on one leg like an obese stork.

'Everyone back to their desks,' ordered Mr McNulty.

Ella stayed crouching as legs jostled around her. She did not dare look up.

'There is a surprise,' said Mr McNulty. The sarcasm brought out his Northern Irish accent. 'Who'd have suspected such a thing? Ella Wallis!' She squinted up at him. 'The very first minute of the lesson. On your first day back. And look who's causing a commotion.' He glanced around the room. Paul Cary, like fat dissolving in a pan, had melted to the farthest corner. He sat, like all the pupils, with his eyes fixed ahead.

'Get up, Ella. Leave the bag down there.' Mr McNulty leant over her. 'I don't want to hear from you again today,' he told her quietly. 'Okay, Year Nine! Last lesson of term. Let's press on with *Pride And Prejudice*, and you can finish it in the holidays. Paul, page 220, start reading please.'

Ella pressed her palms to her ears to black out the voice. She concentrated on the sound of her pulse, like the slow march of boots across gravel. Her possessions littered the floor around her – even *Pride And Prejudice* was out of reach. She dared not bend down for it.

She wanted to be out of there. She wanted the day to be over. She wanted school to be finished, not just for the term but forever.

Two years to go. Less than that. In one year and fifty-one weeks she would be sixteen. That was the day she would walk out of school and not go back. Her father would let her. He knew there was no point in Ella's sticking out six months more of education, to sit a handful of GCSEs she could not possibly pass. She might as well be finding a job – or, at least, getting a place on some government work-scheme.

Ella knew what she wanted to do: work experience at an animal sanctuary, the same as her next-door neighbour's sister had done. Her next-door neighbour's sister got forty pounds a week to clean out the runs at the Cats' Protection League. When her year's training ran out she had to sign on the dole, but she still worked unpaid at the CPL when she could afford the busfare up there. That was what Ella planned to do. Once, she had wanted to be a vet, but that required qualifications. People went to university to be vets. Instead, she would find a sanctuary somewhere. It didn't have to be Bristol. There was a donkey sanctuary somewhere in Devon, it had been on TV. Donkeys would be paradise. Ella had forgotten to include donkeys on her list of Eleven Favourite Things, but they deserved to be way up there, near the top. Donkeys were ace.

She glanced up at the teacher who had recited her Favourites to the class. She wanted to be out of there. She wanted school to be finished.

The crunch of the pulse beneath her hands was slowing. She felt the gap draw longer between each beat. Her head drooped.

The room dimmed.

'Put the lights on,' called Mr McNulty. 'What prat did that?'

No one stirred. Whoever switched the lights back on might get the blame for switching them off.

'Alice! You're nearest. Turn them on. Was it you put them off?'

'No Mr McNulty.'

'Well who was it? You must have seen them.'

'I don't know Mr McNulty.'

'I don't know Mr McNulty,' squeaked the teacher. Only Paul Cary laughed – the rest knew better.

'Something funny Paul?' bellowed Mr McNulty.

'No Mr McNulty.'

A wooden blackboard duster banged against the board and tumbled to the floor. Mr McNulty, thinking it had simply fallen, replaced it on its rail.

As he turned back to the class the duster fell again.

The teacher scowled at it, as though it were a child, mocking him deliberately. His fat behind waved in the air as he scooped the duster up and slammed it, in a spurt of chalk-dust, on his desk.

'Richard, read please.'

A desk lid slammed somewhere. Mr McNulty glared in Ella's direction. She was crouched over her desk, both elbows pressed down. Richard began reading.

An exercise book suddenly dropped beside the boy's feet.

'All right! What is this?' Mr McNulty bounded forward and seized the book. 'Paul Cary' – he read the name on the cover. 'One hour's detention.'

'I never threw it Mr McNulty.'

'Two hours' detention.'

Brief silence, and Richard tried to begin again.

'I will not,' Mr McNulty cut across him, 'have this kind of asinine puerility in my classroom. Is that plain? Shall I make it simpler?' He was almost shrieking. 'Don't fuck with me!'

In the shocked stillness, there was another bang, louder than a desk lid. Mr McNulty jumped, a little convulsion. His ears rang from the noise. Everybody's ears rang – or was the whine something in the classroom?

The teacher glanced down at the children in the front row. Their goosepimple shudders said they heard it too.

'If someone's got a radio in here . . .'

Ella, with her hands still tightly over her ears, could hear the tin-thin tone, pulsing with her heartbeat.

People were shuffling their feet. The noise was working under their skins. It went into the bone like a needle. Wriggling made it worse, as if the whine penetrated deeper with every movement of every muscle, but sitting still was impossible.

Mr McNulty, staring furiously about the room, saw Ella's desk heave up, with her head and arms pressed against it, and crash four-square back to the floor. She jerked back, shocked. The noise got louder.

The door slammed. Someone had run out of the room. The pupils began scrambling to their feet.

'Stay where you are, all of you! SIT DOWN!' The whining was becoming a screech, a thousand fingernails on a blackboard. Mr McNulty shouted over it: 'All right – where's it coming from? Alice, is it your side of the room?'

The pupils, half-standing at their desks, looked around desperately. The noise was everywhere – it was the sound of the air, it was every particle of dust scraping on every breath. It did not come from any one place.

Ella was gripping the sides of her desk. She pushed down with all her weight against the lurching legs. It seemed to be trying to rise into the air, like a table at a Victorian seance.

With a shattering crash the desk tore itself out of her hands and was hurled into the gangway with force enough to splinter the sides.

The deafening whine stopped.

Ella sat breathless in her chair. Mr McNulty stared at her in disbelief.

'The manger!' shouted someone. 'Mr McNulty, look.' In complete confusion, he turned blindly about the room. 'It's on fire, it's on fire!' the pupils were shouting. 'The baby Jesus!'

The nativity scene behind his desk, placed there by the Year Seven children and peopled with plastic cows and sheep, was ablaze. The straw in the stable was burning with a dark, smoky flame. The pickets on the fence, made from old matchsticks, suddenly caught. The purple robe of a wise man shrivelled. The hay in the Infant's manger crackled and flared.

As Mr McNulty caught hold of the display, the straw roof caught light and flames reached for his jacket sleeves. He threw the nativity to the floor, scattering plastic animals and figures and sending tufts of burning straw flying.

The white swaddling around the baby bore no singeing. Everything in the nativity was alight, but the figurine of Jesus was untouched by the fire.

'Get the extinguisher,' he ordered Richard Price, but before the boy was out of his seat, the teacher decided he had no time to wait. He began to stamp out the flames, first the stray straws and then the stable itself. His loose brown Hush Puppies crushed the wood, grinding the fire into black smudges on the tiles. His feet smashed the byre, and the gifts, and the crib.

Sweat was running down the creases of his fat, red face when he looked up. 'Get Mr Evans,' he instructed, as Richard ran back with the extinguisher.

Ella was struggling to stand up the remains of her desk. The floor around her was strewn with books and debris. Mr McNulty, clasping the extinguisher, watched her wordlessly. He was unable to find the words he wanted to say first. The rest of Year Nine, edging back into their seats, followed his gaze. When Ella looked up they were all staring at her.

She hugged the broken lid to her chest like armour and hid her face.

Mr McNulty, the muscles shivering up and down his legs, managed to say, 'Just pick it all up.'

The whine instantly returned, so loudly and on so high a frequency that the big window-panes began humming in their frames.

And then all around Ella, objects began to lift off the floor. Exercise books, heavier text books, pieces of metal and wood hovered an inch or two above the ground and then whirled up. Some of the splinters flew in a tornado straight to the ceiling – other oddments hung at head height, bobbing. A thick book went spinning towards the wall and boomeranged.

The hands of the wall-clock were spinning in a blur, like rotor blades.

The whining sliced off all other sounds. The striplights began to burn brighter and brighter, until they shone like magnesium flares, drenching the room in a two-dimensional glare.

The disjointed remains of Ella's desk hovered in front of her. She had her knees against her chest and her face was buried.

Mr McNulty, scarcely able to stand because of the convulsive tremors through his legs, was on the edge of helpless panic. But the pupils were gripped by a terrified calm. No one tried to leave the room. No one was screaming. In the searing, blazing light they stared at Ella.

She felt a hand seize her hair. Mr McNulty dragged her out of the seat by her scalp and the objects began to fall away from her. He would not have dared take a step towards her, but he knew suddenly he had to have her out of the room. Out of his vision.

Ella, in her utter fright, let him pull her by the hair, half doubled over, to the door. Books and debris were hitting the floor, but the noise of their impact was overwhelmed by the relentless whine. Her shoulder banged against the door as Mr McNulty shoved her into the corridor.

She was suddenly out of sight. The noise stopped.

She stood, not knowing what to do. Her bag, or what remained of it, had been left behind. Holly Mayor was in the classroom too. Where else was Ella supposed to go?

Mr McNulty looked around the door. 'Go and report to the secretary,' he said, quite quietly, but without coming nearer. 'Tell her I am ordering you to go home. Is there anyone at your house?'

'My mum.'

'Go home to your mum, Ella.'

He shut the door on her.

'I hope that shows you all,' he said, stumbling across the littered books and broken desk, trying to keep his voice even, 'I hope you all know now – *never play with matches*. This was an extremely dangerous situation.' He bent to scrape up the charred nativity scene, and saw the white cloth that wrapped the Infant Jesus was not blackened. Mr McNulty rolled the figure between his fingers for a moment, puzzled. He had distinctly seen the manger burning.

Slipping the mysterious plastic icon into his pocket, he continued: 'If the blinds had caught light, the whole room would have been filled with smoke and flames in seconds. We could quite easily have been suffocated and burned alive.'

The vivid idea of a nightmare that didn't happen came as a relief. Some of the girls were sobbing. The children, silent until then, began to whisper to each other.

'Just one stupid girl throwing matches around and we could all have been killed,' Mr McNulty repeated. 'Not to mention throwing books around, throwing her desk around . . .' He raised an uneasy laugh. 'Okay, let's clear it up.'

He glanced at the clock on the wall. Its hands were frozen at eleven seconds and eleven minutes past eleven.

'What was making that noise?' asked Richard Price. Any answer would do – he just wanted someone explain what he had heard.

'She had a radio,' said Flora.

'A radio could never make that noise.'

'I saw it,' insisted Flora.

'Why? Why make such a racket?'

'Some people,' declaimed Mr McNulty, 'are only happy when they're the centre of attention. And the best thing we can do,' he added piously, 'is to ignore them.'

Ella, lingering miserably in the corridor, heard him. She turned and crept out of school, and she was ignored. No one tried to stop her. No one spoke to her in the street, or asked why she was home early. No one phoned from the school, not for her or her parents. Nobody had to tell her to stay away from school, because she did not dare go back. None of her friends wanted to know how she was. None of them was in when she tried to ring.

For a week, Ella hid from her family by leaving at schooltime each morning and spending all the day in the Christmas crowds at the Galleries shopping mall.

Until Holly Mayor came to see her on Boxing Day, no one said a word to Ella about the chaos she had caused.

CHAPTER SEVEN

On Christmas Day snow fell. Juliette kept saying, 'Isn't this lovely, a real Christmas,' as the family walked up Smyth Road to the Pentecostal Church of Christ Reborn. But she did not sound enthusiastic.

The children had to walk in front of their parents, to make sure they did not dawdle. Frank was not allowed to slide or throw snow about.

They reached the church steps ten minutes before the service, almost the first to arrive. The organ-player's wife greeted them, 'Merry Christmas everyone.'

Juliette, Ella and Frank only smiled and nodded as Ken answered for them: 'Christ's blessing upon you on His morn.'

The organ-player's wife beamed. Kenneth Wallis had a lovely way with words, though not as inspirational as his brother, of course.

They took their usual places on the low wooden chairs, second row from the front. Coats were rolled into tight bundles and tucked under the seats. There were no prayer cushions, but each of the four composed their hands on their laps and bowed their heads. Frank closed his eyes tightest. He knew what happened if he opened them too soon. God would not listen to him, and his father would belt him.

On the flat rail that topped the slatted chair-backs, blue prayer-books rested. Ella held one and sat, her forefinger tracing the outline of the white dove on its cover.

Juliette turned every few seconds to check the doorway. Most people would manage to arrive a few minutes early, even at nine o'clock on Christmas Day. The hall, licked by a chill breeze from the wide-open double doors, began to murmur with muffled voices. Chairs were scraped back and forwards. Here and there, earnest voices cut through: 'Peace on earth, Goodwill to all.' 'Christmas joy to you.'

'That woman from round the back of our house is in here,' observed Juliette. 'No sight of her husband still. And she brings her brother's boys also with her son. So where is their mother?'

Ken did not deign to answer. Ella did not dare. Chattering in church was a crime. Juliette did it: 'That's because she's woman,' Ken said, with contempt. Ella was not a woman, only a child, and chattering now would bring her a sound hiding later.

She stared forward at the wall, rows of new bricks interrupted only by the electric organ and a red door. Uncle Robert would come through that door in a few moments. He was Ken's older brother, the lay preacher at Christ Reborn. His sermons were ferocious and very popular, and he never spoke for less than forty-five minutes.

'Look who the cat's dragged in,' murmured Juliette, squinting sideways at a couple, 'fancy that those two should show their faces again. And she still has to wear that coat. She has had that coat as long as I have had my green one, poor thing. She should be cutting it up for dusters by now. Oh, she is seeing us.' Juliette raised a nervous hand.

'You got a new coat,' muttered Ken, without looking around.

'Oh yes. That is what I mean. Sorry. Always I cannot make myself plain. Sorry. She has her old coat but you have buyed for me a new one.'

'That makes us better, does it?'

'Sorry. Sorry. Sorry.'

The red door opened a crack. Uncle Robert edged out, whispering to someone unseen behind him. Then he swung the door shut, with enough force to get the church's attention. He walked slowly to the front of the congregation, clasping a black-bound Bible and smoothing his jacket over his bulging stomach. There was no pulpit at Christ Reborn.

'I preach Christ crucified, Christ reborn and mankind redeemed by Christ's sufferings,' pronounced Uncle Robert. This was the formula by which his father, principal preacher at the church from 1956 until his death, had begun every sermon. Eric Wallis had taught his sons how to speak the Word of the Lord and make people listen. He was fifty-three when the tailgate tumbled open on a lorry delivering newsprint to the Bristol Evening Herald, where he was a printer. Six reels of paper, each three miles long and weighing two tons, had rolled onto him.

That had been 1984. At least twice every month since then, Uncle Robert or Ken Wallis had taken the sermon. After Frank was born, and Ken got made overseer at BK Lewis Printers on the Wells Road, Uncle Robert had taken almost all the duties on himself. Whatever his text, he prefaced it with this homage to his father: 'I preach Christ crucified, Christ reborn and mankind redeemed by Christ's sufferings.'

He solemnly held open the Bible and, without reading, declaimed: 'And when they – the wise men – were come into the house, they saw the young child with Mary his mother, and fell down, and worshipped him; and when they had opened their treasures, they presented unto him gifts: gold, and frankincense, and myrrh. Matthew, two, eleven.'

He closed the book with a noise no louder than a breath, and the hall was so silent, so expectantly still, that every one of the congregation heard the book close.

'And what became of these gifts? Do we see them again in the Holy Story? Do these riches make a posh man of our Lord? What they call, "A privileged childhood"? No. He was a poor man.'

Uncle Robert nodded with approval. He had a coarse, red face, clamped either side by broad sideburns. The hair on his face, bushy and straggling, was peppered with white. The hair on his head – or what was left, for he was egg-shell bald on top – was still black, but wild and uncut like the sideburns. Even the hairs straying from his nose and ears, hair which grew thicker as Uncle Robert grew older, had been left untrimmed.

Ella, who was so proud of her own hair, always stared at Uncle Robert's sideburns. They looked greasy, as if they were growing out of something dirty inside his face.

Uncle Robert had noted her stare before. He thought she was an attentive child, if not very bright.

'But if those wise men had known what they were starting,' he continued quietly, 'I wonder if they would have been so keen to bring gifts. I wonder. Perhaps they would have been content to prostrate themselves at the manger. After all, they were kings, come to worship the greatest King of them all. They must have known their little trinkets would mean nothing to the Son of God.

'But those gifts mean something to us.'

Uncle Robert's voice, mild until now and good-humoured, became louder and suddenly caustic. 'We might not know about those grand-sounding words, frankincense and myrrh, but my, we know about gold. Don't we know all about gold!

'Every man, woman and child on this island, this Great Britain, knows the Christmas story. And they remember just one word of it. Gold! One word, from just one of the four Gospels! One word that can corrupt a whole nation. Gold! What does Christmas Day mean to the world? Gold! Who talks of the miracle of the birth? Who marvels that God sent, on this very day, his only Son, to suffer for us. For us! For every one of you! And for me! And do we thank him? Or are we just thinking of the – GOLD!'

Uncle Robert's eyes locked onto Ella. He felt her intent gaze and returned it. For a second he broke off from his questions and leered.

'What have we taught our children to remember on this morning? What was the first thought in those little heads when they awoke? The Christ-child? No. Greedy thoughts of presents, pagan thoughts of Santa Claus and so-called Christmas trees. And these little thoughts should be so innocent!

'But all through the months and weeks leading up to this holy day, those innocent minds have been bombarded with temptations. Endless adverts on the television. Gaudy dressings in every shop window. Merchandising as far as the eye can see – our children cannot even take their sandwiches to school without being taunted by the siren voices. Buy me! Every toy, doll, game, computer, all screaming – buy me! Desire me! Covet me! BUY ME!'

His voice rose to a shriek, wailing out of his fat body.

The congregation sat forward, yearning for the lash of the words, or else shrank back in their seats. Now Uncle Robert's eyes were rolled upwards, to God and to his own bald head.

'By corrupting Christmas in our children's hearts, we are doing what Herod did. A massacre of the innocents. We are worse than Herod. Worse! Herod slew every child under two years old, in Bethlehem and all along the coasts. But we are not so merciful. Every child! Every child, in every town, village and city, inland and on the coasts, under two and over two, girl or boy. So that there shall not be one drop of innocent blood left unspilled in the country.'

He wrung the black Bible ecstatically. 'And we still think we are worthy of His love!'

Uncle Robert staggered back. His face was dark-red, his fingers white against the Bible's leather. He shut his eyes tightly, and heaved a deep breath. When he looked back at the congregation, calmness was returning to his expression.

'Who here has opened a Christmas present today?'

Hands were raised in every pew, and people relaxed a little. They did not realise how tautly they had been holding themselves, until they slumped forwards a little and their shoulders dropped. The worst was over now. Uncle Robert was even smiling a little, as every hand in the church rose to confess guilt.

He had them now. They were shocked, frightened and penitent. No need for more violence. They would do whatever Uncle Robert bade them. He would order them home, to think of Christ as they ate their dinners. To pray forgiveness for their greed. To resolve to follow Christ's way more humbly in the coming year.

They'd promise him anything, rather than be told again by Uncle Robert that they were not worthy of God's love.

Later, when his blue Jaguar XJS – registration K1 NGJ – was parked outside his brother's house in Nelson Road, Uncle Robert said Grace over the turkey. He had been sermonising, uninterrupted, for twenty minutes about the effects of recession on his petrol station franchise.

Uncle Robert ran the Ufil garage on Coronation Road. As the turkey roast arrived on the dining-room table and Juliette pulled up her chair, Uncle Robert switched seamlessly from economics to ecumenics, 'Dear Lord and Father, on this holiest of days, please accept our humblest thanks for granting unto us, both the bounty that is spread before us, and the gift of Your Son, our Saviour.'

Ella and Frank stayed motionless, hands pressed together, eyes squeezed shut, until Uncle Robert added: 'If I didn't have to pay VAT on the peripherals, it wouldn't be so bad.'

'Right,' answered Ken. 'Pass Robert's plate, Julie.'

'See, £11.99 for a can of oil, that sounds a lot,' said Uncle Robert. 'But you got to remember, almost two quid of that goes straight to the VATman.'

'Right. Do you want breast or leg?'

'Bit of both, Kenny, bit of both. See, I voted Labour, first time in twenty-three years, and Labour gets in, first time in twenty-three years thanks to people like me, and they don't *change* nothing. Like VAT and petrol duty and car tax – does it get any easier for the poor man? Put not your trust in princes, nor in the son of man, in whom there is no help. Them sprouts looks nice, Julie.'

Juliette smiled as she dished them out, but she knew they looked limp and watery. And there was not enough of them, nor of the roast potatoes. Sprouts were such a pain to prepare – all the shelling, and those little crosses in the top of every one. She made sure Ken and his brother got a good serving. Ella and Frank were left with one or two each. Juliette covered their plates with dollops of swede. It was just as nutritious, and a lot easier to cook.

'Wine, everybody,' she added.

'Red for me, Julie, so long as you've got enough to go round.'

'Oh, there is plenty,' she assured him, and there was. Juliette might have misjudged the sprouts, but she had been sure to buy sufficient wine. And a couple of bottles of Beefeater, in case anyone wanted a drop. It wouldn't do to run out of drink at Christmas. 'You must be thirsty, you have talked all the morning.'

'Never seems like I've been preaching two minutes. Then I looks at my watch and I've been on my back legs half an hour.'

'And the rest,' said Ken.

'Ella was paying me attention, I saw. Wasn't you, girl?'

Ella nodded, knife and fork frozen above her plate.

'Always got her eyes fixed on me throughout a sermon.'

Ella dared not look up. Somehow it had not occurred to her that Uncle Robert could see her staring when he preached.

'I almost got you to come and stand up with me this morning. I thought of it. One of those wild inspirations you get when you're preaching off the cuff, so to speak. You know what it's like, Kenny. The spirit of the Lord moves you, and you have to go with whatever ideas come into your head. You wouldn't have minded, would you, Ella?'

She shook her head. Her hands were as white as the tablecloth. Stand up in church with Uncle Robert – she would have shrivelled and died. She could not even have got off her chair. Her legs now, just at the thought of it, were feeble.

'What you want her for?' Ken asked, scornfully.

'Innocence. When I was talking 'bout the corrupted child – the inspiration whispered, "Show them what you mean. Present them with the image of purity, and ask Why. Ask them why we lets it get tarnished. Words like that, they're sharper than the sharpest sword. They slide straight to the heart. One thrust. "Innocence". Another thrust. "Corruption". They're like deadly weapons to the guilty soul.'

'Ella's too old, she ain't no child now,' answered her father.

'She is fourteen,' her mother added.

'That's what I thought,' admitted Robert.

'Not that she ain't innocent,' Ken said.

'It is natural, she is only fourteen, she is pure in that way,' said Juliette.

'She better be,' said Ken.

'No, yes, obviously,' Uncle Robert agreed through a faceful of turkey breast. 'I mean, everyone in the church would take *that* for granted, soon as they looks at her. But purity of spirit. A child's innocence. 'Cos fourteen ain't a child no more, Ella.'

She shook her head again.

'The voice of inspiration passed. Gone as quickly as it come. I reasoned people have got their own image of a child's purity. That is, themself. Their own self, before the rot set in. Before decay took root in their souls. And it were just going to complicate matters if I got a girl of fourteen, even if she is my own niece and Eric Wallis's grand-daughter, and stands her up as an reminder of the Holy Child. If you was two years younger, mind, Ella – I think I would have done it.'

'Okay,' she said, because she felt some response was expected.

'A girl changes about your age,' he pursued. 'Do you know how I mean? She becomes . . . a woman.'

'Ella is not a woman yet,' said her mother.

'But she's on the way, Julie girl. She's got the child's face still. Hair's still childish. Starting to get a woman's body though.'

'She's going to have that hair cut, before long,' warned Ken. 'It's turning into a vanity.'

'Ah. Vanity. Now there's a sin of the woman and not the child. Has your body started to change yet, Ella?'

She looked up, pleading, but her mother and father were glaring at their plates. Uncle Robert, leaning forward, stared straight at her. His greasy sideburns were like feelers.

'Mary would have been about your age,' he said. 'Maybe she was a bit older, but she hadn't started to have her periods yet. That's why God chose her. She was a married woman, of course, but she was a virgin. More than a virgin. Her whole body was pure.' He stuck another potato in his mouth. 'Have you started your periods yet?'

'Ella is a late developer,' answered Juliette.

Ella's face and arms were burning. She could not eat. It felt filthy, to have to consume food next to this man. She realised there were tears on her cheeks – she felt their tracks drying on her hot skin.

'Good thing for a girl's body to stay pure as long as possible,' declared Uncle Robert. 'Girls these days, becoming sexually ready younger and younger. Nine years old, some of them. There's females of thirteen getting themselves in the family way with boys of eleven, in the papers every week. Is it surprising? You look at girls barely in their teens, and you could take them for eighteen.'

Ella clung to her cutlery, fighting to keep herself at the table. Her mother pushed potatoes unhappily around on her plate.

'We get them in the garage shop all the time. Buying sweets. Not even old enough to buy cigarettes, and they're wearing these crop tops. See their pierced belly-buttons. Big breasts.'

Ella dropped her fork. 'Dad, I got to go to the bathroom.' She was already out of her chair.

'Go on then.' He didn't like to say Yes, but it was probably the quickest way to get Uncle Robert off the subject. 'I ought to be getting back to preaching myself.'

'Most Godly thing you can do, Ken, and you, Julie, is pray to keep the devil from that young girl's soul.'

Ella, clutching the toilet seat, started to retch. She vomited so long and hard it seemed certain they must hear her downstairs. Her stomach kept convulsing, until the last dregs dribbling into the pan were flecked with blood.

CHAPTER EIGHT

Christmas Day dragged to an end. Boxing Day came, and brought Holly Mayor round with it. Ella's best friend knelt backwards on Ella's homework chair.

'We ate so much yesterday. Thought I was going to throw up.'

'Me too.'

'Did you have loads of chocolate?'

'A bit.'

'We had masses. We had so much we couldn't eat it all. I finished it for breakfast this morning.'

'For breakfast?' Ella was shocked.

'It is Christmas. Well, Boxing Day's still sort of Christmas.' Holly tipped the chair dangerously on two legs.

'My dad'll flip if he sees you sitting backwards.'

'We'll hear him coming up the stairs.' Whatever Holly said sounded like a question, but she was confident – Ella's father couldn't belt her. 'We had this massive box of Turkish Delight, only it was like the proper stuff, with sugar and everything, from Marks and Sparks. My brother ate 'bout twenty pieces. We all put on masses of weight, we're going to be so fat.'

'Me too.'

'You'll never be fat, you're always going to be really skinny. Look.' Holly pinched a chubby roll on her own arm, then leant out to tweak the skin on Ella's wrist. 'Two weeks to go. Well, thirteen and a half days.'

'Till what?'

'Till we have to go back to school.' This was what Holly had really come round for. This was why she had rung Ella and why she was sitting in Ella's bedroom, when they hadn't spoken for over a week. 'You going back?'

'Yeah. I suppose. Dunno. Why?'

'Well, after you had that car . . .'

'I never stole it.'

'Everybody thinks you did.' Everybody, clearly, included Holly.

'Everybody's wrong. It just got in my bag. It must've been 'cos I were thinking about it.'

'Oh yeah? You thought about it so it drove into your bag on its own?'

'Well, I never took it. I never touched it. But,' and this was sort of an admission of guilt, like she knew it was basically her fault, 'I was looking at it. When we were stood by the table talking. I was staring at it. I never nicked it. I swear I never.'

Holly Mayor was her best friend. Ella knew she wasn't Holly's best friend, only her second best, but surely that was enough. Ella had to trust somebody. Anyway, sometimes Holly and Flora had bust-ups, and then Ella really was Holly's No 1. And if you were best friends, you had to believe everything, and you couldn't have secrets.

'I was thinking 'bout the manger thing when it caught fire.'

Holly stopped rocking her chair. The whole business in the class-room had been taboo. No one had talked of it – they all pretended to accept the explanation about the radio and ignored the rest. They talked about Ella – what a thief she was, what a show-off, how she pretended to be different from everyone else – but they didn't talk about the flying books or the fire. They didn't talk about how Mr McNulty pulled the baby Jesus from his pocket and placed it, clean and unharmed, on his desk, when the whole nativity scene had been charred. Holly didn't want to hear about any of it either.

'My dad says it don't matter what you think, people judge you by what you does and what you wear.'

Ella felt her friend pulling away from her. She knew Holly so well, sometimes it felt like they were the same person. Their outlook was the same, they had the same opinions about other people. Ella trusted Holly's outlook. She let herself be guided. Whatever Holly thought about someone else, Ella wanted to think that too.

But now, when Ella tried to explain something important, Holly was backing off.

Barriers were going up, barriers spiked with fear.

'You know when all that stuff started flying about the class . . .'

'I don't want to talk about it,' said Holly.

'. . . and there was that weird noise . . .'

'Shut up about it!'

'. . . well, I knew it was me, only I couldn't do anything about it.'

'It's just 'cause you're insecure and you want attention!'

'What?'

'You just want everybody to look at you and think how big you are! Mr McNulty said so, everybody just thinks it's pathetic.'

'What did he say?'

'He said you were just showing off and it was probably because you didn't really know who you are or you thought you weren't getting enough attention at home. And I think he's right, 'cause your parents hardly ever give you any attention, specially not your dad, except when he thumps you. That's not your fault.' She conceded the last point.

Ella, horrified that a teacher could talk about her when she was not there, wanted to know the rest. 'So how was I showing off?'

'Turning that radio on.'

'What radio?'

'That awful screaming noise, my brother said it was feedback He said you could do it with a radio and a little speaker thing.'

'I didn't have a radio.'

'He said Jimi Hendrix did feedback and said it was part of the song.'

'There's my radio,' persisted Ella, gesturing at the ancient radio-cassette player. 'It plugs in, it don't even have no batteries in it. How was I s'pposed to get that into school?'

'How did you make the noise then?'

'I didn't. I told you. It was me, but I wasn't making it happen. I wanted it to stop. The more I tried to make it stop, the louder it got. It was like I wanted to scream, but I couldn't, so that noise came out instead.'

'How?'

Holly honestly didn't understand. That was becoming obvious.

Ella could not explain. If Holly could not feel the things she felt, how could Ella make her understand? She wanted to find the words, but she did not know them.

'Did he talk much about me?'

'Mr McNulty? He said we should ignore it, or you'd get the attention you were after, it'd be like we were rewarding you for acting up. And he said you could have caused a really dangerous fire. You could have killed everyone in the class. It was such a prattish thing to do, Ella.'

'What?'

'Throwing matches.'

'I never! How could I? Where would I get matches? No one in my family smokes. And everyone was staring at me. Which I hate! I don't want attention, I just wish everyone'd leave me alone. So how could I chuck matches if everyone's looking?'

'That straw and stuff didn't just catch fire on its own.'

'Look. It's like . . . because I'm thinking about it, something happens. Do you believe I was lighting matches and bunging them? Honest? And I was chucking all them books in the air? All of them? All at the same time?'

Holly sat very still under this onslaught. It was not like Ella to get shirty.

'If you can just think it and it happens, think us some money. Go on, think that we've got a hundred pounds in our hands.'

'Don't be stupid.'

'All right. Think this book into the air.' Holly grabbed a book off the worktop behind her and tossed it towards Ella.

She was scared, but she was ready to be convinced.

The book fell with a slap on the bed. Ella looked at it doubtfully. 'It never happens when I want it to.'

'You just said it was because you were thinking about it. You can think about it now.'

'It's not like that.'

'You're such a wazz, Ella.' Holly got up, relieved. 'No one's going to believe you. Everyone knows you're a liar. People'd like you much better if you weren't. And the teachers would like you.'

Ella didn't argue. She felt the distance between them closing. Holly was trying to be nice. She simply thought Ella was a liar, and that wasn't frightening. Holly understood about lying.

But if Ella persisted, if she made Holly believe in the weird stuff, they couldn't be friends any more.

'Anyway,' she said, trying to keep Holly talking and stop her from going home, 'my dad hasn't said nothing 'bout me going to another school. I haven't had no letters or nothing. They can't just expel me, can they?'

'No,' said Holly, as though she had the final say in these matters, 'but you'd better not do it again or they really will come down on you like a ton of bricks.'

She picked up her coat. It swung heavily. 'I forgot. I got you this. It's a bit boring for a Christmas present, but I know your dad ain't never going to let you buy it or read it at school.' She handed over a wrapped parcel. 'See you. Give me a ring tonight.'

'Yeah, I'll have to ask my dad.'

'He'll let you make a local call on Boxing Day. It's 'bout 1p a minute. He'll let you spend 1p.'

'I'll have to ask him.' Ella had followed Holly onto the landing, but at the head of the stairs she stopped. Her parents were in the hall. 'See you,' she whispered and shrank back into her room.

Holly flicked her jacket over her shoulder and swaggered down the stairs. 'Hi, Mr Wallis, hi Mrs Wallis.' They couldn't hurt her. 'Mr Wallis,' she added, stopping cockily in front of him, 'Ella ain't going to be expelled, is she?'

Ken Wallis was a big man. When he swung around, he was a foot taller than Holly and almost three times her weight. His shirt cuffs were rolled up two turns and his arms strained the polyester sleeves. He bore tattoos above both wrists – a death's-head on Harley Davidson handlebars, and a Celtic cross.

He wore a fat, silver ring on his right hand. Holly suddenly realised that the black, pea-sized bruises she sometimes saw on Ella's face and arms were the marks of this ring.

'Why would she be expelled?' he asked.

'Nothing. Just joking.' She backed away, but he was blocking the hall.

'What's she done to be expelled?'

'You know. Sorry. It was a joke.' He couldn't touch her. If he laid a finger on her she'd tell her dad.

The hand with the silver ring was hovering a few inches above her arm.

'No, I don't know. You tell me.'

'When she nicked that toy car.' That wasn't grassing – Mr Wallis knew about the car,

'Ella says she didn't nick it. Do you know different?'

'No.'

'So why? Why do you think she's going to be expelled?'

'You know. When she got sent home for chucking all that stuff about in class.'

'What?'

He didn't know. The school hadn't told him.

'I thought you . . .'

'Yes? What?'

Holly was pressed against the door of the under-stairs cupboard. The dried-out face of Ella's mother stared blankly at her over Mr Wallis's shoulder.

'It weren't Ella's fault. It just happened. She told me, she didn't want it to happen.' Now she knew why Ella made up those lies. Anything was better than confessing to Ella's dad. Those arms could beat you to a jelly. He looked like he would not be able to stop himself. His hands quivered with the exertion of self-control.

'Want what to happen?'

'Things flew around. There were all these books, and her desk, they just went straight up in the air. She weren't throwing them. I could see, she was really scared. It weren't her fault, Mr Wallis, and there was a really loud noise.'

'When was this?'

'The week before end-of-term. Can I go home?'

'People were throwing books around?'

'No one was throwing nothing, Mr Wallis. Things were flying round on their own. It weren't Ella's fault. But when Mr McNulty sent her home, it stopped.'

'Why didn't Mr McWhat'sisname tell me?'

'Dunno.'

'Are you making this up?'

'Swear to God, Mr Wallis.'

'Has it happened before?' His face was bent low to hers, and he scarcely waited for her answer before hissing the next question.

'Not really.'

'Not really? It has or it hasn't.'

'A window broke. I dunno. I want to go. Let me go.'

He stepped back, and Holly Mayor scrambled past and into the street.

She wasn't ever going back to that house. Nothing on earth would make her step through that door again.

CHAPTER NINE

Nothing was said. The family sat down to tea in silence. Ken had not spoken a word to his wife since Holly ran out of the house, and Juliette was not going to accuse Ella of anything before her husband did.

Ella knew the silence meant something. She wasn't interested in whatever it was. Probably one of her dad's woman friends was involved. Or Auntie Sylvie. Or Mum was in a foul mood because she couldn't have a glass of wine.

She was guiltily grateful for the silence, because it meant she did not have to try and look her mother and father in the face. Ella had opened Holly Mayor's present.

It was a book. A book of drawings. It was the same book they had handed out in Year Nine Human Biology.

Only Ella's father had not let her do Year Nine Human Biology. It meant studying reproduction. It meant sex education. It meant some pervy teacher talking dirty to his daughter.

She didn't need to know about that stuff yet, and it was up to her father, and only her father, to judge when she did.

The school had disapproved, of course, and the school psychiatrist even wrote the Wallises a letter, which Ken ripped up. But many of Ella's classmates envied her. Human Biology *was* a bit dirty. It was drawings of genitals, and people doing it. Proper, educational drawings, but still a bit dirty.

Ella was lucky her dad cared enough to do something about it.

When Miss Chapman handed the books out, Flora Sedgewick tried to make Ella look at one. Flora's parents had told her about reproduction when she was ten, and she had had two boyfriends, though she hadn't done it with either of them. Flora told Holly, in sworn secrecy, that she was going to do it with Richard Price, when she wanted to. Not yet, but when she wanted to, she would.

Of course Holly had told Ella, and Ella was horrified. She began to believe what her father said, that books like that could corrupt your morals. Just looking at them. Even touching them. They helped the devil creep inside you.

So when Flora Sedgewick tried to make her read *Making A Baby: The Story Of Human Reproduction*, Ella refused.

And now Holly had given her the same book for Christmas.

She guessed what it was, but she still unwrapped it. Even while Holly and her dad were talking in the hall – she didn't know why – Ella was wedged against her bedroom door, sliding the big hardback out of its shiny cover.

Most of the drawings were meaningless. Tadpoles wriggling towards a target. A circle filled with bubbles. Something bald and blind, like a puppy, with a tube curling out of its stomach.

But then there were the other drawings. A man and a woman holding hands, with no clothes on. You could see everything. They stood with no shame, not attempting to cover any parts.

There was a cross-section of an erection. Ella could not tell which way up it was meant to be. She had seen horses' willies, when they pee'd, but they looked nothing like this. The diagram of a woman – genitals like her own must be – that made no sense either.

The drawing on the centre spread was different. Everyone could understand that. For a day Year Nine had talked about nothing else. It showed the man and woman making love. Or about to. Not actually doing it, but almost, so you could see everything. The woman was lying down, with her arms reaching up to clasp the man's neck. The man was kneeling between her legs.

Ella closed the book. The hard cover was damp beneath her fingers. The tiny, invisible hairs on her back, shoulders and arms were standing out, bristling against her sweatshirt. She sat for a minute, separating strands in her long, heavy hair, wishing that Holly had never given her the book, wishing she had not opened it and looked. Then she turned to the centre spread again.

The man was clean-shaven. He had no hair anywhere on his body, except for his neat crew-cut and the black bush, like a shaving brush, around his erection. There was nothing like the white hair that overgrew her father's open shirt-collar, or the coarse, grey-and-black sideburns curling down Uncle Robert's face and out of his ears.

The woman had circular breasts, with a couple of pen-strokes to suggest the nipples. The man and the woman were both smiling. They both wore wedding rings. They didn't have bruises, or tattoos.

Ella looked for a long time. She listened constantly for the creak of a foot on the stairs. Then she thumbed through the rest of the drawings, of embryos and blastocysts and foetuses and newborns, and thrust the book under her mattress.

Her silent parents at the tea table seemed disgusted with her. Ella did not blame them. She had done something dirty. Her father had tried to protect her from it, and she had disobeyed him. She deserved their disgust. She was glad they were not speaking, because she could not have looked them in the face to answer.

The book was dirty, and it made her feel dirty. Ella crept to the bathroom and vomited the turkey sandwiches and iced fruit cake. She vomited until her eyes were bloodshot, but she felt only slightly purged.

Just having the book in her bedroom made the whole house dirty.

She could not sleep on a mattress that hid a picture like that. It would be an invitation to the devil. But where else could she hide it? She could not get out of the house to the wheelie bin. The book was slim enough to be pushed through a drain-cover, but she dared not open the front door without asking her father.

The paper was too heavy to flush away. She tried with the corner of one page, but after two flushes it was still spinning in the toilet bowl.

Ella settled for ripping out each page and stuffing it into the shiny envelope of giftwrap. She muffled the sound of tearing by holding the book at arm's length under the quilt. She could not see the pages as she pulled them off the spine. When her fingers felt she had reached the centre spread, she tore it across, again, and again, and again.

At least if her mother found the book before it could be binned, she would know Ella had hated it.

She had hidden the remains in her jumper drawer a few seconds before Juliette pushed open the bedroom door.

'You are very quiet in here.'

'I been . . . doing stuff.'

'That's good. I have come up to say goodnight, because your Daddy and me, we are going to be having a talk. So you are not to come down to say goodnight, okay. Daddy sends a kiss to you.'

Ella jumped up and put her arms around Juliette's shoulders. She kissed her dry, veined cheek – 'Night-night Mum, I loves you. And that one's for Dad.'

Juliette was surprised, but she did not pull away immediately. 'Get ready for bed now – and be very quiet, Frank is already sleeping.'

It was a little before nine o'clock. Ella took her brush and began the blissful, silky tugging at her scalp. When one side was done she leant over to the cassette-radio and pressed the FM switch. Frank had helped her tune it to Galaxy 101. She kept the volume at Level One, so the bland pop and rock was barely louder than her breathing.

She heard her father's voice.

At first she thought it must be a phone-in, and turned the dial a notch higher to hear what he was saying. She did not know why Ken would want to ring Galaxy, but his voice was unmistakeable.

And her mother's voice. Both of them, on the radio.

The brushing paused, halfway, with a thick tress wrapped around Ella's hand.

'I cannot see why Holly could be making it up, it is so odd this thing to say,' Juliette was saying. She sounded upset. Her English was always worst when she was unhappy. When she was happy, and she had a glass of wine or gin in her, she was much clearer.

'She thought she was 'bout to get the living daylights thumped out of her,' said Ken. 'She were too bloody scared to lie to me.'

Her father wouldn't say that on the radio. Surely he wouldn't swear. There was another noise in the background. It sounded like their TV.

Ella crept onto the landing and listened. The voices downstairs were amplified by the radio in her room. It was, by some phenomenon, picking up their conversation. She was not listening to Galaxy 101, she was listening to her parents.

Ella turned the volume back down and put her ear close to the speaker.

'I'll tell you why I believes it,' she heard Ken say. 'My belt. I raised my belt to her and she made the buckle go. I heard it. It was like when a plate breaks on the press, you get a particular sort of noise when it goes. Like an explosion. That were the noise. And it were a silver cross on that buckle. You knows my belt. It were my Dad's, the church gave it to him. A silver cross. You helped look for it. You've Hoovered this whole room since, ain't you? And you ain't found it. It didn't just fly off. I heard it go, 'tweren't my imagining. A silver cross. So what's that if it ain't the work of the devil?'

'Ken, no.'

'Don't you tell me No.'

'I am sorry, I didn't mean . . .'

'You don't never tell me No.'

'Sorry, of course, I am wrong, it just slipped out, I was thinking. I was remembering.'

'What was you remembering.'

'It was when Sylvie was about Ella's age. Maybe a little younger.'

'What?'

'Some things a little bit like this were happening.'

'Your sister had the devil in her too? I believes that.'

'Only it was not like the devil. The priest called it a naughty ghost.'

'Oh yeah. Your Cath'lic priests. We ain't going to give no room to what your Cath'lics say.'

'No. No. Of course. You know I am not a Catholic now. But this is a long time ago. Before I met you. And of course my father goes to our priest. He had a German ghost word for it.'

'What, poltygeist, was it? So what'd it do, this poltygeist devil?'

'Not so bad as Ella. It threw things. Like Holly was saying about in Ella's class. Things fly around. One day it took a cheese, a big round cheese from our goats, and it throws this cheese right at the picture of our dead mother. Crash! The photograph it is on the wall, and it falls down and breaks. Sylvie cried and cried, and then she shouted very loud into the air, "Stop it, stop it, I hate you." And then she stamps on the picture of our mother. She thought the ghost, it was our mother.'

'And were it?'

'Father, he was so angry. He beat Sylvie so hard. I thought he was killing her. And I was too frightened, you know, to stop him. I ran outside. And maybe he was going to kill her, only all the plates on the top shelf, they leap out and crash down. And he is so shocked he lets Sylvie go and she runs away. We do not see her then for three days.'

Ken impatiently cut in. 'So was it the ghost of your mother and did it stop?'

'It stopped. Sylvie came back. Then a few weeks later – I've told you this before.'

'I don't know what you're talking about.'

'She had a miscarriage. You remember. I have told you before. She was not even thirteen years old yet. I didn't know she was having periods. No one knew she was pregnant – even Sylvie, she didn't know. Until she gets these pains in her stomach. She was in her school. I had left school by that time, I was working in the big store. It was a year, little bit more, before I ran away with you.

'So the school phones our house, and our father is there, because he is too drunk to go to the scrapyard that day and work. And they say, Sylvie is not well, can we send her home. But he is so drunk and so rude, the teachers don't like to send her alone, so one of them drives Sylvie in her car. And on the way she started to bleed on the passenger seat.

'The hospital said she was two months pregnant, maybe ten weeks. So I don't know if she was already having the child when she ran away. She told me one time she got raped, she was hitch-hiking and she got in the wrong car. But another time she said our father was messing around with her. And I think he was. I think he was, even if the child was not his.'

Ella, her hair tucked behind her ear as she crouched over the cassette-radio, was struggling to follow her mother's story. She had never met her grandfather. They never went to France. Juliette would say only that she did not have a very nice childhood. Auntie Sylvie never referred to the past – Auntie Sylvie always said, 'Tomorrow's a lovely new day.' No one seemed to know if their father was alive. Or care.

Why did Auntie Sylvie go back, when she had run away? Ella didn't understand. She was interested to hear weird stuff used to happen to Auntie Sylvie, though. Maybe it still did, and everyone ignored it. She would have to ask.

She heard her father say, 'You told me all that. You want me to tell you what I thinks your sister is?'

'Of course. I know.'

'Point is – point is this. It runs in your family. Things flying round. Stuff falling over, falling off shelves. Stuff breaking. And because I don't think our Ella's pregnant – by Christ, she better hadn't be . . .'

Pregnant! How could her father even think that? Her dad! No one had ever said anything that horrid about Ella. She wanted to cry, or hit him with something, or run away, all at once.

Of course, he did not know she was listening. She was spying on her mum and dad, having a private talk. Maybe they always said horrid things about her and Frank, in private. Maybe everybody did. She hated them, and didn't feel so guilty for eavesdropping.

'Of course,' her mother said, 'it is not your fault.'

'I never thought for one second it was my fault. It ain't my family got all this cranky stuff what's in its genes. I know'd it was you, you didn't need to tell me that.'

'It is me, I am sorry.'

'Right. You want to know what I thinks.'

It was what her dad always said when he was arriving at a decision.

'She's got devils in her. Them's what's doing the thieving and the lying and the smashing-up.'

'That is . . .' her mother whispered tentatively.

'That is what I say it is,' Ken Wallis declared with emphasis. 'It ain't what the scientists will say. It ain't what the doctors will say. But there won't be no scientists and no doctors poking round with my daughter no how. 'Cos nobody is going to hear about it. Seems to me her school is more than happy to keep it quiet. And Ella ain't exactly going to tell the world.'

'I do not think she really knows there is anything unusual about it.'

'She ain't the brightest girl,' her dad said, not unkindly.

'Perhaps they are right, the school and Ella. It is better just we ignore anything. Maybe it is all over now anyhow, who can tell?'

'You don't ignore the devil, Juliette. That's the path to Hell. That's the path to eternal damnation. When the devil's in you, you got to cast him out.'

'We must pray for her soul,' said Juliette. Ella thought the catechisms of the Pentecostal Church of Christ Reborn sounded hollow when her mother repeated them.

'I said we got to cast him out,' stated Ken. 'We got to exorcise her.'

'I do not understand . . .'

'Don't matter. The devil is in her, and he got to be struck out. And it's going to take more than prayers to do that, else the devil wouldn't be no problem to the world, would he? We got to ask Robert. Robert'll do it.'

'Can you do it, Ken? I am sure you are as good, you are better.'

'I ain't in practice. In fact, I ain't never done it. Robert can do it, he's good.'

'What will he do?'

'Exorcise the demons what is taking root in Ella's soul.'

Ella clutched her hands to her chest. Where were the demons? Could she feel them? How had they got in? Why her? It was a lie, he was lying. There weren't any demons in her.

Why else, though? Why else did weird stuff happen?

She began to pray. '*Our Father, which art in heaven, hallowed be Thy name . . .*'

'Sometimes your Robert, he is . . .'

'He is my brother, Juliette, that's what he is.'

'Yes of course, I am sorry . . .'

'. . . *Thy Kingdom come, Thy will be done . . .*'

'Sometimes he is very intense . . .'

'. . . *On Earth, as it is in Heaven . . .*'

'You know, Angela left him for a reason. She took both the boys. Now she will not let him see his own sons. It is for a reason.'

'She's a cow,' snarled Ken.

'Okay, I am not any more liking her than you. But it was for a reason.'

'. . . *Give us this day, our daily bread, and forgive us our trespasses . . .*'

'Go on, what? Eh? You going to spread slanders 'bout him, are you? 'Cos that's what the other women does? Robert knows what his cow of a wife said 'bout him. She goes and tells the coppers that he's been touching up little girls and boys, his sons' friends, and she's evil enough that she tells them he's been interfering with his own sons. My nephews. That's what the cops called it, ain't it – interfering? Ain't it?'

'You know I do not rumour people.'

'You're a woman, you're all lying bitches.'

'. . . *as we forgive those that trespass against us . . .*'

'O-kaaay,' said Juliette carefully, after a long silence. 'Always I say what I do not mean to. I did not want to say any bad thing. I do not believe what Robert's wife says about him and the boys.'

'Ex-wife.'

'. . . *and lead us not into temptation . . .*'

'Ex, yes. I am sorry we never can see the nephews now. But I just want to know, how is it Robert will do this exorcise thing?'

'. . . *but deliver us from evil . . .*'

'So you do want him to do it?'

'Maybe.'

'. . . *For thine is the Kingdom* . . .'

'He'll says some prayers over her. Order the demons to leave her body.'

'And he can do this here? It does not have to be the church?'

'Here, if you like.'

'And we can be there all of the time.'

'Don't see why not.'

'All of the time. Yes?'

'Okay,' Ken said.

'Right. And it is just prayers. He will not want to cut her, no blood, nothing creepy.'

'This is Christianity. It ain't witchcraft.'

'. . . *The power and the glory* . . .'

The light on the radio-cassette went out, and no matter how she shook it Ella could not tune back in to her parents' voices. Until gone midnight, when she finally managed to fall asleep, she kept repeating the Lord's Prayer.

'. . . *For ever and ever.*

Amen.'

CHAPTER TEN

Uncle Robert sopped rain off his egg-bald head and surveyed the room. The dining-table and chairs had been dragged to the french doors, and the carpet was rolled back to the table legs. Uncle Robert's blue polyester jacket dripped onto bare floorboards.

'This'll be enough,' he said.

'This back room's the only room in the house big enough,' apologised his brother.

Uncle Robert's footsteps echoed on the wooden boards. 'We want a chair – here,' he pronounced, swinging one of the round-backed, round-seated, green dining-chairs into the centre of the room. The lightshade shone straight down on it. 'Now I got all the candlesticks in the car. Didn't bring them in.' He peered out of the french doors. Rainwater running down the panes distorted his view of the back yard.

'Get him a brolly,' Ken ordered his wife, 'If he's got to go out again in this . . .' He caught his brother's eye. 'Tell you what, I'll get the stuff. Robert's doing this for our daughter, after all.'

Uncle Robert nodded. Raindrops were still trickling off his ears and chin. 'The Jag's only two or three doors down the street. It's all in the boot.' He tossed Ken the keys. 'The gear's heavy, so go careful.'

'Can I get you a cup of tea?' Juliette asked.

Uncle Robert did not turn round. When Ken was not in the room, he would not even speak to his sister-in-law. She seemed to be beneath his notice. He fished his black New Testament with its brass clasp from inside his jacket and began to pace the room, dividing it into quarters, as if he were measuring it. He moved the chair an inch or two. Flicking through the book, he placed his finger on a passage, closed his eyes and began silently to recite. His head was raised slightly and, apart from the rise and slump of his chest as he breathed, his lips were the only things in the room that moved. Dry skin made them flaky.

'Where d'you want these?' asked Ken, a little out of breath as he brandished eight black candle-holders, each four feet long and dripping wet. Uncle Robert gestured a circle around the chair.

The candles had been used before. They were all two inches across, but some had run down to little square stumps while others were the size of baseball bats. Uncle Robert pressed each one onto the metal pin of a candlestick. He took a silver flask of holy water from his breast pocket and then walked slowly around the inside of the circle with a taper, dripping the water and incanting: 'Dominus pater, dominus filius, et dominus spiritus. Amen. Dominus pater, dominus filius, et dominus spiritus. Amen.'

'Where's your boy?' he asked.

'We sent him round to friends.'

'And the girl?'

Ken and Juliette, crammed into the doorway, glanced up the stairs. 'I told her to wait in her room.'

'I'm ready now. Fetch her, Julie. Put the light out, Kenny.'

Ella came obediently, but at the foot of the stairs she hung back. Nobody knew she had been expecting this. They did not know what she had heard. She saw Uncle Robert in his black suit, lighted by candles at shoulder height, and though she had expected it Ella did not know what it meant.

Ken's hand reached around her wrist, to draw her into the room.

'I ain't got no demons in me,' she protested.

Her father's hand propelled her towards Uncle Robert.

'So you know what this is for?' Uncle Robert asked quietly. Ella shook her head. 'Part of you knows, Ella. Part of you has seen this before. Haven't you?' he added more harshly. 'And that's the part we want to get rid of.'

He beckoned Ella's parents. 'Close the door. Ken, you stand in front of the chair – Julie, you behind. Now Ella, you come into the circle. Careful now, mind your hair on that flame.'

His heavy hands on her shoulders pressed Ella into the seat. He smelled of petrol – his skin had been steeped in it for years at the garage. She thought of the candles and cowered in her chair, afraid the fumes might catch. He might explode in front of her.

She dared to look at his face. His brown eyes glittered in the candlelight shining up at him. The underside of his lips and his chin were red in the flickering light.

He smiled.

'Ella, I don't want you to be scared. Remember, Jesus is by your side, every step. What we're going to do is open your heart to Jesus and he'll come in and drive the demons out.'

Her father stood behind Uncle Robert, a candle at each shoulder. He looked grimly at Ella.

'I don't want to!' she burst out. 'Dad, he's scaring me.'

She tried to scramble forward but one heavy hand clamped her shoulder. The other flicked open the Bible with a thumb. Ella twisted to see her mother, but Juliette was deliberately looking away, into one of the flames.

'Mum!'

Juliette kept staring at the candle.

'There was a man like you once, Ella, and his friends asked Jesus to go to him. Just like we're doing now. And that man, he looked after pigs what was called the Gaderene swine, and he did strange things. Just like you do. Your young friends have told us about them, because we're your family and family is the best friends you've got, Ella.

'This man's friends tried to tie him up with chains, but *the chains had been plucked asunder by him, and the fetters broken in pieces.* And Jesus said to this man something very like what I'm going to say to you – he said, *Come out of this man, thou unclean spirit.*

'And the demons in this man, they fled into the pigs and hurled themselves over a cliff, because they was very frightened, Ella. Sore afraid, and that's what you can feel now, Ella. That's your demons, in the dread of Christ the Lord.'

Every muscle in Ella's thin body felt stretched, as though drawn back by wires.

Her stomach felt fat and full of liquid, and she fought the urge to vomit. An acrid bubble of bile rose and burst inside her mouth. She swallowed down the hot taste of sick.

'In the name of the Father, the Son and the Holy Spirit, come out of this girl, thou unclean spirit.' Uncle Robert clapped the Bible to Ella's chest.

A wire-thin whine sang round the room, a sound separate from the rising din of the weather outside. Uncle Robert glanced up. The candlelight glowed on his neck.

'That's the noise of the demon, the unholy spirit, the agent of the devil. And he's afraid. For the name of Jesus makes the devil quake in Hell!'

He lifted both his arms, like wings sheathed in the sleeves of his blue jacket, in an arc above her. 'Come out of this girl, thou unclean spirit.'

The storm's first flash of lightning bleached the window-panes. Thunder growled.

The other noise became two separate strands, scraping on each other. Ella saw her father grimacing, grinding his teeth. She began to lose an exact sense of where her parents, and Uncle Robert, and the candles, were around her.

'Come out of this girl!' roared Uncle Robert, 'Thou unclean spirit!'

She turned her eyes upwards. A shudder ran through her, jerking her so hard that she grabbed on to the seat. Outside, the lightning began to crackle in earnest.

'Filth and corruption of her body! Dirt that infests the soul of this woman yet a child! In the name of the Living Christ – but! In the name of the cleansing flame that will turn her soul to ash – out! In the name of God our Master – out!

'Fire of our Lord – purge this wretched soul!'

'Amen!' burst out her father.

'Fire of Heaven – purify! Purify! Burn in her heart!'

Ella gasped as an intense, searing jab stung her chest.

The room was plunged into blackness. Every candle gave up its flame without a flicker. Each teardrop of fire ran to the top of the wick and vanished upwards. In a brief flare of lightning the figures of the adults stood around her like shadows.

Ella relaxed her grip. The pain in her chest dissolved. She tipped her head forward in relief.

One guttering light spat up again. Uncle Robert, his arms still aloft, turned his head in surprise. The candle, one of the shorter stubs, began to burn steadily, and the high, slicing sound of wire being drawn through the air started again.

A second candle hissed to life. And a third. The noise increased.

Uncle Robert's face became a scowling mask as each flame was renewed. He loomed above Ella's upturned eyes.

'Clasp the book, child! Do not reject the way now!' He thrust the Bible into her hands. 'Truly, you must fight to save your soul. I cannot do it all. Fight the good fight! Take the word of the Lord to your bosom.'

Ella's hands, sweating with terror, slithered on the black leather cover.

Uncle Robert stepped forward and stood with his knees pressing against hers. His stomach bulged over her lap and she shrank back to keep her face out of his shirtfront.

'*And I saw heaven opened,*' declaimed Uncle Robert above the screaming din in the air, '*and behold a white horse; and he that sat upon him was called Faithful and True, and in righteousness he doth judge and make war.*'

He flung his arms higher and let out a bellow like an ox. With his tongue clicking and clucking he plunged his hands down onto Ella's head. His fat fingers combed her hair and dug into her scalp. The words on his lips were like small explosions, bursts of chatter detonating in his throat and forcing themselves out through his teeth. The same guttural, clattering words were repeated over and over.

Ella had seen Uncle Robert possessed this way before. In the middle of a sermon, he had sometimes flung himself upright and begun to kick like a hanging man. Broken sounds fizzed from his mouth.

Ken had told her this was the language of the angels. Uncle Robert owned the gift of tongues. Only the ungodly need fear it, her father said.

To Ella it seemed inhuman.

The hands had worked their way to the back of Ella's neck, wrenching the scalp so hard she thought he would twist her head off. Uncle Robert pushed forward, one fat leg forcing between her knees and the damp jacket flapping against her face. Ella tried weakly to shove him away with the Bible. The candles were blazing with flames a foot high, like gas flares, and the anguished cacophony howled around the top of the room but, above it all, Uncle Robert's gift of tongues boiled over.

His hands reached her shoulders, pulling them roughly. Ella could see nothing but his chest and the fat roll of his neck, with a point of stubble blocking every pore. Sweat was soaking the sleeves of his shirt, and his breath was panting over her hair.

His hands plunged down to her chest, squeezing her ribs, the thumbs digging under the straps of a bra she had never needed to wear. His palms pushed and rubbed against the small swellings that were the beginnings of breasts.

Ella thrust the Bible between his hands and tried to force him back, but his grip under her arms was too strong.

His head was thrown back and his Adam's apple throbbed with his yelps and ululations. Ella's parents could not see what he was doing. His body smothered their daughter. Ella was straining to curl her knees up and shrink into a ball but his fat thigh was in the way. The rigid bulge behind his trousers zip was pushed against her stomach.

A shudder convulsed her, and then another. The spasms shook her as though she were a puppet and something above her was yanking strings. The feedback shrieking became indistinguishable from the ringing in her ears. It did not drown the foul-breathed, ghoulish gabble spilling from Uncle Robert's mouth.

Rain battered the panes in the french doors. The blasts of thunder followed the lightning almost in the same instant.

Then, as the thrust of his groin bruised her and the heels of his hands dug so brutally that the breath was forced from her lungs, Ella's knee jerked up. She did not mean to do it. She would not have had the courage to do it.

The knee powered up with the force of a convulsion. Her thin leg-bone, though there was no weight in it, slammed between his fat thighs so hard that she felt herself connect with the base of his pelvis and almost lift him from the ground. Between her bone and his, Uncle Robert's testicles were trapped.

Uncle Robert's gift of tongues dried up. Before the pain had fully connected, his eyes bulged with amazement. His niece could not strike him, could not dare to strike him, this hard.

Trying not to crumple, he lifted his hands from Ella's body. As she slumped forward, he wrapped his arms over his head, to keep them from the giveaway clutching at his groin. He couldn't stop himself from whimpering, but the tiny noise was drowned by the inhuman shriek around the room.

The leather Bible leapt out of Ella's hands and slapped Uncle Robert across his face. The brass clasp gouged his nose and blood was trickling onto his lip as the Bible hovered a moment and then floated to the floor.

Ella hugged her bruised ribs. The screech was dying. That single kick had contained all her psychic energy. She felt barely conscious, as though the blood was draining from her head, and the adults around her were vague shadows.

Uncle Robert was frozen, squinting between his forearms at the flaring candles.

Ella's father stood, a hand half-outstretched to her mother who was somewhere at the back of the chair.

Uncle Robert, in a cracked voice, recovered his use of English. 'In the name of the Lord, I cast thee out!' The ritual words did not mask his pain.

Ella's mother suddenly cried out.

Uncle Robert motioned Juliette back with a jerk of his arm. 'You will not triumph,' he shouted at the air. 'I will overcome you, even as Jacob wrestled with the angel of the Lord and cast him down.'

Ella, her eyes rolled up, began to rise. With her hands tucked under her arms and her knees drawn up, she drifted up from the chair very slowly, like a bubble of air in thick oil.

Juliette shrieked.

Ella's eyes remained upturned. The noise dwindled to a single wire of sound, and then a sigh, and vanished into the air like a sharp intake of breath. Ella remained hovering. The thunder was suddenly more distant.

'No! No!' Juliette begged. 'Get out of here.'

Uncle Robert turned to scowl at her, and realised she was not shouting at the evil spirits. Her son, Frank, was standing in the doorway behind his father.

His hair and coat were dripping wet, and his mouth was an open circle as he stared at his sister.

'You were told! You were told! You are not to be in here.'

'What's she doing?' asked Frank. 'You got to help her.'

'Keep away from her Frank! Don't touch her!'

But Frank slipped under Uncle Robert's arm and reached up to Ella. He slipped his hands around her legs and drew her back down to the chair. Then he clasped her neck and whispered, 'I ain't scared, Ella. I ain't scared.'

Ella looked around, puzzled. The candle flames had dipped and were guttering. She could not remember why they were there. She could not remember why her father and Uncle Robert were standing over her. Uncle Robert's face was bleeding. Ken's face was white.

She did not understand why her brother, with his hair wet from the rain, was hugging her. She did not understand, though she did not argue, when her father put his arms around them quite gently and ushered them to their rooms. He said he and Uncle Robert had to talk.

Ella must have fallen asleep in her room. She was lying on her bed, face down, when she became aware that her loose grey denims were clinging uncomfortably to her thigh. She twisted over. A thin, dark stain had spread in a fold at the top of her leg.

She unzipped the trousers. Her knickers were heavily stained with blood. There was no pain. For a moment she thought she must have been injured downstairs when . . . when . . . she could not remember what had been going on.

She touched the blood on her leg, and then she realised. She had begun her first period.

PART TWO

CHAPTER ELEVEN

Monty Bell sat at someone else's desk and thumbed through their mail. The other reporters had long since gone home. There was no one to see him nosing about the *Bristol Evening Herald* offices except two sub-editors. One of them was too busy and the other was too drunk to take any notice.

There was nothing unusual about it, Monty poking about the place after eleven at night. He wasn't looking for anything in particular – something to do, that was all. A press release to write up. A magazine to read. Anything, so long as he didn't have to go home.

He talked to himself as he went. 'Policy and Resources minutes – they must be old. November 30. What's she still got those on her desk for? What a mess . . . Nothing up to date. That's the thing about bloody Christmas, eh Jim? Nothing happening.' Whatever he muttered, Monty pretended it was part of a conversation with his colleagues lingering in the office, but he didn't expect them to answer him.

People knew better than to say anything when Monty Bell started talking to them. They'd never get away. He would follow them round the room, desperately plugging away at the conversation. There was no escape, once he had latched on. He had been known to follow people into the toilets, even into the lift and down to the carpark. Still talking, forcing them to reply.

Not that he was a bad reporter. He was always eager, he was always prepared to go to the dullest meetings and stick them out till the last word. He always got his facts straight. He was never ashamed to go back and ask more questions.

Not a bad reporter. Just lonely. But he kept himself smart enough, and clean. Not like Jim Wright, the sub sleeping off his whisky on the business desk, in the same shirt he'd been wearing since Wednesday.

Still, there was something pitiful about a man in his mid-forties, mopping up the jobs a junior reporter should be doing. Monty knew that.

'*Shout For Joy*,' he said, picking an A4 pamphlet out of a pile of papers. 'Yes. *Shout For Joy: Evangelical good news for the Bedminster*

Ministry.' He turned it over. The back page featured a badly photo-copied picture of the congregation at the Pentecostal Church of Christ Reborn. They seemed to be waving, or perhaps punching the air as they shouted for joy. It was hard to tell.

'Yippee,' muttered Monty. 'Have you read the Christmas issue of *Shout For Joy*, Jim? Course you have. Wouldn't miss it, would you? Even if you weren't bloody legless.'

He tossed the magazine back onto the pile of papers, and fiddled with the desktop calendar beside the Apple Mac monitor. Tonight was Thursday, December 31. In forty-nine minutes it would be Friday, January 1. New Year's Eve. Monty turned the date forward and, in despair, picked up *Shout For Joy* again.

Anything was better than going home. Even reading this.

'New Year, New You. Get closer to Jesus on January 1st.' He dug a creased box of Silk Cut out of his trousers pocket, and a pink plastic lighter. Last cigarette. And if he went into a pub now, some prat would want to hold hands with him and sing Auld Lang Syne.

He'd have to go home. There were always some ciggies round the place somewhere. Make a cup of tea and watch Scottish bloody Hogmanay celebrations on BBC1. 'End of a perfect year, eh Jim?'

He looked over at Marielle on features, face so close to her Mac that her breath was probably clouding the screen. Maybe she wanted cheering up.

'Is this how you're going to see in the New Year, Marielle?' he called out. 'Nose to the grindstone?'

No reply.

Monty walked over. 'You going to see in the New Year here?' he repeated.

Marielle snapped, 'Not if I can help it.' She didn't look round. Obviously, she didn't want cheering up. Monty wandered back to the desk where *Shout For Joy* lay open.

He'd just finish this cigarette. Then he'd go.

'Square Dance For Jesus! Why not come along to your friendly evangelical church on Saturday, January 2nd for a toe-tapping night of American-style music? There'll be a ranch-style buffet, plenty of good friends and the chance to jump in with both feet and praise the Lord in a fun way.'

Monty shook his head. Who were these people? If that was what it took to get into heaven, then thanks, he'd be going to the other place. He turned the page.

'The Incredible Power Of Jesus! I had the chance this week to invoke Our Lord's psychical healing force and help a teenage girl, writes *RW*. The popular name for this process is exorcism – though really it is a high-powered method for opening a sick person's heart and letting Jesus in. When Jesus dwells in the spirit, there is no spare room for the devil.'

Monty was still wondering – who were these people? Did they live in the Middle Ages?

'I have performed several exorcisms over the years, but never with such spectacular results as in the back room of a Bedminster home on Sunday, December 27th. The young girl's parents had noted with growing concern that the devil seemed to be gaining influence over her soul. I should add that the girl herself was not to blame – she is the well-brought-up child of a respectable family. I prefer not to identify them, though they are known to you all.'

Monty was starting to get interested. Identify them, he thought. If everybody knows them anyway, let's have their names.

'Demonic powers were at work around the girl, with sometimes chaotic results. Lights would switch on and off, noises were heard and, on one occasion at her school, a small fire was started. Naturally, the child protested her innocence, but these occurrences inevitably caused distress and upset all around.'

That rang a bell. Fire at a school. Someone had been telling Monty about that.

The report continued: 'It was clearly time for drastic steps and so the family's back room was converted, using special equipment, into an amplifier for God's power.'

Monty was thinking – this was a Bedminster parish magazine. His own son, Christopher, went to St John's Lane Secondary in Bedminster. It was Christopher who had told him about a fire. The nativity had caught light, and the teacher had stamped the flames out and, in doing that, stamped Joseph and Mary flat. And the plastic Jesus had survived unburnt.

How had the fire started? Monty didn't remember asking. They'd just been having a laugh about it.

Could this girl, the devil girl, was she a classmate of Christopher's?

He read on: 'The girl was brought in and made to sit inside a circle of candles. It was immediately obvious that the devil had made a great attempt to latch on to her soul. A shrieking noise accompanied the ritual casting out, but the candles were observed to burn very brightly – a visible indication of the Lord's presence.

'When the demon had been forced out of her body, all present can testify that its anger made itself apparent with fearsome protests. Although we knew ourselves to be completely protected by God's love, and that the devil is powerless when we refuse to help him, it was still a disquieting experience. As anyone can imagine, we were glad when the power of Jesus worked its will and the demon was banished altogether from the home.

'I have made a special effort to relate the incident in this month's issue of *Shout For Joy*. Indeed, I am writing less than twenty-four hours after the event. The facts as recorded are, incredible as it may seem, completely accurate, and written down while fresh in my mind. It is not likely that anyone who knows me would doubt me, but in any case the testimony of my two witnesses, her own parents, will bear out every statement.

'Some may find the whole idea of demons and exorcisms hard to accept – it is all so distant from our technological, electronic, materialistic age. As Hamlet remarked to his father: "There are more things in heaven and earth than you dream of . . ." '

Monty smoked his Silk Cut down to the filter as he read the article over twice. When he had finished, he was sure of two things. First, the Shakespeare was wrong – Hamlet never said that to his father. Horatio, maybe. And second: evil voices in the air, demons, castings out, the whole business *was* hard to accept. What did they think – like, *The Exorcist* was all real?

Did anyone really believe in this heavy-duty God-botherer stuff? Who were these people?

Yes – exactly who were these people? Sixty-four thousand dollar question. The writer signed himself *RW* – initials only. Monty flicked through the magazine. Robert Wallis's name appeared at least once on every page. His photograph too.

Wallis, R had seven entries in the Bristol phone book, but only one in Bedminster. It was a bit late to try ringing now, though. Leave it till the morning.

And maybe it was worth asking Christopher. That story about the fire in the nativity probably had nothing to do with this, but it never hurt to ask.

Too late to ring Chris, of course.

Except. December 31. New Year's Eve. Half an hour to go. Christopher was bound to be up. He was fifteen now. No way his mother was going to send him to bed before midnight.

Monty started looking for a cigarette, and he had dialled his ex-wife's number before he remembered he had smoked the last one. Four rings, five rings – no one was answering. Anita was throwing a party, of course. Any excuse. And they were all probably too smashed to hear the phone.

Eight rings. Nine rings.

Maybe Christopher had been sent round to some friend's house on a sleepover. Get him out of the way.

Ten rings. Eleven. 'Hi – yeah?'

'Hi, this is Monty, is Christopher there?'

'Chris who?'

It was him, Anita's latest – Monty knew the voice. A cretinous, English public-school drawl. This creep had been living with Monty's ex-wife and son for two years, and he was asking, 'Chris who?'

'This is Monty Bell, just get my son, will you?'

Long pause. Shouts of laughter and a champagne cork popped somewhere in a different room. Anita was having a party.

'Dad?'

'Hiya. All right?'

'Okay.'

'Your mum got some friends round?'

'Yeah . . .'

Monty tried to grin, but really he was gritting his teeth. Conversations with Christopher always started like this now. They saw each other twice a month at least, but it was like introducing himself to a stranger every time.

'So. Happy New Year.'

'Thanks.'

'Aren't you going to wish me the same?'

'Happy New Year. I better be getting back now, Dad.'

'Sure. Listen. Before you go. You were telling me something last time I saw you. On Boxing Day. Do you remember, about a fire in your school? The nativity caught light, or something?'

'Yeah . . . did I tell you about . . .'

'What?'

'I was thinking about it after. 'Cos you said it sounded weird. I kind of tried not to think about it. Like I didn't want to get into it. But it was weird.'

'In what way?'

'There was this noise. I don't know. It was just weird.'

Christ, thought Monty, this was a bright boy before he went to live with his mother. What did they teach him at that school? Not English, that was certain.

'Did you say there was a girl involved?'

'Yeah. The teacher made her stand outside.'

'And that's when the weird noise stopped?'

'Yeah.'

'Who was she?'

'Just one of the girls in my class.'

'What's her name?'

'Ella.'

'Ella what?'

'Ella Wallis.'

'Wallis! So Robert Wallis is her father! No, not the father – he says her parents were his witnesses. Uncle, grandfather, something like that.

That's what he means – "I prefer not to identify the family, though they are known to you all". Chris, you're a genius. Good story, this. Cracking little story.' Monty was deliberately speaking his thoughts out loud, grateful to be talking to someone. At the other end of the line, his son was squirming. 'Get back to the party now, Chris. I'll speak to you soon.'

They exorcised her! This poor little brat in Chris's class, her own family bloody exorcised her.

Monty folded *Shout For Joy* into the inside pocket of his jacket. He didn't want to give anyone else a sniff of this. Pity it was so late. He was itching to track down this Robert Wallis now. But what timing – New Year's Eve! Maybe it was an omen. Maybe next year was going to be stuffed full of good stories.

Maybe he was going to have some fun with this.

CHAPTER TWELVE

The *Herald*'s deputy news editor read three or four paragraphs and looked at Monty in surprise. It was January 2, thirty-six hours into the new year, and the dep news ed still had a screaming hangover. His face, under the ginger stubble, was grey.

'You worked on this all day yesterday? But no one was in yesterday.'

The *Herald*, an evening paper, never printed on January 1.

'I was in,' said Monty.

The dep news ed shrugged. 'Good story,' he admitted, condescendingly, and read some more. Monty stood patiently behind his chair. Of course it was a good story. The office cat could spot it was a good story. But no one expected Monty to turn in good stories these days. And the simple fact that this one had come from Monty might tend to devalue it, in the eyes of the dep news ed.

'Too late for today's paper, though.'

Monty knew that. He'd been working there fifteen years. He knew what the deadlines were.

'Why didn't you tell me you were working on it?'

'You weren't around.'

'I mean this morning.'

The dep news ed looked suddenly contemptuous. If Monty didn't start showing the proper respect, his story was going to end on the newsdesk spike. Or, crueller still, the copy would go to some twenty-three-year-old whizkid reporter for 'rewriting'.

Monty knew he was expected to apologise. Apologise for bringing in the best story of the day. He'd seen enough like this ginger-faced runt of a deputy newsdesk supremo – they shot up from trainee reporters to 12-hour-a-day superstars so fast, Monty barely had time to learn their names. Then they were off, to radio, or the nationals. When they arrived, Monty would show them the ropes – where the courts were, when the councils met, which cupboard had the teabags. Pretty soon they would despise him, for being twice their age and still stuck on this provincial evening paper.

'Sorry,' he said. 'I should have tipped you off about it sooner.'

'Yes. You should. How am I supposed to run this desk if people like you get all possessive about your stories?'

Monty suppressed the urge to smack him round the back of the head. A distinguished end to a fine journalistic career that would be.

'This girl's parents. The Wallises. Are they going to play for a picture?'

'We got one yesterday afternoon,' Monty answered. 'Well, Roger was around, and when I told him about the story he was interested, so he came out with me. It was easier.' Roger Thompson was the chief photographer. Now Monty was apologising, not just for turning up a front page story but for getting the picture to go with it.

'Pix any good? Is she bending spoons or something?'

'She's just sitting with her mum and dad. Nice picture.'

'Next time you have a brainstorm, let me know straight away, all right? Even if it means ringing me at home.'

'Sure,' said Monty. One last bite of humble pie and he was victorious. 'Good page one splash for tomorrow, eh?'

'Maybe.'

On Monday morning, Monty's story was splashed right across the front, spilling onto half of page three. There were two of Roger's pictures, both used big and in full colour. On the front, Ella, Juliette and Ken stood outside 66 Nelson Road with their arms awkwardly around each other. Inside, Uncle Robert, craftily lit so his sideburns threw shadowy fingers across his face, brandished two burning candles.

The headline consisted of a single word: 'POSSESSED!'

Below that, in smaller type: 'Exorcist terror of church family'.

And barely smaller than that, in white letters on a fat black block: 'EXCLUSIVE! By Monty Bell'.

FROM the outside, there is nothing about 66 Nelson Road to tell a passer-by of the terrors that stalk within.

But one glance into the frightened eyes of schoolgirl Ella Wallis or her elegant French mother, Juliette, and the truth is plain. The ordinary family who live at No 66 have been driven to the brink of Hell in their own home.

What they saw when they peered over the edge makes a story which no *Evening Herald* reader will find easy to believe. It may not be any the less true for that.

And the family can only pray that the paranormal nightmare tormenting Ella, 14, has been ended by a dramatic exorcism during which, they insist, the schoolgirl was lifted into the air by invisible forces while eerie voices were heard.

'It was a confrontation,' declares evangelist preacher Robert Wallis, Ella's uncle and the man who conducted the chilling ritual which, he claims, cast out a demon which was possessing his niece's body.

'We heard the incoherent voice of the Evil One. That isn't a metaphor. I mean every word of it, and Ella's parents will back me up to the hilt. Modern science can't explain it. But what we saw, we saw.

'I wish I had video'd the whole thing. We saw things that would stand the scientists on their heads.

'There's only one explanation – it was a confrontation. The Powers of Light against the Powers of Darkness.'

Ella's mother spoke more guardedly about the ordeal her daughter endured.

'It is all the truth, what Robert says,' agreed Juliette Wallis, 32. 'I don't know how you would interpret it. Robert says it was a demon from Hell – of course he knows a lot more about these things than me. It is not for me to say. But we all saw the same things.'

The stories told by Ella Wallis's mother, her father, Ken, 35, and his brother, Robert, 41, all tally in the minutest details – a circumstance difficult to achieve if their story is nothing but a hoax. All three agree that:

- On Thursday, December 27, Robert Wallis placed a circle of eight candles around his niece in the downstairs back room of her home.
- Clutching a Bible, Robert, who preaches at the Pentecostal Church of Christ Reborn in Smyth Road, began an exorcism ritual which he has used up to a dozen times with other worshippers from his congregation.
- A high-pitched noise immediately began, like feedback.
- An icy wind swept the room. The candles were extinguished, and then relit themselves.
- Robert Wallis began speaking in tongues – a phenomenon he calls a gift from God, indicating the presence of the Holy Spirit. The trance-like state, accompanied by a stream of words and sounds without apparent meaning, has sometimes occurred while he preached before dozens of people at the Smyth Road church.

- The exorcist placed his hands on Ella Wallis's head and chest
  – 'To help the Holy Spirit enter her body,' he says.
- As he reached the climax of the exorcism, Ella was seen to
  levitate vertically from her chair. Each adult present, questioned
  individually, described this incident identically, although
  neither Ken nor Juliette Wallis was keen to discuss it. Their
  daughter, they said, rose six or eight inches and hovered, still
  in a sitting position and apparently in an unconscious trance.
- This continued for over a minute, until the Wallises' younger
  child, Frank, seven, came unexpectedly into the room and went
  to his sister's side.

Ella herself says she can remember nothing of this. A quiet,
small girl, she is visibly uncomfortable at being the focus of
attention. She accepts what her parents have told her – that a
horrific noise was heard, and that she levitated – but she wishes
the exorcism had not been necessary.

'It frightens me,' she admitted. 'I don't understand. I know
my Dad knows all about it so I don't want to go against him. He
knows it was right.

'But other girls I know don't have all this stuff happening to
them, and it doesn't seem fair.'

Ken and Juliette Wallis decided to have their daughter
exorcised after a series of strange incidents, including lights
switching on and off, objects falling off tables and unexplained
noises.

The phenomena culminated, it is alleged, in an incident at St
John's Lane Secondary school in Bedminster, Bristol, where
books flew across a classroom unaided and a fire was started by
an invisible hand in a cardboard nativity scene.

A school spokeswoman refused to comment yesterday. But
one pupil who witnessed the frightening event said: 'It was like
a poltergeist. Everyone knew it had something to do with Ella
Wallis, because the books were coming from her desk. There
was a weird noise, and that stopped when she left the room.'

Opinion was divided among scientists and churchmen today
over the explanation. Psychical researcher Dr Thomas Wathern-
Pickett, of the University of the West of England, said: 'I'm not
surprised to learn there's a fourteen-year-old girl at the centre of
this.

'Paranormal activity is frequently reported around adolescents, and I don't think it should be taken too seriously. Much of it is simply a cry for attention.

'I think the family were wrong to indulge in this superstitious exorcism ritual, however. Glorifying the phenomena won't make them go away, and could give this girl something of a complex. It sounds like she endured a very frightening afternoon. They live at number 66, I hear, though I should have considered number 666, the devil's numerals, to be more appropriate.'

But evangelist theologian Professor Lucius Scudder, of Bristol University, said: 'The Bible is quite forthright about these things. Demons do exist. Possessions do occur. Jesus knew it, and he wasn't afraid to take action.

'It is a perversion of this modern age, that we are prepared to believe in sub-atomic particles that disobey the simplest laws of physics, yet we scoff at truths which our ancestors have understood for millennia.

'This family have reacted commendably. It sounds like the poor girl has endured a very nasty possession, and I hope it's all over.'

Monty knew it was the best thing he'd written for years. The pleasure of it, remembering how good he could be when he wanted, was sensual – his blood coursed in hot shivers when he thought of the intro.

The editor had called him into conference, the newspaper's Cabinet meeting, to tell him: 'Two things, Monty. One, you're barking mad. Two, bloody brilliant story. Bloody brilliant. But we can't run it . . .' and Monty's heart sank '. . . without some kind of disclaimer. What does that David Frost say on the box? "Is it magic, is it illusion or is it beyond belief?" Add that on the end.'

Monty didn't care. If that was the only change his editor wanted, he was well pleased.

Colleagues who turned deaf if he went near them were stopping him to say the same. 'You're losing your marbles, Monty. Brilliant story. How'd you get it?'

All of Bristol was saying the same. It was a fantastic feeling, one he had long gone without – the city was talking about what he, Monty Bell, had written.

He could hardly bear to think that, while he got the glory, someone else would get the big cheque. Bristol's rival news agencies would already be rewriting the story for the nationals. They would pocket the profit.

So Monty took a risk. He broke a cardinal rule in his contract. If anyone caught him, it would mean instant dismissal. He took a copy of the story, slipped out to the Prontaprint shop up the road, and faxed his story – with an invoice for £400 – to the newsdesk of the *Daily Post* in London.

Chapter Thirteen

Until he lifted his visor, the reporter looked like an alien. He stood in Nelson Road, surveying No 66 through the tinted eye-guard of his motorcycle helmet. His body was encased in leathers, boots and suit and gloves. He could have been moulded by alien technology to resemble something human, a Man In Black sent to exact pledges of silence from Ella and her family.

He was not alien. He was a Paranormal Correspondent.

The gloved fist went to his visor and ice-blue eyes gazed out. The eyes betrayed nothing, no flicker of hesitation or fatigue or unease. They were the eyes of Peter Guntarson.

Guntarson studied the Wallises' home. Zipped into a pocket of his motorcycle leathers was Monty Bell's faxed story from the *Herald*. The copy courted ridicule from its first word, but one thing about it had already been proven true: there was nothing about the outside of Ella's home to mark it out from the rest.

Between the front gate and the door were just four stone steps. Along the length of the terrace ran a waist-high, brick boundary wall, which gave each house a tiny front yard. No 66, like most of the houses, grew a bush in the yard. The bush was kept trim, so the maximum light could come through the one downstairs window. Many in the street, including the Wallises, had refitted their window in a modern, aluminium frame.

A tiled porch roof, like a short skirt or the peak of a cap, hung above the door.

There was only one window upstairs – the main bedroom. Everyone in the street shrouded their windows with net curtains. No 66 shared a chimney stack with No 68. The window-frames were painted orange, the only orange frames in the street. That was all there was to see.

Guntarson glanced up the street, at his photographer unbuckling a camera bag from his red Yamaha 850. The two men, helmets glinting blackly under their arms, walked through the gate at No 66 and rang the bell.

When Ella looked up from the television, the newspapermen were crowding through the door. They almost filled the room. Their heads burst from tightly buttoned leather collars, disproportionately small heads, like knights in armour without their helms. Fat black rolls of leather bolstered their broad shoulders. Ribs of black padding guarded their chests and tapered sharply at their waists. The leather on their upper legs glistened tautly. Fans of leather protected their knees, and their immense boots with two-inch soles were buckled all the way up their calves.

They were pulling off their Dainese gauntlets to reveal strangely white hands.

'These men have come all the way from London just to see you, Ella,' said Juliette.

One of the men, the one with swept-back blond hair and shining blue eyes, held out his hand. 'We've been sent by the *Daily Post*.'

So they had not come to protect her. It was a ridiculous idea, but for a few moments she had wondered if her father had hired these men in armour as her bodyguards, to save her from journalists.

Instead, these were the journalists.

She turned back to the television.

'They have come a long way to ask you some questions,' insisted Juliette, reaching over to switch off the set.

'I don't want to say nothing.'

'Your father wants you to answer nicely to their questions.'

Ella stared at the blank screen.

'I am sorry, she is a girl so very difficult sometimes. It is my fault, if I am only more strict with her she can be better behaved . . .'

The blond man ignored Juliette. Squatting a couple of paces from Ella's chair, he unzipped his creaking leathers to the chest, as if he were opening his heart to the girl.

The Dainese gear was embossed with a fox logo. Ella liked foxes.

'Hi. I'm Peter.' His face had the raw lustre that goes with very blond skin. He was grinning. His eyes fixed unashamedly on hers. 'This is Joey. He takes the pictures. I write the words. Your dad's done a deal with our newspaper. He gets some money, a lot of money, and in return the newspaper gets the chance to print a story or two. About you. About your family. Did he tell you this?'

'He don't talk about money.'

'Okay. Well, I'll talk about money.'

Juliette cut in: 'There is no need to worry a girl like Ella with business matters.'

Peter Guntarson smiled at Juliette but ignored the interruption. 'You got interviewed by the local paper, right? They didn't pay you a penny, but they published the whole story about "possession" and "exorcism," and a load of details about your private life too. And when they talked to you, I'll bet they didn't mention this story was going to be all over their front page, with massive headlines and pictures and what-have-you. Am I right?'

'They didn't say much to me 'bout nothing,' admitted Ella. 'It were Dad they wanted, mostly.'

'That doesn't sound very fair to me. In fact, the whole report struck me as unfair.'

As a matter of fact, Guntarson had admired Monty Bell's piece. It did a good job on Ella's parents and her Uncle Robert. They had been stitched up with their own quotes, made to look creepy, and cranky, and cruel to a confused little girl.

But that was not the story Guntarson wanted. He had a different angle.

'Listen. This hasn't been easy for you,' he told her. She was still looking straight into his face. He met her gaze. It was a good way to strike up a rapport. And Peter Guntarson was not going to be stared down by a fourteen-year-old girl.

'I want our involvement to be a positive thing. So that we understand each other from the start – I'm here to help.' Guntarson glanced round at Juliette. 'Do you think we could have a cup of tea? And I'm going to get these leathers off. It's warm suddenly.'

Ella broke off her stare and fixed her eyes on her feet as Guntarson unzipped the armour to his thighs and loosened the bright buckles on his boots. He folded the whole outfit loosely over a chair and straightened his dark blue suit. When Ella looked up he was slipping black Nikes on.

She scarcely looked at Joey, who had discarded his bike gear too and now was rooting inside his camera bag.

'Okay, let's get to know each other. I'm Peter Guntarson. I'm twenty-six. My father's Icelandic – but in fact I was born in Canada. My father brought me to England when I was fourteen, and I don't see him any more. I've got a dual passport. I'm a freelance journalist, which means I'll work for anyone who pays me enough. Mostly it's the *Post* – they like my style of story. I investigate the unexplained. Ghosts, UFOs, parapsychology – I know a great deal about all of it and I've got a very open mind. Also I write well about it: that's why the paper keeps using me. And I've been earning my living like this for quite a while, about fifteen months, since I left university.'

'He's a real brainbox,' chipped in the photographer.

Guntarson managed to smile and, at the same time, give Joey a foul look. 'Actually, I went to Oxford and I've got a DPhil in psychology and parapsychology, but I shouldn't let it worry you.'

Ella looked like it did worry her. She leant back from him, as though he might find out if he came too close what a waste of time it was, talking to her.

'So that's me. What about you?'

After a few seconds, she worked up the courage to shrug.

'Okay. I understand. It isn't easy. A load of strange people, asking you questions. Forget the questions. I'll show you a trick. My mother taught me to do this.' He paused. 'My mother,' he repeated. 'It doesn't work with everyone, but it'll work with you. You're the right type.

'Think of a word. Any word. The first word that comes into your head. And now I want you to imagine you're standing on a sandy beach, at the water's edge. You can hear the waves. There's a ship, right out on the horizon. Nothing but blue water between you and that ship. And you want to tell your word to that ship. So you imagine you're yelling out, as loud as you can. Don't really yell. Just in your imagination.

'Thought of a word?'

Ella nodded. Her eyes were closed.

'Okay. Yell out to that ship.'

Guntarson's eyes flickered, and then he jumped. 'You said it out loud!' But he saw from her face she had not. 'Joey, did you hear her say something?'

'She ain't spoken since we got here,' answered the photographer.

'Wow. I've never heard anyone as clearly as that. You really didn't say it out loud?' He shook his head in surprise. 'The word was "Help". Right? **Help!** Is that what you'd shout out to a ship?' He paused, staring at Ella. 'That's serious déja-vu. I'll tell you what I mean sometime. Okay, my turn. I've got a word, you've got to hear it. Ready?'

Guntarson closed his eyes and let his shoulders droop. Joey watched. He hadn't seen the reporter do this before. Guntarson's jaw clenched and his head ducked forward, but there was nothing to betray what word he was thinking.

' "Friends",' said Ella.

'That's right, that's right.' Guntarson shook his fists excitedly. 'You heard me clearly?'

Ella nodded. There was a short silence. Surely, Guntarson thought, this would be enough. This had to break the ice.

'You think we going to be friends?' whispered Ella.

'We've got to be. I don't want to be on bad terms with anyone who can read my mind that clearly.'

She smiled. It was a nice smile. Ella's teeth were small and white. Guntarson smiled back. His teeth were broader and whiter.

'Let's do it again,' she said.

In a few seconds she called out 'dolphin,' 'Tutu' and 'Rambo'.

He got them all instantly. When Ella spoke aloud she whispered, but her thoughts were loud enough. Guntarson tried to hide his emotion. The power of her telepathic response triggered an intense, disturbing memory. Once, only once before, had he experienced such vivid reception, and it stirred a terror that had lain smothered for half his life.

He choked back the rising bubble of fear, and said, 'Those are hard words. People usually choose easy ones – cat, dog, flower. What's Rimbaud got to do with it?'

'He's my friend's cat.'

'And 2.2?'

'She's Auntie Sylvie's budgie.'

'Ah. Have you got a pet?' He carried on with questions like this, finding out what her interests were, what her friends were called, where she'd been on holiday – none of it stuff that mattered. Nothing he would put in a report. He just wanted Ella to talk to him naturally, trustingly.

His usual technique was easy, a kind of flattery. He just listened. He let the interviewees talk for half an hour or more about their favourite subject – themselves, usually, or their families. People became intoxicated when they were allowed to talk, without check, to an attentive listener. It was a kind of hypnosis. They opened up, they dropped their guard. After a while, a few questions could guide their talk onto the desired topics.

But Ella didn't talk. She never managed more than a few words, a sentence at most, before drying up. Evidently she was pleased to have someone pay her attention – Guntarson guessed she got ignored most of the time. But she wasn't a chatterer.

He could not keep asking her things. Nothing was more sure to make an interviewee clam up than question after question, even the most inconsequential questions.

Juliette brought the tea. 'I hope it is not too boring for you, talking with our Ella. She has not much to say for herself.'

Ella set her teeth and glowered at her own hands.

That was it, thought Guntarson. Challenge her a little. She wants us to be friends – make her show off.

'I suppose,' he said, 'it's been much better since your Uncle Robert cast out those demons.'

'Oh yes,' her mother answered for her. 'Much better.'

'No more weird incidents,' he prompted. Ella still stared at her hands. Guntarson pictured the ship on the horizon and shouted in his mind: 'Smash it!'

Something hurled itself against the skirting-board with a blast like a gunshot. Juliette shrieked.

'Bleeding hell!' said Joey. 'Ha-ha-ha! Did you see that? It was a knick-knack – a cat or something.' He dodged forward and grabbed the three pieces of the ornament. 'Look at this.' He held the fragments out to Juliette.

'What is it? I have never seen it. Ella, is it yours?'

Ella shook her head without looking.

'It's my mum's,' said Joey, still staring at the pieces in his pudgy hands. 'She's got bleeding millions of these things. Ha-ha-ha! She collects them.' He proffered the bits to Guntarson. 'I'll swear it's my mum's. I bought it for her, her birthday, when I was a kid. I don't believe it. It just appeared in the air. Did you see it?'

'I heard it, that's all.'

'I wish I'd had my camera on it. It zapped into the air, just there' – he pointed to a spot behind Juliette's head, about five feet up – 'and it hovered, and I'm thinking what the f-f-flaming heck's that? And then it fell to about here' – ten inches from the carpet – 'and whizzed along, smash into the wall.'

'So it didn't fall straight?'

'I'm not imagining it, Pete. I'm not – I've got the bits in my hand. You don't happen to know my mum, do you, Ella? Ha-ha-ha?' Joey could not stand to let anything go for long without a joke. 'She'll be furious about this. If I can ever make her believe it. She loves her cats. Not your fault, of course. I just wish I'd freeze-framed it. Couldn't do it again, could you? Ha-ha-ha!' He scrambled to the camera-bag to change his lens.

Juliette was not smiling. Guntarson leaned forward, elbows on his thighs, watching Joey's excitement. Ella still said nothing. The sheets of silver-blonde hair about her face did not hide her silent satisfaction.

'When a poltergeist throws something,' Guntarson remarked, 'the object usually appears from nowhere, just like this ornament, and it doesn't travel in a straight line. It hovers, it goes round corners. Just like someone invisible is carrying it.' He saw Juliette's shudder. 'Have you heard of poltergeists, Mrs Wallis?'

'I have seen them. In France, as a girl.'

'In your own family?'

'No.'

Ella shouted secretly, in her head, 'Liar! Radio! Voices!'

Guntarson heard. He didn't quite understand, but he heard clearly enough, and smiled at Ella. She looked confused, and coloured up.

'Often with a poltergeist, there's a young person involved. They're the energy source. And obviously Ella's the energy source here. But I don't think you could call this a poltergeist.'

Joey had his camera in his hand, trained on the air, ready to snap at anything with his wide-angle lens.

'Poltergeists are all the same. No sense of humour, just a lot of destruction and mischief. Things get broken, things fly around. They don't like religious objects, and they don't like parents.'

'I think,' said Juliette, 'I do not know if I believe in what you say, but what has happened to Ella is just the same.'

'No. There's no controlling a poltergeist,' Guntarson said to Ella. 'And I think you can control this if you want.'

Ella shook her head.

'I think you can,' he pursued. 'I have a very strong feeling, you can control much more than you realise. You can think a word as clearly as I can speak it. That's an indication of how strong your mind is.'

Juliette moved to her daughter's side, as though she wanted to step between the girl and the crouching reporter. 'I do not think Ella has any control. Demons, poltergeists, energy – I do not want to under-stand about any of it. You do not know Ella, you did not see her when she was a very little baby.'

'Did things happen then? Even when she was very small?'

'I do not know. No. Of course not.'

'So what does it matter about when she was a baby?'

'I am her mother. I can tell you. She does not control this. It is not what-would-you-say deliberate.'

'I'm not saying it is.' Guntarson fixed his eyes on Ella. 'But you could be in control. If you really wanted it. If you had the right help.'

'The help Ella needs is to be a normal little girl again.'

'That would be a waste.'

Ella kept staring into Guntarson's wide blue eyes.

She had always wanted to be a normal little girl. A normal, loveable girl. She had prayed for that, long before she realised there was anything paranormal about her.

Her prayers hadn't counted for anything.

And now this man came, who talked to her and looked straight at her and did not try to scare her or threaten her. And he said it would be a waste if she tried to be normal.

Auntie Sylvie would say he looked like a lovely Greek god. Ella did not know really what that meant, but to her he looked like a lifeguard from one of the posters on her friends' bedroom walls. *Baywatch* posters.

She didn't know what her lifeguard wanted but, whatever it was, Ella wanted it too.

She breathed in deeply. Guntarson smelled of leather, and of a leathery, lemony aftershave too. 'Most people,' he was saying, 'have weak minds. They picture an image or a word, and dozens of other things come crowding into their head too. Usually things they are trying to repress, the things they don't want to think of. So they can't transmit their thoughts clearly, they can't channel them. They're scared of thinking the wrong thing. It takes a strong mind to switch off everything and concentrate on one single thought. But you can do it, Ella. Your mind is very strong.'

'Her father always says,' sniffed Juliette, 'she is very weak in the head.'

'I can control it,' admitted Ella, quietly. 'Sometimes.'

Guntarson waited a long time, giving her the space to find the words. At last he prompted, 'How?'

'Not the noises. Not when things fall off and break. That ain't deliberate.'

'No one says you're trying to be naughty.'

'I can, sort of, feel other people's feelings.'

'Yes. I understand that.' There was so much he wanted her to reveal to him, and he was having to tease it out, word by word.

'And I can float. When I wants to.'

'Levitate?'

She looked blank.

'Like flying? Your whole body lifting up off the ground?'

'Yeah.'

'Ella!' exclaimed Juliette. The sight of her daughter, suspended above her chair, had been more shocking to her than anything else during the exorcism, and she earnestly desired never to see it again. 'Do not be so ridiculous! What will your father say, if you tell stupid things to these men who are paying us money?'

'It's true.'

'I am so sorry, Mr Guntarson,' pleaded Juliette. 'She lives in her own dream world.'

'Can you show me, Ella?'

Ella felt her mother's anger, like dry heat beating down from an electric heater. Joey was edging closer to her too, cupping a segmented lens in his hand. The lens was malevolent, a fat insect with one glittering eye. She should have kept quiet.

'I can't.'

'Of course you cannot! Stupid girl!'

Guntarson stared evenly at the mother. 'Mrs Wallis, as you just pointed out, my newspaper is paying you a good deal of money. I don't think your attitude is helping matters. Perhaps you wouldn't mind going into another room.'

Ella trembled for him. How could he dare speak to Juliette like that? Ken might find out.

'I am to stay with you. My husband ordered it.'

'Then I must insist you go to the other side of the room, and please don't keep answering Ella's questions for her.'

And Juliette did back off. Ella stared at her new ally with astonished admiration. What made him so brave? He had to be very confident. It was probably because he had such an important job. And he was incredibly, brilliantly brainy. He was bound to earn loads of money too.

And he thought it would be a waste if Ella was normal, if she couldn't control any of the weird stuff. It would be terrible to disappoint him. It wouldn't be worth living if she disappointed him.

'When have you levitated?'

'In my room.'

'When you were alone? Okay, close your eyes. Visualise your room. You're in there, no one else is around. It's dark. You can hear all the usual sounds around you. Focus on that. Now, when you're ready, begin to levitate.'

Guntarson's voice was low and firm, insistent, a hypnotist's voice. He watched Ella breathe out slowly until her body sagged. But her feet stayed on the floor and her hands stayed on the arms of the chair.

Her eyes flickered open. She stared at him and he felt the muscles in his back and shoulders throb, as if he had been weight-lifting. A rush of cold air made his skin tingle. Ella's eyes rolled upwards and she tilted her head, baring her teeth. A shrill note groaned in her throat.

He began to pant, willing her upwards.

Her palms were raised off the armrests. All her energy was being bunched into her body – she had none to waste on a physical down-thrust. Her feet too were drawn off the floor. She began to drift in the seat – not visibly floating but scarcely making an indent on the seat.

With a sudden, sideways lurch, Ella bobbed out of the armchair. One hip struck the wing of the chairback, and she twisted in the air. Her knees were pulled up to her chest, her elbows were thrust out as though something were lifting her under the arms. As she rolled slowly over, to be floating facedown, Guntarson reached a hand out. He touched her foot and pressed it gently. Ella's body dipped away from his fingers as lightly as a balloon. There was no resistance to his touch. She was weightless.

The motor on Joey's camera flickered through frame after frame as Ella rolled gradually to face the lens. Her eyes were all whites, like a statue's. Her lips curled and the skin strained in a transparent mask across her nose and cheekbones. The pulse in both temples of her forehead beat rapidly. She kept on turning on an axis that seemed to run from her crown and out through her stomach, along into her heels. That imaginary line stayed at a constant height, about four feet above the floor.

As Joey flipped the spent film deftly from the back of the Nikon and fitted a new roll onto the drive, Ella drifted downwards. Two or three inches from the carpet, crouched as if on all fours, she suddenly

moved closer to Guntarson. It seemed not so much that a current of
air had wafted her – more as if he had her on an invisible line and was
drawing her in. She came to rest with her head against his foot and
closed her eyes tightly.

Later, Joey rang Guntarson's mobile number from the *Post* darkroom.
'Pete! Pete! I've just developed them films. You ain't gonna guess
what!'

'What?' Guntarson had gone straight from Ella's home to his
Bayswater apartment. He wanted to write the story, but his excitement
was so great he could barely sit down. He stooped now and then
over the keyboard, to tap in phrases and images that seemed to him
to be key. Half-sentences and unconnected words filled the screen.
'Cold . . . oppression . . . her intelligence, almost her whole self-
consciousness, channelled into her psychic force . . . trusting what she
does not understand . . .' His heart was still racing and his hands
punched with the thrill of it.

He'd seen this thing, and it was unbelievable. It was, almost literally,
unbelievable.

Trancelike guitar and drums beat from his music system – U2's If
God Will Send His Angels. Guntarson turned it down with the remote.

'You ain't gonna believe what's happened,' repeated Joey.

'No pictures,' answered Guntarson instantly. 'Blank film.'

'No, they've come out fine. But she's not on all of them. I've got her
rising out of the chair, then I paused a few seconds, then I started
firing again when she started rolling round to face me. Right?'

'On two of the frames, she just ain't there. One instant she's in the
picture, the next she's not, and the next one she is. Then she vanishes
again. Exactly the same camera angle, and everything in the room is
the same. But our little miss ain't in two of the pictures. Even her
shadow disappears.'

Guntarson turned the music back up. He stood at his study
window, three storeys above the Bayswater Road, and closed his eyes.
The image of Ella's body, drifting weightless, floated through his mind.
It did not flicker. He had watched her during every second of the
levitation, and he had not seen what Joey's camera saw – she had
always been there, in front of him. What was he to believe?

He had no reason to dismiss what the camera saw. This girl had
levitated, and there was no rational, physical explanation. If the film
really showed that Ella vanished, it had to be regarded as part of the
phenomenon. For imperceptibly brief instants when she levitated, Ella
might cease to be visible. Imperceptibly, except to a camera.

Guntarson tried to imagine where she could be, when she
disappeared.

CHAPTER FOURTEEN

In the midwinter darkness of Ailish's small bedroom, with only one thin quilt to insulate two large bodies against the cold, Ken Wallis and his Sunday woman lay with their arms around each other. Ailish had slipped her bra back on, for comfort – otherwise, they were naked, and their toes were tucked up against bare legs.

'My Lord, it's cold in here,' said Ken, for the third time.

'That heater's just about clapped out,' she answered. 'Works all right till you get a night like this. Then it can't cope.'

'Weather forecast said it was going to be minus eight tonight.'

'What – Fahrenheit or centithingies?'

'Didn't say. Blooming cold, whatever. It's just coming straight through that window of yours. Why don't you get it double-glazed?'

'Oh yes. Very likely. I'll get an indoor swimming pool at the same time, shall I?'

'Ain't going to be that expensive.'

'Not to you maybe. Not to Mr Millionaire-Sold-His-Story-To-The-*Evening-Herald*.'

'Huh,' said Ken. The pillow talk was lurching in a direction he didn't like.

'How much did you get for that, anyhow?'

'What, the *Herald*? Not a penny.'

'Come on.'

'I don't never tell a lie. You knows that, girl. What's the ninth commandment? Thou shalt not bear false witness.'

'What's the other one? Thou shalt not commit you-know-what.'

Ken sat up sharply and she knew instantly she had gone too far. Fearing he would hit her, she threw both forearms across her face. 'Sorry! Sorry!'

He inhaled hard, the air hissing in his nose.

'Sorry, lover.'

'Don't make fun of it,' he warned her. 'You know not what you do. Don't sneer at the one true book.'

She lowered her arms. One hand slipped to his thigh and caressed it. Her fingers edged up. Ailish knew how to distract a man's attention.

'So you let the *Herald* print all that, your pictures on the front page and everything, and you didn't get nothing for it?'

'They don't pay for stories. They're only the little local rag. I asked them, of course. Said I could give them the full details, like, but I wanted a couple of hundred quid. Proper reimbursement for my expenses. Time, telephone, that sort of thing.' He let his head settle back on the pillow. 'Don't stop girl, you're doing that good.'

'I wouldn't have told them a word,' said Ailish, curling closer and beginning to rub more forcefully. 'Not till I'd seen the lining in their wallets.'

Something else Ailish also knew about – getting money from people. Though she collected a weekly pay-packet, she did not work – and because she did not work, she drew social security. The flat was not hers, but she did not pay rent. She did not sleep with her men for money, but without the men she would not have anything.

Her last proper job had been at BK Lewis Printers, where Ken was in charge of production. Ailish was taken on as a cleaner, during a brief dispute with Lewis's usual contract cleaners. The dispute was soon patched up, and the old firm came back to sweep around the presses and mop the toilets. But Ailish stayed on the payroll. Ken fixed that.

They had been lovers from the third day after she started work. The first time was in the paper stores, with the delivery doors wide open and a freezing draught blowing between the cartons.

They might have been discovered by anyone, at any moment. Ailish liked that. It made her more urgent. She wanted to do it in public – in cinemas, in the park, in the car parked outside Ken's house.

Ken wasn't so eager to be caught in the act. But when Ailish started demanding, his brains cut out and something else took over. He already had one lover, Marcia – the woman he saw on Wednesdays. He hadn't slept with Juliette for more than a year – not properly slept with, not as a man should know his wife, if she be a righteous wife. And before that, it had been years since he and Juliette felt any passion for each other. It had become impossible, Ken reasoned with himself. Passion could not exist in that dried-out, hollow-reed body of his wife's. And no honest man could say he found a husk like that desirable.

He had been obsessed with loving her body once, when there was nothing of the dried husk about her sallow skin and moist lips. He first saw her as she hurried from a shop in an Orleanais village. Kenneth Wallis was twenty-seven, riding in the front passenger seat of a pink VW Kombi camper, with five friends on their way back to the ferry at Le Havre. He ordered the driver to stop and coaxed the girl to take a lift home. She did not need much coaxing – the walk to her father's house was nearly four miles. She squeezed onto Ken's seat, and he found out she worked behind a counter at the shop. Within half a minute they began kissing.

When she slid out of the seat and onto the muddy path leading up to her home, she told them to wait for her at the Artenay junction. The VW stayed at that junction for more than two hours, with Ken holding the car keys and threatening to hospitalise anyone who tried to take them off him.

No one had asked the girl her name. They had no idea why she wanted to go with them, or what she intended to do once they reached Le Havre. But, as she climbed onto Ken's lap and slung a greasy holdall packed with clothes into the back on the camper, it was evident she had made up her mind.

Juliette was smuggled onto the ferry cardeck, crouched under a pull-down bunk, walled in by suitcases. Forty hours had passed since she ran away from her father. She had already become pregnant.

That was a long time ago. They had not been lovers since Frank was two. There had been a reason for it, of course – an event which made it unthinkable for them to carry on sleeping together. The reason had ceased to matter years ago. It did not signify – they would never be lovers again.

They still talked, but they did not trust each other. There were no confessions or searching questions. If Juliette wanted someone to talk to, there was always her sister, Sylvie. She didn't have to bother Ken.

When Ken sold his daughter's story exclusively to the *Daily Post* he did not dream of telling Juliette the details. No more would he tell Ailish.

A man's money was his own business.

Ella was awake too, at three in the freezing Monday morning. The dream had woken her, the same dream about the angel and the demon, the stench and the fire. She was not levitating when she woke up. She knew the word now – levitating. The proper word for it. Peter had taught it her. She had woken, thrashing in her bed, the way she usually did. That was when she saw the lights.

Three lights circled on her wall. They reminded her of something. She had seen them before. They lit the room with a cream glow.

They had no source. Nothing was shining a light through her window. Anyway, her curtains were drawn and her door was closed. She watched them move around each other, each one describing a quick triangle that interlocked with the others. They spun in a blur, and then more slowly. It almost seemed to Ella that they were not on her wall – they were a centimetre or two away from it, spinning discs of light, solid discs. She might have reached out to them, but it was too cold to leave her bed.

Ella lay, one hand draped in her long hair, supporting her head, and she watched as the three lights spun more and more tightly together, until there was only one, bright, whirling disc. She had seen it before. The memory had almost evaporated. Searching for it, she fell asleep.

CHAPTER FIFTEEN

Peter Guntarson was almost weeping with rage. Pressed down on the tank of his black Kawasaki 1100, bowling under the grey sky at close to a hundred mph, he scarcely saw the sluggish Monday traffic on the M4. The top of his helmet was bowed to the horizon, and most of what Guntarson could see, through an angry film of red, was the motorway tarmac skimming under his wheels.

He was almost on top of a metallic blue Porsche 944 before he had registered it. The Porsche was trundling at an arthritic eighty mph, and would not be easing over to let him pass. Guntarson dropped back a few yards, then twisted back the throttle to its limit. The motorbike muscled past on the inside, accelerating hard enough that the car driver did not realise what Guntarson was doing before the bike had drawn level. It was too late to try and block. The Kawasaki jinked in front and kept accelerating, screaming like a Grand Prix racer, and all the Porsche driver could do was stamp his foot down and flash his lights. Before he reached ninety mph, the bike was a hundred yards ahead.

Guntarson wanted to raise one finger in insult, but at 120 mph the throbbing, lunging Kawasaki needed all his fingers and all his strength.

Trimming the throttle, he felt slightly better. Instantly, that made him angrier than ever. How could he let himself be so humiliated, so goaded by these idiots? Did he have to indulge in suicidal overtaking antics to remind himself of his superiority? Did he not have a DPhil from the world's most respected university – Dr Guntarson, actually a doctor, *Doctor* Guntarson? And how intelligent was it to kill himself on a motorbike?

But then, how could he submit to be overruled by that strutting, semi-literate, wine-addled, foul-breathed, coarse, conceited, warted, witless, grotesque imbecile who called himself editor of the *Daily Post*?

They had cut Guntarson's copy. Worse than cut it. Of the copy he submitted after midnight on Thursday morning, more than half had been rewritten for Saturday's story.

He was used to being rewritten. He never complained at the odd word changed here and there – the sub-editors had to do something to justify their existence. But this time they had changed the whole theme. Guntarson had written about Ella's mind. About the confused, secluded character shaped by psychic forces. He had probed beyond the parapsychology, into the real psychology.

And all the *Post* wanted were the weird bits.

They used the pictures. They used about a dozen of Joey's pictures, one of them filling the whole front page. Ella was afloat above the chair, knees drawn up, lying on her side like a baby in the womb. She faced the camera but her eyes were shut, and her nose and mouth were hidden by drapes of hair. Every strand was in perfect focus. It was plain there was nothing to support her.

The headline demanded: 'CAN YOU BELIEVE YOUR EYES?'

The only other words were in the caption: 'This is Ella Wallis. She is a fourteen-year-old British schoolgirl. As these exclusive *Post* pictures unmistakeably show, she can levitate. Turn to pages eight and nine for the full, incredible story.'

The double-page spread inside used another large picture, of Ella rolling impossibly so that her hair hung down vertically from her scalp, almost to the floor.

A montage of smaller blocks revealed the whole sequence, from the moment Ella began to drift from the chair until she settled at last with her cheek against Guntarson's shoe.

The pictures told the story. He admitted that. But where was the depth? The analysis? The balanced, objective dissection which he had revised for ten hours before committing it to the modem? Instead, someone who had never met Ella, some word-grubbing sub, some hack, had drummed up a steaming pile of sensational claptrap and passed it off as a World Exclusive.

What made him angriest was that he had written it at all. He should have taken Ella for his own at the first instant. Now she was sliding into the maw of Post Communications, and Peter was expected to help them swallow her up. He was taking with him to 66 Nelson Road a mobile telephone, a contract and a wide-open chequebook.

Ella did not need to see the *Post* to know her life had changed. She did not have to leave her room or look out of her window. She sensed a swarm, buzzing around her. It felt as if she could hear the city droning, thousands of humming voices as people clustered to talk about her. There was no sound, exactly – the footsteps of her mother, her brother's radio, were the only noises in the house. The droning was a vibration. It was a low-frequency tremble in the bricks and stones. She shivered.

The doorbell was ringing. The droning grew stronger by the

minute. That couldn't be her father at the door – he had his own keys. Sitting at the foot of her bed, gliding her brush under her hair, Ella closed her eyes. She saw the spinning, interlocking discs of light, shining through her closed lids. When she opened her eyes, the lights were not there.

Ella remembered that the discs had fused together in a single light. She remembered how bright it had been, so intense she had been afraid the light might burst under her door and wake her mother. But she could not remember when the light had stopped, or when she had fallen back to sleep.

And she could not remember why these lights meant so much to her.

Juliette half stepped into the room. The rims and corners of her eyes were inflamed. Veins the same colour stood out in her cheeks. 'There are people outside for you. Some of them have a camera, I think they are from the television.'

The doorbell was ringing again.

'I don't want to speak to no one,' said Ella, alarmed.

'It is not up to you, we must ask your father. But there are quite many of them.'

'We promised. We ain't going to say nothing to no-one. Only Peter.'

'I do not know. It is very awful, what will everyone think of us? I have had to take off the phone from its hook. I don't know what the matter is with you, why must all these people have to come and see you?'

'I ain't seeing no one!' Ella shouted after her.

The silent drone was so thick in the air now, it set Ella's teeth on edge. She wanted help. Peter said he would be her friend. Where was he?

She had a sudden impression of speed. A headwind, buffeting her skull and grabbing at her arms. An engine growling under her. Cold, oily air in her nostrils. She sensed Peter Guntarson, as clearly as touching him. He was coming to her aid.

Ella began combing her hair with redoubled energy.

When Guntarson reached Nelson Road, he saw the first effect of the *Post*'s World Exclusive. No 66 had ceased to be a house like any other in the street – none of the other houses had cameras trained on the windows, people crawling over the steps and standing on the wall, cars double-parked on the pavement. The road outside her home was blocked. Guntarson had to shackle his bike in the next street and walk, towering in Dainese leathers, to the corner.

Sometimes with his hands and legs and stomach hot inside the leathers, he fantasised he was a Grand Prix champion, walking to his pole position on the grid.

He turned into Nelson Road and strode to the gate. Some of the other doorsteppers grinned when they saw the newcomer pull his phone from a zip pocket. The locals knew each other – the radio reporters, the agency boys, the Fleet Street stringers, the kids from the weeklies. They saw each other every day in courts, every week at matches. No one knew Guntarson. He was some Flash Harry from the nationals.

'She's got the phone off the hook!' they jeered.

'They opened the door once, for about five seconds.'

'Come far? You needn't have bothered.'

'The mother's around, but she won't talk. Says she wants to see her husband first.'

'The neighbours reckon the girl's probably in there.'

'They don't always send her to school. Apparently.'

'Who're you with, then?'

Guntarson stared flatly, then raised his jaw and closed his eyes. The veins swelled on his temples.

'What're you doing, trying to levitate?' sneered a cameraman.

Guntarson relaxed.

Ella's face appeared from behind the upstairs curtains. Someone's flashbulb went off, and then they were all looking, pointing lenses and fingers, shouting up to her. 'Hi! Ella! Can you open the window? We want a word, we want to talk to you. Do you want to be on television, Ella?'

Her face disappeared again. Guntarson heard her silent shout in his head – 'PETER!'

'How did you do that?' a young woman asked seriously. 'Did you summon her?'

Guntarson looked around. There were figures at every doorway and window in the street. Knots of people gathered at a safe distance from the media crews – over the road, leaning against the walls, ordinary people, sight-seers, some climbing on the lampposts.

If this circus went on, Ella wouldn't be safe at home. Guntarson pushed up the steps. The door opened a crack for him, and he slid inside.

Ella slammed the door and stayed with her back pressed against it, stopping the rest from getting in and Guntarson from getting out. He smiled at her and held out the phone. 'Present for you. Before I forget. In case you need to get hold of me at any time.'

She took it, staring. Her mother said, 'Oh, Mr Guntarson, is that a very good idea? I mean, Ella cannot afford to pay for her calls and . . .'

'We'll pay. No problem. Anyhow, it suits us, having a private line to you. But it's your phone, Ella. You can call whom you like – your friends, TV competitions, anything you want. The Australian speaking clock if you fancy. My editor's paying.' Guntarson would be delighted to see the *Post*'s World Exclusive cost them an extra couple of grand.

'I can't work it,' she muttered shyly.

'Come here, I'll show you. Your mum can make me a cup of tea.'

'We have a little sherry from Christmas, Mr Guntarson, why don't you have a glass? I will have one with you. And I make you tea also.'

Juliette led him down the narrow passage into the beige, crowded kitchen, with its breakfast crockery still scattered over the table and old marmalade chunks creasing the red-checked cloth. The stale smell of food struck Ella as strongly as a whiff from an open wheelie-bin. She glowered as her mother downed a full sherry glass in two swallows. Guntarson took his drink but did not taste it.

He did not seem to notice the grubby fingermarks on the fridge, the chipped rims of the mugs. He had pulled down the zip of his leathers a few inches, to the level of Ella's eyes, and was showing her how simple the phone was. Pull out the aerial, touch the green button with the receiver logo, press 'Go'. It automatically dialled Guntarson's mobile. He began to explain the other presets, but she didn't care. So long as she could ring him – aerial, green button, Go.

They had a brief conversation across the kitchen – 'Hello, Guntarson here, who's that?'

'Ella.'

'Nice of you to call me, where are you? Are you a long way away?'

'No.'

'Nearby, then? Near enough to wave? Ah! Hello! Goodbye!'

'Bye.'

She was very young. At fourteen, he had been sitting his first GCSEs, playing correspondence chess, learning to programme in BASIC. He could hold a conversation with anybody. But then, at fourteen, he couldn't levitate.

'So.' He fished the teabag out of his mug and added a trickle of milk. Guntarson would have preferred soya milk, or skimmed if it had to be cow's milk. Full fat always tasted rancid. He did like to watch his diet. 'This is what it's like. One morning you wake up and you're famous. You look out of the window, and there's reporters everywhere. Hard to get your bearings, isn't it?'

'It is not what we expected. I am sorry, it is probably our fault – my fault – I did not understand this is what will happen.'

'Don't apologise, Juliette. No one expects it till it happens. It's always a shock. Everyone likes to read about themselves in the papers, but they forget the rest of the world is reading the papers too. You're not alone. You'd be amazed how many people open the curtains one day and find ten thousand journalists camped on their doorstep.

Lottery winners, families of crime victims, anyone whose name gets linked with the royals – all basically ordinary people. Nobody is ever ready for it.'

The doorbell was ringing continuously now. Guntarson ignored it, so Juliette did not like to take any notice either. 'It soon blows over. You don't think you'll ever get your old life back, but everyone moves on after a couple of days. The journalists get fed up, they pick on another story – we've got very short attention spans. There's only a very few people whose lives never get back to normal. The Duchess of York, Paul Gascoigne, Brigitte Bardot – they'll always be famous, no matter how much they hate it. They're the exceptions.

'In a few weeks this will be like you had a weird dream, Ella. That's all.'

Ella said proudly, 'I ain't talking to no reporters anyway. I'm only talking to you.'

'That is up to your father,' admonished Juliette. 'He does not know yet about all these people.'

'Well. I ain't.' Ella was made bold by Peter at her elbow. He was not afraid of Juliette. She bet he wasn't even scared of Ken. 'I ain't.'

'Your father's at work? Had he already gone before the media turned up?'

'He goes to Ailish's, Sundays . . .'

'Ella!' hissed her mother.

'Dad don't know nothing 'bout all these reporters.'

'I am sorry, Mr Guntarson . . .'

'Your dad wasn't here last night?'

'Nope.' Ella loved the way all Peter's questions and comments were addressed to her. Not to her and her mother – directly to her.

'Mr Guntarson, I'm afraid . . .'

'Call me Peter.'

'Yes, of course, I am sorry, Peter, sorry . . .'

'And stop apologising.'

'Sorry, of course.'

'*Stop apologising.*'

But that was a little too clever and arrogant. Juliette was not a fool. 'Mr Guntarson, there are some things we are not discussing, never mind about your newspaper's money.'

'Your husband will be coming back here after work?'

'Of course.'

'But he didn't leave for work from here this morning?'

'It is not something I am discussing. It does not matter. You are not putting anything in the papers about our private matters.'

'The story we want to run is about Ella's paranormal powers. But before we take that any further, I am going to have to talk to all of you together, your dad included. It might be best if you came up to London, the whole family. There could be some television involved. We may even be talking about a new financial package.'

'Don't talk about money to Ella, Mr Guntarson. She does not understand. You must wait for Ken.'

So they waited. They played games, because Ella was no less awkward to question than before. It was obvious she had never thought about her powers, that she needed no explanation for them and that Guntarson was making her uncomfortable by pressing for answers. Ella wanted to answer – when he asked how it felt to levitate and what she concentrated on, she gave the most honest replies she could. Levitating felt quite nice. She didn't think of anything, just going up. But she knew these answers were not enough. She knew he'd like her better if she were brainier. The questions were upsetting her, and it showed. So they played games.

Guntarson drew symbols on a pad: heart, circle, triangle, pentagon. Ella guessed them, though she didn't know the word for a pentagon. He handed her the pad. She drew the pictures. He found he knew what she was going to draw before she started: 'House, cat, car,' he said. Ella was clearly delighted but after twenty minutes it reminded him of the repetitive games he played with his three-year-old godson – endlessly rolling a ball, or pulling the same face, until the tedium got unbearable and he had to make an excuse to stop.

This wasn't tedious yet, but it was quickly getting predictable. Ella would think of something and, in her excitement, she would transmit the word or image so powerfully it was almost audible. Then it was his turn, and she could pluck the word from his mind before he had even started to transmit.

He was tempted to try and think of nothing, or to imagine the white noise of an untuned television, or to think in Icelandic – anything to make it harder for her. But she was learning to trust him, and nothing could be allowed to complicate that. There would be plenty of time for experiments later.

Guntarson had been praying to meet someone like Ella, he'd been praying for years. Now was not the time to get impatient.

'Guess what I've got on my head!'

'A star?'

'Right, right.'

'I don't get it,' Ella said.

Peter grasped his blond hair and bowed to her. A star-shaped birthmark glowed on the crown.

'What have I got in my pockets?' he tried.

'A stone,' she answered at once.

Peter was surprised. He had not been thinking of the stone he always carried. His mind had been on the contract Ella's father would sign – that was in his pocket. But she was right: a lump of clear rock quartz was zipped deep inside his leathers.

'Why've you got a stone with you?'

He wondered whether to show it to her. 'It was my mother's,' he said, but that was not quite true.

Ella had a sense of something beyond her reach. Something walled off, behind sheer, high steel. The steel wall was odourless, featureless, containing no clue to what lay on the other side. It might shield one small secret, or a whole life which she could not even glimpse.

'Do you want to see it?'

Ella decided it was Peter's intelligence she could not reach. He had a higher intellect, a mind of steel. Most of his thoughts would be meaningless to her. She was just thick, she knew that.

She trusted him to be her friend. She was sure he was not hiding anything from her. After all, he was showing her his mother's stone.

She cupped it in her hands, a shaft of rock four inches long and clear as glass. Its five sides were smooth, suddenly tapering to a chiselled point. At the other end, the base was rough and cloudy.

'Can you see anything in it?' Peter asked. He was smiling, but uncomfortably. It was hard to see anyone, even Ella, touching the rock.

'I can see my fingers,' she said. 'They're all broken up.'

He laughed: 'That's the prism effect.'

'I can see big cliffs.'

'Can you now? Well, maybe that's the gorge up the road. Someone told me this stone came from Bristol, back when the workmen were excavating for Brunel's Suspension Bridge. They call that a Bristol Diamond, because there's so much of it up there.'

Ella kept gazing at the stone, and then hid it in her hands.

'I always carry it. Can I have it back now?'

She peeped at it through her fingers and then offered the stone to Peter. 'It's gone now,' she said.

'What's gone?'

'There were a face in it.'

'You saw a face?'

'It ain't like a mirror or nothing, is it?'

'You couldn't have seen your reflection, Ella, if that's what you mean . . .'

'There were a face.'

'Some people see visions in crystals, Ella. My mother could.'

'Like the future?'

'Perhaps. Not always. What was the face like, Ella?'

'She were in the water.'

'*What?*' His aspect changed instantly, and he hissed the word with such ferocity that Ella shrank back. 'Now don't be scared, Ella. Describe her face to me.'

'She had blonde hair. Really white. Like mine, but shorter. It were floating all round her. Like the circle round an angel.'

'A halo.'

'But her face was under the water, floating but drowned like. Her eyes was open. They was all rolled up, she weren't seeing me.' Ella's voice was shaking. Peter wasn't even looking at her – he was staring into the stone, blindly, as though Ella's vision could reappear like a television channel on the shining facets.

'Was it me?' she pleaded.

'I've never seen anything in this,' he replied, distractedly. 'I've looked and looked. Christ knows, I've looked.'

'Was it me? Was it? Was it me, drowned? In the water? *Was it me?*'

He met her eyes, but couldn't bring himself to answer. Closing the stone in his fist he dug it deep into his pocket. 'Funny,' he said, shutting the zip. 'Forget about it. Just forget it. Hey, I'm hungry, are you hungry?'

After lunch, they tried the telepathy in separate rooms, or standing on opposite sides of a brick wall. There was no discernible power-loss. They tried transmitting numbers, and then tunes, colours, cities, whole sentences. Ella could sing back melodies she had never heard before, as quickly as Guntarson thought them, though she said she was hopeless at music. She could echo even difficult lines – 'When I'm calling you, oo–oo–oo, oo–oo–oo . . .'

'What film's that from?' he asked.

'Dunno.' And then, picking the answer out of his head, '*Rose-Marie.*'

'Starring?'

She looked bewildered again for an instant, then replied: 'Jeannette MacDonald and Nelson Eddy.' She was still bewildered. 'Are they people's names?'

'You've never heard of either of them, have you? You'd be unstoppable on quiz shows. You could just read the questionmaster's mind.' Could she predict the numbers on a roulette table? Spot the winners on the racing pages? Foretell the lottery numbers?

She was giggling.

'Are you this clever at school?'

'I can't get the answers from other people. Not easy-like. Only you.'

'What about your family? How about Mum?' But Juliette refused to get involved with the game. 'How about your brother?'

She shrugged. 'I never tried.' She wanted to tell him everything, to explain how she could gain a sense of other people's minds, how she could call up a television in her mind and see what her brother was seeing. She wanted to explain that she wasn't very good with words, that she wouldn't know how to pluck numbers and answers out of strangers' heads. She knew she wanted to say all this to Peter, but she did not know how.

Juliette was clutching her mug nervously. Ken had made a big point on Saturday of warning her, 'We got to keep Frank out of this. The papers is only interested in Ella, and that's the way it's staying. No one's going to try and make our Frank go weird and all. He's too young.'

Guntarson was asking, 'Where is he, in school? Could you try sending him a message now? How far is it? See if he responds.'

'Oh! That noise,' Juliette exclaimed. 'The doorbell! Why can they not just leave us alone?'

'Would you like me to go out and ask them to give it a rest?'

'Could you? I am so sorry to trouble you, I know I should be doing this myself . . .'

Guntarson was a full step above the mobbing reporters as he opened the door, and he surveyed them with fatherly contempt. 'A request from the family. As they will not be making any statement until this evening at the earliest, would you be so kind as to desist from knocking, and ringing, and shouting. It isn't doing you any good, and it's very irritating and distracting in there. And the neighbours are complaining,' he added, lying flippantly.

The statement was being recorded and filmed and scribbled down. 'Who are you?' yelled someone.

Guntarson stared with slow disdain. 'I'm Peter Guntarson of the *Daily Post*,' he declared.

A woman with the BBC West camera crew asked breathlessly, 'Have you observed any fresh phenomena surrounding Ella Wallis today?'

'You'll just have to wait and buy the *Post* tomorrow.'

'How much is the *Post* paying Ella's family?' 'How can you justify keeping her away from school?' 'How is she coping with the sudden publicity?'

A commotion at the back of the scrum distracted Guntarson. A heavy-set man in blue overalls was elbowing people aside. One small, dark-haired woman was jerked backwards with a shriek. A male colleague who turned to confront the man was shoved aside with a forearm to the lower ribs. As he reached the steps, the man's hand closed around the bulb of a microphone. Guntarson saw the glitter of a gold signet ring and the mike was torn loose and hurled away.

'Mr Wallis?'

'Let me into my own house,' snarled Ken.

Guntarson took a couple of steps back, almost stumbling as he did.

The reporters, sensing their best chance of the day, were fighting for Ken's attention – 'Mr Wallis! Ken! Hello! Over Here! Could you just look this way, sir! Can we just have a few words!' And then, as the door closed, the questions turned into taunts – 'How much money are you getting for this, Mr Wallis! What does Ella think of this, Mr Wallis! Are you selling your daughter to the *Post*, Mr Wallis!'

Guntarson looked at Ken Wallis for the first time. They had spoken several times on the phone, making their deal, and got along civilly enough. This was the first time they had seen each other's faces. Ken, an inch shorter and thirty pounds heavier, scowled. His fists were knotted as tightly as his features.

Guntarson knew, as clearly as he knew when Ella's telepathic voice spoke to him, that he and Ken Wallis were going to hate each other's guts.

Chapter Sixteen

Juliette dared come no closer than the kitchen door. Her husband's left hand was opening and closing, mindlessly, like a fish's mouth. It was searching to grasp a poker, or a snooker cue – something to use as a weapon.

Guntarson offered his name, trying to introduce himself.

'You don't never come in my house. Not while I'm not here.'

'Mr Wallis, we've talked before. We're paying you.'

'You ain't paying to come in my house and talk to my wife when I ain't here.'

'I beg your pardon. I'd come to wait and see you.'

'This is my house. See? You wants to come and take your photographs of my daughter, you talks to me first. That clear?'

'As I may need to speak with you at any time of the day or night, you had better furnish me with a list of phone numbers.'

'Don't get clever! I don't want to hear no smarmy backchat!'

Ken was so close to him now, that Guntarson stopped trying to smile and leant his weight forward on his left foot, closing his fists.

'You people is going to start showing me and my family some respect! Got that?' Ken swung away abruptly. Juliette flinched. 'Did I say, let this man in?'

'I am sorry, I think it would be all right?'

'Why? When do I ever say, I wants strange men in my house?'

'We have met him before, he was here.'

'Have I met him?'

'I am sorry, of course, you did not.'

'Did I say, I wants him here today?'

'He came, he is here with all the people outside, and Ella wanted to see him.'

'Ella! So it's her what says who can come in our home now, is it? Now she's famous, got her picture on the front page. It's up to her, is it, when I ain't around?'

Guntarson tried to break it up: 'Mr Wallis, if I . . .'

'Shut it!' snapped Ken. 'Where is Ella? Ella, get your arse off that chair and speak to your father proper.'

'Mr Wallis, let's get this straight. We have an agreement – Mr Wallis, would you look at me!' Guntarson had raised his voice now. 'If you want full payment, you've got to co-operate. I meant no intrusion, coming here today. I was waiting to see you and talk business.'

'Come here to shout in my house, have you?'

'I'm trying to make you listen, Mr Wallis. You haven't received full payment yet. If you don't want our money, fine. I'll go.'

'There's plenty of people out there is willing to pay for what I got to tell them, young man,' warned Ken.

'Those people out there? Don't put your trust in them, Mr Wallis. You're fair game to them now. They won't offer you a brass farthing for anything they get out of you. Wait till the paparazzi start after you. They'll be poking their cameras through your windows, down your chimney, but don't think they'll pay for what they get. You've gone public now. You've sold your story. You don't get to sell it again.'

Ken dropped into a chair. He was tired. He felt he was losing his grip. Strangers in his house, shouting at him, in front of his family – not so long ago, this arrogant reporter would have been leaving in a body-bag. The thought of money was making Ken Wallis weak.

He wanted Guntarson's money. And so far, he hadn't been given nearly enough of it.

Ken unfolded a *Daily Post* from his overalls pocket. Smoothing it on the kitchen table, he let his fingers rest on Ella's floating face. He said: 'You wasn't expecting nothing like this. Eh?'

'No one could possibly have predicted . . .'

'I didn't know Ella could do it. Fly, like. I means, hover. Not just when she wanted. We saw her once, but I thought she had the devil in her then. Maybe she got the devil in her all the time.'

'I think there is a more scientific reason than that.'

'Do you? I don't reckon too many of your scientists will be pleased to see this. Turns all their laws of physics inside-upside-down. Makes people believe in miracles.'

'Ella can't be a walking miracle and possessed by the devil too,' Guntarson said lightly.

'I don't think you knows nothing about it, *Mr* Guntarson. Mr *Daily Post*. But you does know how to make people take notice of a fact. I'll give you that. There's not nobody in Bristol hasn't bought your paper this morning, seems to me. And my brother put this same story in his church magazine, first off. It's a pity, that. If he kept quiet, we'd be back to normal now. But seeing as we ain't, and seeing as how you want to sell some more stories about our Ella, let's talk about money.'

'I don't mind telling things to Peter, Dad. He's given us money already.'

'Shut it, Ella.'

'We agreed £4,000, Mr Wallis.' Guntarson pulled up a chair and leaned forward, confidentially. '£2,000 you had already. The other £2,000 I've brought you now, and our contract.'

'Two grand, that's chickenfeed.'

'That's good money.'

'That's expenses, that's all. You're going to want to take Ella away with you. Do some tests on her. I reckon you're going to want to prove your story. Scientifically.' He spat the word sarcastically. 'Cos half of Bristol don't believe a word of it. I've had people coming up to me all morning. They seen the photos. I didn't have no clue what they was talking of, till someone gave me this.' He slapped his paper. 'And then I didn't believe it. I thought it was trick photography, first off. And I seen her do it for real. So if you don't want people thinking you made it all up, you got to prove it. Scientifically. And you can't prove it without Ella.'

'Maybe it would be better for Ella if we didn't prove it. Just left it, one of those unsolved mysteries,' suggested Guntarson, leaning back. 'People would forget about her quite quickly.'

'Bollocks. You're desperate for some more. What you here for unless you wants to print some more? What's all them scum outside my house for? Unless they wants the story too.' Ken grinned greedily. 'Ella's my daughter. You want to get one more word about her – we got to start talking serious money.'

The mobile phone cast a green glow in Ella's dark bedroom. She held it in her lap, the word 'READY' picked out in LEDs, as she brushed her hair. The plastic handset protected her, like a magic lamp. With two buttons, she could summon Peter.

The aerial was out. She would have tried phoning him, but she didn't know if he'd like to be bothered. He'd been at the house all day. He hadn't left till nearly six. He might think she was pestering him.

It wasn't as if she had anything special to say to him.

She rang Holly instead: 'It's me. I got my own phone.'

'Oh. Why're you ringing me?'

'Just to tell you. I can ring you whenever now.'

'Well, don't.'

'Peter gave it me. He's going to put another story about me in the paper, he and my dad done a deal.'

'Well, my dad says he don't believe a word of it. He says you must be making it all up for the money.'

'You know that ain't . . .'

'Everybody thinks so. We just all think you're so stupid, Ella Wallis, so you needn't bother ringing me again on your stupid, poncey, mobile phone.'

Ella began to cry. Holly was her best friend. She kept her sobs very quiet, so Frank in the next room would not hear, but her shoulders were shaking. She put the phone out of reach, on her work top. She didn't want to touch it now.

The light on the phone, blurred by her tears, watched her like one green eye.

Ella sat, chin on her knees, swallowing back her disappointment. There was loads to think about. Loads of pretty good things. Things she'd wanted to tell Holly about. Peter had promised she would go on TV and she'd be famous. That seemed incredible, but she had to believe, because he'd told her so. He said she'd be the most famous person in the world. He said people were going to really like her, and be kind to her, because she could do something exciting.

That sounded really nice. She wanted to talk to someone about that. She wanted to talk about Peter. She wanted to ring someone. But there wasn't the same pleasure in holding her new phone now.

CHAPTER SEVENTEEN

Peter kept his promise. Ella was booked onto a television show within thirty-six hours. The *Post* sent a car, a black Ford Scorpio, to collect her family, and Ella marched down the steps from her house with her collar turned up, holding the *Post* across her face the way Peter had shown her. She was determined the other newspapers would not even get a proper look at her.

She saw Peter, sheltering below the blue neon portico of the Network Europe studios, before he had even registered her car. It was early evening; rain was sweeping over the shining flagstones and breaking up in the headlights' glare. Guntarson stood in a waxed, ankle-length coat, broad flaps jutting over his shoulders, an Australian ranchman's coat. His thick, blond hair was wet, and clung to his scalp.

Ella had the door open as the car was pulling up, and an oily spray from the gutter soaked the side of her seat and spattered her shoes.

'Ella! Wait a minute,' snapped her mother, but Ella was out of the car, coatless, running through the rain to Peter.

He turned his head away as she reached him.

In response to his gesture, a receptionist picked up a phone on the other side of Network Europe's doors of thick glass and aluminium. A liveried doorman hurried out with umbrellas in the green and gold of Post Communications.

When Guntarson turned back to greet Ella, she was standing, hurt and bedraggled, three feet away, in the rain.

'Quick! What are you doing?' He reached out to pull her under the entrance arch, and dabs of rain smudged his sleeve. Ella was drenched already, water streaking her silver-blonde hair and turning the blue velour of her dress a patchy, clinging black. 'You're soaked. What were you waiting for?' She said nothing, but he suddenly knew. 'Did I upset you by not saying "Hello"? I'm sorry, Ella.' He stood, leaning over her, smiling broadly, his hands dug into his pockets. She hunched her elbows to her sides in the January air and looked up woefully.

'I had to let them know you were here, immediately. That's what distracted me. Some very important people want to meet you, Ella. They left strict orders.' He ushered her into the warm lobby as her parents hurried beneath the tent-like umbrellas. 'They had to know the moment you arrived.'

Ella shivered, dripping on the green and gold carpet. Guntarson pointed her towards the desk. 'We'll sign you in. Hey, there's my editor,' he whispered.

A dome-headed man with bushy white hair like a clown's around his ears strode between the palm trees on the other side of the lobby. He wore a heavy suit with a dark tie, and two other men, identically uniformed, followed him. The deep, grey weight of their pinstripes was smothering, descending on her like a blanket.

The man with clown's hair looked Ella up and down, and declared: 'Got yourself a bit wet outside, eh, did you?' He did not introduce himself. The other man gazed at her more closely, as though expecting something extraordinary.

'Mr Wallis!' roared the clown editor. He seized Ken's hand, which was damp from the umbrella handle. 'Here's a turn-out to greet you – quite a triumvirate of Post-Comm big-wigs.'

The other men chuckled but did not stop staring at Ella.

Sometimes a boy in her class caught moths in his cupped hands, and the other pupils crowded round to look. She felt like a moth, with fingertips gently pinching her wings and holding her still. Voices buzzed around her and, shrinking between Guntarson and the desk, Ella understood no more than a moth could.

'Permit me to make the introductions. I am Sir Peregrine Parrish, captain of the flagship. This is Lord Treharris, vice-admiral of the fleet – that is, of Post-Comm – and Mr Dyre, pilot of our satellite.'

Mr Dyre shook Ken's hand. 'I run this TV station,' he translated. 'You're Miss Wallis's father?'

'The miraculous Miss Wallis,' Sir Peregrine cut in. 'Miss Wallis, who seems capable of teaching us that every law of physics we ever conceived is completely wrong. The *Post*'s very own Miss Wallis, I might say.'

'She's my daughter,' Ken growled.

'And momentarily afflicted by an attack of shyness, I suspect.' Sir Peregrine gestured at Lord Treharris, a skeletal man with nicotine yellow around his lips and staining his cheekbones, who was offering his hand to Ella.

'Say "Hello" proper, Ella.'

Petrified by the men in suits, and panicked by the rising anger in her father's voice, she did not move.

'Ella, I ain't telling you twice.'

'No rush, Mr Wallis: it's a young lady's prerogative to be demure.' Sir Peregrine, a professional bully himself, was unworried by men like

Ken. 'To the studio, then – lead on, Mr Dyre, pilot us to the satellite realm.'

Ella tried to stay at Guntarson's side, keeping him between her and her parents, as they were led briskly into a corridor of smoked glass. Framed pictures of the station's soap stars and quiz show hosts hung along both walls. She clung, literally, to the tail of Peter's coat. It was hard to breathe, as though a thick cloth was wrapped around her face. She did not understand where she was being taken, or why they were hurrying. The men in suits were speaking to her, and she did not understand what they said. The confusion was like blindness – her senses were being blotted out.

The smoked glass and thick, lush carpet generated an oppressive charge. She heard her mother's fussing voice and felt a pair of hands on her shoulders, steering her through a doorway. She had no idea where she was, or why she had been brought there. Bewilderment had overtaken her so quickly that she barely knew who she was. She still clutched Peter's coat, but among all these people he was a different Peter, almost as much a stranger as the men in suits.

He was easing the waxed hem from her fingers. 'Do you want your Mum and Dad to go with you?'

She stared at him, terror flickering behind her eyes.

'I'll wait here,' he promised.

'No!' Ella clutched at his coat again.

'I'll be watching you from the wings. They can't fit everyone onto the set.' Peter bent over with his hands on his knees, talking to her like she was a child. 'And I'll be sending you messages.' He smiled and silently shouted, 'It's okay!' Aloud, he added: 'You can still hear me?'

She nodded. Peter straightened up, and a woman took her hand and gently pulled her away. Ella tried to keep her eyes on Peter, but suddenly the men in suits were pressing around her again, and among them all there was a new voice: 'Hello, Ella, you look a little frightened to me, but you know there's no need to be because it's all going to be just fine, just fine, just relax and you'll enjoy it, you'll see, come over here and you can be taking a seat while Alice sorts out your make-up.'

This voice was not talking to her – it was pouring words over her in a cascade. Ella kept her head bowed at first, and did not try to see who was speaking.

Above her head there was a buzz and a muffled thud, and three brilliant rows of lamps burst into light. She ducked and looked up and, in the single instant that she looked into the beams, blue and green triangles were burned onto her eyelids. For the next few minutes, whenever she blinked, the coloured shapes flashed before her.

'Her hair's wet,' said a woman's voice, 'I'll need the drier.'

'Did you get yourself caught in the rain, Ella, it is dreadful wet out there, I nearly got a soaking myself, now you want to be sure you don't catch cold but it's always so marvellous warm in these studios, in fact look at you, you're steaming already from the heat of these lights, you look like a kettle!' The man with the incessant voice patted her arm and Ella cast a glance at him for the first time.

'I've got a good joke – one psychic says to the other psychic, tell me something I don't know, ha-ha-ha, I say, you look like a kettle, all that steam coming off you, look at your shoulders, well never mind, it'll do that lovely dress of yours some good to be dried out, and I don't think Alice'll be needing that hairblower after all.' Every word was perfectly distinct within the gabble. He never stumbled over a sound or paused to think.

He had an accent. She'd heard people talk like that before, much more slowly. He was Irish. Like Mr McNulty.

'Do you know who I am, Ella, have you seen the programme before, do you get Network Europe at home, you haven't got satellite or cable? I'm Phineas Finnegan, this is my show, it's a talk show and the idea is you can say anything you like and I'll do the listening, it's your chance to tell the world about all the things that you've got burning inside of you, the things you're passionate about.'

Hands pressed her down into a chair. The wide rubber rim of a television camera swung on a long arm almost into her face and then slipped away. Phineas Finnegan, his hands constantly adjusting a swirling tie and the lapels and cuffs of his almost-luminous green suit, bobbed in front of her. He was no older than Peter, but a much smaller man. His scalp, beneath waves of thin, sandy hair, was discoloured in patches.

'We get all the stars on this show, you know, are you a pop fan, do you like Life Boys, we had Robbie and Michael from Life Boys on yesterday, what do you think of that, are you a fan of theirs? Robbie was sitting just in that chair where you are now, or was it Michael, right in that chair, we get all the stars, and I'll tell you why' – he paused confidentially for a fraction of a second – 'it's because I choose the guests myself and I won't have anyone on my show who isn't totally fascinating and controversial, so when I saw your pictures in the *Post* I knew, I had to have you on the show.'

Hands were lifting and brushing Ella's damp hair. She hated to have anyone touch her hair. She tugged her head, but the firm hands kept holding and brushing. Ella reached up to free herself, and the insistent hands pressed her back down.

'There's lovely hair you've got, Ella, I bet you never have it cut, but doesn't it take an age to wash it and I bet you've got to do it every night, of course I'm just jealous because if I let mine grow from now till doomsday it would never be long like yours, in fact you wouldn't believe it but I'm going a little bit bald at the back, not so you'd notice because I make sure the girls comb it back properly, it's not vanity it's just television, I wouldn't care for myself, but the viewers are awfully critical, awfully critical, okay are we almost ready Alice, chop chop sweetheart because I want to start in about ninety seconds now, I don't want to keep everyone hanging about longer than we have to because we've got a lot to get through still today.'

The hands dabbed powder across Ella's face and stabbed a buffer on her nose, cheeks and chin. She blinked. Dust twinkled in the bright glare. The powder tasted industrial, like dry shavings of engine grime.

'Okay let's get everybody off the set, that includes even our noble knight, thank you Sir Peregrine thank you, that's it, just a little further back and then we won't have any unfortunate accidents with the camera.'

The suits cleared away, the hands dropped from Ella's face and suddenly Phineas Finnegan dipped into a cushioned, executive's chair. Ella was perched on the brink of one almost identical, but scarlet where his was brown. The lights reflected like moons in the dense glass of a circular coffee-table between them.

Ella caught sight of herself, and the made-up face shocked her with its prettiness.

'Ella it's been grand to have this chance of getting to know each other, I always know an interview will go well when I've had a good chinwag with my guest beforehand, it gives us peace of mind, I feel very positive very optimistic now, there's great human potential in this story, now I want you to be totally relaxed, you're still looking a little uptight, you can lean back it's okay the chair isn't going to roll away, now it's not live, you know that, though actually we encourage the viewers to think it *is* live so don't go saying anything to spoil our little secret, we're just going to record some chat and like I said I want you to talk from the heart, whatever's in your heart I want you to say it to me, I want you to look on me as your friend, as a confessor, think of me like the priest if you like.'

She heard Peter's voice in her head: 'Relax. Relax,' and she twisted round to see him.

'Look at me now Ella,' chided Finnegan. 'Okay we're ready to go, now just be natural be yourself and remember you're the star.' He paused to beam brightly at a camera. Ella did not smile. She clutched the corners of her seat.

The floor manager, waving his hand downwards, cued them in.

'Here we go with my next guest and if you've seen the papers in the past few days you can't fail to recognise all those miles of golden hair, of course I'm delighted to welcome from the realm of the supernatural Britain's newest psychic star, Ella Willis . . . fuck it! I got her sodding name wrong! Ella I'm so sorry that was just stupid of me, it must be these new teeth I'll take them straight back to my dentist in the morning, only kidding, okay are we still rolling, yes? So, let's do it again.'

She began to rock in her seat.

Overhead one of the blazing bulbs exploded like a gunblast. Fragments of glass jingled on the floor.

'Fucking shit! Okay it was just a light. Ella sorry about everybody's language here, it's just the tension I expect you hear worse in the playground every day, fuck that really startled me, okay let's refocus are we ready now no more arsing about now.'

A make-up artist darted forward to dab sweat from under his nose with a Kleenex. If the camera caught his face shining, she'd lose her job. 'I like to dazzle,' Phineas Finnegan warned her every day, 'I hate to shine.'

He ran a hand over his face, pressing his smile into position.

Finnegan rattled into the intro again. Ella stayed rigidly facing him, scared to look away, but her eyes found nothing to focus on and began to wander.

'Ella! Ella!' He was leaning across, patting her wrist. 'It's okay to say something, it's a chatshow. Let's start with the obvious question, can you ever remember when you *weren't* psychic?'

Nothing in his voice made any sense. She saw his lips moving, heard sounds, watched him nodding his head in encouragement, but none of it meant anything. Ella did not know what he wanted her to do.

She rocked a little harder. A second bulb detonated, and something smashed to the studio floor. Finnegan did not swear this time.

'Are all these bangs going off making you a teeny tad nervous, Ella, listen there's nothing to worry about, we don't normally have two of those go off bang in a year and now they're popping like firecrackers, maybe it's a psychic phenomenon, Ella, just don't let it put you off.'

She could hear Peter's voice in her head. 'Sit! Still!' She understood that. With an effort Ella leaned back and stayed there.

'Hey that's better you look comfy suddenly that's lovely everyone's comfy on the Phineas Finnegan show.'

His words, spraying in her face, were still meaningless.

'Now you're the strong silent type really aren't you, you're not one of these silly teenagers who just giggles and chatters all the time and that's good, no one likes a chatterer, but I've got an idea, instead of talking out loud let's try a bit of telepathy doesn't that sound like a good idea, okay well in my pocket I have four envelopes and in each of these envelopes, look they're lovely colours, I've got a red one, a yellow one, here's blue and this is green, I'll just hold them up so that everyone at home can see them, they're perfectly normal envelopes, no clue on the outside to what's on the inside and you've never seen these before have you Ella, you didn't even know we were going to do this . . . I'll take that as a "No" then.'

Finnegan's banter, all silky, salesman's charm at first, was full of needles now. This damn idiot-girl was sitting there like a deaf-mute.

'I've drawn a little picture and hidden it inside each envelope, now I'm challenging you, because we've all read about and been totally amazed by your astonishing telepathic powers, can you read my mind?' He paused.

Ella was staring blankly at the envelopes. Under the heat of the lights Finnegan's personality was wafting at her in thick, sickly waves. She had no idea what was in the envelopes – she did not even know what he was asking her to do. But her impression of his feelings had almost congealed into an ooze. It was as though he was melting with frustration and impatience and contempt.

'Now I'm holding up the red one, I know what the contents are, it's a picture, it's a symbol and I'm concentrating on this symbol, I'm beaming it to you Ella, and you the viewers at home can help too because we're showing you the symbol on the screen so why not suspend your disbelief for a moment and concentrate on that symbol, that's the one Ella's trying to guess.'

'Ella, can you hear me, say something, are you getting any picture of what's in the envelope, it's the red envelope I'm showing you, tell me if you're getting any telepathic contact, hello Ella Ella, it's a yellow star, a yellow star, you can't even see it if I wave it right in your face can you, what's the use! What is the point here!' Finnegan leapt up and hurled the bright envelopes across the studio. 'I mean, who's she supposed to be, fucking Helen Keller?'

Pointing and jabbering, he strode over to Tony Dyre, the studio head. Both cameras remained trained on Ella. The lights stayed up. She did not move from her chair, pressed back into the cushions and grasping the corners. She did not look around, and no one came near her. If she heard her father's raised voice, shouting at someone to watch their language about his daughter, no trace showed on her face.

Her chair tipped slowly backwards.

Ella's eyes still blinked at nothing. Her jaw tipped slightly open as the chair overbalanced and the stand slid upwards. As if a pivot had been rammed sideways through the chair-back, just below Ella's shoulders, the head-rest dipped but did not hit the floor. Ella, her hair tumbling behind her, stayed clasping the seat, as securely as though a seatbelt held her. The chair was hanging in the air, the base pointing above the cameramen's heads.

In the sudden hush of the studio, a silence in which the soundman could hear the rustle of Ella's hair, Juliette shrieked: 'Ella! My God! Stop it!'

Guntarson seized her arm. 'Don't distract her,' he warned. 'She probably doesn't even know she's doing it. She's blanked everything out.'

'Are we getting this?' Finnegan was hissing at the camera crew. 'We've got to get all of this, make sure everyone can see there's no tricks no strings or anything, are her eyes open is she in a trance or what?'

The head-rest bobbed and, cradling Ella like a baby bird cupped in a hand, the chair rose. The director's orders were clearly audible, susurrations from the cameramen's headphones. Lord Treharris, whose skin-and-bones frame made him seem even taller than his six feet three inches, walked slowly to the centre of the floor, mouth open, and stretched up an arm. The chair floated out of reach of his fingers.

'Zoom in zoom in,' Finnegan was urging, 'let's see there's no pulleys or mirrors or anything.'

The chair rolled around and over, as though it wanted to prove there were no wires attached. Then it lofted gently above the level of the lights, into the gloom of the gantries, where dozens of projection lamps were hanging. It stayed there, rocking faintly with each of Ella's slow, deep breaths.

Chapter Eighteen

Phineas Finnegan was on the television. 'I'm Irish and we Irish are accustomed to the improbable, to the supernatural if you like.' His hands were clasped in front of him and he maintained a willing, earnest expression. This was the BBC's *Nine o'Clock News* – easily his biggest audience ever. 'This apparition/phenomenon/ manifestation/I don't know call it what you will, was out of this world. *Out of this world.*'

The television in the Wallis's hotel sitting-room was one of the items which defined their suite as an executive annexe. Forty inches from corner to corner, with satin-grilled speakers curling out from either side, it featured a long-play video recorder and a satellite decoder that accessed more than a hundred channels. Finnegan's face in close-up was almost twice as large as life.

Ella sat by the window, staring at the closed grey slats of the blind. She still had not spoken.

Ken and Juliette were uncomfortable in two billowing armchairs. The cushion-covers mimicked the Chinese theme of the suite – blue dragons of red silk, wise men with white beards, bamboo picture-frames, paper tigers, the Forbidden City and the Great Wall. Ken seemed to be waiting for a Chinese takeaway as he sprawled with his feet dangling over the arm – deliberately disrespectful of the opulent surrounds. The only item in the room which seemed natural to him was the TV remote in his lap.

Juliette, in her lap, was clasping a lead crystal glass. She had found four miniatures of Beefeater gin in the mini-bar, with two bottles of Schweppes tonic water which she had not needed. 'Just a little pick-me-up,' she muttered, shielding the tumbler from her husband. She had been to the bathroom, with its own colour television and towels as big as blankets and wonderful hairdryers and magnificent gilt mirrors and soaps and colognes by Gucci and ice cold marble beneath her feet. She needed a drink after that.

There had been no word from Guntarson. Ella could not remember whether he had come to check she was all right when she left the studio. She was struggling to remember anything at all – it seemed to

her she had been sitting at this window a long time. She had not eaten
– a plate of meat and salad was untouched at her elbow. She wore the
same, blue dress that she had bought for and worn to the show. She
did remember being very, very frightened in the studio, and she knew
she had levitated. People kept telling her. She had been in a trance.

Peter would call her. Soon, definitely soon. Then she would wake
up a bit. She could call him herself but this idea kept slipping away
from her. Everything in her head was hard to hold just now.

'There's how they got you down, Ella,' called out her father. 'See
this? We should of been taping this.' He was much more pleased by
the sight of his daughter on television, bobbing thirty feet above the
floor in a chair, than he had been by the real spectacle in the studio. 'It
needed ropes, like. The lighting boys, they goes right up in them rafters
with you and ties ropes all round the chair, in case it falls sudden-like.
And then they drops one long rope down to the floor and we all pulls
you down. Bit like flying a kite, it was.'

The report filled the first ten minutes of the news. That footage
from Network Europe, which had been broadcast on the satellite
station almost continuously for the past three hours, was replayed, in
slow motion, with video enhancement of each detail, so that every
viewer could see the fact. There were no hidden wires. No pulleys, no
mirrors. The chair flew. That was all. It flew, and carried the girl up to
the ceiling.

The sequence had already been sold to CNN who were beaming it
worldwide to over a hundred countries.

'You're a star, girl. Proper famous now,' remarked Ken, when the
bulletin turned to a studio crowded with experts. With every expert
in every field came a differing explanation – a physicist, two psychia-
trists, a professor of the paranormal and, by satellite link to Las Vegas,
a magician, one of the world's most famous, who 'levitated' nightly
by stagecraft.

Ken was talking, 'We're going to be rich if we handles it right. Have
to speak to our Robert, he's the man, he knows about making money.
We'll probably have a Jag like him. What you think of that?'

He twisted to look over the top of his rolling armchair at Ella. Her
knees were hunched up to her shoulders. She still stared at the blind.

'Shame she's such a miserable little cow,' he mouthed at Juliette.

Neither of her parents came near her, except once, to take her
mobile phone out of her new clutch-bag. Ella let Ken lift the bag, blue
to match the dress, from the table beside her and tip the contents into
his hand as he searched for the phone in its black pouch. 'No point in
running up the hotel phone bill. We don't know if the newspaper's
going to cover it. But we do know,' he added, slapping the mobile
into his wife's hands, 'they're paying this one.'

Juliette rang her sister, to make sure Frank was all right. Sylvie wanted to hear all about the TV programme, and did they know that Ella was all over Sky News? There were magicians on at the moment, and some of them were saying it was all a trick and a fraud ... but some of the others were on the other side of the bandwagon, saying Ella was for real. They said they actually, truly, honestly believed their Ella could fly. Sylvie didn't know what to think – were the TV people making up all of this?

Frank was allowed to speak briefly with his mother too, and he was asking the same questions as well as whining about a headache. Juliette did not want to talk. She was almost as withdrawn as her daughter. She was upset, by all the fuss, or by the oddness of it all, or because her usual routine was broken. Maybe she just didn't like to be in a hotel room, even a luxury room like this, away from her son. Something was bothering her. Ken didn't particularly need to know what it was.

Just as Ken was ordering Ella to get to bed, the flowers came. One of the porters brought them up – the Interflora courier was not allowed anywhere near the room.

The bouquet had to be coaxed into the suite, stems first. The porter could not reach both arms around it. As he propped it against a table, fat yellow magnolias and sunflowers broader than dinner plates spilled out of the cellophane. Sunflowers, in January.

Ella swung her feet onto the carpet and dived at the tag waving on the stalks. She knelt, petals and pollen dropping on her head, as she ripped the envelope open.

'There's more where this lot came from,' said the porter. 'You're going to need vases, loads of them.' And a second carload of blooms blocked the door.

Ella's first bubble of excitement burst when she did not see Guntarson's name. She sat back on her heels and picked over the words of the note carefully.

'Who're these from, eh?'

'Does that note, is it telling you their name, the sender?'

Ella tucked the card between the wet stems and stood up slowly. A third bouquet, all yellow daisies and white daffodils, like a platter of fried eggs, was served up. She walked back to the window.

'She ain't able to read it,' said her father, plucking out the card. 'José Miguel Dóla, says on it. Who's he? Wop name. Someone you know?' he demanded. But Juliette shook her head. The flowers were propped from the door to the sofa. If she took them home, Juliette thought, there were enough to carpet both the rooms downstairs ankle-deep. And they must have cost more than Ken paid for their real carpets.

'José Dóla. Public relations. 110c Kings Road SW1. And there's his phone number. I can't hardly read his writing underneath. "Do not sign anything until you have spoken with me. JMD." Oh yeah. A shark. First whiff of money. Amazing. Well, he can get stuffed.'

But Juliette said, 'I know you are right, of course. I am sorry, I would have very much liked to ring him and say him thank you for the flowers so much. Because he has spent so much. You never see these flowers at this time of year. Daisies, aren't these lovely? And these daffodils, they have been flown all the way from Europe, I am sure. Maybe it could be okay for me to quickly ring and tell, "The flowers are here safely".'

'Be better,' answered Ken, 'coming from me.'

Juliette opened the door to Guntarson when he knocked. He stepped over the remnants of their breakfast on trays outside the door and into a garden of cut flowers.

Every table and shelf in the suite was jammed with jars overspilling with stems and petals. Lilies hung in bunches from the chandelier. Roses were pinned to the sash cord of the blinds. Tall stalks waved from the bars of the grate. Desk drawers had been pulled open and crammed with blooms, and empty champagne magnums had been brought from the restaurant to stand in the corners, single sunflowers teetering in their necks.

'Wow, it's a jungle in here. Did the hotel supply all these?' Guntarson asked. 'Where's Ella?'

'She is brushing her teeth. I think she will be pleased to see you. Come through, there is a sitting-room, this is a lovely big suite. Your paper is so very kind, Mr Guntarson. My husband is through here.'

Guntarson adopted a frosty smile to greet Ken, and instead was confronted by a small man with black hair and a white suit. At his neck, soft and shining like two of the million blossoms he had presented at such expense to the Wallises, was a scarlet bowtie. His crocodile briefcase rested on the dining table, papers spilling out of it. Ken Wallis sat, one of the papers in his left hand and a fat, presidential Mont Blanc fountain pen in his other.

José Miguel Dóla, light-boned and short, blocked the way to that table.

Guntarson took the little man's hand, civilly enough, but looked straight over his head and said, 'Morning Ken. Good breakfast?'

'I understand Ella ate most of it. Her adventures yesterday have apparently worked up a good appetite,' said Dóla, tightly holding onto the handshake and keeping Guntarson from advancing further. 'You must be the lad from the *Post*?'

'I am Dr Guntarson.'

'And I am Dr Dóla. How fortunate – a brace of doctors.' He spoke quickly, with a crisp accent. 'Call me Joe, I don't like pretentiousness. I saw your by-line in this morning's *Post*. You write with great vigour.'

Guntarson's lip twitched as he suppressed a grimace. The *Post* paid him well for lurid journalese, and he was not proud of it. Ella deserved more respect. The obsession which had led him to Ella deserved more respect. He had been searching for a psychic like her, ever since he was her age himself.

'You'll have to excuse us. The Wallises and I have private business to settle.' But the dismissal, which should have brushed Dr Dóla off his sleeve like a fly, rang hollow, and Guntarson knew before Ken even looked up that another deal had already been struck.

'Things is a bit changed now, Peter,' said Ken. 'This time yesterday Ella was getting to be a bit of a celebrity in Bristol. Today the whole wide world is talking 'bout her.'

'Because I discovered her.'

'Because my Ella is a unique girl. Yes, your paper did a good big story on her, and you sold a lot of copies with it. But this morning, we got to think international.'

'Naturally. And I think you will find, Mr Wallis, that there is no international company bigger than Post Comm.' Guntarson's brain was searching for the escape hatch. He had come here expecting to lure the Wallises away from Post Comm, to guide them into his own net. Now he saw somebody else had netted them first.

He should never have waited so long. He should have committed Ella to him in the very first hour. Now his best hope was to keep the Wallises with the *Post* and hope to snatch them away later. 'You know,' he persisted, 'Post Comm is newspapers, magazines, publishing companies, radio and television stations, both terrestrial and cable, film studios, even internet providers.'

'One company, though, ain't it,' said Ken. 'Just one. And I bet every company in the whole wide universe would like to buy a bit of Ella and her magic. If they can afford it.'

'Ah! Money! I thought you might be eager to discuss that today, Mr Wallis. Post Comm's team would like to meet you at their London/ Wapping HQ in,' he checked his watch breezily, 'exactly forty-three minutes – I know Sir Peregrine mentioned it to you. And I'm sure you won't be disappointed in the package our lawyers have devised.'

'They'll be the one's what's disappointed.'

'The *Post* has been exceedingly protective and considerate of your family, Mr Wallis,' said Guntarson, dropping his voice to the level of a quiet threat. 'I shouldn't recommend venturing out from under their wing at this stage. It's a rough world out there.'

'You can leave me to look after my family,' growled Ken.

'I don't think you appreciate how vulnerable Ella could be.'

'I don't think you appreciate it ain't none of your business no more.'

Ken was still seated, but staring up into Guntarson's face with menace. Dr Dóla placed his hands on the table between them, only the very tips of his nails resting delicately on the lacquered surface.

'My client informs me that the *Post* has preferred to mine this vein of diamonds piecemeal.'

'Your client?'

'Indeed. That is, you have not drawn up an arrangement whereby unlimited and exclusive access is granted to the Wallises for any specified period. Which, in the case of a story so evidently remarkable as this, did surprise me.'

'We have paid Mr Wallis a considerable sum for exclusive rights.'

'You've paid him peanuts. I believe I can honestly say I paid more for these flowers.'

'They are so lovely, they must have been far too expensive,' murmured Juliette.

When he smiled, Dr Dóla revealed a ruby set into his left dogtooth. 'Madame Wallis, I confess I excelled myself. I naturally keep a warm relationship with a number of florists. It is in my professional interests. One never knows when a sudden obligation might occur, to appease a disgruntled client or to thank a benefactor. Flowers always say everything. But in your case, I felt the gesture must be spectacular, if it were to reflect the magnitude of your daughter's talent.'

Dr Dóla smiled again. He was delighted with his investment. 'I saw Ella on Sky, and I rang every florist with whom ever I had an account. We found tulips from Amsterdam, roses from Jersey, lilies from the Rhône valley – and I must say you have displayed them superbly, Madame Wallis.'

Juliette smiled her thanks, and forgot to mention that maids from the hotel had made the arrangements.

'You're a PR specialist, I believe,' remarked Guntarson.

'Certain newspaper editors, with their tendency to alliteration, have referred to me as a Media Maestro.'

'So you'll appreciate, the *Post* has the Wallises tied up.'

'Nobody got me tied up, pal,' growled Ken.

'Exactly. You have merely the most nebulous agreement. I have secured, in contrast, the most exact agreement. Mr and Mrs Wallis have expressed themselves most happy.'

'And how does Ella feel?'

'She feels what I tells her to feel,' Ken said.

'You may find, Mr Wallis, that the child has outgrown your reach.'

'Ella is fourteen,' pointed out José Dóla. 'It will be some time before she outlives her guardianship.'

'And has anybody asked her?'

Ella crouched quietly at the archway to the sitting-room. She was hearing what mattered – only one person cared about her feelings. Peter was here, and he was sticking up for her. She wiped her lips on her sleeve one last time, to be certain of eradicating all the breakfast vomit. She didn't want even Peter to know about the throwing-up.

'I am sure Ella recognises,' said Dr Dóla, 'her parents naturally have her best interests at heart.'

'I don't like you,' said Ella.

Dóla spun round. He had not yet seen the miracle child. She was slighter than he had guessed. She did not look like a girl who ate three adult portions for breakfast.

'I likes Peter.'

Dr Dóla inclined his head in a faint bow. 'I'm glad to meet you, Ella. I'm here to help you through a difficult time.'

'I knows what you're here for. You wants to make money.'

'Ella, shut your gob till you're asked.'

She quivered, daring herself to defy her father, and then burst out: 'You wants to smell all nice and perfumy but underneath you stinks.'

Dr Dóla's mouth hung open. His expression, more than the spectacle of Ella enraged, made Guntarson laugh.

'Ella, one more word . . .' warned Ken.

'I am sorry if you don't like my aftershave.' The doctor managed to find the words to make a weak joke of it. 'I appear to be in bad odour with you already.'

'I don't mean the way you smells really,' she said, grudgingly.

'Good. I'm grateful. I hope we can be friends.'

Ella's eyes brimmed with furious, frustrated tears. She did not have the vocabulary to say what she felt. Dr Dóla's personality was stinking the room out, reeking above the daffodils and the roses. Folds of thick, syrupy charm were dripping from him. What was hidden beneath the charm was less nice, like a man who smothers his body odour with eau de cologne.

'Ella, you better be nice to Dr Dóla. He's going to make us a lot of money.'

'I don't want money.'

'No, you'd rather live on air.'

'I won't do nothing except with Peter.'

'Ella,' invited Dr Dóla quietly, 'come and sit up at the table.' But she shook her head and hung back in the archway. 'You have a rare talent. Unique. There's never been a child like you in all history.'

'I don't want to be like that, all on my own! I wants to be the same as like everyone.' Her blood was up, and she was going to say what she wanted. She could stand up to them, because Peter was there.

'I mean your talent is unique. I know you are just a very nice, very ordinary young lady. But most people won't care about that. They'll want to exploit you, and use you, and rip you off, and they won't care about the real Ella Wallis. I can stop that from happening. I can put you in control.'

'Dr Dóla's a pro. He's the best, he can get you on the BBC any time. And the BBC gets respect worldwide – right, Joe?' said Ken. 'Show her your pictures, Joe. He's got photos of him with all his big clients – royals, and the England captain, and race drivers, and the Space Girls. You should think yourself lucky he even wants anything to do with you.'

'I likes Peter,' she said again.

'She likes me,' Guntarson repeated, emphatically.

He'd won. He had won before he even walked into the room. Stupid of him not to recognise it. All that hypocrisy about how wonderful Post Comm was – he needn't have bothered. Ella liked him. Him, Guntarson. No one else.

Ken Wallis had probably signed a paper already which bound him to Joe Dóla for ten thousand years. So what. Ken wasn't Ella. He couldn't do anything without Ella.

But in one way Ken was on the right track. Ella's earning potential was impossible to guess. No one had more than the haziest clue to what she might be capable of, when she was properly trained, when she was investigated, when she was encouraged.

What Ella needed was a freelance. A PR guru. Someone who knew everyone. Someone who knew the value of a contract. Someone who could screw millions out of Post Comm before Ella ever had to levitate a finger. Someone like Joe Dóla.

But if Ella didn't like Joe Dóla and didn't want to co-operate with him, she was going to be worse than useless.

Ella wasn't going to be useless when Guntarson was around. Ella had performed for him from the first – telepathy, levitation, even just opening her mouth and talking. He triggered her. He was her enabler.

All that passed through his mind in a fraction of a second. The speed of thought, of the electrical impulses firing across synapses, comes close to, maybe even exceeds, the speed of light. Guntarson saw the light.

'Ella needs more than your media contacts,' he said.

'She deserves better than Post Communications,' retorted Dóla.

'She needs an enabler.'

'A what?'

'Someone who provides the right environment for her powers. A catalyst, a trigger, a familiar if you like. Someone she trusts. Someone to get the magic flowing.' He was leaning back on a couch, lounging, smiling victoriously at Ella. And she was smiling back.

'Are you suggesting,' asked Dóla, with drawn-out irony, 'that Ella is only capable of producing her paranormal effects when there's someone from the *Post* around?'

'Forget the *Post*. You can ring the *Post* and tell them to start advertising for my successor.'

'Ring them yourself,' said Dóla. The treacle-thick charm was draining away.

'Ella, would you be happy if I weren't around?'

She shook her head, looking anxious.

'Would you feel more confident if we linked up? Like a team?'

'My Ella's been paranormal long before you was around, pal,' said Ken.

But Ella was smiling and nodding her head. Guntarson could hear her shouting in his head: 'Friends! Friends!'

CHAPTER NINETEEN

The Independent, Friday, January 15:

It has the appearance of a miracle. Rising effortlessly, without visible support, defying common sense as well as the established laws – the unstoppable upward momentum of José Dóla's career defies explanation.

At forty-six the PR guru from Oporto, Portugal, has lifted his biggest prize, an exclusive deal with the psychic wonderchild Ella Wallis. Slipping in beneath the noses of outraged executives at media giant Post Communications, Dóla made off with their paranormal protégé – securing, so it is rumoured, an astonishing twenty-five per cent of her earnings after the first million pounds is banked.

Dóla lost no time in throwing a cloak of mystery over what is already the most baffling instance of paranormality ever to command the world's attention.

Fourteen-year-old Ella and her family were whisked from their Kensington hotel suite to a secret location outside London, ostensibly to protect them from the world media crush.

The *Daily Post*'s distraught editor, Sir Peregrine Parrish, who had been due to complete a contract yesterday morning binding the Wallises to Post Communications for the next two years, is said to have launched a counter-attack already, hiring professional psychic Bill Durrant to ferret out Dóla's bolthole. Durrant terms himself 'an out-of-body private eye,' able to visualise the whereabouts of missing persons, using a technique known as 'remote viewing'.

Parrish also ordered a blood-letting, something which has become a ritual under his tenure whenever good exclusives are poached. First sacrificial victim was due to be star reporter Peter Guntarson – who had apparently read the morning tealeaves and faxed in his resignation twenty minutes before the *Post* even knew they had lost his story.

Sir Peregrine, who once dismissed an entire team of features sub-editors by standing on a desk and screaming, 'You're all ****s,' was not told of Guntarson's escape for more than three hours. At length the *Post*'s news-editors worked up their courage and bribed a secretary to slide the incriminating fax into Parrish's office. So the rumour goes.

By six o'clock last night, there were a thousand stories like this floating around the newsrooms of London and heading out to the Press Association and Associated Press and Reuters. Stories that materialised from nowhere and kept being blown higher, despite feeble attempts by sceptics to knock them down.

Wags said José Dóla was beaming tidbits telepathically into the rumour mill. That may be so – but he is placing his faith on the more conventional press conference, promising to produce Ella's parents for the media's scrutiny at London's South Bank centre today at 11am.

Ella, the wonderchild, will not be there. Officially, she is too sensitive to bear cross-examination by a room of baying hacks. Unofficially, Dóla does not wish to jeopardise the energetic bidding war between TV channels to broadcast Ella's next manifestation. Already, Sky look to have secured the rights, bidding two million pounds in association with their US sister station, Fox, but that may change at any moment, such is the frenetic interest of the major US networks – NBC, CBS, ABC.

Ella is being sold much as a boxing promoter sells a prize fighter, but she must be screened from the frenzy. After all, the stress of a press conference, being staged just across the Thames from that decidedly paranormal spire, Big Ben, might just set off her levitation node again. That would amount to a free show for the world.

And before any more miracles happen, José Dóla wants to get his miraculous contract firmly tied down.

Daily Telegraph, Friday, January 15:
In any group photograph of celebrities, he is the man at the perimeter. Smiling enthusiastically, dressed immaculately, but never at centre stage. Never the focus of the picture.

This is not an accident. Dr José Dóla has perfected the technique of whisking a bystander into the foreground, just before the shutter snaps. 'Come, come,' he cries, 'let the public get a better look at you. Nobody wants to see my ugly fizzog. My word, your gorgeous gown, we'd better have a picture of that!' He has a hundred phrases like this. They all work.

The bystander, flattered into star billing for this photograph, either is already a client of Joe Dóla or soon will be. Whom the doctor wants, the doctor gets.

This knack for ducking out of view extends to his personal life. Even his most trusted staff do not get to meet his wife, Carmilla, or visit his Queen Anne town house in Kensington. His teenage sons, José and Ricardo, board at Marlborough – a school so steeped in offspring of illustrious parentage that the Dóla boys go quite unnoticed.

Dóla insists his low profile is part of the successful *modus operandi*. When public attention swings towards one of his clients, he does not wish to siphon off any of it. That would diminish the effect, and thus his effectiveness.

Yet he clearly is not a shy man. He dresses to impress – suits whiter than Dulux Gloss, bowties as lurid as Las Vegas. His teeth are capped, one of them ornamented with a round ruby. A visit to his hairdresser in Soho Street, unfailingly at 9.30am on Monday mornings, keeps his hair lacquer-black.

The son of a prominent businessman in Oporto, Portugal, he was expected to take over the reins of the family cork export business, founded by his grandfather, Jesus Juan Dóla, in 1922. But a spell in Paris during the early seventies, studying law, awakened his taste for a lifestyle not easily satisfied in Oporto. Attracted as much by the prospect of fine lunches as by the potential salaries, he entered advertising. He makes much today of the fact that his first pay packet contained just £47.60.

Dóla insists he stuck at his studies long enough to earn the title *docteur en droit*, though there does not appear to be any record confirming this at the university. Whatever, it is certain that Joe Dóla never practised law. His family, of course, had never intended that he should. Nor had they intended the heir to the firm to start work as a copywriter at £47.60 a week.

He quickly switched from copywriting to PR, though

not before he invented the 'Dial-a-Smile' logo that accompanied the GPO phone system up to the inception of British Telecom.

In the meantime, he married Carmilla da Portelegre, daughter of a family friend, and the woman who has stayed discreetly at the docteur's side for twenty years. Their first child, a girl, died aged three days. She was named Maria Anna, in a hasty baptism at the bedside.

Two healthy sons followed, and for a time friends speculated that Dóla would become a father in the dynastic, Portuguese tradition. But the shock of losing a child seems to have engendered caution, and Dóla quite candidly announced in the mid Eighties he was having a vasectomy.

It did nothing to sap his vitality. His PR talent had grown into a genius for brazen promotion. No client was too tacky, no field too tasteless for Dóla's manipulative touch. Young women expecting the love-spawn of earls, drug addicts who made secret videos of rock-star orgies, convicted fraudsters who formed dubious business relationships with minor royals – these people were the backbone of his agency.

By the early nineties he had acquired a particular reputation among mistresses. Britain's invisible economy is immensely rich in these women – and Dóla is fond of saying that if mistresses were outlawed, the nation would collapse. Whether he is among the virtuous few who eschew their blandishments, he does not say.

His professional mistresses, the ones he represented, include Lady Alicia Stedding, the baronet's widow whose book of illicit photographs featured two Cabinet ministers, a dozen peers and a sports commentator. Zsuzsa Peppar, the Hungarian actress who shared a bed with a woman chief constable and her husband, is another.

His signing of Ella Wallis and her family might seem a leap upwards in moral standards. It remains to be seen whether Joe Dóla will drag the flying psychic down to his level.

'Don't read the newspapers,' Dr Dóla advised Ella's parents. 'Measure the stories but don't read them. It will only make you angry. They get everything wrong. I don't think I ever saw a report where every fact was right. It makes you want to pick up the phone, start correcting every inaccuracy you see. Then they just start printing more inaccuracies. And if you sue for libel in this country, you're liable to go bankrupt. Believe me, I know. It's better to ignore it and stick to counting the money.'

'Got to read the papers,' said Ken slyly. 'We wants to know you're making our girl rich and famous.' He lounged in the big beige leather bucket seat of the Mercedes 600 V12 stretched limo, chauffeur-driven, a mahogany table unfolded across his lap and a glass of champagne on the table. Ken almost never drank alcohol. It was a weakness, the kind of temptation from hell to which women succumbed. He knew Juliette liked a drink, more than she ought. He was stronger.

But this was a Merc, a limo, with a chauffeur in uniform and a cap and everything. You got to have a bit of champagne.

'Look at me,' he crowed, sipping the bitter bubbles and grimacing. 'Drinking and driving!'

Dr Dóla smiled. Everyone made that joke. He sat in the pavilion that passed as a back seat, with Juliette, who was laughing loudly to mask the hiss as she poured herself another glass.

'Rich and famous, fame and fortune,' repeated the doctor. 'Rich is what matters. Famous is part of the technique for getting rich. By being famous, you help sell newspapers, and books, and films, and videos, and CDs, and so you generate money for people. My job is to ensure you get a fair percentage. But you might not enjoy being famous. I'm just warning you. It can be a pain in the neck, people always recognising you. They hound you for autographs. Maybe they even stalk you. The paparazzi sink their teeth into you. They invade your privacy. They shout out the same jokes all the time. With me it's 'Who are you blackmailing today?' Very unfair, because I don't blackmail people. Quite the opposite.

'Your daughter probably won't enjoy being the centre of attention. We shall have to protect her, as much as possible. Without prejudicing her earning potential. Every time she walks down the street, people will be yelling "Come on, fly around for us. Show us your wings. Go on, hover like a helicopter." '

'She can just ignore them,' said Ken.

'There'll be a lot of questions about Ella today,' Dóla continued. 'Have you thought how you'll answer them?'

'I'll do the talking,' said Ken. 'Juliette ain't going to start making the statements unless I okay it.'

'Fine. It helps to have one person as the focus. But you should sound sympathetic to her. Think, "Strong and gentle". Okay? You don't want anybody to start saying you're exploiting Ella. Absolutely the reverse – you're guiding her. Shielding her from a hostile world.

That's why she's being kept away from this press conference. Out of the glare.'

Ella was in a safe house. No one knew she was there – no one except Guntarson, who was there with her. Baby-sitting. The house belonged to a Scandinavian acquaintance of Dóla's, who used it for six weeks of the year and let the publicist have it free of charge all the rest of the year. For Dóla it was a tax-free perk – for the Scandinavian, whose ex mistress had for a brief and unfortunate time been a client of Joe Dóla's, it was a convenient way to pay a debt. Dóla used the house regularly, and the world never got to read about the Scandinavian and his ex-mistress.

Because it was one of the doctor's known bolt-holes, Ella would not be invisible there forever. The reporters would find her. For a few days, however, until Dóla and the Wallises found their bearings, the house was safe enough.

Juliette drained the champagne bottle. Her nervous fingers turned it round and round by the neck.

'And another thing. Don't mention this friend of hers, this Peter. I don't know where he fits in yet.'

'Nowhere,' said Ken.

'She likes him. She needs people to give her confidence, help her grow. You don't want her to shrivel under all these bright lights. But we want to take care and listen to what he's saying to her. She's very vulnerable, I suspect, to ideas that are planted in her head.'

'That girl ain't never had an idea in her head, her whole life.'

'Mr Wallis.' Dr Dóla sounded deeply earnest. 'When the reporters start asking questions about your daughter, I only want to hear you say the most positive things.'

'I ain't going to look at the telly,' vowed Ella. 'And I ain't going to see none of the papers.'

She stood at the window, watching the garden become a kaleido-scope through thick rivulets of rain. The lawn and the slender poplars ran into each other, and the gravel path washed against the high stone wall that hemmed all of it in. She could see two faint reflections of herself, slightly out of alignment, in the double-glazing.

Over her shoulder, a television flickered. Guntarson sprawled, not watching it, with one long leg hooked over the arm of his chair and the *Telegraph* in his hands.

'You'll have to get used to being the boss,' he said. 'What you say, goes.'

She did not answer for a long time. The poplars were straining towards her in the strong winds, and gusts were squeezing through the window-frames and stirring the curtains. It was cold where she stood. The window rose to an arch, twice her height. She looked a very small girl, standing there, between drapes of faded yellow satin like twin pillars. The room behind her was furnished with eight or ten chairs, which did not begin to fill the floor space. A long dresser, black with age and roughly carved, stood by one of the two doors, facing the fireplace.

Ella had never been in a room like it. She supposed it must be the kind of stately home she had seen on school videos, but there were no tourists here. The house felt dry and there was no dirt, but when they arrived it was empty. No one to clean or cook. No butler, even. Breakfast had been delivered by a boy in a van.

'Big house,' she said at last.

Guntarson laughed and craned round the chair-back to see her. 'Do you want to explore? I saw a suit of armour up on the second floor.'

She liked it when he laughed. It was a deep, full noise, that came from his chest. She wanted to make him laugh again, but did not know how.

'No one's here but us,' she stated.

'Nope. We can go and search every drawer in the building, and there's no one to stop us.'

The thought of so many rooms daunted her. So many people, living in them, using them. Knowing their way round the house. Rooms which had been there for hundreds of years.

'Let's stay here.'

He shrugged and agreed: 'We don't want to miss the press conference. It must be almost over by now – there'll be a report on the next bulletin. I bet your mum and dad were nervous.'

'My dad ain't never scared.'

'I would have been.'

Ella turned round and looked at him proudly. No man had ever talked to her honestly before – her teachers, and her dad, her Uncle Robert, they all fed her the official version. She had never been worth the effort that honesty required.

'I were scared,' she said, 'I were shitting myself on that TV thing.'

Guntarson burst out laughing. 'You were *what*? I thought you were too perfect to use words like that.'

'Why'd you think I'm perfect?'

He was still laughing, now at the surprise on her face. 'Just the way you look.' He was teasing her.

'I ain't perfect,' she said seriously. 'You don't know.'

'You must be fairly perfect, or you wouldn't be able to float. You'd be weighed down by all that sin. But you shouldn't be scared of television cameras. That was my fault, I should have given you a lot more support. I'm sorry. I'll be more use next time.'

He laughed, he was honest with her, he said he thought she was perfect. And she was alone in a house with him. Ella thought she must really be happy. And she would try to do anything to make Peter happy too.

'Because there will be next times – I want lots of film, to show the whole world. Film of you levitating, film of you mind-reading, of objects appearing. We'll make an absolutely thorough record of it, to show the close-minded scientists your PK energies. Psychokinetic powers. Then no one will be able to deny them.'

'If you want – I ain't doing it for no one else, see. Not for that doctor what my dad's hired. Not on chatshows again, neither. I'm only doing it for you.'

Guntarson laid his newspaper down and leaned forward, looking intently at Ella. 'If you're really scared, we're going to have to do something about it.'

'I ain't scared of you.'

'That's good. I feel honoured.' He wasn't teasing her now. 'But no one will pay attention unless you can demonstrate your capabilities for lots of people. Not just me. I'll always be nearby, with you, if that's what you want.'

Ella nodded. That was what she wanted.

'But I want you to be yourself, be natural with other people too. Are you scared of that?'

'Dunno.'

'Have you ever been hypnotised? Do you know what hypnotism is? I don't mean like TV entertainers do. Not stupid stuff. Proper hypnotism.'

'I ain't been hypnotised,' she said worriedly. 'It's not that what makes me leveltate.'

'That's not what I mean.'

'My friend, well this girl in my class, Flora, her brother went to see the hypnotist when he was at Ritzy's in Bristol. And he said this woman was hypnotised and she had to eat an onion and she thought it was an apple and . . .'

'That's not what I mean.' Guntarson smiled – it might be slow progress, talking to Ella, but at least he was getting her confidence. He had never heard her string so many words together. 'I'm not going to make you eat onions.'

'Are you going to hypnotise me?'

'Only if you want me too.'

'Can you do it?'

'I'm good at it. I did it at university all the time. Hypnotism doesn't make you lose control, it puts you in control. It makes your mind stronger.'

Ella looked at him, uncertain.

'I'll make sure you're totally safe.'

That was all she needed to know. 'I wants you to hypnotise me,' she said.

CHAPTER TWENTY

'All I'm going to do,' said Guntarson, 'is make you feel relaxed. You won't feel funny, you're not going unconscious or anything. You'll remember everything that I say to you and everything that happens.' He swung his feet off the arm of the chair and dropped onto the carpet. 'Come and kneel opposite me. Sit cross-legged if it's comfier.'

Ella was wearing a fake Hard Rock Café T-shirt over loose jeans. She tucked her feet underneath her and clasped her hands in her lap. Their faces were no more than two feet apart.

Guntarson flicked off the TV with the remote. He spoke quite softly, pronouncing each word carefully. 'As you relax, you will become more aware of everything around you. The sounds in the room will become clearer to you. Your thoughts will feel clearer. Everything will be simpler and stronger. I'm looking into your eyes. You are looking back at mine. I want you to be aware of the sounds in my voice. You can hear every tiny detail in every word. Every sound is clearer than water to you.'

Ella could hear the rattle of water on the windows. Raindrops dashing against the gravel path. Somewhere in the house, on another floor, a heavy clock ticked.

'Breathe in, slowly and deeply. You can feel the faint chill of the air as it passes through your nose. Feel your lungs fill. That's oxygen. With every breath you are feeding your body. Hold that breath, and now, let it escape slowly from your mouth. All the tension is flowing out with that air. Feel how your shoulders are falling. The tension that bunched them up is leaving you. As you breathe in again, straighten your back. Feel how strong your muscles are. All that strength and control, at rest. That is how your mind feels. Relaxed and strong. Relaxed and in control. You don't feel like I've hypnotised you, do you?'

'You ain't started yet.'

'I've finished. That's all I'm going to do. Your mind is very receptive, Ella. It is a very strong mind. It obeys easily, when the orders are good.'

'Are you going to snap your fingers, like, when we stop?'

'We are in a state of relaxation. When we're ready to stop, I shall simply tell you. For now, I just want you to breathe each breath, letting the oxygen refresh every fibre of your lungs. And when you're ready, feel yourself breathing out and all the anxiety and the fear drifting away.'

He leaned back, one palm spread on the floor behind him. Her eyes were still fixed on his, but all her attention was focused on each breath. Guntarson too was relaxed. Her clear, unmoving gaze was like a mirror, channelling the mesmeric energy back to him. He saw the details of her face as if each hair in her eyebrows had been painted with a separate brushstroke.

She seemed unreal, like a figure sculpted in flesh. He was faintly surprised that he had no sexual feelings for her.

She seemed to be looking down slightly on him now. Guntarson broke the gaze and saw Ella's knees and feet had lifted three or four inches from the carpet.

'Ella, can you feel that you're floating?'

She was intent upon the long, steady breaths. Guntarson watched for several minutes, as her body stayed weightless and stationary. Ella's look of acute concentration was softened by a faint smile.

What buoyed her up? Guntarson's eyes searched for signs of a force, but there was no hint of a disturbance about her. Her outline was clearly defined, without haziness or distortion. He stretched an arm, tentatively, beneath her body. Her hair and the folds of her clothes hung ordinarily, as though they were subject to gravity. The carpet beneath her was unmarked. Ella seemed simply to have forgotten to stay on the ground.

But she did not rise any farther. She remained kneeling, perfectly balanced, without swaying or rolling or drifting.

His own body strained, as he tried to imagine that he too was light enough to lift into the air. His toes and fingers drove into the wool pile. The muscles in his upper arms trembled. He did not levitate.

'Do you know how you do it?' he asked. 'Could you teach me?'

Ella floated silently.

'It's all right. I understand,' he whispered. 'You got born like this. I didn't. I help, though, don't I? You've got more strength when I'm here. I am an amplifier to your powers. We'll show them. People like my father, people who think it's all just hocus pocus, we'll show them this time.

'You know what you make me think of? A place called Snowflake. My mother went there once, and she told me Snowflake was the place that changed her life and Snowflake was the reason I got born. And that's the reason my mother started to get so interested in crystal energy, because snowflakes are crystals. Crystalline, frozen water. Crystals have got such incredible energy in them, they're almost intelligent. I showed you my rock crystal. I always have it with me, always, and nobody knows about it but you. My mother. Her name was Ruth.

'Shall I tell you about Snowflake? It was way, way back. About 1971. My parents had been married five years or so, and my mother was bored. She had this job, graphic artist or something for a design agency. That was in Winnipeg, where I was born. And my father – I'll tell you now, I don't like my father at all, so he's liable to come out rather badly from this story – he was a construction engineer. He was from Iceland. Guntar Einarsson. He insisted on teaching me Icelandic. He lives in London now, with his ugly girlfriend – or last time I spoke to him, he did, which was about six years ago. For my twenty-first birthday he gave me a flat, in Bayswater, and I still live there, and £200,000-worth of shares in his company. Which I promptly sold. I've got the money still, naturally, in offshore bonds and stuff. It helped me through my DPhil. But the deal was this – I had nothing more to do with my father. I didn't ring him up for money, I didn't get my allowance any more. In effect, I wasn't going to be his son any more. Which suited me very nicely.

'But that's not what I was telling you. You want to hear about Snowflake.'

Ella, noiseless and distant, showed no sign she could hear Peter's murmurings.

'Snowflake was where my mother went to find herself one day. She had a map, all the places around Winnipeg. There's the lakes, and there's a fishermen's settlement called Reykjavik, about 220K from their city apartment. They had a hut out there, I think just simply because my father came from Reykjavik, Iceland, and he thought it was this big joke. We're just driving over to Reykjavik for the day. Ha, ha. I must have heard him say this about a thousand times. Well, the joke was on him, because Reykjavik was where my mother ended up living with her lover.

'Snowflake is nowhere near Reykjavik. Snowflake is on the border with the United States. Right next to Crystal City. And there's Turtle Mountain, and Swan Lake. And my mother had never been to these places. Her family were Jewish, they had no car, because they hadn't had a lot of money when she was growing up. Everything they owned was in Germany. They got out in 1933, and they had to leave a lot of my relatives behind. My mother's paternal grandparents, and their brothers and sisters, and their children, they all died in the Holocaust. In the camps. My mother said to me, more than once, "We were poor, but we were alive." What money her family did have, all through the fifties, they saved. Saved to emigrate. But when all the family had enough for tickets and they were ready to up sticks, *en masse*, and claim their plot in the Promised Land, my mother had just met my father. They were in love, and she'd got her career off the ground, and he was just starting out in the construction industry. And they didn't want to give up all of that. Anyway, they couldn't get married and tag along, because my father wasn't Jewish. Lutheran Christian, in fact, same as me, nominally. So you didn't know that about me, did you – technically, I'm Jewish? The son of a Jewish mother is always fully Jewish. But I didn't have a Jewish upbringing, so I'd tend to call myself half-Jewish. You see?

'Snowflake – I'll get to Snowflake. My mother was tired, you see, of hearing about construction industry politics, all the infighting, stuff which my father lived for. It was all right for the first few years, but after a while it was just more of the same. My mother was a terrifically imaginative woman. She needed new horizons. So she thought, maybe having children is the answer, but my father was opposed. Totally. He's always said this to me, that he never actually wanted a son. Or a daughter. No desire to see the line carried on. Children were trouble, trouble and expense. Which is fair enough, providing you acknow-ledge that's how you feel and you're not a hypocrite. It's how I feel, as a matter of fact. The difference is, I've no children.

'Snowflake was the first place my mother tried to picture in her imagination. She wasn't going to have children, she'd taken her job as far as she could, she was married to a man she had once been very much in love with but now he was holding her back. She wanted a family – me, she wanted me – and he wouldn't agree; she said, "Let's move on, New York, Los Angeles, London, somewhere that isn't Winnipeg," and he wouldn't agree to that either. Building up his precious firm, you see.

'Snowflake became a symbol for her. This intriguing little name on her map, that suggested something fleeting and fragile and waiting to be caught and held, just for an instant. It touched her imagination. So she tried to envisage it, in her mind. She'd just started meditating – late sixties, early seventies, remember – and so she got down cross-legged and started to meditate on this word, Snowflake. Picturing it.

'Snowflake is, I don't know, two or three hours drive from Winnipeg. My parents had a car each, by this time. So one day my mother headed off to Snowflake. It took a lateral leap to do it – going off exploring, on her own. But she did. And here's the thing.

'Snowflake was exactly as she envisaged it. The streets, the houses, the people. Not just the general look of the place, which I suppose she could have guessed. But individual buildings. Signs in shop windows, flags above doors, trees. She told me she walked into a restaurant to get a cup of coffee, a restaurant she had pictured in her mind, sat at the table she had imagined to be there, and the waitress who came to serve her had the face of the waitress from her meditation. It was as though my mother had created the whole town in her head, and made it real.

'She tried to tell my father about Snowflake, which was a waste of time. He thought it was her hormones playing her up, or too much meditation sending her brain screwy. In fact, he ordered her to stop meditating, which she didn't. She just tried the experiment with another town. Notre Dame de Lourdes. There really is such a place in Manitoba. And my mother pictured it to herself as minutely as she could. The gardens of houses, the faces of children, the light on the Pembina Mountain. She tried to experience these details vividly in her head. And in every detail, she was right.

'She was psychic, Ella. A different kind of psychic to you, because her intuition was highly evolved and intelligent. And my mother couldn't understand that nobody believed her and nobody was interested. So she decided to learn for herself everything that was mysterious, and she started sending off for books and magazines, and she was at the library every day. Till my father got quite worried. Psychic powers meant nothing to him. He couldn't put up an office block with psychic powers. He started to think my mother was losing her grip on sanity, which would have been bad for the firm. He would have become, not the managing director any more, but the managing director with the mad wife.

'My father confided in his friends, if you'll believe he had any, and they said, "Well it's obvious isn't it? She needs children, same as any woman. Obvious." And I think maybe they dropped hints, man-to-man hints – Ruth is driving out of town every day, she has this weird story that she is visiting places from her imagination . . . "Are you sure, Guntar, she doesn't have a man friend? Are you sure? Are you doing enough to make certain she doesn't want a man friend?"

'And that's how Snowflake led to me.

'My father said to me once, he would have wanted children eventually but not until the firm was safely grown. Maybe when he was fifty. When my mother would be fifty, too. He was saying, in other words, he had married at the wrong time, to the wrong woman.

'All through the pregnancy, my mother was reading about religion, the Kaballah and the Bible and the Koran, and about the occult and the paranormal. Anything she could get hold of. She said she went into hospital, in labour, still clutching a book. Trying to have a baby and read at the same time.

'Then she took a lover. Of course she hadn't been carrying on an affair when my father suspected her. But when I was three months old, she began sleeping with a man who'd been her colleague at the agency. And of course my father suspected nothing. My mother told me – she told me most things – that she had sex with this man, not because she found him attractive but because *he* found *her* attractive. After the pregnancy and everything, he still wanted to sleep with her.

'When I was quite little, she took up something more serious, with a man in Reykjavik. He was a boat-builder from Minnesota called Clarence. Clarence was around all through my childhood. My father found out about it, took it very calmly – probably because it was very much what he'd been doing himself for years. I don't know if my parents ever talked about it. It was just tacitly accepted. I grew up spending half my time on the shore of Lake Manitoba.

'There was something else more important than that. My mother saw a television programme, that galvanised her psychic awareness. This guy was on who could bend metal through mindpower. He touched a spoon and it bent. He was urging viewers to try it themselves.

'My mother could do it. She was good at it. She was awesome. She could sit stroking the stem of a spoon and after about five minutes the metal went like Plasticine. If she kept stroking, the end dropped off. I tried, and tried, and tried, as I got older. My mother always said that as I was a child, it should be twice as easy for me. Maybe I had a mental block, or maybe I wasn't born psychic enough, but I've never bent a spoon in my life.

'I could read her mind, though. When this TV guy concentrated telepathically on an image, she could get the picture just by watching his eyes. She told me she could already pick up on my thoughts, but she thought at first that was a mother thing, something all women did with babies. She started to practise. She developed this technique for planting a word in my head – shouting it, from ship to shore, like I showed you, Ella. And I found I could do it back, but only with her. Once or twice I've got telepathic messages from people, especially when I put them under hypnosis. She taught me how to do that too. But until I met you, Ella, there was never anyone who could read my mind like my mother.

'Clarence tolerated this stuff, I think. It was all too weird for him, when she was trying to make things move by PK, and talking about auras. But he didn't mind it . . . my father, he hated it. Hated it. And I hated him for hating it. I blamed him, I supposed, blamed him for the gene in me that blocked my powers. My psychic node didn't grow very big, and maybe that's genealogy, and if it is then it's his genealogy.

'More than that – sometimes I seemed to have a negative psychic charge. Sometimes I actually drained my mother. I came into her bedroom in the cabin once, just barged in, when I was about nine years old. My mother was meditating, concentrating on a candle. She must have been there ages, I remember the candle was burnt right down low. And I was getting concerned about her. Or maybe I was just looking for some attention – anyway, I walked in and the candle went out. As though I switched it off. It wasn't the draught, the flame didn't seem to blow out. It just went off.

'My mother looked at me, daggers. Daggers. I felt so awful – I had none of my mother's ability, I wrecked what she was doing, I wasn't wanted. Some matches were on the floor, and I jumped forward and tried to relight the candle. Somehow I set light to the bedspread at the same time. Almost burned the cabin down. My mother was so angry. Angrier, I think, that I'd wrecked the meditation with all these negative vibes, than she was about the damage.'

Peter stopped his murmuring. He was staring vacantly at Ella. She floated before him, her hands clasped between her knees, as if she were locked in the deepest prayer.

'My mother's dead,' Peter said at last. 'I hadn't told you that. She's dead. I don't know what made me tell you any of this. I don't think I want you to know it. Perhaps it would be better if you forgot it. You're going to wake up soon, Ella, and your mind won't recall any of that story. It doesn't matter to you anyway. It's not relevant. Not to us.'

Ella sank quietly from the air. Guntarson watched her for several minutes more, listening to her soft, long breaths. Her smile was radiant, literally radiant – her face seemed to be glowing, as though she had been running on a cold day. The lustre offset a hint of hollowness under her eyes and in her cheeks. Watching her, Guntarson thought for the first time what a thin child she was. No wonder she ate three breakfasts when she got the chance.

'Ella? Ella, you have been in a deeply restful state. You are totally relaxed now. I want you to start moving around again now. Stretch your arms and legs, that's right. You will feel perfectly normal, but very rested. And very strong. In control. You won't be frightened of situations now. This strength will stay with you. You're free to talk now, do whatever you like.'

Ella stood, blinked at him and walked to the window. 'I been listening to the rain. Strange what you can hear when you really try, like.'

'What did you hear. A voice?'

'No, dim-brain! Rain can't talk!' She stopped and glanced round suddenly, as the first wave of her habitual fear returned. She had just called a grown man 'dim-brain'.

It was all right. He was smiling. Now Mr McNulty, he'd have blown his top. Peter was different.

'What did you hear?' he was asking.

'Splashes. It was like I could picture where every drop was when it hit the window. And I could even hear it being soaked up in the grass.'

'You're a very good hypnotic subject.'

'Really, honest?'

'You have a terrific mind, ultra-focused. In a way, in a very important way, you are as clever as I am.'

Ella shook her head. She knew he was wrong. But it was wonderful to hear him say it.

CHAPTER TWENTY-ONE

Ella sat very quietly in the corner, half-hidden by a curtain, and pressed Last Number Redial on her phone. Peter had ridden off on his big black bike, back to his flat for the night. She would have asked him to take her too, she would not have been scared to ask. She was still on a confident high from the hypnosis. But her dad would never let her go off for the night, so what was the point of asking?

Ken and Juliette were getting a lesson in media management from Dr Dóla. He was replaying the tape of their press conference, and tactfully offering criticisms. 'Perhaps it might have been better to phrase that like this . . . I don't think you need to be so frank there . . . you must not allow reporters the satisfaction of feeling they're putting pressure on you . . .'

Ella was invited to join in, but she shied away. She did not want to read stories about herself, or see her face on the TV.

Ken, conversely, was enjoying it. The only thing that bothered him – and it must have been nagging at him, for he mentioned it three or four times – was his waistline. 'That's not a good camera angle, makes me look like I got a gut. Can we ask them only to film me face on?'

Juliette had smuggled two bottles of white wine out of the reception room after the conference. She wrapped a cardigan around them, figure-of-eight fashion, to keep them from clinking in her shoulder-bag. In the back of the limousine, out of sight from Ken in the front seat, she slid one out. Dr Dóla stared. She deftly, silently opened it. Apparently she kept a corkscrew in the bag.

She saw Joe Dóla's dismay. 'They were there for us,' she hissed. 'I did not think it is stealing, no one will mind if no one sees.'

'It won't look very good in tomorrow's papers if someone has sneaked a piccy of you, tucking the maison blanc under your purse.' He smiled; he liked Juliette. More precisely, he felt sorry for her, living with Ken. In French, he murmured: 'Leave it to me – I'll make sure you don't die of thirst.'

Now she sat, gazing inattentively at the TV, stewed enough not to care if Ken saw her pouring another small glass of free wine. They were only little glasses, and it would be a pity to waste it.

Ella held her mobile phone tightly. Aunt Sylvie in Bristol answered the ringing.

Last Number Redial. Ella had never rung Auntie Sylvie before, and that meant someone had pinched her phone to make their calls. That meant Juliette. Well, she could keep her thieving hands off. It was Ella's phone.

She nearly rang off. The thought of speaking with Frank kept her there.

'Is my brother there, Auntie Sylvie?'

'Ella! Are you ringing me? Well this is an honour, I don't think I've ever spoken to a superstar before. Won't it be nice when I see you to get your autograph!'

'Don't.' Auntie Sylvie always teased her like this, making her squirm.

'But you can tell your mumma, I will not be doing what your dadda's horrid, horrid brother did. I might need the money, we all need money sometimes, but I just thought it was so-o nasty, what he said. You've seen all the papers, of course?'

Ella wished she had put down the phone in the first place. 'I ain't going to look at none of the telly or the papers, nothing.'

'Well, good for you. What your Uncle Robert said about our family, it was so-o mean, it does not bear repeating. I am glad you didn't read it, and you must tell mumma not to look at that paper. It was the *Daily Post*, the paper who paid your dadda too. Of course, perhaps your Uncle Robert did not say any of it and they just made all of it up.'

'What'd they say?'

'It's better you don't know. I have been so-o upset, all the day. He told them horrid things, all about me. And I don't know what I have to do with it, just because you are going on television and doing these things, I really don't. All my private life, dragged out for people to look at. And it is better for these things to be in the past. I don't know why your Uncle Robert thinks it is any business of his. Just because he is a church minister he thinks he can go about preaching to everybody, like he is some kind of saint. Well we know he isn't don't we Ella?' Sylvie's words were stumbling over each other, as she rushed to keep herself from sobbing. 'We know very well what people say about your Uncle Robert, and I know it's not very nice. And it's certainly none of my business. How would he like it if his private life was suddenly all over the papers? Well, he might find out, except I wouldn't stoop that low.'

'Can I speak to Frank, Auntie Sylvie?'

'Yes, yes, you don't want to sit gabbing to boring old me all night. But don't keep him long, Ella, he's only little and he should be going to bed soon. And he has had a horrid headache all day. Tell your mumma, she must remember, it is not fair on Frank if all this is getting stressful to him. I know it is very nice for you to be rich and famous, and everybody is interested in you, and I'm sure your dadda will be making some nice business deals, now you are clever and famous. You are *so-o* clever, Ella. But maybe it is not as good for Frank.'

'Hi, Ella!' Frank got the phone at last. 'Where are you?'

'Dunno.'

'Is it a big hotel?'

'Dunno. Don't think so. It's more like a house.'

'Is there room service and waiters and all that?'

'No.'

'So why don't you just come home?'

Ella had no idea. She did not know what else to say, either. She liked talking to her little brother on a mobile phone. It was really cool. Maybe Peter would buy one for Frank too, and they could phone each other up, like on walkie-talkies. She wished she could think of more to say, though.

'Auntie Sylvie said you got a headache.'

'I'm okay. It's just Sylvie, she's talking and talking. Makes you feel ill,' he whispered. 'She was real pissy with Uncle Robert, 'cos of what he told the papers. She said she'd go round and see him, only she was scared she'd kill him.'

'Kill him! With what?'

'I dunno. Maybe she got a gun hidden in her knickers!' Frank stopped to think about this for a moment. 'I read the newspaper, anyway. When she was on the toilet. Auntie Sylvie says it's a pack of lies. Most of it's just about you, boring stuff. There's one bit about Mum and Auntie Sylvie and their dad, and that's what she's pissy about.'

'Yeah?'

'It says Mum and Dad only just got married in time before you were born. And Sylvie weren't allowed to go to the wedding by her dad, but when she got pregnant he threw her out and she came to live over here. And she didn't even get married when the baby was born, and she tried to look after it on her own, but she had it adopted because it got too much work.'

'I never remembered that.'

'It was when you were two. And I weren't born then. Auntie Sylvie don't know I read it. So I can't ask her nothing.'

'That baby was really lucky,' said Ella. 'I bet it got given to a really nice family.'

'You going to come home soon, Ella?'

'Dunno.'

She dialled Peter's mobile after that. She got a woman's recorded voice, telling her the number was unavailable at that present time and asking her to try again later. For a long time, she dialled and listened. In the end, she tried his home number too, though she didn't like to – his answerphone would always cut in. The answerphone paralysed Ella: she listened silently to the message and stayed silent when the bleeps came.

The battery light was flashing on her handset, but she ignored it and rang Holly too. 'If I'd known your uncle was going to slag your family off, I could of told Miss Meese loads more,' said Holly.

'Who's Miss Meese?'

'She writes in the *Daily Mail*. My dad says the *Mail* is loads better than the *Post*. More upmarket. My dad says twenty per cent of *Mail* readers are in marketing group ABC1 and the *Post* don't have no ABC1s at all.'

Ella said nothing. She was listening, but she did not understand and so she had nothing to say.

'The *Daily Post* is gutter-press, my dad says. I suppose anyone who reads that is a Z. I wouldn't never have talked to the *Post*. My dad says they must have paid your uncle loads, either that or he must hate your mum and your Auntie Sylvie. He probably got thousands for saying all what he said. I got a hundred pounds, but my dad said I could only tell Miss Meese facts. The *Daily Mail* only has facts.'

'You talked to a paper and got a hundred pounds?'

'My dad said I'd be stupid not to,' retorted Holly combatively, 'when you were making stacks and stacks of cash.'

'What you tell them?'

'Read the paper tomorrow. I ain't said nothing that's not true. Anyway, you don't care, you're rich now. Have you bought a car yet?'

'No.'

'Are you getting it all paid into your own account? Have you got a bank account? You ain't, have you? I knew it! My sister Brooke said your dad wouldn't let you get ripped off, but I bet he is. I said so. Serves you right, Ella Wallis, you think you're so much better than the rest of us, but I bet you don't end up getting a penny. You won't even get a hundred pounds like me. That's what you . . .'

The winking light on the handset died. Holly's voice faded. Ella tried to ring back. She wanted to tell Holly she didn't mind if her friends talked to the papers. She wasn't going to read any of them, so it wouldn't matter. She didn't want Holly to be worried about it.

There was no dialling tone. The battery was drained. There was a socket on the handset, for plugging it into the mains. She needed Peter to show her how it connected.

And Peter wasn't there.

CHAPTER TWENTY-TWO

Rainwater was swilling across the gravel drive and running in folds from the bonnets of the cars outside Dr Dóla's hideaway house when the BBC team pulled up. It was eight o'clock and not yet light. As the Range Rover crunched up to the front steps, its headlights swept across the wet foliage smothering the stone walls. Dripping water sparkled on dark green leaves.

When the last of the daylight was long gone and the team returned to London, the downpour had dwindled to an oily drizzle. Red and yellow tail-lights glittered in the wet windows of shops and in the shimmering tarmac and trickling gutters.

Emily Whitlock watched the cameraman over her shoulder. He sat across the back seats, hunched above his Ikegama with one eye pressed to the viewfinder. His fingers, confident like a touch-typist's, flicked between the Rewind and Replay buttons. For a few moments he watched, then ejected the tape into his hand. He had repeated the ritual every ten minutes of the journey.

'Still there?' asked Whitlock.

'I'm going barmy,' admitted Fraser Bough, unzipping his camera bag and counting six more video cassettes. 'It's just what Guntarson said, it bugs me – if you video something paranormal, the tape disappears sometimes. Dematerialises. Okay, they're all here – I am barmy.'

Eric Williams, the lighting electrician, in the driving seat, said: 'He's the one that's barmy. Not you, Fraze.'

'I imagine,' remarked Whitlock, in the same dry tone she always used to her team, 'living with that girl would drive anyone barmy.'

In the Number Two editing suite at Whitlock Majestic Productions, she was relieved, though she kept it to herself, when each of the day's cassettes tested smoothly. Sharp pictures, clear sound. Each tape marked with the start and finish times. Seven hours of images – they had kept the camera running every minute. Seven hours of proof that the extraordinary Ella Wallis was not a fake.

Seven hours to be cut down to ninety minutes.

'Let's break the back of this now, shall we? At least identify the sections we have to keep in. Just in case we come back tomorrow to find everything has dematerialised. Or been erased.'

'Don't even think it,' warned Fraze. But he too wanted to start the editing immediately. It was Saturday night. Better to be working till two or three in the morning, than still to be snipping and shaving out seconds at 9.15 on Monday evening. The closer came the deadline, the less accurate were the edits. He knew. He'd been there often, with ten minutes to go before broadcast and twenty minutes of video still to cut.

'Don't start at the beginning,' said Emily. 'That wasn't the best stuff. Where did she start levitating – third tape? Fourth tape?'

Fraze loaded the third cassette: '11.15am – 12.30pm,' and spooled it forward. 'It's on here. Here.'

'Okay, we'll start with the indispensable stuff. Anything that's not indispensable . . . we shall have to dispense with.' Miss Whitlock looked nervously at Ella's flickering image, rolling towards the ceiling.

Emily Whitlock had been Dr Dóla's first choice to interview Ella. It was lucky she had leapt at the chance, for there was no second choice lined up. Dóla needed someone respected, conservative and powerful, a journalist whose opinions would not be laughed at. A journalist who could turn the production round in a couple of days and elbow it into a prime-time viewing schedule. Someone with selling power to networks around the world.

Emily Whitlock, with her own company making current affairs programmes and her ten years as presenter of BBC1's *Spirit Of Inquiry*, was as highly regarded as any broadcaster of her generation. At thirty-nine, she had hosted Radio 4's *Today* programme, been an influential champion of women priests and put religious television back on the serious agenda. She had been a war correspondent, filming from the front line in Bosnia and Beirut. She had won an Emmy, and BAFTA trophies two years in succession.

Emily Whitlock's opinions would help millions make up their minds about Ella Wallis.

There were other journalists of her calibre, if only a few. But Emily Whitlock met Dr Dóla's other, essential requirement. She would not overawe Ella.

Dóla himself, with a lifetime's experience of winning trust, terrified the child. He used simple language and a kindly tone, shone smiles at her and tried at every moment to make eye contact. She cringed from him. She answered him in half-words, mumbled between clenched teeth, and jumped from her seat to avoid him if he entered the room. She endured him when forced to do so by her father. 'Listen to the doctor,' Ken had snarled when Dóla proposed the Whitlock interview, 'he knows what's good for you.'

There was no question of taking Ella to a TV studio. She had already been uprooted from her home and school, separated from her brother and her friends. Something was needed to restore a vestige of security.

She trusted that motor-cycling lifeguard, of course. Nordic blond and built like Conan the barbarian. The first thing Guntarson had done in Dóla's earshot was to ditch his job. Since then he had appeared to do nothing towards finding other work. He had not even attempted to clarify his position with Ella. She had no formal contract with the fellow – how could she have? She was still a minor. And Ken Wallis would be just too pleased to see the back of him. No handouts there. So what did he think he was going to do for money?

Ella trusted Guntarson, but it would have been fatal to let him conduct the interview. He had zero credibility. Inexperienced, unknown and puffed up with his own pride. Who could tell what sorts of stunts Guntarson might pull, if you put him in front of a camera?

And in the event, his ridiculous behaviour almost wrecked the Whitlock interview.

Dóla made the correct choice. Emily Whitlock won Ella's confidence right at the start. The Wallises were eating breakfast when the television team arrived. Ella was munching a large bowl of cornflakes in half a pint of full-cream milk with her usual mechanical swiftness. Each heaped spoonful arrived at her lips before she had barely swallowed the last, and she never took her eyes off the Tim Henman endorsement on the back of the packet. No doubt she burned off her breakfasts in psychic energy, because she certainly did not seem to get fat. Dóla had never seen her fail to clear her plate, no matter what she was served. Her father insisted on it – at every Grace he repeated with menace: 'And let us not fall into the sin of ungratefulness, by wasting the bounty which our Lord provides.'

When one of Dóla's cleaners let the TV crew in from the rain, an excited yapping and a scramble of paws on stone tiles echoed in the hall. Ella emptied her bowl in three lightning strokes and hung off the edge of her chair, silently imploring her father.

'Get down, then,' he said, and she ran from the breakfast-room.

In the hall, pressed back against a far wall while Dóla greeted the three strangers, Ella gazed at a wet puppy on the doormat. The dog saw her and froze, halfway through shaking off a cloud of spray. Its whole purpose in life was suspended, awaiting her orders.

Ella pictured the puppy, leaping onto her lap. It bounded at her, and she crouched to scoop it up. The dog tried excitedly to clamber out of her hands and over her face.

'That's Cleo,' called Emily. 'She likes you – have you got a dog? Can she smell it on you? Then you must be a terribly nice person, because Cleo gets very cross with people she doesn't like.'

Emily Whitlock was lying. Or using journalistic licence, at least. Cleo was a fourteen-week-old retriever. She liked everyone. Ella did not like everyone, but she could not help taking to Emily.

Ella consented to sit in front of Fraser's camera, under the four hundred watt glare of Eric's lights. She tried to answer Emily's questions, when her family gave her the chance. And at 11.11 am, the crew from Whitlock Majestic got what they had come for.

Ella flew.

She did it on command. Emily had been probing for half an hour. Did she like living away from home, missing lessons, being on TV? Being famous? Did her brother have the same powers? It was all asked very gently, very obliquely.

When Ella was perched next to Guntarson on the sitting-room sofa, Cleo in her lap, Emily steered the questions around. She had brought a little picture with her. At home, last night, with no one around, she had drawn this shape – or thing, or diagram – and sealed it in an envelope. The envelope was in her pocket. Could Ella tell her, if they both concentrated hard, what . . .

'Christmas tree,' said Ella. 'Like, a Christmas tree with a circle in it. A smiley circle.'

Emily Whitlock, eyes shut and eyebrows raised, dipped into her waistcoat pocket and tore open an envelope. She unfolded the sheet of tin foil inside it, and took out the enclosed scrap of paper before the camera. On the paper she had drawn a Christmas tree with a round, smiling face in the branches.

'This,' commented Emily to camera, 'is one of those moments that leaves you in no doubt. It's something that has to be personally experienced. The vicarious medium of film cannot do it justice. I realise that. No one watching at home can be certain, as I am, that Ella knew nothing of this experiment. She did not know this was what I'd drawn, in my own home, in my own kitchen with no one around. She could not have seen it, through the paper envelope, through the tin foil. She didn't know I was going to do any experiment like this at all. I mean, I'm totally convinced. There's no trickery. But it's like any issue of faith. Everyone has to find out for themselves.'

'I think,' added Guntarson, 'we can convince all the doubting Thomases. Ella?'

She turned to him. The puppy was insensible over her legs.

'I want you to look at me.'

His eyes were ultra-violet, masked by a sheet of thick ice. She stared into them.

'Breathe in. Feel the air in your nose, in your throat, in your lungs. That is all you can feel. When you breathe out you will be relaxed. All the weight and tension will flow out with that breath. Breathe out.'

Her head sank forward as she exhaled. Almost instantly her feet lifted, pulling her forward from the seat. The back of her head stayed touching the sofa, so that she swung upwards from that point, turning on its axis. When she was upside-down, with her knees still drawn up in a sitting position, her head drifted off the chair-back.

For a few moments, she stopped rising. Her eyes were open but blank. Her hair cascaded over the cushions.

'Look at the dog,' whispered Emily.

The puppy, asleep and oblivious, remained in Ella's lap. Its curly ears hung back, pulled by gravity, but there was nothing to keep it suspended. Ella was not holding it.

Emily reached up gently and cradled her pet. It dropped into her hands like a fruit. Ella, her own hands slowly stretching out before her, began to rise again.

The blazing bulbs tracked her. They shone on her feet, her shoulders, her hips and on the ceiling – anywhere a wire might be attached.

In the cutting room of Whitlock Majestic, Emily let the silent tape roll on. 'I could not think of anything to say,' she murmured, watching as Ella drifted to the ceiling and bumped along it, like a bubble. 'I had all these questions, and suddenly they seemed – just banal.'

Off-screen, Ken's voice said: 'I don't want you hypnotising her, mucking 'bout with her mind.'

'Ella, I want you to come down now,' said Guntarson evenly.

'I'm her father. Ella, git down here.'

'Let's not alarm her, Mr Wallis. She could be hurt.' He maintained the same tone, and it obviously annoyed Ken.

'I don't know what right you thinks you got,' he hissed, 'acting like my girl's your property. You can get out of here, 'cos I don't want to see you round Ella no more.'

Ella was sinking to the floor, drooping with each long breath. Juliette took her hand. Fraser Bough shuffled on his knees to bring Guntarson and Ken Wallis into shot, still keeping Ella in the picture. The men's faces were revealed on screen as Ella's blurred body dropped down the frame.

Guntarson glanced across. Ella was safe.

'Listen!' Ken, standing at Guntarson's side, grabbed his arm and pulled him round. The younger man tipped back his head, stretching his advantage of height. 'It's you I'm talking to.'

'I am not "mucking with her mind". I am helping her to deal with this pressure. And you are not.'

'I'm telling you,' ordered Ken quietly, 'to get your arse out of this house. And I mean now.'

'You can huff and puff all you like. I'm not in this house for your benefit.'

The camera focus pulled back, leaving the two men as shapes without detail, locked against each other. Ella, kneeling on the floor and recoiling from her mother's hand, became sharp in the foreground. Her face was almost luminous. She stared at the floor, breathing hard.

'You can get out now, Mr Poncey Smartarse, or I can throw you out. And I'm telling you . . .'

'You'd be ill-advised to lay a hand on me, Mr Wallis.'

'. . . if you makes me throw you out, you ain't going to be going home 'cept in an ambulance.'

'Shut up!' said Ella.

'What you say, girl?'

'Don't shout at Peter.'

'Right, this is it! You – on your bike NOW! And you, my girl, are going to get a hiding to . . .'

A hand, José Dóla's hand, clamped over the lens and blacked out the screen. Dóla's voice could be indistinctly heard, arguing with Fraser above Ken's shouting. Dóla lost the argument, and a few seconds later the camera wobbled down to the carpet and then found Ella's face.

'Keep that in, keep it, it's gold' said Emily. She and Fraze were crowded so close to the video screen that their breaths were clouding it.

'Mr Wallis, Kenneth!' Dóla was exclaiming. 'Let's keep our emotions in check. Remember we have guests.'

Ken jabbed a finger at Fraser: 'You ain't taping this.'

'That's not the idea, is it?' persisted Dóla. 'We invited them here to film. Now everyone will understand it's a tense time for you all. But we can resolve our problems without shouting.'

'She ain't no *problem*,' said Ken. His tone was suddenly and sarcastically reasonable. 'She'll soon remember she's got to honour her mother and father, don't matter if she's gone all famous.'

'I ain't doing nothing without Peter.' Ella's face scowled with fear. She had never opposed her father. Now she had started, she did not dare back down. 'You can't make me.'

'We'll see 'bout that.'

'I ain't. Peter's the only one what understands.'

'Yeah? Well *Peter* can go and find himself some easy money somewheres else.'

'Greed. That's it, eh, Mr Wallis? You know why you can't beat Ella to a jelly any more, don't you? Because you're greedy for all that money she's making you. She means a lot more to you than ever she did before. Doesn't she?'

'You ain't a father,' growled Ken. 'What do you know?'

'I know you can't think of anything except money.'

'And don't you just want a part of it!'

'If it comes to that, I'm more deserving than you. Ella needs me around. She can do very well without you.'

'You're after a pay-off, right?'

'Money's not what I'm about. I don't even care to have a formal contract.'

'You ain't getting one. Ella's still a minor. I'm her legal guardian. And I ain't signing anything with your name on it.'

'You will, when Ella wants you to. You won't have a choice.'

'I ain't doing nothing for *you*,' Ella wildly declared to her father. 'All the money you makes out of this, it's like you're thieving it. You ain't done nothing to deserve it.' She smiled, proud and terrified, at Peter. He was not looking at her. He was out-glaring Ken Wallis's glittering, porcine eyes.

'You thinks you're so clever. Just wait, Mr Smartarse. You'll be out on your ear before you knows it.' He walked to the oak door and turned. 'And you, my girl – I hopes you repents your evil words one day, good and proper. The devil's got his hold on your heart. You don't know enough 'bout God's way now to even be shamed when you've spoke such base and wicked words to your father.'

'Mumbo-jumbo,' spat Peter.

Ken shook his head solemnly and wisely, like he had never raised his voice in his life. 'You made Our Saviour weep bitter tears for you today, my girl.'

CHAPTER TWENTY-THREE

Emily Whitlock jabbed Ken's beer gut on the screen. 'Pause him there. How long was that? Eleven minutes? A shade over. All one take – Alfred Hitchcock, eat your heart out. '*Our Saviour weeps bitter tears.*' I wish we could get some shots of this guy preaching, but there's just no time to set it up.

'Okay, cut to . . . we need to establish who this blond guy is. Guntarson. Everybody else is obvious: Ella, her parents – maybe I'll have to insert half a sentence of voiceover, right at the start, to introduce Joe Dóla. But the viewer's going to be wondering, "Who's the tall one?" Boyfriend? I don't think so. He doesn't act like he's sleeping with her. And she's obviously not a tarty type. She's a child. So we've got to establish where he fits in.'

Fraze handed her another tape.

'3.30 pm to 4.45. This is the one where he goes upstairs, right? That'll do it. I said to him, something like, "Why are you intruding on the family?" Can you find that?' She watched the tape run forward. 'Okay, it's after this, this is where I was trying to get the mother to say something, anything. And having no success. Okay – play from here.'

Peter's face was in the frame, as he stood silently behind Juliette Wallis's chair and watched her daughter. Every few moments he shut his eyes and pursed his mouth. The camera tracked around to Ella. She was hiding a smile behind her hand.

'I didn't know you'd shot this,' murmured Emily. 'Ella and this Guntarson, they don't know you're watching either. It always amazes me, Fraze, people just don't see you filming. You go invisible. Is it paranormal?'

Ella shut her eyes with her fingers and began nodding her head, as if she could hear a tune. 'What planet is she on?' asked Emily.

'I thought when I was filming,' said Fraze, 'he's sending her messages. Mind messages.'

'A secret conversation,' breathed Emily. 'No wonder she trusts him. We've got to work this in somehow.'

From the TV her voice asked, 'Peter, some people would say you're intruding on this family. Ella's father has expressed very clearly his wish that you should leave.' Ken and Dr Dóla were out of the room. 'Why do you stay here?'

'Ella wants me around.'

'But in fact, you've only known Ella a few days, haven't you? You're not an old friend.'

'So?'

'So why do you think she is suddenly this much in need of you?'

'Because suddenly, her life has changed utterly.' He spoke quietly and certainly.

'You were very much instrumental in that change.'

'I . . . alerted the world. Yes.'

'Are you glad you did that?'

'Of course. But you should understand – I was assigned to the role. I didn't choose it.'

'The *Daily Post* newsdesk might just as easily have assigned another reporter?' suggested Emily. 'And that other reporter would be standing here now, in your place, insisting on being with Ella?'

'Of course not. It's nothing to do with journalism. Come and see something,' said Guntarson. He turned at the door. The camera watched Ella's anxious face. 'Ella, do you want to come?'

'Her father says she stays here,' said Juliette. 'Until he is come back.'

'Will what you want to show us take long, Peter?'

'Couple of minutes. Then you'll understand.'

The picture cut to an upstairs landing with a window at one end and doors on either side. A cuirass and a helmet like a tin bowl hung on the wall. Facing the stairs was a half-moon table with a laquered surface like satin. On it stood a brass bust.

Guntarson weighed it in his hands and passed it to Emily Whitlock. 'See the inscription?'

'Our Dear Dan.'

Eric Williams played a light on it, so the brass glittered. The sculptor had cast an unconventional pose, with the face propped on one hand. The features were a little irregular, and slender. The fingers that cupped the hand and cheek were almost impossibly long and delicate.

'Dan,' said Guntarson, 'is Daniel Dunglas Home. A Victorian spiritualist. A medium.'

'Table-rapping, messages from the dead, that sort of thing?' replied Emily. 'A charlatan, in other words.'

'I don't suppose the sculptor thought so,' said Guntarson, replacing the bust on the table. 'Neither did anyone else who ever met Home.' He pronounced it 'Hume'. 'Just about every Victorian you've ever heard of went to one of Home's seances. Dickens, Thackeray, Ruskin.

He was a guest at most of the palaces of Europe. And nobody ever detected a fraud. Home was for real. And the point is – he levitated. Just like Ella. He was a superstar for a while. Dozens of people saw it happen. He'd be sitting or standing at a seance, he'd probably be in a trance, and then he'd start to levitate.

'Sometimes he went straight up like a rocket, sometimes he took his chair with him. One time he flew out of a window three storeys up and then in through another.'

Behind the camera, Fraser laughed.

'It sounds comical,' agreed Guntarson, mildly. 'I shan't be in the slightest bit surprised if something comical happens to your video footage. You'll play it back and it might be ruined. Or simply vanished.'

Emily asked: 'Are you going to tell me Ella is a reincarnation of this man, Home?'

'You're missing the point. All the facts are here, before us. We don't need to invent connections.' He slapped his fist on his palm, 'Look. Ella's never heard of Home. Dóla's never heard of him – I asked. Dóla just uses the house. It's not even his, he doesn't even live here, it's just a hideaway.

'So for years he comes to this place and for years he's walking past, completely unawares, this bust of Our Dear Dan. And then the good doctor brings Ella here. The world's most famous levitator. And here's a bust of her predecessor.'

Emily's shrug was audible as she said: 'Nice coincidence.'

'How can you deny something so obvious? The plainly undeniable?' Guntarson was almost shouting in exasperation. 'There is a guiding intelligence at work here. When you are shown a sign, why dismiss it as coincidence?' He raised his hands and clutched the air in despair – then suddenly looked brighter. 'Still, if you could see it, there would be less need for me.'

'How do you mean?' Emily probed.

'I told you, I have been assigned. As Ella's interpreter.'

'Assigned by whom?'

'You're too literal. Psychic power has its own personality. It can pick and choose people, order events, just like we can. Being psychic isn't just the obvious stuff – levitating or whatever. It is being in possession of a non-human intelligence.'

'Non-human? You mean alien?'

'No. I don't mean that. Some people choose that explanation, and some people choose the God explanation, but I think it is perfectly adequate to say psychic power contains its own, self-contained intelligence. Including the power to bestow itself upon particular individuals.'

'So Ella wasn't born psychic? Her powers chose her?'

'They may even have chosen *me* first,' declared Peter. 'After all, I was on the planet first.'

'And where do you fit in? What's your rôle?'

'I am her enabler. Her catalytic converter, the key that unlocks her, the essential piece in her jigsaw, the spark which ignites the engine. Whatever metaphor you choose, you have to understand that without me Ella is just a random psychic generator. She can't control it. She can't understand it. She can't make sense of it.

'And then I come along, the enabler, because she is old enough now to be a useful channel for her psi energies. And I put it all in focus.'

Emily said: 'Wouldn't it be rather simpler just to say Ella was born with unusual abilities?'

'Oh come *on*. You don't seriously think all this is a natural human function? Her powers are something she was born with? It wouldn't be very logical, really, would it? Otherwise a doctor would be able to perform surgery and find her levitation node. You know, a lump in the brain or something. This isn't physiological. It isn't a gene thing, she won't be able to pass it on to her children. Believe me, I'm living proof.'

'How?'

'There were psychics in my family. That's what set me off to research it. I've spent half my life reading up on every aspect of the paranormal. I moulded my degree around it – the whole drive of my psychology studies was to learn how the psychic interacts with the psyche. My own psi energies guided me down this path. Ready for the day when I could enable Ella.'

'Who were they, your family's psychics?'

'Just relations.'

'Did any of them levitate?'

'No. Ella's exceptional. But it's our combination of energies which make her exceptional. That's why I know we've naturally gravitated to each other. Our psychic energies attract.'

'Some people might consider your theory a little . . . ego-centric.'

'I know you think I'm bats,' he countered. 'But just for a moment, consider the power involved in this little "coincidence" or synchronicity, for want of a better word.' He patted Home's bust. 'It is arranged that this bust is made, and displayed here, and left, and a hundred years later it's sold, and then years after that someone comes to the house who is *relevant*. And she brings with her someone who will see the sign, and interpret it, someone who will know who Home was and what the significance is. And explain it to you.'

'Yes. Okay.' Emily wanted to move on.

'Think of the power manifested. It leaps across a century and closes up the gap with a pinch of its fingers. When you can get your head around that, all you can feel is awe. Small wonder it can pick Ella up and blow her round the room like a feather.'

'What if the energies decide they want to do something you don't like. Say it conflicts with your morals. They've got their own intelligence – how will you cope when there's a difference of opinion – and I don't mean between you and Ella, I mean between the human intelligence and the psi intelligence?'

Guntarson shook his head, smiling. 'You put it a different way and that's exactly what her Jesus-freak father is scared of. Okay, sorry, let's stick to parliamentary language. Ella's father is an evangelical Christian, he takes the Bible very literally, and he's scared that his daughter could be possessed by demons. I don't imagine he's so much scared for her soul – it's just that he is about to make a great deal of money out of Ella. And it's probably a sin to make money from the demoniacally possessed.

'He needn't worry. And you needn't either. Ella has been chosen because she is good. A very pure-minded child. An innocent. The innocent are beyond the corruption of demons.'

Emily stopped the tape. 'It's a pity,' she said, 'but we're going to have to lose that last bit. Too libellous.'

'Do you have to leave any of it in?' demanded Eric. 'The guy's just blithering.'

'I have a feeling he's going to stay in the big picture. He's an integral part of the Ella phenomenon. And we're the first people to link him with the story. He colours the way you look at Ella. Don't you think? It stopped me from projecting my own agenda, my own wishlist, onto what she is doing. Because someone else has got there first.'

'In that case,' cut in Fraze, flipping open cassette 4.40–5.55 pm, 'we've got to put this in, too. It's right at the beginning here. I've been dying to play this back. We'll see if it's for real, or just malarky.'

He scrolled through footage of the family at the tea table. Ella and Juliette were eating, Ken and Joe Dóla were talking vigorously with plenty of fingers jabbed at the ceiling and fists banged on the table.

Peter Guntarson was sitting back, detached from the group, not touching his food.

The brass bust, when it fell, seemed to hit the table at a sharp angle, as if it had been thrown from behind Ella's head. It hit the teapot, base-first, in an explosion of crockery. A pool of steaming tea flooded the tablecloth. The bust rolled twice and lay quivering at the edge of Joe Dóla's plate.

As the teapot shattered, Juliette jumped and screamed. Her husband was struck dumb and motionless. Dóla touched the object gingerly.

'Give it to Ella,' instructed Guntarson. 'It has come to be with Ella.'

'I ain't never seen it!' protested Ella. She inched her chair back to avoid the dripping tea.

'Our Dear Dan,' answered Guntarson, grasping the brass head and leaning towards the camera. 'It's Daniel Dunglas Home from upstairs. Now you have to believe me: this bust is a sign.'

Fraser paused the film. 'Steady as a rock,' he said proudly. 'I think you'll find my camera never trembled once. Even though,' he added, winding back the video, 'my knees turned to jelly after.

'Now look. Frame by frame. The object comes in from the left. So is someone chucking it? Out of the frame? Watch their faces at the table – is anyone looking up, looking for an accomplice? Waiting for this thing to be thrown? I can't see any hint of that.'

'Guntarson's not eating,' pointed out Emily.

'True. He's just staring at the teapot. Let's move it on – one, two, three . . . four frames. Five.

'There it is! See – almost centre of the picture. So where's that come from? We'll go back a frame. No trace of it. And forward – it just materialises. That's all you can say. It appears from nowhere, in mid flight. And the next frame – see, it's travelled about three inches, and it's a couple of inches lower. What would you say: six inches off the cloth? And it goes another couple of inches. It's falling pretty sharply. And the next frame . . . Gone! It's not there. Vanished! Back one, it's there. Forward one, it's gone. Wow. And the next frame, still not there. So where is it? Did it seem to come and go, do you think?'

'I just saw a blur.'

'Unbelievable. It's back. And it's still here, it's going to hit the teapot next frame. And bang!! One more frame – look at that image.'

'It reminds me a bit,' remarked Emily, 'of those stop-motion photographs. You know, a bullet going through an egg.'

'Only this is a brass head hitting a full teapot. If it is a sign . . .'

'It's got to be. It must mean something.'

'All right. Say he's right,' conceded Fraser. 'Mr Guntarson claims it's intelligent, meaningful. Okay. It's meaningful. So what in God's name is it supposed to mean?'

CHAPTER TWENTY-FOUR

Sun, Wednesday, January 20:
ONE ELLA-VA MIRACLE

Britain went paranormal-potty yesterday as tales flooded in of incredible phenomena across the nation while millions were glued to the box.

BBC1's fly-on-the-wall documentary on airborne psychic Ella Wallis sparked off a mind-boggling string of copy-cat episodes.

- In Burnley, mother-of-three Michaela Nixon levitated uncontrollably onto her roof and had to be rescued by neighbours with a ladder.
- In Falkirk, the Kennedy family's antique grandfather clock floated horizontally to the ceiling and remained there for over two hours, still ticking.
- In Mousehole, Cornwall, schoolboy Richard Wellington, ten, was apparently able to make objects disappear and rematerialise, simply by pointing at them.
- In Aberdovey, Wales, water from Charles Tidworth's bath flowed up the walls and soaked through the ceiling.

Minutes after Emily Whitlock's day-in-the-life *Panorama* programme began on Ella and her family, The *Sun*'s newsdesk phones were red-hot with calls from baffled, excited and frightened readers.

Embarrassed BBC chiefs admitted their own exchange was blown out for four-and-a-half minutes by the surge, with many callers simply pleading to be told they were dreaming, or that this was an Orson Welles-style *War Of The Worlds* hoax.

By 11 am most high street camera stores across the nation were cleaned out of camcorders, still cameras and every kind of film, as tens of thousands rushed to capture their own private miracles through the lens.

The hysterical response easily dwarfed the impact of Swiss psychic Rudy Zeller, who had viewers bending cutlery and restarting broken watches in the mid-seventies. This time, every incredible report was unique – not one caller reported a phenomenon identical to any of the others.

But they all had one thing in common – in every house a TV was on, and tuned to BBC1.

Even our own staff were not immune. Crime correspondent Niels Hammer – not normally known for his flights of fancy – said: 'My watch vanished from my wrist, about ten minutes into the programme. I know I was wearing it. It turned up this morning, in a shoe.

'What's really spooky is I can't get it to work. It stopped at 9.41, exactly the time it vanished. It's always been totally reliable, but I think I'll have to get a new one.'

Niels's surprise was minor compared to the shock in store for BBC weathergirl Janice Chauncey, watching the documentary on studio monitors after presenting her 9.25 pm bulletin.

'The empty chair next to me began to levitate,' she said. 'I think I must have shrieked, because the producer stuck his head round the door to check I was okay.

'It's a closed studio, so I instantly thought, "You can't tell anyone about this – they'll think you've dropped off your trolley." But then I realised I wasn't imagining things – my producer was frozen in the doorway with his jaw dangling round his ankles. Staring at this flying chair.

'So I reached up and held its legs. And the chair kept going up. I couldn't bring it down. I'm eight stone, and I was pulling as hard as I could. But in the end it was pulling me off the floor. I had to let go. I only fell three or four inches, but it had definitely lifted me off the ground.'

Last night Ella Wallis, still living at a secret country hideaway with her family and her guru, ex-journalist Peter Guntarson, was said to be as bewildered as the rest of Britain by the paranormal pandemonium.

'She can't explain it,' said a spokesman. 'She doesn't know why things happen to her – so she's got no idea why it's affecting other people.'

Pages Two and Three: Inside Ella's Topsy-

Turvy Flying World.

Pages Four and Five, plus Centres: *Sun* Readers' Incr-Ella-dible Stories.

Pages Eight And Nine: Growing Up With Ella – Her Best Pal's Story.

The Independent, **Wednesday, January 20:**

Give thanks for the video recorder. It has saved fifty million people from social oblivion.

More than half the viewing population opted to give *Panorama* a miss on Monday night, tuning in to the European Champions' league game between Man. United and Juventus on ITV instead.

Big mistake. For one thing, the match proved a rather colourless, 1–1 draw. And for another, *Panorama* turned out to be the most momentous event in broadcasting history.

If you didn't see it, and your cat didn't levitate, and your furniture didn't start waltzing round the living room on its own, then your outlook for the next few months is decidedly bleak.

If, on the other hand, you did enjoy a phenomenon or two, and you had the presence of mind to capture it with a camcorder, you can expect to see your footage endlessly replayed on Miracle Video Compilation shows hosted by the likes of Denis Norden and Jeremy Beadle.

For weeks to come, the talk at every dinner party and in every pub will focus exclusively on what happened to fellow guests and drinkers. Office gossip will consist solely of who was seen levitating with whom. The man on the No 19 bus will regale you with the terrifying occurrence which overtook his sister in Acton.

Fortunately, there's the official video. Research appears to show that strange things could happen, and even keep on happening, in the vicinity of any TV where the Ella Wallis documentary is being reshown.

Every time you press play, the table will take off, the piano will start playing itself and eerie voices will emanate from the floorboards.

Hallelujah! You are saved! Just buy the rush-released video (Whitlock Majestic Productions, £19.99, ninety minutes, Certificate E but carrying a stern warning: This Video Could Cause Paranormal Occurrences In *Your* Home).

> Alternatively, just do what everyone else is doing – let your
> imagination run riot and make up some very tall tales.

For Monty Bell, the exhilarating flush of triumph had rapidly gone
down the pan.

The credit had been his, for a day or two – but like all Monty's
credit, it quickly got swallowed up and his reputation was back in the
red. The chief reporter, the news editors, the assistant editors, all his
seniors, were quick to heap extra work on him, on the pretext of
covering him with praise. 'Monty, I've got just the job for you – needs
your touch, your insight, your experience,' they said, and sent him on
a flurry of fool's errands.

Monty tried, he was even enthusiastic. He believed his seniors when
they flattered him – at first, at least. He really thought his career was
going somewhere, finally. It wasn't the first time he'd been stitched up
like this but he fell for it, the way he always did. So off he set, to chase
stories that weren't there.

And when he failed to deliver sparkling copy, and his seniors
stopped flattering him and started slagging him off, Monty felt he had
let himself down.

He had let himself down, further and further, until today he had
been given the bollocking of his life. In the middle of the office, in the
middle of the day, with every reporter on the staff in earshot, Monty
Bell had got his nuts cracked by the chief newsdesk editor. Monty was
nearly twenty years older than the chief newsdesk editor, but he had
to stand and listen while this laddie handed out the kind of bollocking
that no one ever ought to take. No one with a scrap of dignity. No
one but a middle-aged reporter whose hopes of finding another job
anywhere were nil.

Monty took the bollocking. It came on the feeblest pretext – something about a misspelt name. He was humiliated, but that was only a
side-effect. The main aim was to let the staff of the *Herald* know that
Monty Bell was back at the bottom of the heap. The editor, the
assistant editor and the news editors would be taking the credit for
Ella henceforth.

The staff got the message.

Now it was late, and Monty had not gone home. He knew why he
was staying on, and on – in the office he had to keep up appearances.
At home, he would probably have left the television on, made a
sandwich and not eaten it, gone to bed and wept. In the office he had
to stay jaunty.

Keep smiling. I'm Monty, I've seen it all before, I don't care. My
skin is thick.

Marielle from features walked past his desk. 'I've had better days,' he remarked, but she didn't answer. She didn't even look at him.

'Oh yes, I've definitely had better,' he continued. Another Monty trick for side-stepping humiliation: when people ignore you, keep talking anyway. Act like you were just talking to yourself. 'Swings and roundabouts, that's what it is. Ten days ago, I'm top dog – tonight, I'm not fit to clean the print-room bogs. Oh well, keeps us in our places.'

He stood up and wandered over to the vacant newsdesk. The dictionaries and directories were locked neatly in drawers. There was nothing to read. A massive Apple Mac had landed since the New Year on the chief newsdesk editor's desk. Monty switched it on.

'It's my own fault. I come up with a cracking story – and it was me who started the Ella story,' he reminded the Apple Mac, 'even if every man and his bloody dog is claiming the glory now. I mean, look at our front page yesterday: UPLIFTED! Up-bloody-lifted. And the editor's got his own by-line on it. How Ella Levitated My Television, by *Herald* Editor Andrew Archibald. Not the most exciting pheno-menon in the world, as it happens, but the Big White Chief has to get in on the act. Uplifted! How many times does he mention Yours Truly? Precisely none. How many times does he mention himself? Two-four-six, about fifteen.' Monty stood, tugging the paper between his hands, staring at the front-page story. 'I mean, it's not even well written.'

He sat down in the high-backed chair reserved for chief newsdesk editors. 'Only got myself to blame. Ella was my find. I let them all take her off me. Prat.' He sighed. Poor old Monty Bell, everybody bollocked him. He even got bollocked talking to himself.

'There was a kid at my school, he was younger than me and all, used to nick my dinner money. He was younger but he was well hard. Him and his pals gave me a good kicking once, and after that I was too scared to argue. I handed the dough over soon as I saw his face. Prat. I should have kicked him in the nuts and nicked it back.'

He pointed the cursor at the programme launcher and clicked on a small blue icon embossed with a ship's wheel. A window flashed up, with the night sky for its backdrop and the legend Netscape Navigator 3.01.

'Here I am, forty-seven years young, still getting my dinner money nicked. Kick them in the nuts and nick it back,' muttered Monty. 'If I knew how.' He watched Navigator load. 'So how does this work then?'

He spent the next few hours finding out. Marielle went home and, by 11 pm, Monty and the security guard were the only people in the building. The guard wandered past around midnight but he knew better than to speak to Monty – it might be hard to get away.

Navigator was some sort of Internet programme. That was why this Mac was on the newsdesk. It had a modem in it. Monty had never used the Internet, but he had a rough idea about it – millions of computer archives, including thousands of newspaper libraries. The *Herald* was supposed to be putting its front page on the Internet each day. He wondered whether he could find his Ella story there.

Navigator would not even let him weigh anchor without name and password. He typed 'Monty Bell' more in hope than expectation and got the brush-off: User ID not recognised. Cancel or try again?

Try again, of course. If at first you don't succeed, try, try, try again. Kick them in the nuts. Nick your dinner money back.

He typed in the editor's name: Not recognised. He typed in the chief newsdesk editor's name, and scored a hit. Next question: Password?

Monty tried Herald, Evening, Bristol, news, paper, story, Internet, logon, password, newsdesk, editor, copy, headline, deadline. Each time he had to input the chief newsdesk editor's name. He tried using that name as a password too, and he wracked his memory to recall the name of the laddie's girlfriend. He tried all the editor's favourite obscenities. He tried all the reporters' clichés – shock, horror, probe, boffin, scoop. He tried Ella.

Ella worked.

A screen scrolled down, filled with starry blue artwork and words in bold blue type. Monty clicked the cursor randomly round the page. New screens appeared. He found nothing very interesting. A toolbar stretched across the top: 'What's cool?' it asked, 'what's new? Search?'

Yeah, okay. Search.

In the panel that flashed up, Monty typed 'Ella'.

Navigator searched, and returned 295,611 matches for 'Ella'. They couldn't all be Ella Wallis, of course. There must be thousands of different Ellas on the net. He tried 'Ella Wallis' and got 173,011 matches.

Which one was his?

He clicked on the first few and read newspaper reports from Sydney and Wellington. There was a personal account on something called Mervyn's Home Page of a spectacular levitation in Cleveland, Ohio – dining-table, family meal and two grandparents. Monty laughed, but he couldn't decide if it was meant to be funny. He found more home pages, more eye-witness accounts. Maybe there were Bristol home-pages. He accessed the help-notes for using the search function, and got a coffee. It was 1 am.

By 2 am he was executing accurate searches with several engines: 'Ella Wallis' + 'Bristol' + 'Home' scored thousands of hits, because people filing entries on Ella usually listed her address. But by adding 'Clifton' to his search, Monty narrowed the field to three hits – all of them net-users up Bristol's posh end. Three eye-witness accounts of inexplicable phenomena during the *Panorama* documentary.

It was a start, but it wouldn't get his dinner money back. Monty could have walked into any pub in Bristol and found three eye-witnesses to the Ella phenomenon inside three minutes. Keep trying.

He tried 'Ella' + 'Guntarson'. Numerous hits, but the pages he checked seemed to mention Guntarson with no more than a passing nod. Who was the guy supposed to be? Did anyone have a back-grounder on him?

He tried 'Guntarson' + 'Biography', 'Guntarson' + 'School', 'Guntarson' + 'Career' without success. 'Guntarson' + 'Nationality' threw up an interesting snippet – Ella's friend was born in Canada. Maybe that awfully English accent was put on.

'Guntarson' + 'Canada' was a disappointment. Monty remembered Peter had altered the spelling of his name, probably when he was busy losing the colonial accent. What about 'Guntarsson' + 'Canada'?

One hit. But a very palpable hit.

The address was a newspaper archive, the *Winnipeg Free Press*, based at 300 Carlton St, Winnipeg, Manitoba. The cutting was twelve years old. Monty cross-referenced all the names in the copy, to squeeze every last fact from the *Free Press* archive. That was 3 am.

He wrote up the story at his desk, on the *Herald*'s input system, printed it out and marked it: Copyright © Monty Bell. Then he wiped the copy from the system, taking care not to leave any duplicates in the blacks field.

He switched on the newsdesk fax and despatched his copy to the *Daily Post*. This time the bill was £800 – twice what he had dared to ask last time. Monty Bell was getting his dinner money back with interest.

That was 5 am. Monty was due on at 6.30, so he went for a walk round the city. The following morning, the *Post* led on his story. They'd unearthed a Guntarsson family snapshot during the day, and gave it the whole front page.

By the weekend, Monty Bell had left the Bristol Evening Herald to become the full-time, fifty-grand-a-year Paranormal Correspondent on the *Daily Post*.

Daily Post, Friday, January 22 [or Thursday 21]:
ELLA GURU'S SECRET TRAGEDY

The mysterious guardian of wonderchild Ella Wallis saw his mother drown when he was just thirteen, amazing hidden documents revealed yesterday.

Ex-*Post* reporter Peter Guntarson has never discussed the

secret heartache which destroyed his own childhood.

But last night forgotten facts came to light, via the Internet. They show the Canadian-born guru, who featured in this week's world-shaking TV special on fourteen-year-old psychic Ella, has been living with nightmare memories.

Ruth Einarson's death thirteen years ago upended her teenage son's existence – an existence already blighted by a bitter family split. The forty-three-year-old former graphic artist sank to her doom while boating near the wreck of a fishing vessel on Lake Manitoba near her home in Winnipeg, Canada.

Peter was forced to watch helplessly as his mother, a strong swimmer, got into difficulty and drowned just yards from their rowing boat.

And within weeks of her funeral, the boy was sent to public school in England by his father – even though Peter had lived only with his mother since the break-up.

For years, Ruth Einarson put her career at a design agency in Winnipeg above her hopes for a family – an attitude which suited her ambitious husband, a construction engineer whose practice, now based in London, has always specialised in eco-friendly materials.

Friends said her decision to have a child put an impossible strain on the marriage, and before Peter was three his parents had drifted apart. By 1981 the split was permanent, and Ruth was living with her lover, a boatbuilder named Clarence Robson.

Robson was one of the rescuers who saved all but one of the fishing boat's crew when it ran aground and capsized in the hundred-mile-long Lake Manitoba. It has never been discovered why, a week after the sinking, Ruth Einarson chose to row to the stricken boat.

Last night her son refused to comment about the tragedy – a stance he has always maintained. Until Peter Guntarson decides to tell the whole story, the reasons for that ill-fated venture to the wreck will always be shrouded in mystery.

Daily Post, inside pages, Friday, January 22:
TEN Things You Never Knew About Ella's Screwy Guru – Ex-*Post* Reporter Peter Guntarson Exposed:

1) You can trust him – he's a doctor! Dr Guntarson's DPhil thesis

at Christchurch, Oxford, was wackily titled 'Spaceship Fins And Alien Eyes: UFO Imagery In Modern Design'.

2) Despite his 6'2", 175 lb build, he never shone at team sports – but represented his county at Under-eighteen 200 m.

3) His favourite 'sport' is bonking. One ex-girlfriend told how he liked to make love up to *FIVE* times a night in his student days.

4) He's so proud of his Mensa-busting IQ score that he once planned to spend £1,250 on the numberplate PG183 – his initials plus his genius-level rating.

5) He launched his freelance journalistic career with a series on a local poltergeist for the *Oxford Journal*, but was furious when the sceptical editor toned down some of the more amazing ghostly phenomena.

6) A health faddist, he never touches dairy products or wheat-based food . . . but he definitely isn't a vegetarian and loves tucking into red meat cooked rare.

7) Aged fourteen he was sent as a boarder to the Lutheran Academy in Theakston, Yorkshire – where he excelled in every subject.

8) At Oxford he toyed with Roman Catholicism, Spiritualism and the Campaign for Nuclear Disarmament. But he never let outside interests interfere with studies, and scored a first in Psychology.

9) His parents, Guntar Einarson and Ruth Friedman, married in 1964. In his father's Icelandic tradition Peter was named 'son of Guntar' – Guntarsson – but shortly before taking GCSEs at a Yorkshire boarding school in 1988, he changed the spelling, dropping an *s*.

10) Money's no problem. His millionaire father, Guntar Einarson, provides him with his London home and gave him for his 21st birthday a six-figure portfolio of stocks and shares – which Guntarson boasts he sold, investing the proceeds in low-tax, off-shore bonds.

CHAPTER TWENTY-FIVE

Ella sat at a writing-desk in the big room, her right arm crooked round a sheet of paper and her head bowed on her wrist. With a Biro gripped in her left hand, she was filling the paper with thick, black loops and lines. For nearly three hours she had been drawing like this. Around the chair were scattered twelve or fifteen sheets, all scored with the same patterns.

With her face almost touching the paper, Ella could not see what she was drawing. The constant, heavy movement of the ballpoint was automatic. She was looking at something else.

She was seeing what Peter Guntarson was seeing.

She was watching the world through his eyes.

To begin with, Ella had simply been picturing where he was in the house. While he went exploring on the third floor or picking through the damp library in the next room, she stayed with her mother in the sitting-room and followed him in her mind.

Juliette had been watching the television since before 6 am. She said she had not been able to sleep. She said she had breakfasted before Ken went out for the day, before anyone else was even up. She was drinking, and not trying to hide it today.

For the past couple of hours, Juliette had been talking. Maybe she was on the phone. Ella didn't care. She wasn't listening.

When Peter picked up a book, it was like she could see the book in the dark swirls under her arm. Not really see it, not like a book in her hand. But all the impressions were there. The frayed hinges of the spine, the decaying gilt letters, the stain of moisture like a ripple at the base of the jacket.

He turned the pages and the lines of type were clearly visible. His eyes skimmed over them, too fast for her to pick out the words, but she knew he was reading them.

When Guntarson stared at the wall, or his hand, or the shelves, Ella saw them too. It was a good sensation. She had often caught an echo of his thoughts, but never a glimpse of what he was seeing. She had never tried, either – this was the first time. She had been concentrating for hours, and her vision was becoming clearer and more confident.

She was not spying. She wanted him to know that, and sent him messages: 'I'm watching you.' 'I can see you.'

He always sent back: 'I can hear you.' Once he added: 'Are you okay?'

What was Ella supposed to reply to that? She did not know where in the world she was staying. Her mother was across this strange room from her, with a gin bottle. She was not at school. She could not speak to her friends or her brother. Her father might be coming back at any time.

How could she know whether she was okay?

She just answered, 'Yes.'

Ken did return, and Ella saw it through Peter's eyes. The rain was coming down in billows, fold after fold that swept across the drive. Dozens of cars were clustered around the house, their tyres sunk glumly in the gravel. She saw them so clearly that the registration plates were legible – B612 FLY was the nearest. The cars had been there since dawn the day before, when the location of the hideout had been discovered. Cloudy windows, rolled up against the downpour, hid the journalists and their cameras. The international crews lurked in their satellite trucks, the antennae out and the dishes open, collecting water.

They had been promised by Dr Dóla there would be no appearance by Ella today. The promise was honoured. Of the fifty cars and photographers' motorcycles there at dawn, more than half and skulked away.

One or two of the reporters had discovered Ella's mobile number. They dialled and dialled, but Guntarson had the phone in his jacket. He had not bothered yet to recharge it.

A fat BMW 750il, racing-green that shone black in the twilight, rolled gradually up the gravel. Its new owner was zealously cautious for the paintwork. Ken Wallis had not owned a brand-new car before. He had never driven an engine so powerful, not even when his brother grandly lent him the keys to the four-litre Jag.

It had been worth the wait.

Raindrops came down like mortar-shells on the bodywork. Every detonation threatened to gouge a dent in the gleaming paint. Ken switched off the ignition and suggested, 'Let's get the press to picture me with the Series Seven now.'

Joe Dóla was buttoning his coat. He had been hearing Ken's suggestions all day. Since eleven o'clock, when Ken first caught sight of the car in Kensington's BMW showrooms, every sentence had referred to the 'Series Seven'.

'It's too wet.'

'It's their job, ain't it? If they can't stand a bit of rain . . . their editors won't think much if they ain't got no pictures of Ella's dad's new Series Seven.'

'You'll get drenched.'

'They can picture me through the driver's window. Like this, like a movie star, you know, that picture of Clark Gable, at the wheel.'

'The light's not good enough.'

'What's the matter? Don't you want good publicity photos in tomorrow's papers?'

'These guys have been in their cars all day,' said Dr Dóla. Ken had been wearing out his patience all day. 'They probably slept in their clothes. They won't thank you for getting them soaked now. Come on, let's get these bags in.'

But at the front door, sheltered by the portico, Ken turned and beckoned to the huddled journalists. His hands were full of varnished paper bags, with gilt cords for handles. The photographers, who had been edging their lenses through part-opened windows, reluctantly turned up their collars and stepped into the rain.

'What are you doing?' hissed Dr Dóla.

'Giving them a statement.'

'No! For Christ's sake!'

'Don't,' warned Ken, turning sharply and jabbing a finger at the smaller man. 'Don't blaspheme. I know you're foreign and you got a different religion and everything. But don't never take our Lord's name 'cept in holy reverence.'

The snappers were edging forward, shielding their long lenses with cupped hands. They had apparently been summoned into the rain to witness an argument.

'I'm a Catholic.'

'It's a good job for you,' said Ken seriously, 'you never told me that to start with.'

'Let's get inside.'

'I got a statement,' he insisted. 'Gentlemen of the press! Come on, get nearer, I don't want to shout. Okay, that's close enough. Sorry to get you wet and everything. But I read the papers. We gets all of them delivered, posh ones and all. And I know some of your editors have been saying, like, that my Ella ain't for real. They says maybe it's all made up, in the imagination. Hysteria. That's the word they been using. Hys-teria.

'Well, you seen what I'm driving today. Brand new Series Seven BMW, top of the line. Classiest car in the world. Probably better than what any of your editors is got. It ain't British, I knows that. Few years ago, I'd of got a Jag. But you got to face facts. We're in Europe now. And the Germans is the strongest nation in Europe. Make the best cars.

'That Series Seven cost me £75 000. And I paid cash up front. It ain't on tick. It's paid for.

'That sound like hysteria to you? Do you think you're imagining that Series Seven?

'See the names on these bags? Harrods. Harvey Nichols. I got presents for my wife and my boy. And Ella, she got something in here too. Lot more than what she got for Christmas, too. So these bags, is they hysteria? You listen, I'll tell you this – soon we'll have our own house with gates to keep you lot out. Okay, you can get back in your cars now.'

'Mr Wallis, can we come in and dry off a bit?'

'Nope.'

'Come on, Ken,' called someone in despair. And then, as the door was closing, another voice appealed to Dr Dóla. 'Joe, let us in. Be reasonable.'

The door shut.

Peter Guntarson, standing at the first floor window looking down on the drive, watched the journalists trail back to their cars. Ella, crouching at the desk, watched too. She was frightened of the men and women who clung around her house. Waiting for her. She did not want them to be wet, but she was much too fearful to go outside and talk, or take them hot drinks.

Guntarson heard Dr Dóla in the hall, complaining: 'That was a stupid thing to do, that was not good. Why don't you listen to me? I know about these things. They're going to hate you for that.'

'It's their job. Tough. I don't give a toss, it's their lookout. They don't like it, they can go get proper jobs.'

'You're a printer, aren't you?' Dr Dóla remembered.

'Like my father before me.'

'If you want to keep driving nice cars, you need journalists to help you. So help them.'

'Listen, I've stood on picket lines and seen journalists walk through.'

'Old animosities are not going to be of assistance.'

'I said then, them's going to take over our jobs. Rob men of their wages. And I was right, weren't I?'

'Do not make them your enemies,' snapped Dóla. 'Or they will show you what it is really like to have enemies. Aren't you paying me enough? Don't you believe I know what I'm talking about? More respect!' He stalked away.

Guntarson, leaning in the darkness at the top of the stairs, looked down as Ken Wallis swayed angrily for a few moments. With a deep breath to compose himself, he scooped up the Knightsbridge shopping bags and banged into the sitting-room.

'Julie girl, you look what I got you. And then you come and see what's outside.'

Neither Ella nor Juliette looked up.

Ken swung the bags onto the sofa. 'Take a look inside them. And that's just the trimmings, Julie girl. Wait till you see what's on the drive. I worked out,' he added with casual pomp, 'we spent nearly eighty grand today. That's more than what I earned in three years total. Before tax. And that weren't half of what we still got in the bank. I seen the bank manager, I wouldn't of spent a penny unless he promised me we got all that dosh for keeps. All them cheques have cleared. Mostly, it's the publisher's advance. We got to collaborate with the writers on Ella's book, but it don't matter to us if the book don't sell much. Don't matter if it never makes a penny. Don't matter,' he reasoned confidently, though no one was listening, 'if the book don't never get published. We still keeps the advance money.'

No response.

'Open the bags then!'

Ella and Juliette were saying nothing. Only the television was answering him back.

'What you watching?' He flicked the off-button. Without the light of the screen, the room was grey.

Juliette was still staring at the set.

'You been drinking.' He said it with a preacher's soft incredulity, amazed at the devil's wiles. He had dropped his guard for a few hours and sin, like a viper, had nestled in his family's bosom. 'Where's the bottle?'

Juliette raised her head.

He seized the gin flagon and a heavy, crystal tumbler from the floor. A tonic bottle lay on its side, dribbling bubbles. Holding the glass as though it stank, Ken tipped the dregs onto a newspaper and stuffed the paper in a bin. Only a trickle remained in the bottle.

'You drunk all this?'

Juliette sucked air in slowly, trying to move her tongue without forgetting the need to stay sitting upright. 'I,' she said, 'had two.'

Only the scratching of Ella's ballpoint pen irritated the silence before Ken spoke again.

'My father had a quote, he used to tell me: "All wickedness is but little to the wickedness of a woman",' and he added, 'Ecclesiasticus. That's one of the Bible's apocryphal books.' Ken was proud of his knowledge.

He looked down pityingly at the dregs of his wife. She could not hear him or understand. All that was left for him was to conduct himself with dignity equal to a modern Job. 'It ain't the Christian way to offer censure. I got to find forgiveness in my heart. But first, you got to be sober enough to repent. I ought to make you sit out in that rain, that'd bring you round, only you'd probably catch your death.'

'Good,' hissed Juliette.

'And you a mother. Ain't you grateful for what God's given? You don't want to go to His judgment yet, do you?' Another thought struck him. 'You ain't trying to kill yourself? Julie? Have you taken tablets? Is that it? Where are they?' He scrabbled on the floor, searching for empty bottles of paracetemol. Looking up, he saw Ella, twisting round in her chair to watch.

'What you looking at!'

She snapped away and hid her face.

'You just been sitting there? Staring at your mother and letting herself get in this state? You seen her taking tablets? Answer me!'

'No Dad.'

'No what?'

'I ain't seen Mum doing nothing. I weren't looking.'

'No, you don't take notice of any of it, do you? Living in your own world, ain't you? You don't even see when your own mother's got a bottle in her hand. 'Cos them demons don't want to see, do they?'

'She can have a drink when you ain't here,' pleaded Ella. She wanted to run to Peter. She could not see where he was now. She did not know why he was not coming to help her.

'I'm always here, girl. I'm your father. I'm the master in my home, and I don't have to be here in body twenty-four hours a day to be keeping order. You ought to behave like I'm watching you every minute.'

'I do, Dad.'

'I ought to take my belt to both of you. But she wouldn't feel it' – he gestured at his wife, struggling to rise from the sofa – 'and you ain't got the wit to learn from it.'

'What day is it?' asked Juliette, thickly.

'Found a voice, have you? Don't even know what day it is. Wednesday.'

'Didn't 'spect you. Back. On Wednesday.'

'I brung you presents. And a car. I wanted you to see, but you ain't in no fit state to go out and look. It's a Series Seven BMW.' He let his fierceness abate. It did not seem reasonable to stay so angry, with a Series Seven parked outside. Anyway, Juliette would suffer for her sinning. It wasn't going to be his hangover.

'Wass'name?'

'BMW 750il – fuel-injected long-base, that means.'

'Not the car. Your Wednesday woman. Marsha. Mar-see-urr. Marcia.'

'Leave it, Julie.' He gave forgiveness one last try: 'Come on, I brung

you presents. Pretend it's Christmas. I even got stuff for Ella.' He
tipped out a bag on her desk and swept the patterned papers aside.
'You been doing homework? What's this, art? Good girl. Mustn't let
your studies suffer while you ain't in school. Now see this. It's a
portable CD. Got headphones so you can listen anywhere. 'Cept at
the table, you got to turn it off when we're eating. It's got recharging
batteries and everything – best one in the shop. And,' he lifted up
another bag with a flourish, " 'cos a CD player ain't no use without
CDs, I got you all the records in the Top Twenty. What do you say?'

'How much was it?'

'Don't matter. I can afford it.'

'No. How much was it?' she repeated.

'You don't say that. You says, "Thank you Dad".'

'I don't want you going spending all this money. You should of
asked me.' Ella faced the rage filling her father's face again. She had
defied him once, on Saturday, with the TV crew there. With Peter to
support her. It wasn't that hard a second time. 'I don't want all this
crap.'

'You'd better mind your tongue.'

'You wouldn't have no money, if it weren't for me.'

'You wouldn't have nothing if it weren't for me,' he retorted.

She couldn't argue with him. She didn't know how. He always had
answers. All Ella could say was what she felt.

'It ain't your money.'

'Oh yes it is. It's in my bank account. My personal account. Nobody
wrote no cheques to you. 'Cos you're only fourteen, and in legal
terms, girl, that means you ain't nobody when it comes to money. I'm
going to do what's best with it, and you're going to accept that.'

'I don't want you spending it. I wants Peter to look after it.'

'Well Peter ain't going to get his greedy fists on one penny of it.' His
face pushed her back on her elbows against the desk. 'Fine. You don't
want your presents. Frank'll get them. You're the one what's wasting,
not me.'

He turned his back on Ella's pale, bony face. Juliette, lolling with
her fists on her knees, tried to taunt him as he grabbed the bags off
the sofa. 'Mar-see-urr,' she rasped.

Ken flung the bags across the hall. CDs scattered over the tiles, and
fabric wrapped in gilded tissue spilled under his feet. 'Joe Dóla,' he
yelled. 'Who's been giving booze to my wife?'

He ducked through the doorway and, grasping the gin bottle by its
mouth, swung it over his head. The green glass shattered against the
frame. Ken brandished the jagged neck. 'Joe Dóla!'

Guntarson, standing two feet from him, remarked: 'The doctor's
outside dispensing hot soup to the needy.'

Ken spun. 'You! You been snaking round, listening. You been plying my wife with gin.'

'Nothing to do with me.' Guntarson raised his hands as the broken glass switched under his chin. He did not try to push Ken away. He did not want to wrestle a big man with a bottle. He did not step back either.

'Right. It ain't nothing to do with you. You ain't got business with any of my family. And I'm telling you now to get out.'

Ella, eyes clenched shut, edged to the doorway. Peter was there! He had been outside the room, all the time she had stood up to her father. He had been ready to help her. He was standing guard.

Her hands were over her face. The luminous points of the bottle-neck swam before her, just as they waved before Peter's eyes.

'You get on that bike, now!' Ken yelled. 'Or do you want to leave in a body-bag?'

Guntarson kept his language calm. 'I'm someone you can't bully, Ken. What does that feel like?'

Ella felt the jagged glass pulled swiftly back. She sensed the soft flesh of Peter's throat, open and vulnerable.

She shrieked, 'No!'

Ken hurled the weapon against the floor. Sweeping his arm back, the back of his hand, not even bunched in a fist, slapped into Guntarson's cheek. The younger man stepped backwards.

In a smooth movement, brutally agile for a man of his weight, Ken pivoted on his left foot and drew his right knee up to his chest. His foot hammered out, in a Bruce Lee kick from his teenage fighting days. The move came back like an instinct. His right heel took Guntarson in the middle of his belly, doubling him over.

The second part of the move, the knee into the face, would have come with the same automatic certainty, twenty-five years earlier. But a moment's breathlessness slowed Ken after the kick. He lowered his foot.

'Leave him alone! Leave him alone!'

Ella's face looked foreign to him. He saw it in detail suddenly. She stood, impotently clawing the air between them, her wide eyes circled with red and her lips drained of blood. Her skin was almost trans-parent.

She did not look like a daughter to him. She was a shrieking demon.

His wife made no sense to him. The man he had kicked meant less than nothing to him. Ken reached into his pocket, to check the keys to the Series Seven were there, and walked out of the house.

Ella ran to Peter and let him lean his weight on her shoulders as he struggled to stand up. 'What's he done to you, are you okay?' she kept asking.

The anger passed quickly off Guntarson's face. 'I'll live,' he promised, and straightened up. 'He's gone now.'

He wrapped his arms across Ella's back and, pulling her face onto his chest, hugged her hard.

Chapter Twenty-Six

When Ella was alone she tried intensely to recreate the sensations of that hug from memory – the textures, the components of touch and aroma and temperature – all the things which she sensed powerfully but could not analyse.

She imagined her white cheek was crushed against his blue cotton shirt, the corner of her eye pushing at a rib, the side of her nose rubbing a ridged button. The roots of her hair were burning, because his arms across her back were pulling the locks down.

Heat, after the sudden excitement and adrenaline, was rising off his chest, and a pungent deodorant, like grated lemons, was rising with it.

Her own hands reached tentatively around him, and found his waist, and rested lightly above his belt. The muscles in his sides were hard and elastic beneath her fingers, unlike any surface of her own body.

His heart beat frighteningly fast, like two fists battering at a wall. He held her for no more than a few seconds and then, sliding his hands up to her shoulders, rested on her. She let go of him and, uncertain what to do with her hands, dared to clutch carefully at his forearms.

'You do,' she asked, 'you do . . .?'

Guntarson raised his eyebrows and gently slipped her grip to rub his sore stomach. 'I do what?'

Surely he knew? He must know what was in her mind? 'You do . . . *like* me?'

'Of course I like you. You wait and see, you're going to be very popular. Everyone will like you. I can't say I'm terribly fond of your family, though.'

Guntarson took Ella's wrist and patted his chin with her hand. 'Yow, that's sore. Am I cut? There'll be such a bruise.'

She thought for a moment he was going to kiss the palm of her hand. Her whole arm was limp.

The front door closed softly. Dr Dóla, shaking his wet hands, said: 'Sorry, didn't mean to break anything up.'

Ella jumped guiltily.

Guntarson grinned. 'Where were you to break things up when we needed you?'

'I saw Kenneth thundering out and racing away in his new car. He wasn't going for a joyride? So you've been fighting with him.'

'He's been beating seven bells out of me. Though he might not have liked it if I'd felt like hitting him back.'

'What about Juliette? He hasn't struck her?'

'She's out of it. Watching TV.'

'Wife-beating's very difficult. Publicity-wise. This business presents enough complications without your father throwing his fists around. Have you ever seen him hit your mother, Ella?'

Ella stared mutely. To answer would be disloyal.

Dr Dóla looped his dripping coat over a hatstand. 'I wonder where he's off to. Especially as the shops have closed. Ah, my dear Madame Juliette, have you passed a pleasant day?'

Ella's mother stood, head upright but buckling into the door-frame from the knees. Her skin, usually waxy and taut, was swollen, as if blisters lay under the skin. She stared grimly at the wall opposite, but shut her eyes helplessly as a mouthful of clear, stringy liquid escaped from the corner of her mouth.

'Peter!' commanded Dóla. 'Help her, hold her up.' But as Guntarson reached for Juliette's arm she folded, falling onto her knees and trying to keep her head from the floor by clutching at his leg.

Like a splash from a bucket, vomit hit the stone floor. A second convulsion sent it spuming across the front of her dress, over her lap and onto Guntarson's and Dóla's shoes. Then she slipped, hitting the tiles chin first and retching viciously. With every cough she brought less up and fought harder for it.

Ella slithered behind her and tucked a hand under her chin and an arm about her waist. She kept her mother's face lifted and her throat open. Ella knew about being sick.

Dr Dóla, to escape the stench, hurried down the passage to the kitchen, to find a bucket and some cloths. Guntarson, though the sight of Juliette's spew, like glaze on his shoes, was revolting enough, forced himself to grip the woman under her bony arm and lift her up the stairs to the bathroom. He left Ella there with her and quickly slipped away.

There was blood on Juliette's chin. It might have been from the retching – Ella had seen blood in her own sick, more than once – but when she held her mother's mouth open, a tooth was loose. It had been knocked half into her mouth, and Ella might have tugged it out if she'd dared. She did not.

Instead, she undressed her listlessly conscious mother and helped her to sit in the bath with the iron taps pressing in the small of her back. Ella plugged in a shower-head and for a quarter of an hour rinsed her with the feeble spray.

When she had wrapped her mother in a robe and rolled her onto a bed, she returned downstairs.

Peter had already gone.

Ella searched for him, in the dark of her own room. Dr Dóla was somewhere on the next floor, trying to polish the tidemark of Juliette's vomit off his shoes. The journalists' cars and motorcycles were still thronged outside, jamming the drive and spilling across the lawns, their engines chugging intermittently to keep the blowers hot and the cassette players running. The Series Seven had not returned. Ken was probably back in Bristol. With Marcia, the Wednesday Woman. Juliette was still with Ella, but not conscious. Frank was in Bristol, sleeping in Auntie Sylvie's front room. Ella felt something damp and cool had been laid across his eyes, and could not understand what it was. She gave up trying.

So Ella looked for Peter. She lay and listened to the whine of the wind in the poplars, and imagined he was hugging her. She rubbed the edge of her sheet on her face, pretending it was his shirt. She crossed her arms and placed her fingers above each elbow, pretending to hold his arms. The smell of grated lemons rushed in and dispelled the damp mustiness in her room.

She pictured his face smiling down on her, her eyes on his lips. She tried to reach around him and pull him closer, but her own body felt skeletal compared to the thick layers of muscle she wanted to imagine. His face evaporated and she felt as though she had been dropped onto her mattress, cold and alone.

So she started searching for him.

She concentrated on what he was seeing but, wherever he was, the room was dark. A flickering blue glow, perhaps a television to the left of his vision, was not bright enough to help. She waited in case her eyes became accustomed to it. There was something there, she was sure, but it refused to be seen.

Ella tried to listen but the wind kept blowing in the poplars. She tried shouting out to him but he did not seem to want to hear her. She kept searching to see.

After fifteen or twenty minutes of patiently staring into darkness, Ella saw something. Orange light flared in front of her face. A match. It burned, steady and white, after a moment, and a girl's dark face, framed by black curls, appeared. She was lying with her head on a pillow, lighting a cigarette. Her neck and shoulders were bare, and Ella seemed to be looking straight down on her, which meant Peter must have been kneeling or crouching above her.

The girl blew a column of smoke up. Ella smelled it, coarse and bitter. She jerked her eyes open. She had never seen the girl before. She never wanted to see her again.

CHAPTER TWENTY-SEVEN

Daily Mail, Thursday, January 21:
We have lift-off! A week ago, levitation was a phenomenon credited by no one but mystics, eccentrics and crackpots. Now, half the world believes in it as a certainty.

Half the world either grew invisible wings and flew during Monday's epoch-making TV broadcast, or watched someone (or something) else take flight before their eyes.

Evidence like that cannot be ignored – or forgotten. These experiences will be remembered, not merely as a media sensation but as family legends, to be polished and embellished and passed on down generations. History has been made.

The world knew about levitation, of course, for centuries, but the big proof has been a long time coming. All we've had until now has been the little, isolated incidents of proof. Take St Ignatius Loyola. In the sixteenth century, without the benefit of television, and video, and satellite links, Loyola founded the order of the Jesuits. But even among the faithful, the story of his miraculous levitation at Barcelona in 1524, when he was seen to be raised several palms from the ground and the room was filled with burning light, must have been hard to believe.

St Joseph of Cupertino, the patron saint of pilots and astronauts, did achieve worldwide fame for his flights. Ambassadors and popes and princes made pilgrimages to the Franciscan friary at Grotella, to witness his ecstasies.

Joseph was a simpleton, born in a stable the illegitimate son of a carpenter in 1603. Desperate to lead a religious life, he sadly proved incapable of acquiring a monk's education. His hot temper kept him even from holding down the job of cobbler at a Capuchin monastery, and it took years of fasting and self-mutilation before the authorities decided a monastic life was the best thing for him.

They quickly regretted it. Joseph fell into an ecstatic reverie at the least reference to God. The sound of the choir, a peal of bells, any story from Christ's life, the Holy Virgin's name, the names of any of the saints, the mention of heavenly glory: anything set him off.

Joseph's Franciscan brothers helpfully kicked him, knocked him down, ran needles into him and burned his body with candles, but the trances could not be broken. Only the voice of his superior could break the spell.

Frequently in these ecstasies he levitated. Numerous eye-witnesses swore to the fact. The grace of his posture, lifted from his feet as though by a heavenly hand, was usually spoiled by his tendency to let out shrill, excited shrieks.

These were not mere suspensions. St Joseph sometimes flew thirty feet or higher, into treetops. The Spanish Ambassador to the Papal Court, the High Admiral of Castile, watched him sail at head-height across a church to embrace a statue of the virgin. At Osimo he seized a wax image of the Infant from a statue above the altar and flew back to his cell, cradling and cooing over the baby.

Fearful that a cult could spring up around him church elders denounced him to the Inquisition. St Joseph spent his last years in miserable ignominy, shunted in secrecy from retreat to retreat. It is said that even when he was dead, his body hovered three inches above its bier.

In one of his engrossing essays on Catholicism and the paranormal, Father Herbert Thurston lists more than twenty holy men and women whose reported levitations seem to be beyond doubt.

St Teresa of Avila, the Carmelite reformer, described the sensation: 'You see and feel it as a cloud, or a strong eagle rising upwards and carrying you away on its wings.' St Philip Neri said: 'It seemed to him as if he had been caught hold of by someone and in some strange way had been lifted by force high above the ground.' Both saints fought the raptures, but were sometimes surprised or overcome by them.

From the Norman Conquest to the turn of the century and beyond: Giovanni Batista della Concezione, reformer of the

Trinitarians; the Mexican missionary Anthony Margil; St. Edmund, Archbishop of Canterbury; the theologian Father Francis Suarez; Sister Mary of Jesus Crucified, a Syrian nun; none of them sought recognition for the miracles visited upon them, and most were embarrassed to be discovered in ecstasy.

Not so the Victorian medium Daniel Dunglas Home, a Christian Spiritualist who willingly subjected himself to every examination imaginable during his flights. Home may have been the most psychically gifted man in history. As a young man he dreamed of a visit to the spirit world; his intensely detailed description tallies closely with modern accounts of near-death experiences.

At twenty-five, he was an international celebrity. The Emperor and Empress of France, and the Russian Tsar, were converted to Spiritualism by the miraculous seances he held for them. In brightly lit rooms, massive pieces of furniture would glide and waft. Tables walked up walls. Musical instruments floated and played unearthly tunes. Hidden voices sang. Hands materialised and melted away.

When the lights were dimmed a little, spirits would manifest themselves and burn like phosphorous. Flames flew from one sitter to another. Stars burned in the air and on Home's face.

You probably suppose he was a conjuror of genius. So did everyone, at first. But Home was so keen to prove the existence of the spirits, so filled with his mission, that he welcomed every kind of sceptic at his innumerable seances. As he wore himself to a shadow, defying feeble health to perform daily sittings, his investigators tried everything to catch him out.

They held his feet, his hands, his arms. They crawled under chairs and tables. They demanded obscure snippets of personal information from spirits. They stripped him, searched him, required him to give seances at a moment's notice, presented him with pianos and accordions which he must make play without laying a finger on them and, after his departure, subjected their homes to minute searches for traces of trickery.

None was ever found. In more than thirty years of seances, Daniel Dunglas Home was never once discovered in deception. It is hard to believe he was for real, but harder still to prove he was a charlatan. The phenomena that accompanied him all appeared, even to the most sceptical observers, to be genuine.

The most spectacular of them was levitation. Sir William Crookes, who became President of the Royal Society and was one of Victorian Britain's foremost scientists, wrote: 'There are at least a hundred recorded instances of Mr Home's rising from the ground, in the presence of as many separate persons. On three separate occasions have I seen Mr Home raised completely from the floor of the room: once sitting on an easy chair, once kneeling on his chair, and once standing up.'

The most extraordinary levitation occurred on December 16, 1868, at a seance on the third floor of a house in Ashley Place, London. Home's three sitters were Lord Lindsay, Lord Adare and Adare's cousin, Captain Charles Wynne. They all saw Home leave the room in a trance, and heard him lift up the window.

In a testimony which exactly matches those of his friends, Lindsay writes: 'Almost immediately afterwards, we saw Home floating in the air outside our window . . . about seventy feet from the ground. (Home) raised the window and glided into the room feet foremost.'

Lindsay and Wynne saw tongues or jets of flame leaping from Home's head. When he broke from his trance, unconscious of what he had done, Home was deeply disturbed and spoke of a terrible urge to hurl himself from the window.

Home the extraordinary is almost forgotten today. Many people accepted that his countless, respectable witnesses were honest, and that he was genuine. But they still could not believe in the phenomena he provoked. They preferred discreetly to nudge it to one side, and forget him. The books written about Home, once printed in bulk, are now scarcely to be found outside specialist libraries. The dedicated researcher might find copies behind the doors of the Society for Psychical Research, or in the University of London's Harry Price Collection, where the doors are opened to the public only once a month.

The fate of Ella Wallis will be different. Thousands have done more than simply witness her miracle – they have experienced it for themselves. And that can never be brushed aside.

CHAPTER TWENTY-EIGHT

Sun, Friday, January 22:

THE DAD FROM HELL-A

Miracle girl Ella Wallis's father is today exclusively revealed by The *Sun* as a double love-rat.

The born-again preacher who told the world last week, 'My No 1 job is protecting my family,' has walked out to live with one of his *TWO* mistresses.

And friends believe that while Ken Wallis's French wife Juliette knew about the other women in his life, she has never till now known of the biggest shock – her husband's secret family, just two miles from his own home.

Unemployed actress Marcia Collins bore Ken a baby boy named Luke three years ago, when Ella's brother Frank was four years old. A family friend said last night, 'Ken never told his wife, though each week part of his pay-check goes towards Luke's upkeep.'

Marcia Collins lives with Luke and her twin daughters, Esme and Esther, six, in a council flat in Hartcliffe, one of Bristol's poorest suburbs. Social security pays her rent and heating bills.

She has always refused to disclose the name of her baby's father to the Child Support Agency, while making little secret of Ken Wallis's weekly stop-overs – which earned him the nickname 'Wednesday Man' with neighbours.

Yesterday the couple refused to comment as they unloaded Ken's collection of jazz LPs from the spacious boot of his brand new BMW into her flat.

But a workmate at BK Lewis Printers, where Ken is works manager, said: 'If he's taken the albums, it must be serious. He's got pretty much everything Sinatra ever recorded. Ken reveres the old jazz stars. I think most of the records were his dad's – he used to go to all the clubs in the 40s and 50s, and Ken told me he just grew up with those sounds.

'That's how he chose his kids' names – Frank for Sinatra, Ella for Ella Fitzgerald.'

Ken's other mistress is believed to be fifty-three-year-old Ailish McLintock, a part-time cleaner, of Easton. Yesterday the curtains of her flat overlooking the M32 were drawn and no one answered our reporter's calls.

'Oh, this is just brilliant. I am so happy,' said José Dóla. 'I really needed this. I don't need to remind you, do I, that I have yet to gain one single, solitary penny from this? And all I asked in return was a little honesty?'

Juliette sat meekly on the sofa, turning a cup of cold tea in her hands. Dóla was trying to sit facing her, but he was too agitated. He kept hopping to his feet and slapping a rolled *Sun* against the heel of his hand.

Guntarson sprawled in a round-backed wooden chair, watching in evident amusement. Dóla was too upset to notice him, or to keep his voice down and avoid upsetting Ella. She was hunched at her writing desk again, with a vast pack of coloured felt-tips which Dr Dóla had brought. Today she was drawing stick people – thousands of them packed onto each sheet, hip to hip, with bodies the width of a pen-stroke.

'So how are we going to turn this round? Why didn't you tell me in the first place? Why?'

'Sorry,' murmured Juliette.

'Sorry, well of course. Sorry is very helpful now. What did I say to you? When we first started? "If you've got anything you don't want in the papers, anything from the past, skeletons in the closet, tell me. Tell me," I said, and you said, "Oh no, we're Christians, we lead good lives." And I know, it doesn't seem fair to blame you for your husband's sins, but you knew, Juliette, didn't you? And you could have warned me.'

He ran a hand across his scalp. The black sheen Dr Dóla's hair acquired on a Monday had worn thin. This was Friday, and the strands no longer slid slickly back. They rebelled, and sprouted between his fingers like straw.

'I could have prevented this. So easily. A few pounds here and there, and it is all hushed up. Everybody denies it. Or we could even turn it into some kind of virtue. Say the child is not Ken's, it's his cousin. Or his godchild.'

'She is Jamaican,' remarked Juliette.

'So? So? This is a multi-racial country. I'm not English, you're not

English, he's not English.' He pointed at Guntarson. 'Everything can be explained. If . . . *if-if-if-if-if*,' he sputtered, stamping his foot so furiously that Guntarson laughed, 'if we get to the facts first. It is not funny!'

'Sorry,' said Juliette, though she had not laughed.

'Okay. Enough recrimination. It is not nice for you, I realise, to learn about this kind of thing from the tabloids. And you are worried about your little boy, Frank. And it has all been a bit of an upheaval.' He sat down helplessly. 'So what can we do to build on this? Okay, first of all, your husband.

'I have not been able to contact him. Fair enough, he is avoiding the reporters. He stirred them up like a flock of bees and now he is hiding from them.'

'*Swarm* of bees,' Guntarson corrected. Dóla ignored him.

'He has my number. He has not attempted to contact me, and you say he has not contacted you. So I have to terminate my association with him. Breach of contract. In fact, my whole contract with the Wallis family is at an end.' He stretched his legs and folded his arms dramatically.

'However. It would not be right to leave you in the lurch. You need guidance, more than ever. So I propose we take court action to have Ella made solely your ward. And I will handle publicity for you only, not Ken.'

'Not court,' said Juliette anxiously.

'But yes. It has to be. We fear for your safety, for the child's safety.'

'You are saying divorce.'

'It was a natural assumption. He has left you. Moved in with another woman.'

'It only is what the *Sun* says.'

'Juliette, you must be honest with yourself. I have checked it. The facts are correct. He really does have a son by this woman.'

'He will not stay with her.'

'Possibly not. The way he spends money, I do not think he can afford to stay away from work very long.'

'We are not going to divorce,' declared Juliette. 'He always comes back. There is Frank. He cares for Frank, really he does. Much more,' she added in a whisper, 'than for Ella. And there is my Church.'

'Do born-again Christians never divorce?'

'I am like you. Catholic. In my heart. Ken does not understand that. He has never known what is in my heart. It is secret. Secret God.' She was nodding her head hard. 'So there can be no court, no divorce.'

'I think that means he can contest your claim to Ella's earnings.

He'll demand all of it. He'll probably have a right to half. One way or another, you're going to end up in court. Then the only people who make money are the lawyers.'

'Why not,' Guntarson cut in, 'just give Ella the money she earns?'

'Stay out of this, you,' snapped Dóla. 'When I need your expert opinion, I'll ask, but this discussion is not about making you rich.'

'Ella and I have regard for more than just the monetary implications.'

'Juliette. I propose we negotiate a new contract. We very visibly set up a trust fund for Ella, beyond her father's reach. Or anyone else's,' he said, glowering at Guntarson. 'I take twenty-five per cent of gross earnings, as before. We hit the tabloids with a charm offensive – Ella being very mysterious and distant, because she is best in small doses, but you being most considerate to all the reporters and making photographs available, providing daily updates on your daughter's health, her education. Be demure and forgiving about your husband. We can make you into a saint. If – again we come to that word – if you can promise me, no more nasty surprises. Okay? No more skeletons in closets?'

Juliette cast her eyes down.

'What is it? Are you worried about drink? Because I told you, we're going to give you all the support you need. There's no alcohol within a mile of here. So you can forget temptation. You will be strong, I know you will, I know you want to put drinking behind you. I will help. Ella will help.'

'Sorry. It isn't drink. You are quite right, of course. I have given it up. Forever. It is quite easy, without Ken around. It is all to do with my will-power. And when he comes back, I will have forgotten about drinking.' She still stared at her feet. 'It is not that. There is something else.'

'Tell me. Whatever it is, I am unshockable. I've seen it all, much worse than you can imagine. Tell me now, and I will deal with it. Don't tell me, and it is the tabloids who will deal with it.'

'It is . . . personal.' Juliette leant forward, her knuckle on the cushions, and mouthed the word.

'A relationship?'

She shook her head. Shaking a thumb over her shoulder at Ella, she whispered, 'She must not know. It is in my medical records. I know someone will publish them. If that happens I would die.'

'An abortion?'

She cupped her hands to his ear and hissed into them, 'He gave me something bad. A disease.'

Dr Dóla's face betrayed nothing. 'A disease. You're talking about syphilis? Gonorrhoea, then. Ken gave you the clap. It's something people get every day. It's not unique. After Frank was born? You are okay now? Fine. No problem. You see how much better it is to be open. No one will see your records. I will have an injunction placed on them. And on Ella's records, just for effect. We'll say it is for genetic reasons. People will be intrigued. See? We make a good thing out of something bad. And anyone who publishes so much as when you last took an aspirin – they'll go directly to jail, don't even pass Go!'

'Thank you. Sorry.'

'For God's sake,' he smiled, 'it's not your fault. And let's get out of this house, shall we? I have only just realised how much I dislike it. It is so gloomsome. We'll go where you like. Ella, how do you fancy the seaside?'

She ignored him.

'Fresh sea air would do everyone good. Let's plan our next step.'

'The next step,' said Guntarson, 'is scientific validation.'

'By which you mean?'

'We need a paper published in a scientific journal. We want the stamp of approval. Experiments, tests . . . I have it all arranged. I have been busy on *Ella's* behalf, not just her parents'. And before you ask, there isn't any money in it.'

'Peter. Why don't you go and make us a cup of tea?'

Guntarson grinned. He enjoyed watching this self-important little sham of a man, all trussed up in braces and silk bow-tie, making plans for something he could not possibly control.

'Tomorrow afternoon, Ella and I have been invited to meet some people.'

'Tomorrow afternoon, we will be staging a press conference. Though your presence, of course, will not be necessary. I don't see when it ever is.'

'Double-booked,' exclaimed Guntarson, affably. 'We shall offer up our dilemma – Ella, would you like to go with me tomorrow, where we discussed, or with Dr Dóla?'

'Go with you.'

'You don't sound very sure, Ella,' remarked Dóla. 'In fact, you seem a little distant with your friend Peter today.'

She still ignored him.

'Nothing wrong?'

Guntarson projected the words, 'Sit! Here!' at the back of Ella's head. She turned round, beaming, and crossed to lean on the arm of his chair. He patted her hand.

'Ella and I have an invitation. We shall visit the Raglerian Laboratories in Oxford, with the co-operation of the *Journal of the Scientific World*, and the most brilliant physicists and psychologists of the university will put their white coats on, and Ella will completely freak them out with a little psychic display.'

Dóla stared, not believing him.

'I couldn't tell you why,' added Guntarson, 'but I have a feeling Ella's power is cyclical. It rises and falls. Like the tide of an ocean. It's always there, it's always immense, but sometimes it's higher than others. And tomorrow, I have a strong premonition her power will be at a peak.'

'You are joking?'

'Why should I be?'

'You can't take her to a science lab.'

'Why shouldn't I?'

'God! You understand nothing, do you? Try and think. Ella is a mystery. Very profound. A mystery affecting life, and religion, and the way we perceive reality. Things no one can ignore. And like religion, like life, everybody has their own theories about Ella. Everybody wants answers to the questions. Is she a fraud, is she an angel, do we all have these powers, is she a witch or a miracle-worker? And you want to go to a laboratory and dissect the mystery.'

'Yes.'

'Like cutting open the goose that lays golden eggs. Suppose the scientists find out what causes Ella to levitate? End of story. End of interest. End of mystery.

'And worse still, suppose they don't find out a solution. That frustrates them. Embarrasses them. They have their professional pride. So they declare Ella is just a hysteric. That's all it is. A fourteen-year-old girl's nerves. Everyone will seize on that answer. You have no idea how quickly a story can dry up when public interest goes. Today, the papers are "Ella, Ella, Ella". Tomorrow – nothing at all.'

'You're suggesting we should deprive the world of the most out-standing opportunity ever for research into the paranormal – just to sustain a publicity campaign.'

'And to assist Ella's trust fund.'

'Very pious. I didn't hear much mention of trust funds before this morning. And what became of your promise to take no cut from the first million pounds? Are you going to quietly forget that?'

'Listen you.' Dr Dóla leapt smartly from the sofa, his finger at Guntarson's face. He did not trouble with charming words now. 'I've warned you about talking money. This is the last time because, believe me, you aren't ready to play with the big boys. Get me?'

'I refuse to hold a conversation in your Pidgin English.'

'You want me to spell it out. Okay. Where are you Tuesday night? I know the answer. Wednesday night? I know. Last night? When the pictures are developed, I'll know that too.'

Guntarson had stopped smiling. He was sitting up, and brushed

Ella off his chair. 'I was at home last night.' His words came thickly.

'And whose home were you at the night before?'

'I don't believe you'd be foolish enough to think I could be black-mailed.'

'I would not take the trouble. I think it is simply time, as you want to throw a little weight around, that you find out what it's like, playing rough.'

Peter suddenly rocked back, and laughed. 'You asinine balloon of a man. Inflated with grand self-importance. You're a national laughing-stock. I can scarcely be bothered to puncture you. Pitting my wits against you would be a waste of intellect.'

'Fine. I am sure you won't be a laughing-stock, when the world sees your Oxford-educated bottom with its trousers down.'

'I have no idea what you're talking about. And neither have you.'

'Wednesday night. Where were you seen, do you think, with your trousers down on Wednesday night?'

'Wednesday night. That was when Ken had attacked Peter, and they had both disappeared, and Ella had gone searching for what Peter could see. And all she had found was a girl with a dark face, lighting a cigarette.

That face, seen for a moment, had been watching Ella in her mind ever since.

'Wednesday night? You really care what I was doing Wednesday night? Okay, one: I can do what I like. Two: If you've been spying on me I think you're very sick and very culpable and it will be a pleasure to see you in court – first the criminal, then the civil. Three: All I did on Wednesday was watch TV.'

Ella believed him. It was simple – a girl's face, her naked neck and shoulders, blowing cigarette smoke straight up. It was just an image on his television.

'And four: Upset me and you upset Ella. Because Ella and I are best friends, right Ella?'

She smiled, and writhed, and jammed the toes of her right foot under her left sole.

Dr Dóla laughed, a knowing little snort. 'Ella is only fourteen. Mind it isn't you that ends in the criminal court.'

'Think what you like. I'm Ella's best friend, right?'

'Yes,' she said, 'yes. Right.'

Chapter Twenty-Nine

From: John Potts-Style,
    Raglerian Professor Emeritus, Christ Church

To: Other members of the Ella Wallis Working Group,
    Raglerian Laboratories, January 24.
FOUR COPIES ONLY.

Confidential – Not For Circulation Or Publication

These notes being dictated at 19.20, January 24, four hours subsequent to the completion of investigations into the psychic capabilities of Ella Wallis under laboratory-controlled circumstances.

Taken from detailed notes made during the experiments, and following only limited discussion with colleagues present of the phenomena observed.

To be compared with records and impressions noted by my colleagues.

Present at the investigation, commencing 11.00 today: Myself; Prof Siegbert Bronstein, Nobel prize winner (physics), University of Wittenberg, and discoverer of the Bronstein Effect; Prof Hannah Samson, formerly of Durham University, author of papers regarded as the definitive study of *déjà-vu*, now on the board of directors, ICI; Dr Bernard Massey, editor-in-chief of the *Journal of the Scientific World*, the well-known illusionist David Bentwich, president of the Magic Sphere, who attended in his capacity as consultant to the *Journal*, Col K——R——, military intelligence observer; Lord Quentin of Dursley, Master of Christ Church.

Professor Bronstein and Samson have been frequent investigators of suspected psychics, and were willing to avow themselves convinced of the subject's peculiar powers, even prior to the examination. They had personally experienced phenomena of an anecdotal nature during a television broadcast which purported to show the subject in levitation. I myself, without experience of procedures for establishing the presence of so-called psychic energy, brought counter-ballast, being like the Master a life-long sceptic.

Col R—— was the Master's guest, and for the benefit of our other observers was referred to throughout as Prof Wilson. His interest in the investigation was not declared to the visitors, who were:

Ella Wallis, a psychic, fourteen;
Dr Peter Guntarson, a journalist, who claimed to fulfil the role of Ella's enabler or familiar. An acquaintance of Prof Samson, it was he who proposed the investigation, which offer was readily taken up by the college.

Procedure:
Our aim was simply to establish whether demonstrations of paranormal activity could be convincingly and repeatedly produced under closely monitored and controlled circumstances. Specifically, evidence was desired of psychokinesis, telepathy, levitation and, owing to particular interest from Col R's governmental department, remote viewing. Equipment will be discussed in relation to each experiment.

Observations:
Subject and companion arrived by motorbike at 10.40. Subject was considerably excited by circumstances of journey — she had not ridden pillion before. Academics were equally excited, perhaps, by the opportunity to investigate such fresh and apparently powerful phenomena, and an atmosphere of nervous jollity dominated early proceedings.

Ella proved to be a child of few words, daunted by adult attention and the mood of expectation pervading the laboratories. Her reticence was more than counter-acted by the confidence of Dr Guntarson.

After introductions, an attempt was made to gauge, in a general way, her intelligence, which was by no means apparent in her conversation. A simple IQ test was presented, and at first Ella, with Dr G at her shoulder, seemed to have few difficulties in completing it. Neither Ella not Dr G spoke during the test, and he did not appear to be supplying visual or aural prompts. Nevertheless, when Prof Samson suggested Ella attempt a similar test without Dr G beside her, an utterly different result was achieved — one which on its own would suggest the girl was barely numerate, and only half-literate. Naturally, no conclusions can be drawn from such a casual examination.

Before the commencement of experimentation, Ella consented to a thorough search of her person with a magnetometer and a hand-held, airport-issue metal detector. The purpose was to detect hidden apparatus; none was found.

Experiments:
1) For historical reasons, the first apparatus recreated an experiment in psychokinesis by Sir William Crookes, OM, FRS, first carried out in 1870. One of the first reputable

investigations into the paranormal, its subject was the Spiritualist medium, Daniel Dunglas Home.

A wooden plank was balanced, one end on a desk, the other supported by a tripod and secured to a spring balance. Ella was invited to place her fingers lightly on the plank where it touched the desk, a tip of wood about two centimetres long, five cm wide and three cm thick. The balance showed a downward pull of 1.5 kilos. Prof. Bronstein, who weighs 86 kilos, demonstrated that by standing on the desk and resting his whole weight on the near end of the plank, he could extend the balance at the far end by only one kilo.

In contrast to the antiquated tenor of this experiment, no fewer than five video cameras were placed so as to record the phenomena from all angles.

Ella, who had previously been encouraged into a calm and compliant state by Dr G, rested the fingers of one hand on the very end of the plank. An immediate increase of three kilos was recorded on the balance. Her own body weight, fully clothed, was afterwards established to be thirty-seven kilos. The inference is ludicrous, though hard to refute: that this waif exerted a pressure equal to 250 kilos, with the fingers of one hand.

The sensation caused by this archaic demonstration was considerable, since it had been introduced merely as an amiable homage to the past.

2) At the commencement of the investigation proper, while the attention of the observers was temporarily focused inwards and not upon the subject, she appeared unmistakably to levitate.

Standing in a corner alone, unobserved and some distance from the cameras, she rose vertically about ninety centimetres and hung with arms outstretched, as though supported by a harness. Naturally, no such apparatus was present. When the effect was exclaimed upon by Dr G, her floating body seemed lifted by the heels, until she was horizontal. The conjuror David Bentwich, despite pleas by Profs Samson and Bronstein, insisted on approaching and passing his arms in a loop along her full length, to satisfy us all there was no physical means of support. As his examination was completed, Ella fell quite sharply to the floor. She did not remember the elevation, and insisted she was unhurt.

2a) This levitation threatened to disrupt the entire investigation. All present declared their inability to disbelieve the evidence of their eyes, yet the occurrence fell outside the controlled environment and therefore was inevitably, from a scientific viewpoint, inconclusive and strictly warranting to be struck from this record. Furthermore, the levitation could not immediately be reproduced in the controlled environment, the subject protesting she was tired and frightened and did not wish to 'fly' again. Her companion took her part, warning that extension of psychic power against the subject's better judgement could be highly deleterious.

An interval of thirty minutes thus occurred before the attempt at psychic communication. This took another traditional form: that of the Rhine cards. Five cards were each marked with a simple, distinct symbol — a cross, a circle, a star, a square and a wavy line. The subject was then placed in a large, windowless, sound-proofed cubicle, well-lit, with a single chair and a microphone. The cubicle acted as a Faraday cage, with wire mesh woven through the walls to block out any electrical signal. Earlier tests had proved the impossibility of any stimuli from outside the cubicle seeping to the occupant.

The famous Rhine cards were then shuffled and presented, one at a time, to Dr G who was with the observers outside the cubicle. In turn he 'telepathically projected' the symbols to the subject. Almost instantly as he received the cards she spoke the symbol into the microphone. The pack was reshuffled and revealed five times over, with the subject achieving one hundred per cent accuracy. Dr G claimed the subject had never seen a Rhine set, and could not know of the symbols. Furthermore, he pointed out, she had no way of knowing when a card was being revealed, except telepathically.

The Master suggested Dr G might be utilising a hidden, electronic communication device, featuring some new technology which might penetrate the 'cage' woven by our venerated forefather, Faraday. The Master therefore asked to adopt the role of telepathic sender. There was a drop in the result, with the subject being aware of new cards on only six out of ten occasions. However, when she did offer an identification, it was with perfect accuracy.

In Rhine experiments, chance dictates twenty per cent of predictions will be on target. A score of thirty-three per cent is generally taken as evidence of telepathy. Frequent failures with supposedly telepathic subjects have been blamed generally on the inpropitious surroundings of laboratories.

3) The only notable suspicion of trickery or fraud arose, curiously, not during experimentation but at lunch. Dr G having earlier warned us that the subject would be uncomfortable in the grandeur of the college refectory, we dined in the less rarefied atmosphere of the lab canteen. The child ate heartily for one of her size and, while others were finishing their desserts, urgently requested to go to the lavatory. Prof Samson, our only representative of the fairer sex, offered to show the way. The subject was adamant she should go on her own. Our master magician David Bentwich suggested, more as a possibility than a challenge, that practised fraudsters might take advantage of time alone during ablutions to adjust hidden equipment and so forth — assuming that any equipment might have eluded our

searches. The subject became very agitated, insisting she must be permitted privacy. Of course we concurred — and it is hard to imagine what secret apparatus could possibly have influenced the subsequent occurrences. Nevertheless, her insistence on privacy remains puzzling. During lunch the Master expounded with great energy and no little wit on the vital importance that the Church should embrace what he termed "the global X-Files culture". His alarming contention that more Britons now believed in the existence of alien life-forms and UFOs than believed in the Resurrection did meet spirited opposition from Dr Massey and Prof Bronstein; his fervency of prayer that science and religion should soon share a closer understanding, the one better to illuminate the other, elicited warm admiration from all present.

3a) The experiment in remote viewing had been introduced at Col R——'s request, and proved a disappointment. The subject was provided with map references, with a request to report what the mind's eye imagined to be at those geographical points. Despite some prompting by Dr G she could not provide any information; being unable to visualise what might be the physical form contained within a set of co-ordinates, she was clearly unwilling to guess at or invent an answer.

Col R——, apparently having previous experience of experiments in remote viewing during an association with the CIA, opined that favourable results were often obtained through 'out-of-body' experiences — the subject imagining an instantaneous flight to the designated locale, to see it 'firsthand'. Ella denied any familiarity with 'out-of-body' travel, and her cursory attempts to comply met with predictable failure. Dr G refused to assist her efforts by hypnosis, insisting that the only probable result would be a recurrence of levitation and that this would probably deplete her psychic reserves so gravely as to render further experimentation impossible.

4) All the investigators were in warm anticipation of seeing the feat of levitation repeated, this time under our prescribed conditions. The child herself was showing some symptoms of fatigue, including an almost luminescent pallor and trembling in her fingers. She requested at least twice, barely audibly, that Dr G would 'take her home'. His assurances that the tests would soon be over quieted her.

The subject was returned to the telepathy cubicle, where this time the microphone had been replaced by three micro video cameras. The compartment offered sufficient room for the subject to lie prone, corner to corner, and a blanket was spread on the floor. When she expressed reluctance to lie down, a chair was offered. She continued to complain of no longer wishing to undergo the tests, and repeated her desire to be taken home. Dr G placated her, insisting the favourable outcome of the investigation and, by extension, of all her aspirations, depended on a verifiable instance of levitation.

During this reassurance he gripped her hands, a circumstance which had a visibly favourable effect on the subject. He then proceeded to induce a fairly profound state of trance with relatively few hypnotic suggestions. At no time during the hypnosis did he order her to levitate.

The subject was led to a wooden chair placed in the cubicle by myself and Dr Massey. She indicated a need for motherly reassurance: her precise words were, 'I wants my mam!' Dr G was unperturbed, assuring us that the phrase was unconscious.

The heavy cubicle door was closed. This action appeared at first to break the trance — the subject stood up violently, knocking the chair over, and called out. Her precise words are not known, since the box was sound-proofed and the microphone had been removed, but it seemed clear the subject desired to leave her confinement.

The Master immediately offered to cancel the test, and Prof Samson voiced her agreement, but Dr G proposed the investigation could be allowed to run a few moments longer. The agitation would shortly subside, he predicted, and accurately so. It was replaced by an apparent collapse: the subject buckled and sat on the floor, her face bowed to her ankles. Again Dr G recommended non-interference — the subject was likely to pass into a deep trance, and levitation was certain to follow.

The subject's behaviour at this point reminded me strongly of experiments on young primates (chimpanzees, etc), particularly where the subject has been forcibly separated from its family group and perhaps been obliged to witness the destruction of one or more of its colleagues. In this case, the human subject was observed to slip into the foetal position with knees and elbows shielding the face. There was no movement other than a periodic convulsing of the chest. Prof Bronstein voiced concern that this might herald respiratory difficulties, but Dr G assured him that, in a relaxed hypnotic state, such crises were not possible. Whatever distress the subject might be suffering was most unlikely to be a response to external stimuli and was probably a reaction to something much more deeply rooted. Furthermore, the appearance of distress could well be misleading. He remained convinced that a remarkable levitation was heralded, hinting at concomitant phenomena, and succeeded in calming all aspects of anxiety among the investigators.

At this point, the subject's body, dressed in dark clothing, was clearly defined on the light-coloured blanket.

As the video-tapes confirmed, her disappearance was instantaneous.

At the moment Dr G was most confidently predicting a psychic manifestation, the form of his protegée vanished from the screen.

Col R— was the first to shake off the immobility of disbelief. While we others were gaping at our monitor, now displaying an empty cubicle, he and Bentwich went rapidly to the door and opened it. The unit was unoccupied. All seals were intact.

All the thin air ducts were examined. It was impossible that the subject could have left by any conventional means — quite apart from the evidence of our eyes and our cameras.

David Bentwich made a perhaps unnecessarily elaborate show of circling the cubicle, tapping its roof and then the inside walls in his search for hidden trapdoors. Although he is an accomplished escapologist, he quickly confessed himself baffled.

The immediate jubilation at having induced and recorded an unmistakable instance of human dematerialisation was much muted, however, by concern for the subject's safety. Dr G's optimistic assertion that she would soon rematerialise was not borne out, and after several minutes of increasing anxiety his mood suddenly switched from one of confidence to abject shock.

The ludicrous impossibility of alerting anyone to the disappearance — she could hardly be reported to the police as a conventional 'missing person' — emphasised our bafflement. The urge to re-examine the cubicle, as though her presence under the blanket or in one of the corners might have gone undetected, was hard to resist. Instead we realigned our bearings, and attempted to calm Dr G, by asking him for details of any person or place to which she might be 'drawn'. He named certain friends and family, whose telephone numbers were easily obtained, but there arose then the difficulty of contacting these people in a manner calculated not to arouse alarm.

Dictation paused, 20.40, January 19; to be concluded tomorrow.

CHAPTER THIRTY

At the same moment Ella was in Oxford, pleading for her mother, Juliette was in London. She too wanted to leave. She was hissing at Joe Dóla, 'I can't do this, you read it to them,' and the microphones were picking up her words and whispering them round the floor.

Dr Dóla, possessing a perfect instinct for photo-opportunities, had chosen a Bond Street hotel named the Royal Palace for this press conference. Its lobby and first floor had been refurbished and fashioned into an airy atrium, which stood to one side of the tower block of bedrooms. Two spiral staircases wound up to the centre of a broad ring, where guests usually dined. A curved bar stood on part of the rim. The ceiling was glass, and looked straight up to the heavens. Journalists and TV crews, present strictly by invitation, were seated around the tables. They had been presented with flowers, and plates of cheese snacks, and glasses of white wine.

Juliette sat close to the stairs, at a square table which trailed two dozen cables. Arc lamps shone down from all sides. Her face was partly hidden by a nest of microphones.

Dr Dóla was at her side, leaning back and squinting past the brilliant lamps at the grey sky through the ceiling.

It had not started well. They had lunched at the hotel, and been recognised. Other guests kept slipping over for autographs, and to share stories of what they had experienced during the *Ella* documentary. Dr Dóla explained to each fan that the time for autographs was after a meal, while Juliette simply shrugged and silently signed napkins and menus and the backs of business cards and the back of a man's shirt. She accepted she was famous now. After all, she was Ella's mother.

She was distracted and short of words. Dr Dóla sympathetically supposed she was anxious for Ella, being made to jump through hoops for anonymous scientists.

Juliette was not worried for Ella – and Dr Dóla's assumption that she should be worrying made her feel worse. She wanted a drink. Thursday and Friday, poisoned by the gin, she had coped without fresh alcohol easily enough. Today she was not coping. She was shivering, and had no appetite. The bar beyond the stairwell was open, with fat bottles of spirits draining into optics and racks of tonic and ginger ale tinkling below the till.

The moment Dr Dóla stood up to sign the check, a fat man in a tweed jacket hurried over. Clamping an arm round his back, gripping his bicep, he murmured: 'José, José,' and offered a pumping handshake without letting his other arm slip.

Dr Dóla let himself be led away three or four steps. People with a lot of money to spend often used this very physical approach.

'My name's Barry Green, I'm on the *Star*.'

Dr Dóla stiffened. The fellow was just a reporter.

'Listen, I've got a good one for you. We can let you in on it for nothing. I bet you're about ready for a break, aren't you?'

'Yeah, you bet,' agreed Dr Dóla. He could treat anyone he'd known for longer than four seconds as a close confidante. 'I'm working hard for my cut this time. Correction. As you probably know, I'm not taking a cut this time.'

'You're not getting nothing? Doing it for free?' Barry Green's face was a picture of incredulity.

'It's only fair. This girl, Ella, she's a wonderful child but . . . a child. She needs to be protected. I shan't be taking a penny before I see her safely into the harbour.'

'Joe Dóla, it don't matter what folks says about you, you're a solid-gold saint.'

'Of course, why do people find it so hard to believe?' The doctor chuckled. He was pleased to bandy words with this man from the *Star*. Barry Green was evidently an insincere, untrustworthy bullshitter. Good. You knew where you were with people like that.

'The problem we're having,' confided Green, 'how do you get a grip on this story? I mean, you can't predict what's going to happen one minute to the next.'

'A running story, and you've got no idea where it's running to!'

Green roared. 'Very good. Like it. Runaway running story, got it in one.'

'If you can't get a line on it, how do you think I feel? This family won't tell me the truth one minute to the next. First it's all happy families, then mistresses start popping up all over the place. And the girl's gone all doe-eyed over this Adonis of hers . . .'

'Really?'

Dóla doubled back. 'I'm exaggerating. The point is, I'm trying to groom these people, but they're yokels. We're off the record, Barry. But it's so hard to get through their thick heads. They can make a tidy sum, if they'll only play the game. Set themselves up for life. But you can't trust them to behave for a minute. Stick them anywhere near a camera and it's guaranteed chaos. You know what they say, never work with children or animals. I tell you, never work with children, or animals, or the Wallis family.'

Green was nodding sympathetically. 'And Ella, turns out she's got the hots for this Viking, then?'

Dóla would not slip a second time.

'No, no. Pay no attention, Barry, I'm rambling. So what's your deal today, then?'

Green checked that Juliette was nowhere near. 'We've got the grand-dad. Ricard Deyonne. The old Frog geezer. He's actually here, in one of the rooms as it happens.'

'Juliette's father? I don't think they've seen each other . . .'

'Since she legged it to get her leg over Ella's dad. *Exactement*. If I can slip into the vernacular for a moment there.'

'*Alors, nous parlons Français.*'

'Ace, you talk the lingo. Course you do. Well that's good news, cos the Frog doesn't speak one word of English and I'm buggered if I know what he's spouting about. Anyway, so I gather, he and Ella's old girl haven't seen each other for fifteen years. Wouldn't have met up ever, if it wasn't for all the fuss. I don't think he can read, and he ain't even got a telly, but somehow, right in the back of beyond of Frogland, word reaches him he's got a granddaughter and she's famous all of a sudden.'

'Maybe he simply smelled money,' remarked Dóla.

'I think he just wants to bury the hatchet before he snuffs it,' said Green. 'He's this really old geezer. Looks like he stepped out of a Gauloise ad.'

'What are you whispering?' Juliette demanded.

Dr Dóla spun round, and before he had finished his turn a smile was hammered to his face. He introduced Green.

'What are you telling him?'

'It is more what he's telling me, Juliette, some good news for a change.'

'What?' Her eyes tightened suspiciously, and then sprang open in shock as she read the answer on his face. 'My father – no, not my father? Oh no, no, no. You have been to dig him up, is it? Or did he sniff the chance to steal some money? You tell him to crawl back into his hole in the ground. And tell him I hoped, his daughter really, really hoped, he was dead.'

Green tried to keep looking confident. It was not hard to imagine someone undead in the Wallis family. Ricard Deyonne had the face for it.

'Juliette,' Dr Dóla soothed her, 'maybe now is a good time for building bridges. Dealing with the past. But I promise, if you do not feel strong enough to achieve that today, you do not have to meet him. I'll make sure of it.'

'I never want to see him, if I live a hundred lives.'

'He seems very mild-mannered now,' lied Green. 'Course, I don't know how he used to be like. But maybe you'll find he's changed, mellowed with age.'

'People like him do not change. He is bad. It runs all the way through him.'

'Okay Juliette. Let's try to focus on the conference now.'

'You want to know why I hate him? Do you? Can you guess?'

No, Green was shaking his head innocently. Attentively. Dóla was trying to ease her away, but Juliette pulled back.

'When my mother died, what did he do then? For his physical needs? What do you think? And when I ran away, how do you think it was for my sister Sylvie? You people in the newspapers, you drag it all up again. First of all – no, *you* shut up,' she told Dr Dóla, shoving him away. 'First of all they publish all the lies my brother-in-law tells them. He knows nothing about my family. Nothing. And then they bring that horrid, bad, bad old man here.'

She was shouting, and she kept on shouting as Dr Dóla led her firmly away by the waist. 'You ask him,' she yelled at Green, 'why he made my sister have a poor, sick baby.' And then Dóla steered her into the ladies' toilets and clamped the door shut with his heel.

'Control yourself! Control yourself!'

She flung her fists on his shoulder and wept onto them. Dóla supported her awkwardly.

'Come on. Brave face now. The boys from the press are out there.'

'Sorry, I am sorry. You don't know what is being brought back alive for me.'

'I get the picture.'

'He made Sylvie have his baby. Me, I killed two of them. I had abortions. I thought I would never have more babies, but I got pregnant with Ken the very first night. Maybe that is why Ella is strange, I sometimes think so. Because she has the ghosts of my two dead babies in her. Her own grandfather's babies.'

'Come on. This is not helping you. Think of something nicer.'

'That is what Sylvie says. Be Happy. Don't Worry. She teaches that song to Frank. I don't believe Sylvie is happy. It is just another way to be unhappy. He made her have the baby. Our father, he decides it. She was sixteen. It was born blind. And mad. When he saw it, he wanted it killed. First he will not let her have the abortion, then he sees his own son, out of his own daughter, and he says, "You must drown it".'

'I'm glad,' said José Dóla, 'you're telling me this in private.'

'Is that what you think? Maybe I was wrong to tell the reporter something without first we charge him money?'

'He'll make plenty out of anything you say. It's your life – you might as well get paid for it.'

'What difference does money make? Don't you care about the little baby?'

'It's long, long in the past.'

'So why am I crying today?' She straightened up and regarded her pale, stained face in the mirror. 'I see that awful face every day. I do not like to look in a pram, or see a baby poster in a shop, because Sylvie's sick little animal is in their faces. It had one swollen eye, and it could not eat or even breathe very well. She had it wrapped all in jumpers and things she begged off people in the motorway services. She hid in a car because she had no ticket on the ferry. Same as me.

'And she found me in Bristol, and brought the baby to me. And after two nights it died in our kitchen. So Ken took a spade and went up in Leigh Woods and dug a hole for it. That's what he did. And we said prayers for it. Maybe you want to dig it up and sell its tiny bones?'

'Come on, Juliette. Dry those eyes. I expect it feels worse today because you'd like a drink.'

'It always feels like this.'

'It is better to spit it all out. Get the taste out of your mouth.' He took her elbow. 'They will be waiting for us now.'

She did not want to face the press, and she was still pleading to go home when Dóla pressed her into a chair behind the microphones. He tapped on a glass for attention.

'My friends of the media – for I think I know all of you here, with the exception of some from more far-flung places.' He peered past the camera at tables circled by journalists, curving away beneath the sloping sheets of glass. 'I'll keep this brief. I'm sure you understand this is a trying time for Ella and her mother. Ella, in fact – and I know you'll be disappointed but perhaps not surprised – will not be here this afternoon. She is working with very eminent scientists at Oxford, it's all very hush-hush so I can't reveal any further details today. I'm sure whatever comes of it will be fascinating for us all.'

Someone shouted, 'Who is behind the experiments?'

Dóla ignored the outburst. 'Juliette, Ella's mother, has been anxious to meet you all and answer your questions, and I know you'll be very gentle with her. We're all human – many of you, I know, will have had your own, tragic marriage difficulties. Try and bear her feelings in mind, for decency's sake, and I hope we've all got a lot to gain from this afternoon.'

Juliette pressed her statement flat on the table with one hand. The other clasped a microphone stem, manouveuring it to her mouth. This way her hands would not been seen shaking. Forgetting her orders to keep facing the cameras, she showed them the top of her head and read: 'Following much speculation in many quarters, I wish to set straight the record regarding the relationship between Ella's father and mother – my husband Ken and me.

'I have been fully aware for some time of Ken's relations with other women, and I have always felt the most dignified course was to ignore them. Furthermore, as a mother, my first duty has been to provide love and support for my children . . .'

She spoke steadily, without injecting a scrap of meaning into the words. They did mean nothing. José Dóla had written them for her.

At the foot of the page she paused. She did not know whether she was supposed to turn over the sheet. She scarcely had the energy to care.

When the silence had held for a couple of seconds, a woman two tables back leapt up: 'Juliette, I'm Millicent Armadale of the *Mirror*. May I ask . . .?'

For an instant there was a shadow over the glass ceiling, and Miss Armadale never asked her question. One of the oblong panes broke with a crack like a tree-trunk snapping, and the huge shards creaked in their frame before dropping. They fell with a faint swish, like spears in the air, and plunged through the stairwell to shatter on the tiles below.

And Ella Wallis, her body curled in a tight ball, crashed onto her mother's table, spilling the microphones and sending the camera crews reeling.

CHAPTER THIRTY-ONE

During the confusion, no one could be sure of what they had seen, how they had reacted. But the photographs showed José Dóla leaping back, his mouth round with horror. He stumbles over his chair, as if the object hurled down before him is a bomb.

Juliette is screaming. Her hands are flung over the crown of her head and she is shrieking between her arms. Huge spears of glass lie everywhere, splintered on the tablecloths and carpets, but none of the pictures show injured journalists. Miraculously, no one had been hurt.

Ella lay motionless for several seconds. With her back bent and her legs pulled tightly up, it was not instantly clear what she was. Her face was away from the cameras. Her clothes were the clothes she had been wearing in Oxford a few moments before.

Anyone guessing the object was human might have taken her to be a suicide. Someone who had thrown themselves from a bedroom high above, through the glass ceiling.

One of the Sky news team touched her first. He laid a hand on her shoulder, to roll her over, the way he might have touched a corpse at a roadside in Bosnia.

Ella raised her head. Suddenly everyone was shouting her name.

Her mother was shrieking it. The photographers were yelling it, hoping she would look into their lenses. The reporters were urging it, desperate to ask questions. Dr Dóla, as he lunged forward to separate her from the pack, was hissing it. 'Ella! *Ella*! *ELLA*!'

The rattle of cameras was like hailstones on glass. Someone who already had the pictures he wanted shouted for a doctor, and the pack took up the cry: 'Get a doctor, call the ambulance, she needs paramedics! Don't touch her. She must have broken every bone in her body – don't touch her, you'll kill her!'

Ella crawled off the table. Dóla scooped her up – she seemed to weigh no more than a cat – but she wriggled through his arms and caught her mother's hand. She did not look scared, or bewildered. She expected to see Juliette, and Juliette was there.

Dóla pressed them into one of the lifts and kept out the baying pack by spread-eagling his arms and legs behind the doors as they slid shut. The dim lift seemed a lightless hole after the halogen glare of the lamps. Bellows followed them up the lift-shaft: 'Ella! Ella!'

Juliette was whimpering. Ella was calm and silent. 'Are you hurt? Juliette blurted at her. There was not much affection in the question.

At the eighth floor they were ushered out. Dr Dóla was looking nervously around. 'We've got a room, I booked a room. I've got the key. So we wouldn't have to go back to the house. 1111. It's probably this way.' He stood, hopping left then right.

The lift-bell rang behind them.

'Come on,' decided Dóla, pulling them left, and stopping at once. '1001, 1002. We want what – 1111. Shit. This is wrong – shit. Back in the lift.' But the lift doors clamped together, stranding them on the wrong floor, and the next-door lift opened up to reveal a crowd of journalists bristling with cameras.

'Ella, what happened? Did you fall? Did you jump? Did you try to kill yourself? Ella, are you hurt?'

Dóla, leading her backwards, fending off the questions with his palms, glanced down at her. *Was* she hurt?

'I ain't cut or nothing,' Ella answered.

Dóla looked more closely and was amazed to see she was speaking the truth. 'Ella, how did you fall?'

'I didn't fall.'

'Tell us what happened.'

She was being backed down the landing, clutched by her mother. Dóla looked frantically around for stairs.

A hand caught her sleeve, and another her wrist. They were feeling her, as if to be sure she was real. She tugged away.

'Where did you come from?'

'I was in this little room.' She looked up at Juliette. 'Where's Peter, is he here? He was making me leveltate. And then I landed on the table.'

'But where were you? Were you upstairs?'

'I was in this place. Oxford.'

'What?' And then all the questions started at once, each of the journalists barking and howling her name. Behind them another pack spilled out of the lifts, pulling and carrying their gear.

Big Barry Green, jabbing with the patched elbows of his tweed jacket, forced his way towards them. He was brandishing a key on a fat, round fob, like José Dóla's. The number on it was 1016.

'Joe, come on, this way.' The man from the *Daily Star* hooked one arm across Dr Dóla's shoulders and the other round Juliette's waist. Ella was shoaled between them, into the throng. 1016 was two doors up. Dóla did not attempt to resist. The key sprang the lock so swiftly that Ella almost fell into the hotel room. Green was behind her, shoving the cameras away and slamming the door.

'God!' murmured Juliette, and sank to her knees.

From the neck of the room, between the bathroom door and the wardrobe, they looked into a square bedroom lit by wide windows. On the nearer of two beds a long pair of legs stretched.

As Green guided Ella towards the window, the legs swung to the floor. Ella glanced up at the man as she passed. He was tall – taller even than Green. His face was cracked like dried mud. His long nose had been smashed flat, more than once, a long time ago. The scorching stub of a cigarette was screwed into the corner of his mouth.

Juliette, on her hands and knees, stared at the man's buffed and scuffed brown leather shoes. Instead of looking up, she sank her chin on her chest. The way these feet were planted on the floor, well apart, one twisted inwards – it sent an acid spurt of recognition through her stomach. These feet had kicked her often enough.

'Go away,' Juliette asked, hopelessly.

'Stand up,' commanded her father. He did not call her 'tu'. He spat out 'vous'. It was beneath his dignity, to admit any connection to the woman at his feet.

His voice curdled her stomach, the way it had in all her nightmares for twenty years. She had fled from his barbarity, and in two words it caught up with her again. 'Stand up!'

Dr Dóla stepped forward. 'I am here to insist,' he began in French.

Ricard Deyonne did not deign to look across. He reached out one knotted hand, thick bristles on each finger, and took hold of Dr Dóla's bow-tie. Lifting him by the throat till his head rapped on the ceiling, Deyonne flung the little man against the door. The air was knocked out of his lungs in a cough.

'Ricard,' shouted Green, grabbing at his elbow, but the Frenchman did not turn.

'Don't make me stand you up,' he ordered Juliette.

With her back against the wardrobe she slid to her feet. 'What have you come for?'

'You.'

'What do you mean?'

'You and the girl. You can come back to France with me.'

Green looked across at Dr Dóla, who was also climbing shakily to his feet. 'What are they saying?' Dóla did not have the wind to answer.

'I am married,' said Juliette.

'Your husband, does he want you?'

'Why do you want us? You never did before.'

'Your husband, I said. Does he care to keep you? No. Then I must.'

'You don't really think we will go with you?'

'Is that the child?' He gestured backwards at Ella. 'She is a witch. Hard work and the back of my hand will quickly knock the magic out of her.'

'You think she doesn't know what a blow feels like?' muttered Juliette.

'I refuse to permit you . . .' Dr Dóla struggled to begin again.

'Shut up. Next time it's the window for you.'

'How much do you want?' persisted Dóla.

'I want my daughter.'

'I am not your daughter!' shouted Juliette.

'Blood is blood!'

'And money is money.' Dr Dóla knew he was getting through. 'What are you asking?'

'For what?'

'To go away.'

Deyonne stared down at his cowering daughter. Then he leaned back, lit another blunt, white cigarette and never looked at her again.

'You are offering to buy what is not for sale.'

'I don't want to buy anything. I'm paying you to go.'

'No.'

'Five thousand.'

'What!' Deyonne looked truly shocked. 'Fifty thousand.'

The horror was repeated on Dr Dóla's face, until he realised they were talking francs. 'Okay. Okay, look, I'm writing you a cheque.'

'Don't give me that shit!'

'What do you want? Cash?'

'Of course?'

'How much do you think I carry?'

'I don't think. I don't care. You pay me cash, that's all.'

Dr Dóla looked at his watch. It was Saturday afternoon. The banks were shut. The bureaux de change, though, would be open. He scribbled, 'Pay the bearer' and the sum across a cheque and thrust it with his Gold AmEx card at Green. 'Get that cashed. Take him out and give him his money, and don't let him start talking to anyone else.'

Deyonne snatched the card from Dóla's hand.

'Tell him it's useless without the number. Oh-one-oh-nine. And only use it if you have to. And absolutely no more than fifty thousand francs. Got that? Francs, not pounds. That's the limit on my card. Don't let him tell you anything else.'

Green was pushing the grinning Deyonne to the door. 'I'd get back round the corner,' the newspaperman advised Juliette.

The door opened and, in the instant it took to shunt Ella's grandfather out, the room was filled with shouts. 'Ella! Are you all right? Ella! What was the shouting about? Can we come in?'

Light from camera flashes blazed for a moment around the edges of the door, until Green pulled it shut.

Dóla gave Juliette his arm, helping her onto the bed. Her father's gangling hollow was still pressed into the blankets. Juliette sucked the tip of her thumb and bit the nail.

'I ain't going with him,' said a voice from the corner.

Dr Dóla glanced at Ella. He had forgotten she was there. 'Don't worry,' he said.

'Why ain't I with Peter?' she demanded.

She was shaking. Her knees were drawn up to her chin and her shoulders were jerking with convulsive quivers. There were specks of blood on her cheek, as though she had bitten her lip and then wiped it on the back of her hand.

'Don't be frightened of that man,' Juliette told her tiredly, without looking up. 'He doesn't care about you. He just wanted money.'

'What am I doing here?' answered Ella. 'Where are we? What happened?'

Her body shook so violently that her chairback started rapping on the glass. José Dóla walked across and gazed out. The window, in a tower-block of rooms stretching high above the hotel's foyer next-door, looked down onto the atrium with its smashed roof and its debris-strewn tables. Rain had started to drip through the jagged hole.

'If you don't know how you got here,' he said, resting a hand on Ella's leaping shoulder, 'no one else does.' He held her hands. They were icy. 'You're suffering from shock. I suppose it has only just hit you. Would it help if I tried to hypnotise you?'

She shook her head vigorously.

He pulled a Kashmir blanket over her. 'I would not know how, anyway. These are better.' He unzipped a pouch from his jacket and popped two round, white pills through the foil of their plastic tray. 'I'll get you a drink with them.'

'What are you giving her?' said Juliette. She still did not look up.

'Something to make her feel better.'

'I want some too. What I want is a drink.'

Dr Dóla looked at the pills in his palm. Juliette already knew one route to oblivion. He did not want to teach her another. Taking two bottles from the mini-bar, he poured tonic water for Ella and a gin for her mother.

Juliette did look up when she heard the seal on the bottle-cap crack. She saw the little brown fridge and smiled.

Dr Dóla was helping Ella to lie on the other bed and straighten her legs, tucking the blanket under them, when his personal mobile rang. Only a few people had the number – it could be his wife, one of his children. He answered.

It was Juliette's sister.

'We have Ella here,' he said. 'She turned up unexpectedly. I'll pass you over.'

Juliette took the phone and lay, propped up on an elbow, listening to Sylvie's nervous gabble. Peter, that Canadian man, had phoned, and she had been so-o worried because he said Ella had run off. He said not to be concerned, but how could she not be concerned, if that poor little child was all on her own and no one knew where? And thank goodness she was safe, all she had wanted was to be with her mother, and Sylvie was so-o glad.

Juliette told her about their father. She took pleasure in it, knowing the news would upset Sylvie the way it had upset her. And then she shouted at her little sister for being frightened. Sylvie would not have to see the foul old man. He had gone now. Juliette had seen to that. It was her money that had paid him off. So what was Sylvie snivelling for?

There was a long silence between the sisters. Neither wanted to end the call. It was a comfort, knowing the other was listening, waiting for something to be said.

'How is Frank?'

'Oh,' said Sylvie, 'I do not want to worry you about him. You have so many other things bothering you.'

'What do you mean?'

'Let me take care of this.'

'Of what?'

'I was not even going to tell you . . .'

'Sylvie, if anything is wrong . . .'

'He has these headaches, that is all.'

'Still?'

'It has only been a week.'

'Have you taken him to the doctors?'

'He did not feel like going.'

'He's too ill to go to the doctors? Call them out then.'

'I do not like to, they are so-o busy. You know.'

'Sylvie, if Frank is ill, he must have the doctor. Do it now.'

'Okay, Okay. You are always shouting at me. Just stop shouting. It doesn't help.' She was sobbing again.

'Call the doctor.'

'I was going to take him tomorrow anyway.'

'Why tomorrow?'

Sylvie did not answer at first, and the question came again. 'I was not going to worry you with it. It is nothing. Okay? He will be fine. Look, Frankie had a bit of a . . . fit. Oh God, oh God. I knew I should not have told you.'

Juliette was screaming.

'I thought maybe, epilepsy. Or just something he ate. But if you want,' she said, trying tremulously to calm the boy's mother, 'I can call the doctor now. Okay? Yes, I'm doing that. I'm calling now.'

'I want to be there with him. Tell the doctor I'm coming home,' shouted Juliette. But her sister had rung off.

Dr Dóla was pressing another tumbler of gin and tonic into her hand. 'We're going home. Now,' she ordered.

'We're rather stuck here at the moment.'

'I don't care.'

'The hotel has security people, they'll be evicting the rabble. We can wait till the coast is clear.'

'I want to go now.'

'I think Ella needs to rest.'

'Ella! It is always Ella! I have another child, you know. He needs me.'

'When Barry gets back, then. He has my Gold AmEx.'

'Ah!'

'We can't get anywhere without it,' snarled Dr Dóla. He hated any implication he would put money above a client's well-being. 'I'm sorry if Frank isn't well. Yes, I've seen the picture of him, you showed me. Sorry. Of course I'll see it again. Yes, he is a lovely-looking little lad. You know, I have two boys too. There now. We can go and visit him. As soon as that reporter gets back. I'll order a security escort.'

Green needed an escort himself to get back into room 1016. The journalists had been cleared from the corridor and the floor was sealed off. Police had been called. A forensic team was checking the broken sky-window. The Royal Palace's deputy manager insisted on joining Barry Green to see Dr Dóla.

'Soon as the old Frog got his dosh,' said Green, 'one of the intellectuals grabbed him. Guy from the Torygraph. So providing they've got someone who speaks haw-hee-haw, you'll be reading all about Granddad tomorrow.'

Dr Dóla understood. The *Telegraph*, most of whose staff owned timeshares in Provençal gîtes and spoke exquisite French, had bought up Ricard Deyonne. Small wonder Green looked choked.

'I'll have my card back, please, Barry.'

'You'll read my obit tomorrow too,' persisted Green. 'I haven't told the boss yet, that I've spiked his front page.'

'I'm sure you can salvage something of it.'

'What? We got no pictures. And I never understood one word he was saying. No, you got to slip me something else, Joe, or I'm dead and buried. We paid a fortune to get that geezer over here. And paying for this room.'

'Okay,' admitted Dr Dóla. 'I am not ungrateful for this room.'

'All I want is five minutes' chat with Ella.'

'No, that, I'm afraid, is not possible. I had to give her something to help her rest.'

'She can't be blotto yet?' Green looked around for the girl, and saw the deputy manager, standing in awe at her bedside.

Ella was unconscious. She lay on her back, her endless locks spread over the pillows. Between her body and the blankets was a clear three inches of air.

Astounded, Green and Dóla watched the motionless, floating form, waiting for a movement. Only the faintest breaths and a flickering pulse beneath the eyelids disturbed the apparition.

'I got to have a snapper,' whispered Green. He had never witnessed anything remotely like this, and excitement brought sweat out on his forehead.

'No photographs.'

'Come on. You got to see this to believe it.'

'It'll take too long. You'll just have to rely on your powers of description.'

'Let me talk to the ma, then.'

'She's not really in any state to be interviewed.'

'Stinking, is she?'

'Just shocked.'

'Joe, I don't think you understand. You owe me. And I need a deal.'

'Okay. Okay, I was saving this, but you can have it.' He pulled an envelope from his pocket and tipped ten strips of negative from it. 'Clarissa at my office can give you the lowdown to go with these. And you've got a major bargain here. I'm going to go bankrupt, giving stuff like this away.'

Green held one of the strips to the window. There were no images of Ella on it. There was a girl, but she was not Ella. She looked to be dark-haired and dark-skinned. She was wearing only underwear. There was a man with her. He was naked. A blurred bar obscured the left edge of each frame. These pictures had probably been shot through a window or a chink in a door. The couple did not know they were being photographed.

Green checked the next strip. The man was clutching the girl. His face was to the camera. The face, in negative, was hard to discern, but Barry Green could guess who it was.

This was the guru. The Viking. Ella's pal. Peter Guntarson.

CHAPTER THIRTY-TWO

Ella woke in her own bed. She had not lain there for a long while. She did not remember going to sleep there.

She did not remember going to sleep at all.

Light streamed around the edges of her curtains. She was wearing her clothes. These two things made her think she must be dead. This would be how it felt, being in a familiar place and unable to say why. Not knowing the time. And the inviting light, waiting to be greeted.

Ella was not afraid of the light. She would be glad to walk into it. She hopped out of bed and tugged the curtains aside.

In next-door's concreted yard, which offered the only view from her little window, four or five men in quilted anoraks pointed camera lenses like ships' cannons. She rested her hands on her windowsill, which dripped with condensation.

She heard Peter, shouting in the room below hers.

From the top of the stairs, she could make out his words. Ella was glad he was there. The world outside her home still seemed shrouded in a dream, and she could not recollect when she had last seen him. Or how they had parted. She listened.

'It's because of what you're after. Money, money, money, money. The more you want it, the less you'll have it. You imagine you're on a meal ticket. Ella is a ticket to something much bigger.'

'Don't tell me,' she heard José Dóla's mocking answer, 'don't tell me you're so saintly. Everybody knows what you're getting out of fame and fortune. They read it in the *Star*.'

'Greedy! You don't just want the money. You don't just want to cheat Ella out of every penny she deserves to have. You want to feel you've got some moral right too. Well, Dr Greed, I'll spell it out. My lifestyle hasn't changed just because I met Ella. I'm a single man. To your average *Daily Star* reader, who comes off worse here? Me, exercising my bachelor freedom? Or the dirty little blackmailer who spied on me, and took peeping-Tom pictures, and flogged them in the gutter for a nice fat profit?'

'I can assure you that not one penny was paid for that distasteful story.'

'Then you even managed to betray you own code of conduct. You gave something out for free.'

'You keep forgetting. I am making no money here. This has all been an investment of my time and expertise.'

'And you'll never see a return. There is an intelligence involved, of which you have no conception. A just intelligence. The more you yearn to squeeze money from Ella, the more wealth will flow out of your own pocket.'

'Oh, keep the voodoo to impress your girlfriends.'

'Think about it. How much money have you spent so far? What has this cost you? The harder you try, the harder you will hurt.'

'And who precisely dispenses this justice?'

'Who? I can tell you who *you* are. You're a blackmailer, an old-fashioned hypocrite of a blood-sucking blackmailer. A hundred years ago you would have stolen other people's secrets and sold your silence. Now you barter what you've stolen to the papers. It's still blackmail. If we are reincarnated, that is what you always have been. In every life. For thousands of years. A peddler in guilt.'

'As you are a peddler in bullshit.'

Ella had crept down the stairs. She stood at the edge of the doorway to the dining-room, where the men were, and where her Uncle Robert had tried to exorcise her. Juliette was along the passage, in the kitchen, sitting with her fists on her eyes.

The kitchen curtains were pulled shut, to keep out cameras.

'You all right, Mam?'

'Fine. Fine.'

'Why are we at home?'

'Because we live here. Put some water in that.' She handed Ella an empty tumbler. It smelled of drink. Ella rinsed it thoroughly.

'Peter and that man is arguing.'

'I can hear them.'

'Why's it dark in Frank's room?'

'What?'

'Frank's in his room and it's all dark.'

'I left him watching telly up there. It is not dark – I opened his curtains.'

Ella nodded. She was not anxious to contradict Juliette. But it felt strange. In all the rooms of the house, she could sense daytime. Except in Frank's. In Frank's room it seemed dark.

'Mam?'

'Yes. What?'

She could not say. She had to hold her mother's arm, and pull her away from the table, and lead her up the stairs to Frank's room.

The curtains were open and the TV was on. Frank was awake,

lying on his bed. Ella sat beside him and gave him a hug.

'Is Auntie Sylvie coming back?' he said.

'Why do you want Sylvie?' asked his mother.

'She said she'd make my headache go away.'

Frank's headaches, his sickness, his pallor, his headaches were no longer earning him sympathy. The symptoms got dismissed as the reaction of a boy whose sister is suddenly in the limelight and whose parents cannot see him every day.

No one supposed he was about to die of neglect.

Ella was hugging him. Her hair was getting in his mouth. He tried to wriggle away, but he wanted to keep hold of her too. The next time he spoke, he sounded very puzzled, the way all seven-year-olds are when they don't know the question to get the right answer.

'Mam. Mam, I can't see nothing.'

She caught him by the chin and forced his face up. His eyes stared blankly past her. She snapped her fingers in front of his face. Frank's hand searched blindly for hers.

Juliette seized her son by the chest and the head, wrapping her arms over him and dragged him towards the door.

Dr Dóla held her hand in the car. Juliette was weeping, the helpless, shivering tears of a woman who saw she was losing everything. She had been pushed into the back of the Bentley with a shawl over her shoulders and her face, and the boy was shoved in beside her. Ella wanted to follow but Dóla would not let her near the front door. He almost elbowed her away.

The chauffeur crawled out of Nelson Road, over the kerbs, behind the shunting press cars that cleared the way. Cameras were thrust at the windows. A steady stream of traffic tailed them, across the river, through the centre, following the signs for the Bristol Children's Hospital.

Dr Dóla murmured, 'You have to be brave. Be strong. For Frank's sake.' He looked out of the window as he said it. He could not look at Juliette. He could not keep his mind off Guntarson, either. 'It bewilders me,' he remarked, 'that a girl with such insight into people's minds can be so easily duped.'

Frank sat very stiff and still.

Outside the Hippodrome, at traffic lights, while the chauffeur's feet twitched on the pedals, Frank suffered a fit. His body rode up the seat and rocked sideways, knocking his head against the window. At first Juliette thought he was trying to drive the headache away and she told him, not unkindly, 'Don't do that, Frank.'

But his legs began to jerk and rip at the seat in front, and when she pulled his face to her, his jaw was locked. The tip of his tongue was caught on a tooth and blood leaked down his chin. His eyes were white. His breath came in grunts, as if the air was being beaten out of him.

Juliette was kneeling on her seat, shaking her son by the ribs and screaming at him to stop it, stop it. And then she turned to the privacy partition which protected the chauffeur from her and she hammered on the glass, screaming, 'Go! Drive! Help me!'

José Dóla had no knowledge of First Aid. He could no more control Juliette than she could control herself. All he was feeling, as he shrank from her flying arms and saw the red drool on the blind boy's face, was revulsion.

Ella crept downstairs to sit with Peter. He had shredded a copy of the *Daily Star* and it hung in tatters over the rim of a wastebasket. The newspapermen were pushing the bell and rattling the letterbox and tapping on the windows. Dr Dóla flight with Juliette and her son had excited them. Where was Ella? Had she dematerialised again? Did anyone know where to look for her? Or had she been abandoned, alone in the house?

Like someone who lived beside an airport or a foundry, Ella had learned not to hear the noise.

Guntarson looked at her. His face still burned from the argument with Dóla. 'What's the matter with your brother?' he asked bluntly. Then, making an effort to be more sympathetic, he added: 'I'm sure he's going to be all right.'

Ella was grateful. If Peter thought Frank would be okay, she could worry a bit less. Peter was as brainy as any doctor. But she knew his mind was not on Frank, or he would be sending mental notes of reassurance to her. It didn't matter. Frank was her brother. It was her job to worry about him.

Peter was worrying about that man. Something in one of the papers had caused it, she knew, but she wasn't going to look. She didn't care what the papers printed. She felt venomous anger radiating from Peter, and shut her mind against it. She didn't want to know about it when Peter was angry. All adults got angry, she understood that – she just didn't want to know about it right now. And she never wanted Peter to be angry at her. That would be the worst.

Still, she sat at the table, watching him pace. It helped to be near him. When he went to the kitchen, she silently followed. When he went abruptly upstairs, she waited.

The curtains were all drawn, against the besieging journalists. As she sat, silently staring at their folds, one curtain lifted slightly, as if the kitchen window had opened and a drought was blowing.

A beam of light, so thin it was no more than a hair-strand, shone through the chink onto Ella's face. The dust in the air made the light almost opaque, with a silvery aura. For just a few seconds it fell on her forehead, so focused it might have come from a laser. Then the curtain dropped back, cutting off the light.

After two hours of silence and no call from the hospital, Ella said: 'I wants to go on the telly.'

Guntarson stared at her. 'I wasn't thinking about that,' he answered in surprise.

'I weren't guessing what you was thinking.'

'But I expected . . .' Guntarson had been hoping for another idea to worm into her head. He had been focusing on it, waiting for it to drift across. Not transmitting the idea, just leaving it lying around, for her to pick up.

Guntarson was not used to hearing original thoughts from Ella. 'Why do you want to go on TV?'

'For Frank.'

'We don't know what's the matter with Frank.'

'He's got a thing in his head. Behind his eyes. I think it's blocking out all the light.'

'What kind of thing? Like a bone?'

She didn't know. She couldn't explain. She just wanted him to understand.

'A cancer?'

'I wants to go on the telly.'

'But why, what's the value? They're just holding you up as some kind of freak-show. If you ask to go on, that just encourages the wrong point of view.'

'It's for Frank.'

'Listen, what I was thinking, it's much better. People must learn to respect us. They have to be educated, now. And the best way . . .'

'If you can't sort it for me, Mr Dóla can.'

'You what!' Guntarson gawked. There was a stone of challenge in Ella's voice.

'He can get me on the telly, that's what he's paid for.'

'You damn well dare.'

'Then you do it.'

'All right. All right. That's what you want. You've done things for me. We're a team. I'll sort this for you. It's Sunday. There'll be some chatshow on one of the channels, bound to be. Whoever they've booked, they can kick off. Ella Wallis wants to go on television – Ella Wallis *goes* on television.'

Chapter Thirty-Three

Ella carried her black £200 Arai Rapide 3 motorcycle helmet proudly. It was another gift from Peter, and with her silver tresses tucked inside it she looked like a space-child. She followed Guntarson, through the doors to the security checkpoint at the BBC studios on Whiteladies Road. On the dark forecourt outside, cameras flickered like lightning.

The two women on the reception desk were itching to dive forward and seize her hands, tell her what an extraordinary gift she had, warn her about letting fame go to her head, get a treasured autograph. They held back. The security guard acknowledged her with a wink and a smile, but he too said nothing. The technicians and the canteen staff and the reporters crowded to the doorways and looked at her, but stayed away. They all had strict orders. Don't do anything, don't even whisper.

Only Hattie Maysfield was allowed to approach. Ella would know Hattie's face. She might even feel she knew Hattie. Everything that could be done to make Ella less nervous, must be done.

Even Karl, the producer, who had issued the instructions, kept his distance.

Hattie crossed the foyer, beaming. She wore gold whorls the size of saucers on her ears, and gold eyeshadow. One tooth in her glittering grin was gold. Thick, golden rings overlapped on her fingers. Her scarlet blouse was hooped in gold.

Her dark brown eyes in a rich brown face shone at Ella. Ella smiled back.

'You'll have to be a little patient with me,' Hattie whispered, clasping Ella's shoulders and brushing her cheek. 'I'm so nervous! I'm not used to interviewing *really special* people like you.'

After that Ella felt ready to tell Hattie anything.

Hattie Maysfield was one of the BBC's favourite reporters. Colleagues and viewers loved her. When Guntarson rang, to announce his protégé wanted to make an appearance, the receptionist transferred his call straight to Hattie. No one else deserved the task.

'Did you come by motorbike? Is this your driver? Hi Peter.'

'I seen you on the telly loads,' said Ella.

'Am I fatter in real life? You can't usually see my hips on the screen.' Ella giggled.

Peter, loosening the buckled throat of his leathers, glanced down at her. He did not ever remember hearing Ella giggle.

'Come on through here, there's all these corridors and one of them leads to a dressing room.' Ella followed briskly, clasping an oversized yellow envelope marked Clinical Radiology Unit. A sheet of film crackled inside it. She was full of energy. This appearance was her decision. She wanted to do this. It showed.

'We're going to record something. That way we can both "um" and "er" and make as many mistakes as we like, and it won't matter. No one'll see our bloomers.'

Ella giggled again.

Peter was not laughing. 'I wanted this to be live.'

'It would have been really hard to get the whole network to agree. Live television is always an unknown quantity. Even if Ella was the president of America and I was prime minister, they wouldn't just clear a slot for us. The best you could hope for is twenty minutes around midnight. And what if it takes us twenty minutes to relax? We just start chatting and click, it's goodnight and closedown.'

'I don't want to be on live,' said Ella.

'What? But you insisted . . .'

'Ella's right,' Hattie grinned. 'Smart potato.'

'So when is it broadcast? A month next Tuesday?'

'Tomorrow. Seven o'clock, probably. Half-an-hour, more if it's needed. Don't worry. You're getting Auntie Beeb's ultra-red carpet treatment. Trust me. I know. We are aware,' she added, 'I mean, we're flattered. That you chose the BBC. Let's face it, Oprah Winfrey would fly out here to do a personal interview and she wouldn't think twice. I'm glad you chose us and not Oprah.'

Guntarson stretched his legs out in the corner of a tiled, white dressing-room and stared at Ella as the make-up was dusted over her face. How nervous the make-up girl looked, he thought – almost too excited and scared to move the brush.

The tie between them had weakened yesterday. When her body vanished from the Oxford laboratory, she had not broken away from him, but she had strained at the bonds. Part of her had wanted to escape from him. And it was becoming daily more essential to Guntarson that Ella should be under his influence. Only his. Completely his.

And now she was chatting away to this presenter.

She should be distraught at her brother's blindness. Instead, she seemed to be drawing strength from it.

Guntarson watched her. He would not allow her to get away from him. He would not allow a gap as thick as a sheet of paper to open between them.

Hattie said, 'My cats were most surprised to see me setting off tonight. On a Sunday? They expect to be cosseted and stroked and fed bits of chicken all evening on a Sunday. Actually, now I think about it, they've been moody all day. Maybe they sensed something. All cats are psychic, aren't they?'

'What your cats called?'

'Helmutt and Helga. Do they sound like silly names to you?'

'Dunno.'

Guntarson saw Hattie's face, and smirked. 'Did you think this would be easy?' he thought. 'Did you suppose you could turn on instant rapport? Now you know why Ella needs me.'

Ella was still thinking about the question. 'If I was a cat, it'd be lush, having names like that.'

Thick ice glazed Guntarson's blue eyes. His stare remained frozen on Ella.

'Got any pets?'

'No. My dad won't let me. The woman 'cross the road's got a cat though. I feed that sometimes.'

'I think,' said Guntarson, 'we might find a way of getting you a pet now.'

'Really? Honest?' For a moment she was almost bounding out of her seat at him. Then she remembered the envelope of black X-ray film in her lap. Getting her own cat hardly mattered, compared to that.

The X-rays had come from the hospital. It had been Ella's idea. To obtain it, Guntarson had tried threats, flattery and cajoling, applied randomly to anyone who would come to the phone on a busy Sunday afternoon at the Bristol Children's Hospital. At last Guntarson stepped aside and allowed Ella to make the attempt, and with a gentle plea to a doctor she was successful at once.

The doctor had seen Frank. With the same gentleness that Ella had spoken to him, he tried to tell her how it was with Frank.

Guntarson sent a taxi to collect the film. They did not step out of 66 Nelson Road until nearly 7 pm.

It was Hattie who suggested letting Guntarson onto the set. 'He doesn't have to answer the questions. But would you feel happier, having a friend next to you?'

'Yeah,' said Ella, nodding hard. 'Peter's my friend.'

Ella took the middle of the sofa, and Guntarson the far end. Hattie, in a high-backed swivel chair on castors, faced them. Hattie's interview arena had been designed to resemble an office, with a desk and a

hatstand and a year-planner pinned behind her. All this paraphernalia
had been removed, to establish a less formal air. Now, the seats looked
bizarre, as if they had come from a charity furniture shop.

Ella tucked the yellow envelope at her side. She had told Hattie she
had something to show viewers. That was the whole reason for her to
be there. But they would not talk about it at first, Hattie explained.
They could build up to it. First of all, they would talk about Ella.

Hattie wanted to know what levitation was like. She made a joke
of it – no one could imagine a big girl like her floating away, could
they? Anyway, her earrings would weigh her down. So how did Ella
feel when it started to happen?

The interview had no formal beginning. There were no announce-
ments, none of the spiel that had terrified Ella at Network Europe.
Red lights winked on the cameras but they stayed well away. Peter
was sitting beside her, arms spread wide, legs crossed, head drawn
back into his neck. She felt safe to talk.

'I can't usually tell when it's starting,' she said. 'Normally, I'm asleep
or something.'

'It happens in your sleep? Aren't you scared you might fly out of
the window, and wake up in the clouds?'

'No!' She was giggling. Everyone treated her levitations as something holy, to be spoken of with reverence. Ella knew people laughed
about her behind her back. People always had done. But no one had
made jokes to her face before.

'Do you like it when you're floating?'

'It don't feel bad or nothing. It's just like, the whole world's really
heavy and I ain't. I don't feel weighed down. Sometimes, I can think,
"I want to go over there" and I just sort of drift. I can feel almost like
a breeze round me then, or when there's a current in the sea. Most the
time, I don't know what's happening. Peter can hypnotise me, or I'm
asleep, and I start dreaming. I suppose unless I get woke up, I don't
never know it happened.'

'Do your dreams wake you?'

'There's one dream. Sometimes I seem to have it when I've just woke
up. It's always like I'm remembering something what really happened.
I think I must of been really little. I ain't never thought of this before.
I ain't told nobody, not even Peter.'

He was sitting forward. He asked, 'Why?'

'Just forgot about it. It's not like a story or nothing. It's just lights.
I see these three round lights. They're all going round, and then they
start going round each other, and they get really fast. And then they
roll up into one light, really bright, and I wake up. But they ain't real.'

'What do you mean?'

'They make the room really bright. Like, you know when there's a fire and everything goes all wavy in the hot air. Things look like that. But the light's only in my room. Even if my door's open, it don't shine out. So nobody else don't see it. But it were real once. I think there really were these lights, I saw them when I was maybe two. Or three. Like, really small.'

Peter rested his hand on hers and told her, 'That's the force. That's the intelligence. The entity which actually gives you the power. You can see it.'

Ella looked uncomfortable. Her hand, under the warm weight of his, stayed still, but her toes twisted on the studio floor.

'Peter knows about it. I don't,' she muttered. 'Like, he can tell me, why it's happening to me, and not him. He can explain it, make it proper and plain. I can't. I understand it when he says. I do. But then later, I can't keep all the ideas in my head.'

'All of Ella's life,' said Guntarson, 'people have told her she doesn't understand things. So when she really wants to get to grips with the facts, she's afraid that she can't. It's a confidence thing. She's actually one of the most intelligent people I've ever met. Honestly. You are, Ella.' He squeezed her hand and let it go. She was scarlet. He patted her head. 'Fantastically focused mind in there.'

'Why do *you* think these powers have come to you? And not Peter?' asked Hattie. She made a small motion with one gleaming hand, to damp Guntarson down and give Ella space.

'I think . . . Peter says it's like I'm the car but he's the engine. It looks like I'm moving on my own, but really I wouldn't be going nowhere without him.'

'Ella,' cut in Guntarson, 'is a message. A living message. And it is up to the world to listen. We don't know quite what that message is yet, so we've got to listen hard, to understand. I believe it is imperative we get to grips with her message quickly. Her phenomenon already has worldwide implications, and it's obvious to anyone that her message is of global import.'

Guntarson was speaking rapidly now, spitting his words out to the camera. 'All of this is confirmed by the Bible Code – quite fascinating. By subjecting the original Hebrew text of the Bible's first five books to a computer code, mathematical patterns can be identified among the configurations of letters. Prophesies emerge, foretelling everything from Alexander the Great to the Third Reich, even the Gulf War. Even,' and his voice sank, 'the threat of Armageddon.'

Hattie tried to silence him, but Ella was staring at Guntarson and a forcible interruption now might create a hostile atmosphere. So Hattie let him talk. If the man would not shut up now, the editor's scalpel would silence him later.

'The decoded book of Exodus,' he was saying, 'connects the word

Diana – this is incredible but the proof is irrefutable – it connects Diana with "car accident" and "death". The Princess of Wales's tragedy was prophesied at the dawn of history. Even the year was named: 5757; which corresponds in the Jewish calendar to 1997 AD.

'And so,' Guntarson drove on, 'by using "Ella" as a keyword, the Book of Genesis – which God is supposed to have dictated letter by letter to Moses – turned up the phrases "beyond this world" and "our regeneration", "prayer" and "hope", "angelic" and "international". In other words, Ella's whole mission was prophesied, thousands of years ago, in the world's holiest book.

'The coming of the millennium is certainly not without relevance here. In fact, the Bible Code speaks clearly of a doomsday in the very near future, and it is my belief Ella may have been chosen or sent to prevent precisely that. The doomsday scenario. I truly believe Ella can save the world.

'In fact – do you know what her name means in Hebrew? Goddess. Ella is Goddess. Break it into two parts, El-La: El is their word for God. And La means, "to her". That's to say, her name means, "God To Her". "God is given to this girl." In Arabic, the almost identical word, "Lillah," mean's "for God," or, "to God". Now, do you think her parents were aware of that when they chose the name? Somehow I doubt it.

'Oh, you can look at me like that. What do you know? Has your whole life, like mine, been reaching for this point?' He was speaking lightly. 'I know no one will give the faintest credence to my words. I have resolved not to care. It's better to speak the truth. But you can't hide the scepticism and cynicism on your face, and that is why it is time for Ella to become something more than a performing sea lion for the media's amusement.'

'Ella,' asked Hattie, 'you tell me. In your own words. What do you think?'

'Yeah. I think Peter's right. I don't want to be just in the papers for being weird all the time. I don't like that.'

'But what about your psychic, mystical, whatever? Where does that come from?'

'It's like what Peter says.' Ella was growing less and less happy. The cameras had crept closer. She liked Hattie, but she didn't like this conversation. It whirled around her without making sense. 'I can't explain none of it proper. But I know now that it's really important. I didn't used to know. But I got this really strong feeling, like inside of me.'

'Now, all of a sudden, you've found yourself thrust into the spotlight. Famous. How are you coping with that?'

'It's okay.'

'Do you enjoy it?'

Ella shook her head. 'I want to say about Frank,' she whispered to Guntarson.

'There's been a lot of stress on your family. Does it upset you, seeing all this stuff about your mum and dad in the papers?' Hattie was keeping her tone as sympathetic as she could, but she knew she was falling into the trap of hurling questions at a girl who did not know how to answer. Ella simply said she did not read the papers. She had stopped looking at Hattie's face.

In the dressing-room, Ella had talked a little about her father. She had said there was an argument before he left, and she seemed to blame herself for the split. Hattie wanted to get back to that. Her own parents had separated when she was small, and she knew about the guilt. How Ella would feel her family was being punished for her own failings.

But they were drifting a long way from the heart-to-heart that Hattie wanted.

'Do you miss school? Your friends? I bet you don't miss homework.'

Guntarson said, 'I intend engaging private tutors. Of course there's no question of her returning to the classroom.'

That man was blocking her. No-one could get close to Ella while that man was there. Inviting him on set had been a bad error.

'My brother Frank's blind,' Ella blurted.

'Frank? Is this the thing you wanted to talk about? What's that you brought along?'

Ella scrabbled to pull out the sheet of film. 'He went blind today. He's been being sick. And he's got headaches. My mum took him to hospital. She got an X-ray. He's blind and he might die.'

Chapter Thirty-Four

Hattie had not been warned. They had told her, Ella had a purpose behind the interview, but not what that purpose was. 'You've got the X-ray there – can we see that? If I hold it up to the light, can the camera see it? And this is . . .?'

'It's Frank's face,' said Ella, leaning off the sofa. Her anxious enthusiasm rushed back. What she was going to say was so important. 'Here's his eyes, the dark bits, they don't X-ray proper. And his nose, his teeth – see, the hard bits show up better.' She was pointing.

'Frank's seven. His birthday ain't till April. Everyone says he don't look like me, but he does, a bit. Only he's much more like a boy than I am, I mean, he's always on his bike and stuff. And Dad lets him get away with stuff more. 'Cos he's a boy.'

'You obviously love him a lot.'

'He's my brother. Only when I went to London, he had to stay at school and live with Auntie Sylvie. And he starts getting these headaches. And my mum thought it was just Auntie Sylvie was giving him too many cakes and biscuits.' Ella was spilling her words out, and making every statement sound like a question. 'Only then he has these fits.'

'And he's losing his sight?'

'He woke up today and he couldn't see nothing, but he didn't say. He waited for us to find out.'

'Do the doctors know what's wrong?'

'I could sort of feel what it was, I could feel his headache and I knew it was dark in his head but I didn't know why. But then I got this cold feeling behind my eyes' – she thrust her thumb and forefinger against her eyelids – 'and it's this.'

She rubbed her fingertip on a white blur in the centre of the X-ray. 'It's hard and it feels like its got sharp points. Like, did you ever see a piece of coral? From the sea? It feels like that in my head.'

'You can feel,' asked Hattie, 'what's making Frank ill? But you're not going blind?'

'I am blind when I'm seeing in his head. That's why I know it's dark.' She shrugged. She could not explain. Anyhow, that part did not matter. 'The doctors, they don't know if they can operate.'

'What is this white thing? The coral?'

'You know,' said Ella. 'Cancer.'

'In his brain?' A stupid response, but what was she supposed to say?

'If they try and cut it out, he's always going to be blind. It might even kill him. They say it's growed very fast. It's going to grow more. That's what his headaches is, this thing getting bigger and pressing in his head. And that's why.'

Hattie was shocked by the brutality of the X-ray. Ella's little brother was very sick. Ella could feel the sickness, but did she know how serious this was? If what she said was right, Frank might be dead within a few days. Did Ella understand that?

'That's why,' Ella repeated.

'Why what? Why you've come today?'

'Why I got powers,' whispered Ella. 'To make Frank better. That's why it's got to be me and not Peter. 'Cos he can't see in Frank's head. He can't feel it. He ain't going to know when it's gone.'

'You think you can make the cancer disappear?' There was awe in Hattie's voice. No disbelief.

'It would all make sense then. All the floating, and the dreams and voices and stuff. 'Cos up till now – that's why people don't know what to think. Even if things happen to them and they have to believe in it, they don't know what to think 'cos it don't have no meaning. And everything in life's got a meaning. Well, if Frank gets well again, that's the point. That's what it all means.'

Ella had been thinking about it all day. She knew what she was trying to say, but even she was surprised when it came out the way she intended.

'How can you make him well?'

Ella was sitting straight with her hands clasped. Her face was firm and earnest. She was going to get this right.

'It ain't just me. It's everybody. When I was on the telly last week – right? – people watching got the same powers as me. That's true. Peter said so. People just started floating, and things disappeared and stuff. So that's because of something about the telly.'

'How do you mean?' asked Peter. Ella had never talked like this, trying to explain.

'It don't happen when I meets people. Like Hattie. Just 'cos if I leveltate, don't mean she does. But if it's on the telly, she might.'

'That's true,' nodded Guntarson, acting as if the concept had occurred to him before. 'The psychic power is not bestowed on people around you, but it is transferred to television viewers. That collective energy activates the powers.'

'I wants everyone watching,' pursued Ella, 'I wants them to help. I wants them all to pray.'

'Pray for Frank,' Hattie repeated.

'Don't matter how they prays. 'Cos everyone believes something different, don't they? They can be Evangelkle or Catholic, even something what's Moslem or something – it's the prayer what matters. We got to pray that Frank's cancer goes. 'Cos otherwise he's always going to be blind. And he's only really young.'

'Do you want to say a prayer aloud?'

'I ain't no good at that. My dad does that. I just want to pray inside my heart. Everybody concentrate really hard. Get a picture in your head and concentrate on it. A picture of what you really wants to happen. Like, Frank can see. Frank's well. Get that picture, that's what's going to happen. You got to really focus on it.'

She clamped her eyes shut. The cameras watched her still, pale face. Hattie too closed her eyes. Golden circles of eyeshadow hung like pennies on her face. Guntarson bowed his head and folded his hands, like an uncomfortable Christmas church-goer.

Ella bunched her body tightly and held her clenched fists beside her face. She desperately wanted to float. She knew that was what people wanted to see. She wanted them to be rewarded for watching her and believing, so that they would believe even more. So that they would pray harder. To cure Frank.

Beyond the studio, behind the monitors, the producer was the first to be sure of what they were seeing. Hattie and Guntarson had closed their eyes, and the cameramen, watching through viewfinders, were too close to be certain at once. But the monitors showed it clearly. Ella's head and shoulders were radiating light.

The studio lights were dimmed at the producer's order. The effect grew by the second. Ella was surrounded by brilliance. Light shone from her silver hair like strong sunlight off the sea, and her face was flooded with radiance.

Her face was upturned, and with a sigh she lifted from the cushions into the air. Her limbs relaxed and stretched slightly, but the intensity of her prayer was still displayed in the way she held her hands – balled, quivering, clutching with all her strength at Frank's last hope.

The last lamp in the studio was extinguished. All the light came from Ella. The shimmering glow surrounded her like a star blazing beneath her skin. Like a fiery orb descended from the heavens upon her. Like a halo.

Frank woke from a sixteen-hour sleep, about forty-five minutes after the interview was broadcast. He had no recollection of where he was. His headache had gone.

One of the nurses told him, around 9 pm, that his sister had been on television and had asked everyone to pray for his recovery. 'And you know,' said the nurse, 'you're a very lucky boy. Lucky that someone cares so much for you. After all, it might work. Prayers do work, I can tell you that. And she's certainly got something, your sister. It's not all just clever public relations. I can tell you something else, too:

'Five minutes after that programme finished, there's a little girl in the wards who's been in and out of here ever since she was born, with cerebral palsy. Spastic, you'd call her. Her parents, they're lovely people, and it breaks their hearts to see their little lassie like that, but there's some things you can't do very much for. Not everything's got a cure, even in this day and age. So what do you think? She's sitting up with her toys, not one hour ago, and she rolls onto her tummy and starts wriggling along. She's halfway down the corridor before anyone spots her. And when the orderly picks her up, she can't stop the giggles.' There were tears on the nurse's face, tears she had not shed in a hospital for more than twenty years. She smeared them away with a rub of her rough sleeve, and said, 'Now this is a girl who hasn't been able to lift up her head or make one sound you could understand. Just like that, she starts crawling. I ask you – if that's not a miracle, what is? And if it can happen to her, who's to say it won't happen to you?'

'Can I watch television?' asked Frank.

'No you cannot! What time do you think it is? The best thing you can do is go straight back to sleep and wake up for breakfast like a good boy. But I suppose you want to see your big sister on the programme, is that it? Well, maybe someone has video'd it.'

She stopped at the next child's bed and turned around. 'And what would you want with looking at a television?'

She cupped his face gently in her hands. 'Frank?'

He stared intently back.

'Holy blessed Mary! You can see me, can't you?' And she ran shrieking for a doctor.

Ella prayed on Sunday. The world watched, and prayed with her, on Monday. Dr Dóla obtained the new set of X-rays and sold them both to Reuters news agency on Tuesday.

On Wednesday morning, *The Times* carried the images across the full eight columns of its front page. Two X-rays, side by side, the time and date of each burned into the top corner. On the left, an image which twenty-nine million people in Britain alone had seen and which was viewed by maybe a billion more as the BBC syndicated the interview and projected it over the earth to the satellite stations of one hundred nations. It was a picture of a seven-year-old boy's skull, oval and symmetrical and missing two milk teeth. And stamped between the eyes with a white cancer the size of a watch face.

The second X-ray was identical, but without the cancer. The smudge on the black film, like one of death's white fingerprints, had been wiped away.

The impact of Frank's miracle was muffled by other events in the hospital that evening. Things happened which the staff had never dared hope for, and could scarcely believe. Doctors at first were reluctant to contact parents, for fear the breath-taking changes in child after child might evaporate as quickly as they occurred.

Some of the children had watched Ella's interview. One of the girls, a smiling, talkative creature with grey shadows ringing her eyes and a tartan bobble-cap covering the baldness of her chemotherapy, was lifted into the air. She lay with her head back and her eyes rolled back, and had to be clasped around the waist and drawn back to the floor by her friend. There was great excitement at the sight, and when the child woke from her trance she was filled with more energy than she had been for months. But no one suspected there might have been a cure.

Almost a day later she was given a blood test. Her leukaemia, it transpired, was in complete remission. As if it never had been there.

'It might have been the drugs,' the specialist reminded her parents. 'That's what they're designed for – curing cancer.' But her mother, holding the doctors hands and thanking him again and again, her cheeks varnished with tears, said: 'It was that girl. That Ella. When she was on television, praying, I was praying so hard with her. I said to myself, "Okay. I can pray for her little brother. Of course I'd like him to get better. But next to Suki, I don't really care about any of the other children." It wasn't very nice, but it's true. I didn't. When your own child's ill, nothing else matters.

'I made a deal in my head. I'd pray for the little boy, if part of her prayers went to help Suki. I've been praying ever since, I was up all night. I made my husband sit up with me. I just really felt it would work. I *believed* it.'

The specialist nodded. For twenty-three years he had been asking parents to have faith. To pray. Miracles did happen. He had never seen a malignant tumour vanish from a child's skull, the way it had happened to Frank Wallis. But he had seen crippled children walk, and dying children live. Sometimes, occasionally. This wouldn't be the first time.

'I'm glad,' was all he could say.

The specialist did not want to get caught up in the euphoria. He was afraid of seeing cures where none had happened, and aggravating illnesses by imagining they were cured. He treated colleagues with suspicion when a teenage victim of a hit-and-run driver came out of his six-week coma. He was sceptical when they told him about the girl with shrapnel wounds – she had been flown from Bosnia, after a landmine had torn off her legs. The shock had worked steadily on her kidneys, and in the afternoon she had been close to death. By the morning, her kidneys were functioning normally, and appeared to be whole again.

But when the bandages were changed on a baby boy's face and his skin cancer was gone, as if it had been peeled off – then the specialist sat in the half-lit ward, beside the cot, with the sleeping infant in his arms, and wept himself, and began thanking God for miracles.

Letters, *The Times*, Wednesday, January 27 to Friday, January 29:

From Dr A Y Henver

Sir, Without in any way wishing to dissuade the credulous from their self-fulfilling fantasies of renewed health in the aftermath of the 'psychic schoolgirl' television appearance, I feel I must protest at the ludicrously stage-managed so-called phenomena which formed the climax to that questionable broadcast.

It was no surprise to see the studio lights turned off as the pretence at 'levitation' commenced; after all, it would not do for viewers to detect the wires which must undoubtedly have held La Wallis in that semi-comic suspension.

However, the absurd conceit of creating an artificial halo around the girl's dangling form was worse than pretentious; it bordered on the blasphemous. There can be no doubt that the effect was produced by camera trickery, or even by the crude means of daubing the child in phosphorus. The halo is a visual metaphor for sanctity, especially relevant to the Christian faith. It is particularly associated with the Blessed Virgin, the Mother of God, and indeed with the Infant Himself. Were the whole business of Ella Wallis and her theatricals not so manifestly bogus, it would be offensive, and the Broadcasting Complaints Commission shall certainly be hearing from me.

Yours faithfully,

Dr A Y HENVER, (Secretary, Society for the Observation of Anomalous Phenomena), Cirencester. January 26.

From Dr Niall Jameson

Sir, Those correspondents who assume (Letters, Wednesday, January 27) that a halo cannot be naturally produced by the human body are quite wrong. The evidence for this lies not only in the legends of Christianity and the traditions of its art, but in attested medical investigations.

Put simply: under certain circumstances, human skin glows. The 'glow' of good health, brisk exercise, true love and pregnancy is, of course, so common as to be not a phenomenon at all. The more spectacular radiance of the ecstatic is much less frequently seen but is nonetheless a matter of fact, not invention. Doubters may examine the archives of this newspaper (*The Times*, May 5, 1934) for a report from a Milanese correspondent of how moving film had been shot of the Luminous Woman of Pirano.

The Luminous Woman was no circus freak. She was a devoutly religious person whose beliefs had taken on an obsessive character. Dr Protti of the University of Padua investigated her case, and put forward a theory that the intensity of her credo was affecting her physiological make-up.

Fear causes adrenaline to flow, and the heartbeat to increase. It is very difficult to will one's heart to beat more quickly; it is even harder to slow it when one is scared. Extreme fear can cause much more striking changes – the overnight bleaching of hair, for instance. This is well known. What Dr Protti suggested was that other emotions could produce analogous effects.

Protti believed that the Pirano woman's strict fasts, which were devotional, caused her glands to produce an excess of sulphides. This theory was supported by the appearance of dark marks on her skin wherever she wore silver jewellery. Sulphides become luminous when exposed to ultra-violet light.

As we all know, blood can be radiant – that 'glow' of good

health and warm exercise. When the heartbeat increases, the blood flows faster, and the radiance increases. This radiance is ultra-violet.

When excess sulphides are present in the skin and the blood begins racing, the effect is inevitable. A halo forms. The skin can appear impossibly bright. In this way many human auras can be explained.

In Ella Wallis's case, it is evident from her build that she is not a great eater. Whether she fasts, we have not been told, but the casual observer might almost wonder whether her waif-like thinness is a symptom of some eating disorder, such as anorexia. We do not know, either, if her heartbeat increases during her levitations; hopefully, serious experiments will soon be conducted. At any rate, the possibility cannot be ruled out that the Luminous Woman of Pirano and the Radiant Schoolgirl of Bristol demonstrate the same signs of a mild physiological disorder.

Yours etc,

Dr NIALL JAMESON Trinity College, Dublin. January 27.

From Mr Geoffrey Hendrik

Sir, The simple and evident solution to the Ella Mystery is unfortunately regarded by modern society as 'politically incorrect'. The idea that this female is a witch – a practitioner of magic, as primitive as pagan blood sacrifices – must surely have occurred to many who dare not speak out for fear of incurring the vituperative hostility of the Feminist Brigade.

I understand that her family – who are ironically good Christian people – feared at first the girl was possessed by demons and took steps to 'cast them out'. This, unfortunately, will not work in the case of someone who is actively working with and encouraging the demons. It is not then a case of mere possession: it is collusion. In short, witchcraft.

Ella Wallis's eagerness to exploit her disturbing abilities by putting on a public show makes her true nature very clear. She wishes to profit from her devilry. It is no surprise to read this morning that her business manager, Mr Guntarson, intends installing her as the head of some commune or cult, from which she will be able to issue her prophesies and to which, no doubt, the gullible will be encouraged to donate all their money. There is but one way to designate her; as a witch.

Yours sincerely,

Mr GEOFFREY HENDRICK, Cheddar. January 27.

From the Countess of Bannockburn.

Sir, How delighted I was to read your correspondent's view that human luminosity has a simple, natural explanation (Letters, January 28). I daresay in the Middle Ages, thunder and lightning were held to be inexplicable, supernatural phenomena. No doubt in months or years to come, science will be able to explain levitation and faith-healing in equally clear-cut terms, and then we shall all look pretty silly for making such a fuss about a rather dim, provincial schoolgirl.

Yours Faithfully,

BANNOCKBURN, House of Lords. January 28.

From Miss Amy Roberts,

Sir, Like most of the country, and probably half the world, I have been absorbed and entertained and agog as the Ella Wallis story unfolded. I compared far-fetched theories with friends, I expanded the little story of my own phenomenon (a disappearing, reappearing pencil) into a full scale epic, I took to buying three or four newspapers each morning and swapping them with colleagues to ensure we none of us missed the smallest snippet.

You can imagine the atmosphere of cheerful excitement when my mother, my sister and I sat down at seven o'clock on Monday to see Ella's latest appearance.

Our attitudes changed forever when she asked us to pray for her sick brother, Frank.

My own brother is an invalid. He is also called Frank. He was born with Downs Syndrome, what my classmates used to call a Mongol. When we held each others' hands and closed our eyes to pray for Frank Wallis, the image of Frank Roberts inevitably came into our heads. Our Frank's condition is genetic. It is caused by a chromosome disorder, and nothing can cure it. But we prayed for him anyway.

On Wednesday morning *The Times* printed the X-ray pictures

which proved Frank Wallis's cancer had vanished, but by then
my family was past being amazed. The overnight change in our
own Frank had drained us of every ounce of amazement. The
hospice where he lives called us early on Tuesday to beg us to
come and visit him. They were sorry they had not called earlier,
but there were seven similar cases – seven! – and there simply
had been no chance to contact us earlier.

We rushed around. The Frank who greeted us was the most
wonderful blessing I could ever have prayed for. He looked the
same, of course. No more tidily dressed, no slower with a smile
and a hug. He is Downs, and Downs is chromosomes, and
nothing can change that.

But the *pain* had gone. The pain and the frustration, which
had always been present and which, I suppose, the rest of us
had learned not to see, that pain was gone. How do you describe
it? As though a malignant electricity generator inside his body
had been switched off. When he spoke, he was not fighting
himself for words any more. When he stood, there were no
spasms in his legs to make him grimace. His hands were open
and still, not flexing and bunching themselves into fists, the
way they always had. A peace has settled inside him.

My tears are wetting the paper as I write. For the first time in
his life – can you imagine it? I can't. A whole life of torture and
now – the pain has gone.

All because of Ella's prayers.

She is much more than an entertainment to my family now.
She is a benefactor, a miracle worker. A saviour. I truly believe
she is the closest thing to an angel that ever lived on the earth.
Perhaps that is just what she is – an angel. Sent by God.

Yours sincerely,

Miss AMY ROBERTS, Chester. January 28.

PART THREE

CHAPTER THIRTY-FIVE

It was ten months before Ella was interviewed again. She became more famous every day, but she did not speak to a journalist for 303 days. As more and higher barricades were built around her, she ceased speaking almost to anyone. Only Guntarson.

She did not watch herself on the Hattie Maysfield interview, and ten months later she did not read the account by Aliss Holmes of their meeting. But later, when she looked back, it seemed to Ella as if the two interviews stood like bridgeheads on opposite sides of her life. In the chasm between, her voice was taken from her. Her mute image was delivered to the public in a series of carefully arranged packages. Her messages were supplied by Peter Guntarson.

Guntarson became the figure of international importance he had always desired to be. Power was piled into his arms so fast he could hardly keep hold of it all. But this story is not about Guntarson; it is Ella's story, so the mere facts of those ten months will suffice:

On January 26, the day after Frank is cured, Guntarson announces Ella will be making no statements personally. Whatever she has to say, she will say through him. She is dispensing with José Dóla.

In Wolverhampton, Ian Richards, aged nine, overcomes severe autism to speak to his parents for the first time. In Oban, baby Callum McCloud's disfiguring facial birthmark disappears.

On January 27, the house in Nelson Road is under siege from well-wishers, journalists, people on crutches and in wheelchairs, pilgrims with desperate prayers, cranks. Dr Dóla claims he still represents Juliette Wallis, as she and Frank fly out of Bristol airport to Schiphol, Amsterdam, for rest and healing at an unknown destination.

Psoriasis sufferer Aubrey Trace of Gibraltar claims he could feel his skin condition melt away as he prayed with Ella. In Toronto, Nina Setton, paralysed by a stroke four years before, regains sensation in her left side. In Reading's Royal Berks Hospital, Sharma Shabnam, aged nine, watches her first-degree body burns vanish as her parents pray by her bedside.

By January 28, the Maysfield interview has been broadcast in fifty-eight countries. In many it is rescreened repeatedly. The X-rays of

Frank's skull have appeared in more than 1,000 publications, and the children's hospital has made more than a million pounds from royalties on the copyright.

On the 29th, Guntarson declares life in the tiny family home has become unbearable for Ella. Security guards bar every door and window, and scuffle constantly to prevent break-ins. Chippings are hammered from the brickwork day and night, for souvenirs. Ella has blacked out her bedroom windows and is afraid to walk down the stairs. Police roadblocks seal off the roads around Nelson Road, police motorbikes rend the air and police horses dirty the streets. No Derby match between the Bristol teams, City and Rovers, has ever generated such intense security as this vast tide of pilgrims to a fourteen-year-old girl's front door.

Ambulances are everywhere, bringing the desperate to within a few hundred feet of Nelson Road. Every hotel and boarding house for thirty miles around is fully booked. Bristol's airport has to double its staff to contend with the surge in traffic.

Ella's images are painted on flagstones and walls across the city, a stick figure with long hair and angel's wings. Slogans are spray-painted or scrawled in coloured chalks: 'Ella is real'.

Guntarson appeals for a benefactor to provide a safe, practical retreat for Ella. Seven thousand offers are received from around the world.

In Auckland Keanu Frayling, a thirteen-year-old spina bifida patient, announces he has been reborn after praying with Ella. His new name is Frank Ella Peace. He does not have spina bifida.

By January 30 a World Wide Web site on the Internet, set up to record reports of healing, lists 156,000 cases from media reports and eMail postings. Website records showed seven million hits a day – more hits than the Mars landing, more hits even than *Playboy*. The Post Office's sorting office in Kent Street, Bedminster, unable to deliver to 66 Nelson Road, holds 193 post-sacks of mail. This mountain of fan letters, thank you letters, donations and appeals for help doubles in size every two days.

On February 1 Guntarson takes Ella to a sprawling house in Leigh Woods, a secluded suburb across the Avon Gorge from Bristol. The building is permanently loaned by a businessman who also owns a castle in Scotland, a mansion in Paris and a football team; he and his family will be permitted to meet Ella on occasions when she is strong enough.

The house – though noone but Juliette remembers – is less than one hundred yards from the place where Sylvie's baby lies buried and hidden.

Guntarson launches The Ella Foundation. 'Our aim is to protect and to help,' says the press release. 'To protect everyone who prays with Ella, from sharks and scoundrels, from profiteers and false prophets. To help people use the healing power and cure the sickness in their lives.'

The security guards – there are more of them than ever at the new house – are ordered to identify the most persistent pilgrims and photograph them. Not media men – just the fans, the devotees. Guntarson examines about twenty faces on film and asks for seven of them – four girls, three teenage boys – to be brought to him. They are offered jobs inside the house, cleaning, cooking and sorting mail. All accept, and are required to sign a non-disclosure, confidentiality contract prohibiting them from revealing any detail of the Foundation for 101 years.

Within a week, while a fortune in donations languishes in untouched post-sacks, four more recruits are brought in to open letters.

Around the perimeter, innumerable mobile broadcast units are ready for breaking news. Transmitters are turned to satellites that can relay live images of this house to every inch of the globe. Many of the journalist are veterans of the OJ Simpson stakeout and trial, and they all agree the Ella phenomenon dwarfs everything.

Ella appears on the front covers of *Newsweek* and *Time* simultaneously. Twice. One edition of each is a 'stand-alone', entirely devoted to Ella. It is an unknown accolade.

From *Newsweek*, March 29:

Prayer is Power – How Your Message To God Becomes Ella's Message To the World

Who believes in God? Who is God anyway? Is my God the same as your God and, if not, are they on speaking terms?

Most of us admit we don't know. Those who say they do know tend to be fundamentalists – put any three of them in a room and logic dictates that at least two of them must be completely wrong.

But there's one thing about God we all do believe: He's listening. And He's answering our prayers.

A *Newsweek* telephone survey of 750 people two years ago revealed eighty-seven per cent of us believed in prayer power. A similar survey run this week returned a phenomenal 99.6 per cent hit rate. Just three of those questioned said they did not believe prayer could make any difference to their lives. And, who knows, by the time you read this they may have been converted.

What is incredible is that only twenty-nine per cent of these
people counted themselves as devout. The rest admitted they
had not prayed regularly during their lives, had skipped church
or the synagogue or the mosque or the shrine or the temple,
had never really believed there was an actual, for-real God
somewhere out there. And they're still not sure.

The paradox is clear, but no one seems to care. What matters
is the Ella Factor, the Ella Effect. People know prayer works,
because they see what happens when Ella Wallis prays and
when they pray with her. Good results. Miracles. That's what
prayers have always been supposed to deliver.

At the turn of the year, Ella Wallis was unknown. Six weeks
ago, she was known but not understood – even her psi-guru,
Peter Guntarson, admitted he had no idea what her message
was supposed to be.

PRAYER IS POWER. We all know it now. And now that we
know it, what are we going to do with it?

On February 4 Guntarson makes his first TV appearance alone. Ella,
he says, is too exhausted to travel. She is not sick, but drained by the
demands on her psychic reserves. She does not regret anything, he
insists. She is overwhelmingly happy that so much good can come
from sharing her prayers. But she is tired. The public must not expect
too much of her.

The Ella Foundation, says Guntarson, will not make profits.
No sponsors, no endorsements. But running costs will be huge,
and everyone is invited to contribute, by investing in Healing
Shares. These shares will not pay a cash dividend – but spiritual
dividends are guaranteed. In many, many thousands of cases,
explains Guntarson, renewed health is the dividend which has been
already paid.

Surplus finances will be ploughed into every kind of prayer
programme – prayer initiatives in hospitals, in research, in schools.
Why should there not be an Ella Prayer Hospital, where conventional
medicine can work alongside miracle cures? As Director of The Ella
Foundation, Guntarson's ambitions are limitless. Ella, he says, shares
the vision. He employs a team of fifteen lawyers and accountants to
run his finances.

Hundreds of companies are pleading for Ella's endorsement on their
products, for Ella's face in their commercials and on their billboards.
Guntarson refuses them, as he refuses the top movie studios who bid

for her life story. No fee could be enough to justify cheapening the Ella miracle.

By March, the house has been made secure. An electrified fence runs inside the perimeter wall. Guards with mastiffs, Rottweilers and German shepherd dogs patrol the arc-lit grounds. Guntarson arrives and leaves only by helicopter. Ella does not leave at all. Workers at the Ella Centre are called disciples, and may come and go only with the Director's permission. No less than twenty-five motion detectors and closed-circuit TV cameras with infra-red lights are installed to cover every corner.

On March 13 the backlog of post has been processed. Every letter has been answered. Every cheque from every investor has been cashed. Every appeal for help is honoured with a colour photograph of Ella, in levitation. The disciples have signed every one, 'Pray With Me – Ella'.

On March 26 Juliette Wallis claims she has been turned away from the Ella Centre and is not permitted to see her own daughter. She has been staying in Florida since January. Initial media interest in her was intense – now it is starting to dwindle. She is an unreliable television guest, because of her drinking. Her history has been told in full, her autobiography has already been sold and syndicated. There are five unauthorised biographies which scrape together every black-and-white picture from her childhood, tattered images sold from the photo albums of forgotten friends. Now her celebrity image is sad and tawdry – she is the all-too-human mother of an earthbound angel.

The Ella Foundation states on March 28: 'Ella longs for a reunion with her parents and brother. She deeply desires to see her mother and father together, as a family. As long as the recriminations go on between Juliette and Ken Wallis, Ella fears too much pain would result from her meeting either of them. For the sake of the family, she urges them to forget their differences.'

After Ken flies to Florida, without Marcia Collins but with their son, Luke, the chances of any reconciliation are nil. Juliette has the Miami Beach police department evict her husband from her apartment in Coconut Grove. She fears he will kidnap Frank and decamp with both the boys. The story is blazed across the front of the *National Enquirer*.

In late April, Laura Pittens becomes the first disciple to quit the Ella Centre. Her story is bought by the *News of the World*, and becomes a sordid tale of three-in-a-bed romps with the Director and another disciple. Very little detail of life inside the house is revealed. Laura seems almost never to have seen Ella herself. But there are rumours that Ella is sick, too weak to speak and too depressed to eat.

There is no official rebuttal, but accosted by reporters on his way through Heathrow the Director, very informal in a Gianni Versace jacket and RayBan sunglasses, makes an informal statement. Ella is stronger than she has ever been. She knows the whole purpose of her life lies in healing, and she devotes every minute to her prayers. Her spiritual strength for this life of solitude and self-denial is immense. Of course she is reclusive, of course she does not waste time on chitter-chatter. As to suggestions she is not eating – anyone who knows Ella will know she has a formidable appetite. He happens to have a photograph of her, in his jacket. She is at the table, behind a mound of fish and chips. She is trying to grin. The Director hands the picture to a reporter.

The picture does not show Ella hunched over a toilet afterwards, her eyes suffused with blood, with a toothbrush jabbing deep into her throat, retching every atom from her stomach. It has to be a toothbrush, or a Biro: her fingers alone no longer do the job.

Ken Wallis, repeatedly denied access to his daughter or his daughter's earnings, sues The Ella Foundation for twenty-two million pounds. The brief court case which he loses destroys the last of his funds. His clumsy attempts to play publishers, and newspapers, and sponsors against each other for extra cash, turn against him. No one wants to buy his endorsements. He declares himself bankrupt and returns to his printing job on the Wells Road – this time as deputy assistant to the new foreman.

In June Ella stood on a stage with two million people overflowing Bristol to see her. Around the world, an estimated three billion watched live. The event was The Miracle In The Meadows.

Beside her stood Guntarson and the Prince of Wales. The world had been given six weeks to prepare. Together, more than half the souls on the planet would pray for global healing.

Guntarson was leaning sideways to whisper the Miracle Mantra at the Prince: 'Not only individuals, but nations – not only sickness, but wars, famines, poverty.' And the microphones caught the whisper and sent it hissing above the heads of two million people congregated to pray for nations.

The venue was Bristol's Ashton Court, the vast grounds of a mansion which once belonged to the city's wealthiest land-owner. Now the park, and the mansion, belonged to the people. Guntarson made the point, frequently, that this would be a symbol, of how the world could belong to its people too.

For the first time, coverage would be live. Images of Ella had been beamed and rebeamed around the world, but never at the instant of the miracle. The Ella Effect seemed limitless. Could it be greater still when TV bore live witness?

Guntarson had promised that world leaders would join hands on the stage, taking their place beside Ella, and as the moments ticked away before the Miracle was to begin, it was clear his promise had been kept. The stage, with Ella at its centre, was ninety feet long, and none of those crowded on to it was insignificant. Every continent was represented by at least one head of state – no more than three or four countries had declined to send any official representative.

Britain's deputy prime minister had agreed to attend, before the scale of the event had become apparent to the PM himself. The deputy PM had insisted on keeping hold of his invitation, and now he was smiling smugly, hands clasped behind him, looking forward to the coverage which would seem to cast him, to watchers around the world, in the role of Nation's Leader.

During the previous weeks Guntarson had been interviewed seven times by CNN, for *Insight*, *Q+A*, *Impact* and *Larry King*. He was photographed at summits with every politician who could get close to him. In the international arena, only the immaterial were ignored by the Director, and no statesman could afford to be immaterial. Hourly bulletins revealed the stellar guest list – Michael Jackson, Pavarotti, the Hanson boys, Sting, Elton John, Diana Ross, Tina Turner.

Guntarson had promised a confluence of world powers, and he had promised that security would be simple. The prayers for peace would keep evil-doers away.

Security arrangements for The Miracle In The Meadows were, in fact, immense. And immensely confused. (The only feature more chaotic than the security was the on-site plumbing – long before the Miracle began, every mobile toilet between Bristol and the Severn estuary was flooded.

Leaders from more than 200 countries, principalities and states were present, and each nation insisted on keeping overall responsibility for its own politicians' safety. Their safety was ultimately assured by a transparent, rocket-proof screen which surrounded the platform, and a cordon of bodyguards ten deep. The stage was continuously scanned and searched for explosives. The grandees were set down, one by one, from an endless relay of helicopters and transported the fifty metres to the stage in a shell of secret service men.

Senior Metropolitan police officers involved in planning the funeral of Diana, Princess of Wales, were recruited for their expertise by Avon and Somerset police, and had to wrestle horrendous logistical problems – for while the funeral had been a moving procession, this was a convergence, massively concentrated on a single point.

The pilgrims filled the grounds, shoulder to shoulder. Far more than half the two million never caught sight of the stage, but were able to watch it on massive video screens set up across the city. Five hundred thousand people headed into the area and gave up, miles from their destination. Pilgrims crowded into people's houses all over the West Country to watch on television the miracle they had travelled from around the globe to witness. Giant video walls were erected in sports stadia and city parks around the world, and the streets and shops were empty as people crowded around screens great and small.

Peter Guntarson possessed a video of a favourite news report, which he played to anyone who dared doubt the enormity of the miracle. Reporter Judith Sykes, reporting for NBC four hours before Ella was led from a helicopter to the stage, told the camera: 'Wherever you are in the world, thank God for the BBC – because the BBC is providing coverage of this event to one hundred and ninety countries.

'Britain's other big network, ITN, is supplying twenty more. CNN say they are making the pictures available in two hundred and ten countries, with three start times for different zones around the globe. The planet is truly covered, and the actual number of viewers may never be known. The British audience is projected at a record thirty-five million.

'In all the history of the media, there never has been an event like this, nothing ever reported so widely in one hundred years of broadcasting. Bristol's media facilities have registered more than five hundred reporters. The Foreign Press Association has registered over six hundred during the week's run-up. The British Press Association says it has literally lost count of the hundreds of foreign pressmen and women to whom it has given accreditation.

'Countless more technicians, producers and anchormen and women are in Bristol to cover this expected Miracle. Americans are in the West Country in the greatest force. Our three networks, including NBC, plus CBS and ABC, have boosted their London bureaux with almost three hundred extra staff and naturally have given the event over to their biggest stars to host and present.

'Smaller broadcasters are having to make do with hiring time in front of the BBC cameras for their reporting. Because of the crowds, the Corporation has fixed its forty-five cameras onto protective, raised, blue platforms.

'One Australian reporter summed it up best for me when he said, "It is a bloody nightmare trying to move around."

'The cameras are feeding footage into thirteen mixing desks which then pass pictures to the BBC's huge broadcasting trucks. I've counted over thirty engineers using fifty screens to mix footage for British screens and to supply a feed to the satellite transmitters on the Telecom tower to send across the globe. We've seen mass coverage before – think of the Louise Woodward trial, when almost every channel in

America broadcast the 'Guilty' verdict live. But the Miracle in the Meadows is blasting far beyond that level of attention. Whenever you are in the world, whoever you are, whatever you're doing at three o'clock today – you will have to be aware of Ella Wallis.'

NBC did not remark on the convoys representing every religion, though there were at least as many priests of all faiths as there were journalists. Countless thousands of nuns arrived, from every town on every map. They came from Peru, from Tibet, from the Western Australian desert, they came from Calcutta in the sanctified name of Mother Teresa, to be at The Miracle In The Meadows.

The almost saintly presence of Princess Diana could also not be missed, with tens of thousands of pilgrims bearing her image on placards and banners, invoking her spirit, weeping for her. Mourned around the world, her death had been most deeply felt in Britain, and many who spoke to reporters declared they would pray for her soul.

Around the world, via satellite to two hundred and thirty-two countries, the event was transmitted live to one hundred and eight stations. The public address system was six times more vast than the Stones' PA for their '98 tour. Bristol International Airport was jammed for a fortnight with private helicopters and government jets, emblazoned with company insignia and national flags. Transport flights brought bullet-proof limousines and brigades of secret service men.

The estimated audience was wider than anything known before. The miracle was viewed across China. It was viewed by scientists at the South Pole. It was viewed in Washington and Tokyo and Baghdad and Melbourne. And at the centre of it all was a girl with silver-blonde hair to her elbows, a girl as thin as a strand of hair, with her round eyes tightly closed.

From the moment she stepped on stage, she was praying. The politicians were clasping each other's hands and beaming proudly at the ocean of disciples, where the fervent were shrieking, weeping, singing, laughing, reaching out, baying in ecstasy, pleading, kneeling, murmuring, howling, pushing, hugging, waving, chanting. Chanting Ella's name. But Ella was simply praying.

Clocks around the world watched the seconds drip away, clocks where it was midnight and where it was dusk, dawn clocks and midday clocks and the atomic clock at Greenwich, where it was counting down to 3pm. At 3pm the world was joined in prayer. That was the Miracle.

Guntarson, grasping Ella's wrist, lifted her hand into the air, almost pulling her fragile body into the air. The roar from two million mouths reverberated around the world. Ella kept her head bowed, like a doll, as he counted down.

'Ten seconds to go. We're going to show the world now! The greatest unleashing of healing power in history! Sweep away the unbelievers! *Three! Two! One! PRAY!*'

He let Ella go and adopted an exaggerated pose of fervency. She hunched meekly at his side. Amid the welter of celebrities and solemn dignitaries Ella seemed to be alone. She was alone, among the mass of half a million around her, alone among the three billion people sharing their prayers.

Many who came in wheelchairs were standing to cheer her, even before the prayers began. Tumours shrivelled, cataracts dissolved. Cameramen struggled through the crowd, looking for the newly cured. One girl said she came to pray for her mother, and already her own toothache had gone – she felt certain her mother would be healed. A man, dying from sickle cell anaemia, said he felt refreshed, as if he had stood under a jet of cold water.

The banners proclaimed, 'Ella The Messiah'. In English, in Hebrew, in Arabic, in Gujerat, in Chinese, in Tibetan. All faiths have faith in a Second Coming. The banners say, 'Ella will save us'. 'Absolve us, Ella.'

There were levitations reported throughout the crowd, though Ella herself stayed earthbound. Overhead, the din of helicopters was deafening.

By six o'clock, when Ella had lapsed into an exhausted trance and was slumped on a chair at the back of the stage, five thousand cures had been reported in the meadows. Around the world, it was hundreds of times that number.

In Britain, the miracle got more press coverage than even World War Two's most momentous events. The London clippings agency, Durrants, calculated that newspapers in early May, 1945, devoted up to twenty-seven per cent of their columns to the defeat of Germany. Ella was given forty-five per cent.

One story was repeated over and over, giving the mass miracle a handle, a face:

In Philadelphia, fifty-year-old Simon Weinstein prayed for the soul of his son. The child died nearly thirty years ago, from a cancer in his blood. Born in the nineties, that boy, Harry, might have had a chance at life. Born in the sixties, he had no chance. He died a week before his second birthday, and his parents said prayers for his soul and his memory every week. Simon had been a widower for eight years, but he had not forgotten the boy. He said a prayer for Harry every week, just as he prayed for the soul of his wife.

Simon grieved for Harry all the harder, because he had also lost his younger son, Michael. Mike and Simon had fallen out long ago. They last saw each other at Mike's mother's funeral, and hard words were spoken. Words which were not likely to be forgotten.

And then the miracle began.

Mike rang Simon at the precise moment Simon was praying for Harry's memory. He said, 'Dad. I've been watching the prayers on TV. I want to make peace between us.'

Simon said, 'Yes?'

'I've got a wife, you've never met her, her name's Fleur, we're living in Oregon now. And we've got a son. Dad, I want you to do something for us.'

Mike was in tears, sobbing into the receiver as he spoke, and though he was suspicious as to why his estranged son should offer peace out of the blue and immediately ask a favour, Simon could not speak a hard word. So he said, 'Yes?'

'We called our son Harry.'

'That's beautiful.'

'Is it? He's got what your Harry died from. Cancer. In his blood. He's had every treatment there is and he isn't getting better. He's gotten a lot worse these last two weeks. He's in hospital. And on Tuesday, if God grants him that long, he's going to be two years old. Dad, will you pray with us? Pray for Harry? Please?'

Simon did pray. He prayed all day and night for the grandson he had never known. In the morning he rang a local radio station to tell them his story and to ask its listeners to pray with him. City TV picked up on the story. Then national TV. By next breakfast-time, the day before Harry Weinstein's second birthday, all America was praying for the child. He became a symbol, of how prayer could fight illness and more – bring a broken family together. Bring a nation together.

On the morning of his second birthday, when he should have been at death's door, Harry Weinstein was cured.

CHAPTER THIRTY-SIX

From the *Observer*'s *Life* magazine, Sunday, December 12. Front cover features aerial shot of mansion, sub-titled 'What *Really Goes On In The Ella Centre*'

International Exclusive – *for the first time ever, a report from inside the secret world of Ella Wallis and her disciples.* **ALISS HOLMES** *spends a week behind the locked doors of the Ella Centre, with unprecedented access to Director Peter Guntarson, and gains an audience with the reclusive miracle-worker herself.*

Aliss in Ella-Land

No one had warned me Peter Guntarson would be at the party, because no one had known. These days, he expects to be allowed to walk into any building he chooses, dressed however he likes, and be welcomed, seated, served. No doubt he could stroll into the Houses of Parliament if he desired, still zipped into his glistening black bike leathers, and back benchers on every side would wave their order papers and demand a speech. This is not such a silly idea – after all, Director Guntarson has become a regular guest at Highgrove House, visited the White House thrice, even favoured No 10 with his presence.

This, then, is precisely why no one expected him to walk into an after-show party for a West End premiere. The date was November 29, the production was Eric Osborne's latest, and the party was promising to be an endurance test, because Eric hadn't bothered to turn up, because every bore east of Windsor had been invited and because the actor I was supposed to be interviewing was already rat-arse drunk. Now imagine the shockwave rippling through the room when a square-jawed tousled blond superman in an orange all-weather mountain coat walks in.

Half the crowd does a double-take. The other half is rubber-necking round him, to see if he's brought the angel girl with him. Is it possible? Are they actually in the presence of Ella?

Of course it isn't possible. She never goes anywhere with him. She never goes anywhere. She has not been out of doors since June. Everybody knows that. And nothing annoys the Director more than people who look disappointed to see him, because they were hoping to see Ella.

I did not look disappointed. God knows how I did look – tongue hanging down by my boobs, probably, and ice popping out of my double Martini. Because Director Guntarson in the flesh is ten times as ravishing as his photographs, partly because he is taller than you would believe and partly because he radiates power. The smile, the stance, the handshake, the clothes – there is nothing conciliatory about any of them. He does not need to make people like him. He is used to being adored.

He made himself pretty adorable to me. Topped my glass, whispered a secret about one of the other guests, listened intently to my babble. It's easy to see why he's had the angel girl wrapped around his finger since Day One. Later on, I heard myself mouthing inanely, 'Has anyone ever told you you're irresistible?' The Director has that effect: cogent, sceptical brains reduced to jelly. Maybe it's a paranormal power. When I asked what he was doing at a theatre knees-up, he said, 'Looking for a beautiful woman.' Anyone else would have been sponging Martini off their shirt-front – the Director was treated to my red-face, legs-in-a-twist, 'Aw shucks' routine. 'I like women with strong psi-power,' he added, and when I protested that I couldn't float in a swimming-pool, let alone levitate, he showed me how to project messages telepathically. 'You just close your eyes, and imagine you're shouting the word from a desert island to a ship on the horizon. See if you can hear me.' And we closed our eyes, and telepathically he made a very obscene suggestion.

I said Yes immediately. Or it may have been Yes Yes Yes Oh God Yes. And that's how I came to be invited to the Ella Centre.

The approach by helicopter is so splendid, it's almost mystical. Hot-air balloons hung like map-pins in the sky. We buzzed between them in our five-seater Bell JetRanger, following the tin-foil glitter of the river in the gorge below. And then Brunel's Suspension Bridge, stretched like a necklace from cliff to cliff, loomed before us and we flitted away, over the woods, and dipped onto the helipad, grey-with-an-orange-H, behind a square, sandstone edifice. Two youths came loping out, ducking below the rotor blades, and slid back the door for the Director. He helped me down with exaggerated chivalry, like Raleigh assisting Queen Bess over a particularly wide puddle, and the youths seized my bags and loped back into the house.

It wasn't what I was expecting. I didn't know what to expect, of course – maybe Ella, floating out of an upstairs window to greet her guest, or columns of nuns trooping across the gardens, bowed heads hidden behind their wimples. When I followed the Director through the conservatory into the congregation room, nine or twelve teenagers were lounging over books and magazines. Some looked up and said, 'Hi.' Some didn't. On a low table, where you might have expected a television to be, was a Monopoly set. Beside it were at least a dozen computers and a nest of cabling to their printers. More teenagers were hunched there, online, down-loading the daily thousands of eMails.

The Director was darting in and out with a mobile phone in each hand. I stood in the middle of the room, wondering where my bags had been taken. No one gave me a second glance.

'Hungry?' he asked on one fleeting appearance. 'Brooke can fix you scrambled eggs. She knows just how I like them. I taught her well. Brooke, cook – now!'

An eighteen-year-old with a puggish face and sweater-girl breasts slapped down her James Herbert paperback and hauled herself off – to the kitchen, I supposed.

'Where's my room?' I asked.

'Whatever do you want a room for?'

He showed me to the master bedroom, the Director's suite, up a flight of wide wooden stairs and behind a locked, oak door. The window looked out across the grounds and the gorge, but he kept the blinds down. Two chandeliers hung, one either side of a massive, crimson bed. No, not crimson – blood-red. The bed looked hot. And soft. There was almost nothing else in the room – a fitted wardrobe, a mirror above a shelf, a small table where a digital Sony camcorder stood. And a polar bear rug.

'From my father's native Iceland. I shot it myself. No, that's cobblers – I was forgetting you're a journalist. Never joke with journalists, they don't have any sense of humour. Actually, I bought it in Anchorage last time I was there. It's been dead decades – trapped in the thirties. About as politically correct as fur can be. Feel it, it's coarser than you'd think. Nothing fluffy about polar bears. Sit down.' He sat beside me, pushing his fingers through the fur beside my thigh. 'You'd be shocked how abrasive this rug can be. Against bare skin.'

'Why have a camcorder?'

'Oh, I don't know. In case Ella does anything unexpectedly marvellous.'

A nervous tap on the door, and the girl with bazooka boobs brought our eggs. She stood fidgeting in the doorway, anticipating further orders, but she was dismissed with a flick of the Director's fingers.

'Her sister Holly,' he remarked, 'was at school with Ella. Brooke Mayor. So she knew Ella, of course, this time last year. And no doubt never spared her a sideways glance. But by the time I'd presented Ella to the world, miracles left, right and centre, poor Brooke couldn't keep away. Started living outside Ella's house, sleeping in the road, trying to break in, trying to take photos through the windows. Completely obsessed. Couldn't believe she'd actually known Ella. Which made her an ideal candidate to come and live at the Centre, help us with housekeeping, correspondence, all that. All the kids you saw downstairs are just the same. Rock stars have fans and groupies. Ella and I have disciples.'

'Where is Ella?'

'Praying,' he answered, vaguely.

'Praying where?'

'In private.'

'I really want to meet her.'

'So does everybody.'

'But that's why you brought me here.'

'Is it? Is it?' For a moment he was huffy; then his white-knuckled wrist was clamped round my arm and twisting me down, playfully, onto the rug. 'Is that why I brought you *here*? To my boudoir?'

'You haven't locked the door.' I tried (not very hard) to dodge his lips.

'So? Are you going to try to escape? You won't get far. The dogs will be loose in the grounds by now.'

So I had to submit. I didn't emerge for three days.

The Director was snatched away by the helicopter, in the end, and I got some uninterrupted sleep for the first time in seventy-two hours. Then I lifted the blinds and sat, watching dusk settle in the gorge. Across the lawns and over the glass-topped wall, beyond the barbed wire, photographers sat in the trees – heavy, black shapes, like ravens with zoom lenses. Their digital cameras could transmit images directly to Apple Macs on waiting newsdesks anywhere in the world. No need for film.

Flood-lamps bleached the garden, spilling sheets of light that seemed to fizz and zing with whiteness. Three immense mastiffs, torpedoes on stilts, ambled across the grass. They stopped, quivering, their muzzles a few yards apart. One took a step forward and the others sprang away, repelled like magnets.

In the congregation room, four disciples sat cross-legged round the Monopoly board. 'Hi,' one greeted me eagerly. He was the only boy. The girls ignored me.

It occurred to me he was the only black person I'd seen at the centre. He was wearing a Mother Teresa T-shirt and blinking through John Lennon specs – not so much blinking, more scrunching every muscle in his face. His shaggy curls were shorter one side than the other, a classic kitchen-scissors haircut-at-home. 'I'm Stewpot.'

'No one calls you Stewpot,' muttered one of the girls. 'Just Stu.'

'It's what my mum always called me.'

'I'll call you Stewpot if you like,' I offered. It was about time I made a friend. 'Who's got the hotels on Mayfair?'

'Me,' he admitted. No surprise. The girls looked too bored to roll the dice, let alone add up the rent owing. 'Do you want to join in?'

'Is this what you do with your spare time? Monopoly?'

One of the girls said, 'Pah!'

'What's "pah"?'

'Spare time,' she said, not looking at me. Her hair, spread over her shoulders and hiding her face, was shining, thick and auburn.

'What about it?' I asked, thinking that the Director's trick of picking disciples from attractive girls and nerdy boys must create some sexual imbalance in the household.

'How much spare time have you had since you got here?'

'True,' I said, 'I've been flat out since I got here.'

'So wait till he gives you a sack of photos to sign, and you've got a thousand envelopes to write, and it's your turn for washing-up.'

I explained I hadn't come to do the washing-up. They explained they hadn't been expecting it either. They had come to be companions for a lonely Ella, and as junior managers in The Ella Foundation. Nothing had been said about washing-up.

'So why don't you leave?'

'Why don't you?' they countered.

That was ridiculous. I could leave whenever I wanted.

'Oh yeah?' said the sulkiest, a black-haired teenager named Xenia. Like the other girls she wore no make-up, no jewellery, plain clothes, and she looked bright. None of them looked vacant. 'So leave then,' she challenged.

'You don't get rid of me like that. But if I wanted, all I have to do is walk out the door.'

'And get eaten by the hounds from hell.'

'All right, I'll just pick up the phone.'

'What phone?'

I had my mobile, I told them. Obviously.

Only I didn't.

'He's taken it! Bastard! He's taken my phone! Bastard!'

'No one's allowed to phone from here,' they told me. 'The Director has to control all the statements coming from the Centre. Even our eMail outputters are disabled. You won't get your mobile back – he'll say he confiscated it to stop one of us getting our hands on it.'

'But you're not prisoners?'

'We come from all kinds of backgrounds, but we're all servants,' explained Stewpot. He seemed happy about it. 'The

Director has to be able to guarantee continuity. And that means establishing our long-term commitment.'

'I'm not a servant,' I said primly.

'What are you then?' Brooke wanted to know. 'A sex slave?'

I made a note to avoid Brooke's scrambled eggs next time. They might be poisoned.

But the atmosphere changed when I told them I worked for the *Observer*.

'You mean the Director's really going to let you write something? Bet he never does.'

'He's got to. Or my editor sends the SAS in to collect me,' I said smugly.

'You've got to put the truth then,' said Brooke.

'She doesn't know the truth,' said Tamara.

'We'll tell her,' said Xenia, eagerly.

'You know Tim and Nick?'

'They were the two who carried your bags in.'

'You probably didn't notice them. But there's Sadie as well.'

'Sadie's the worst. She's the rotten apple in the barrel.'

'Are you really going to write all this in the paper?'

Well, no I'm not. For one thing I kept getting lost, and for another it's all impossibly trivial. But I pretended I was very interested, because it was better than being hated by everyone. All the casual student needs to know is that the Director keeps his disciples busy with factions. Everybody is jockeying to be closest to Ella. There's Tim and Nick, who take her food in each day. 'They're just waiters!' said Xenia. There's Sadie, supposedly sleeping with both these waiters. And there's another boy, Daz, and to hear him tell it the real villainess of the Ella Centre is Brooke because she, being depraved and libidinous, has a special hold over the Director. The nicest of the bunch really did seem to be Stewpot. He was genuinely unhappy as he sat, long after midnight, with two boxes of colour prints and a marker pen on the table before him.

'I mean, in one way it's a privilege,' he reasoned, neatly following the template beside him as his marker traced: 'Peace ... Harmony ... Health ... Love Ella,' on each picture. 'Sometimes we use a signing machine, but I'm not allowed to, it always breaks when I touch it. Of course Ella can't sign stuff herself. She's got to pray. The Director says every prayer saves a life. And it takes me about twenty seconds to get a photo out the box, straighten it up, write on it, put it in the envelope, and then it's at least forty seconds to decipher the address and copy it down right. So that's a minute. And it never takes a minute to say one prayer.' He recited the Lord's Prayer, without garbling it and without making it mean anything either. 'Eighteen seconds. So there's one way of looking at it – every time I sign Ella's name I give her time to say three more prayers. And that's three lives.

'But then I worry: what would people think, if they knew? They get Ella's photo – it probably means a lot to them. To think Ella wrote the words, left her fingerprints on the pictures. Maybe some of her energy would be imparted through those prints – tiny unique evidences of her. That thought might be helping them get better. So in that way, I feel a bit of a fraud. Or worse. What if there's someone really banking on this signature? Really focusing on it, trying to draw Ella's healing power out of it, only there isn't any because actually it was me that wrote it, me that left my fingerprints. So maybe they don't get healed. Or maybe they're cured but it's only because of their own healing energies, triggered by their belief. Because Ella never touched their picture.'

'If people aren't cured,' I said, 'surely that's because Ella's a fraud. Not you.'

Stewpot shook his head. Then he smiled. 'She's for real. Do you want me to show you? Come and see her? Okay, we've got to be very, very quiet. For one thing, it's not nice to disturb her. For another, I'm not really allowed to go to her room. Only Tim and Nick can go. They take her food, and the dog too. Have you seen Furbag? He's a spaniel, the Director bought him for Ella. But because she's in her room, all the time, the dog gets bored. Plus it needs to be walked, and the Director just won't let Ella go outside. In case she's photographed. It's all to do with mystique. This puppy, Furbag, it kind of attached itself to Tim, and he has to do all its grooming and feeding, and every day he takes the dog to see Ella. Sometimes he's tried leaving it with her, but it whines and scratches to be with him. He's a bit paranoid about it, because of all the killer Rottweilers in the grounds. He has to be careful of when he takes it out to do its business.

'So I'm supposed to see Ella only when she comes downstairs, and that's about every six weeks. But I sneak up and look most nights. That's why I sit up late, writing extra photos, till everyone's asleep.'

He led me through the congregation room, where Daz was sleeping on a sofa, his feet in unlaced Reeboks. 'He's a slob,' breathed Stewpot. On the first floor landing, he whispered a name at each door: 'Xenia. Her light's off. Nick. His light's off, he's probably listening to headphones. He's a Nirvana freak, Kurt Cobain posters everywhere.' Stewpot sounded disgusted. 'This is Tim's room.' Muffled grunting behind that door. 'Tim and Sadie, I suppose. Yeah, here's Sadie's room, light off, door open.' He shook his head, like a fifth-form dormitory monitor forced to turn a blind eye to bed-swapping among the upper sixth. 'Okay, up these stairs, but step right over the second. It squeaks.'

The second floor was blacker than a dungeon. And cold. I put a hand on Stewpot's shoulder and let him lead me along a passageway, swirling with icy air. We stopped in silence, with the darkness wrapped around my face like a blindfold.

He slid back a cover in the wall, allowing a glimmer of light to show, and then blocked it with his face. When he stood back he wordlessly pressed me towards the chink.

And there was Ella.

The room's single window was boarded up. The lamp in the corner was not lit. But a stream of thin radiance leaked from the girl in the centre of the room, as if something were burning deep inside her.

Her hands were clasped in her lap, and she was kneeling. The pose was more like a little girl waiting to be told her bedtime story than a saint at prayer. Her magnificent, burnished hair billowed around her. Her eyes were partly closed – or rather, her hollow-boned face was in repose. The luminous skin was stretched across her forehead and cheekbones, and was sucked into cavities beside her mouth and below her eyes. She looked haggard and ethereal – and half-starved.

And of course, she was in levitation. Her body was tipped forward, so the knees were nearest the ground, a hand's-breadth from it.

'She's awake,' hissed my friend. 'We'd better leave her.'

I took a last look at the room – no furnishings, no books, a soft, green teddy on the untouched bed – and slid the spyhole cover shut.

We passed Ella's bathroom, a cubby-hole with a toilet and a shower next to her room. On the stairs Stewpot began to whisper again. 'I can tell when she's asleep, because the light changes. Do you remember how she said she saw three spinning discs of light? I've watched them. Sometimes I've stood there for hours. Literally. It's freezing up there but you forget that after a while. I've watched her praying and, if she's very focused, she gets that glow. What you saw is nothing. Sometimes it's dazzling, like the whole room's on fire. But when she relaxes, I suppose her mind wanders a bit, and the glow goes out. Just now, it was like embers. She'll be asleep soon. I didn't want you disturbing her. No offence.'

'None taken. But isn't she cold? I'm frozen after five minutes.'

'I've thought about that. I think she's drawing the heat into her. Taking energy from the air. And if you stand there for a while, you can almost feel the energy being taken from you too. She never wears different clothes, anyway. It was the same, just jumpers and trousers and stuff, in the summer. We handwash them with olive oil soap. The Director says she mustn't get her head turned by all this attention, and lots of clothes could make her vain. He made her get rid of most of her old clothes even, specially merchandise-type stuff with logos on it.

'She's not always praying,' he added. 'I've seen her sitting on the edge of her bed, combing her hair. Great long brush strokes, right from her head to the tips. I don't like to watch, then. Everybody needs private time.'

'Would you mind if she came and watched you while you were sleeping?'

'She doesn't even know who I am! She's seen me about three times, right in the background. I'm just a minion.' He said this with a laugh. 'Anyway, when I've stood and stood there, watching her fall asleep, and there's the glow like you saw and slowly it fades, and the room is totally dark – then if you stand there long enough, three discs of light appear. Spinning. Just like she described them. On the wall, circling each other, faster and faster, till they're quite bright and merged into one. And then they separate gradually, and slow down, and it becomes like a cycle. Spinning, blending, pulsating, getting bright, separating out. It's like the heartbeat of some huge, invisible being, a very slow heartbeat. And you get this strong feeling that it's watching over her. Guarding her.

'I feel sad for her sometimes. But, you know, there's a Hindu belief we must suffer before we attain bliss. Well, if that's right, there must be a whole lot of bliss waiting for Ella.'

When the Director's away, the mice will play. And what they play is Monopoly. Or Sim City, on one of the Apple Macs. And that's it. I didn't hear anyone swear, didn't see anyone smoke or have a drink – since all their provisions come in by van every other day, the disciples have to put up with what they're given. So they've got no way of acquiring bad habits, even if they wanted to. I said 'Shit' once, and got looked at like I'd farted during Holy Communion.

I was pretty drained of sexual urges, but none of the boys was worth flirting with anyway. Cult-mentality geeks one and all, and that's finding something nice to say about them. We won't mention bodily hygiene. If Sadie really was sleeping with Tim, she must have had a pretty strong stomach.

Stewpot wore me out with his eager enthusiasm for every detail of the angel child's existence. He was an astrology nut, and spent ages trying to make me understand how Ella had not been born under any of the ordinary astrological signs. Apparently, around her birthday in mid-December, the sun takes a holiday from the zodiac and nips off to a nearby constellation called Ophiuchus the Snake-Charmer. 'It's really important,' – he said about eighteen times, 'because the earth has been shifting off-course for 2,500 years, ever since the Babylonians drew up the star charts. And it means Ella's sign is Ophiuchus, and that's the sign of positive thinking. Not Sagittarius. I'll tell her all this one day.'

'Why make her life harder than it already is?' I asked, but

poor Stewpot was completely deaf to sarcasms. I didn't have the heart to tell him to stick a sock in it, so I just tried to amuse myself, getting him to explain the Ophiuchus thing over and over again and then saying, 'So that makes her a Gemini, right?'

Eventually, even this riotous entertainment paled. So I spent two days stroking Furbag, and rolling dice, and listening to bitchy whispers about whoever wasn't in the room at the time.

And then the Director came back, and I got to talk to Ella.

Chapter Thirty-Seven

The *Observer*, Sunday, December 19. Front of *Life* supplement for the second week – a distinction never previously awarded. The cover shows simply a ray of light, streaming down from the right edge to the left:

Aliss in Ella-Land, Part Two – The Miracle:

Ella was produced as a grand gesture. Other men might fly a mistress across the Atlantic for sex in a five-star hotel, or present her with a gruesome, bloated gemstone. Peter Guntarson gave me Ella.

I had started asking for her as soon as the Director returned, and kept asking all through the night. By lunchtime he stopped saying, 'We'll see,' and was promising, 'Yes'. By teatime he really seemed to mean his promise. The disciples passed the day in a nervous flurry, cleaning and arranging and tidying and straightening. At eleven minutes past eleven, when people began to despair that all their hopeful duties had been pointless, the Director guided Ella down the stairs.

She looked ill. Now she was standing up, I was struck so much harder by how thin she was. This was not the Ella I had seen on television. It went beyond the amphetamine-waif look some people accuse her of affecting. It was not the gaunt health of an ascetic, either. She looked neglected and plain ill, painfully ill, like an anorexic or a bulimic. Her eyes were deeply withdrawn into their heavily ringed sockets, and their colouring was stagnant, with dark rings around them. Her mouth hung open a little and her lips drooped. The skin on her hands looked transparent and brittle.

She was clinging to the Director's big ruddy hand and when he steered her onto a chair, she clung on determinedly. He settled himself, cross-legged on the floor, beside her. The rest of us were standing as we were bidden, in a line with our backs to the double doors, and one by one the disciples were permitted to kneel before Ella and touch her hand. I had to join the ritual. Discreetly, I switched on my miniature tape recorder.

Her hand was cold and her face showed me nothing. She looked disconnected, as if someone had pulled the plug out. Perhaps the Director had interrupted her prayers, and there was a half-said supplication still hanging in the air in her cell, waiting to be finished.

The disciples were sent away. I saw the looks of longing that Stewpot cast over his shoulder. Of all the disciples, he was the only one whose eyes seemed to tell of love for the real Ella and not the icon.

The Director said, 'This lady has come to talk with you. She's a special friend of mine. I wanted her to meet you, and see that you're special too.'

If Ella felt anything during this little introduction, none of it showed on her face. I wanted to feel sorry for her, but in this shell of a girl there was nothing I could relate to.

'I want to ask you some questions. Are you okay with that? You're not too tired?'

'Can I have Furbag?'

'Dog, dog,' said the Director, snapping his fingers, 'that's her dog.' He jumped up to the doorway and called into the passage, 'Can we have that Fleabag thing? Thanks.' The dog was brought to him; he gave it to her. It seemed every instant of contact with Ella was a gift wholly in the Director's granting. No one communicated with her by accident, not even to bring her the dog.

'Do you like it here?'

Her hands stroked the spaniel from its collar to its tail. It showed no sign, drooped in her lap, of being very happy. I began counting the strokes – twenty-seven, before she said: 'Peter's here.'

'Is that all you want?'

'No.' She thought about what she did want for another thirty-three strokes. 'I wants to pray.'

'You could pray anywhere.'

'Peter says the energy here is right.'

'These cliffs are full of rock crystal,' he cut in. 'Bristol Diamonds, fantastic for magnifying psi and healing power. Ella's prayers boom out of here like they're coming through a speaker stack. And we're on a ley-line like a motorway, pumping energy through this house in lorry-loads. It's because of the Suspension Bridge – it's become one of those focal monuments, like Stonehenge or Glastonbury Tor, and the Pyramids, of course. It's key point in the natural energy web.'

'And that helps?'

'Peter can explain it,' muttered Ella.

'What about school?'

'We have an on-going tutorial programme,' said the Director, though no one had mentioned it to me before. 'We prefer not to talk about it.'

'Don't you miss your family?'

'I got Peter. And Furbag.'

'A dog's not much of a substitute for your mum and dad.'

'They didn't never let me have no pets. I got this furry bundle here now.' Her hands, just bunches of twigs, tried to pull Furbag up to her face, but he gave a wriggle and slipped to the floor.

'And I'm a better person with Peter. Cleaner.'

'How cleaner?'

'You know.'

'No. I don't know.'

'I don't . . . bleed.'

For a moment I thought she meant stigmata.

'You know,' this fifteen-year-old child added, 'bleed. Every month.'

'You don't have periods?'

'Not no more. I had one once, but then I come here. My Uncle Robert told me, the Virgin Mary didn't never have one. So I kind of feel better, 'cos I know I ain't as clean as her. Does that make sense?'

What do you say? Was the Holy Mother as pale and bloodless as this creature? She didn't look healthy enough to menstruate.

'You look quite frail,' I tried.

'I eats all my food.'

'So everyone says. But it doesn't seem to build you up much.'

The Director stepped in again: 'No one realises the energy

Ella burns. Think of it, the fantastic cures she empowers people to make in themselves. Thousands upon thousands of human lives enriched. And she asks nothing in return. We do everything we can, of course – utilising the ley-line, giving her absolute peace, protecting her from prying eyes, running all the business aspects. Everything to maximise the power she has. But we can't ask her to go easier on herself. She has a huge responsibility. It's painful to see the toll this exacts from her body, but I know she is protected by the force which gives her this healing power. It is not for us to impose limitations.'

'What do you think about when you pray?'

'It's not good asking Ella a question like that. Her nature is intuitive. She doesn't think, she experiences.'

'So what are you experiencing during prayer? Or tell me – what are your feelings, right now? What do you want?'

'I wants Peter.'

'I'm here,' he said, 'you've got me.' But he was looking at me, wanting me to be impressed at his importance and his selflessness.

'Is that all? Is that what you want when you pray?'

'Peter says for me to pray for world peace.'

'What does that mean, do you think?'

'Peter explains it proper.'

'Come on, Ella. Tell me. When you're praying – what's at the heart of every prayer?'

'I wants everybody to feel good. I don't want nobody to feel like me.'

'You don't feel good?'

She shook her head.

The Director started to speak, but her whisper gained strength and I was able to hang on to it. 'I got to help people get better. That's the point. That's why I got born. I worked that out. When I been praying. Sorted out what I feels. 'Cos my dad didn't want me born. Meant he had to marry my mum. And he made her sad too, and he gone off and spent all my money.'

That word, 'Money.' made the Director flinch. I saw it.

'Now I helped Frank get cured and other people too, so they're not sad. My mum can't be sad no more, cos Frank's better and she might not still have him if it weren't for me. Peter says they gone to America, 'cos of the sunshine making Frank stay well, and that's brilliant, really, 'cos Frank always said he wants to go to Disneyworld. And when they comes back I know they'll want to come visit me.'

'Doesn't it make you happy, knowing millions of people feel better because of you?'

'Of course it does!' the Director declared, with a jolly swing of his arms. 'Ella simply expresses herself badly sometimes, don't you?'

'I ain't no good with words. Peter explains it proper.'

'I want to hear *you* say it. Your words. Not his.'

'I just . . . it's like I swallows up everybody's bad feelings. When I helps people get better, it's like I takes the sadness away and I put it inside myself. Like I got a big heavy weight of sadness in here.' She held her stomach.

'Come on.' The Director prodded her tummy lightly. 'Anyone can see there's not much in there. You're just tired.'

'I am tired,' she said. 'I knows I got to keep praying. I wants people to get better. I really does. But sometimes I got so much sadness in me I just wants to be dead. It'll be good when I'm dead.'

'Come on. Come on now,' Peter Guntarson told her sharply. 'That's nonsense. You can't say that. It's been too much of a strain for you. I shouldn't have let you prattle on so long, it's bad for you. Come on. Sleep time. Rest now.' He scooted her out of the room, that grey mass of opaque sadness clenched in her transparent body.

When he burst, grim-faced, back into the room less than thirty seconds later, his first demand was: 'Tape!'

I was ready for this. In a few fumbling moments I had switched the minicassette in my machine for a blank one, so that what I flipped obediently into the Director's hand was not the precious interview, her declaration of a deathwish.

'Of course, we can't print this. I should never have let you keep her up so late. I know, your editor will want something. We'll give him quotes. Don't worry. This is what we'll say. This will satisfy him – Money and Power. Ella talks about Money and Power. Think that'll whet his appetite? So I'll give you some ideas and you can make them sound like they came from Ella's mouth. The way she speaks, and so forth. Think you can do that?'

'Sure,' I said. Why argue?

'Okay.' He gripped his temples between his thumb and forefinger. 'Money: We want people to invest in the Ella Centre. They buy our shares – there's no fixed price, they just send what they can afford. But I want to urge people to examine their souls before they write that cheque. If they've prayed with Ella and been blessed with a miracle, what is that miracle really worth? Just a few pounds? A few dollars, a few yen? Can it be brushed aside so easily? Or is it something life-changing, something for which they'll have cause to thank the Ella Centre for the rest of their lives? A cure, a new lease of life, refreshed health. If not for them, then for someone they love. Isn't that worth a sacrifice from your savings? A change in your will?

'If Ella's miracle has yet to touch you, don't be sceptical – you never know when you will need her power for yourself. And if the miracle has saved your child, or your parent, your much-loved husband, wife, brother, sister, your friend – why, then, isn't it worth so much more than a miracle that might have saved your own life? Don't leave it to the person who was cured to make the donation. Think of yourself as the true beneficiary, because you gained a loved one. Remember – the best way to say thank you is to help the miracle happen to others.

'What do we want to do with the money? Prayer hospitals. I'm in constant negotiation with all sorts of health groups, including the NHS and the biggest US insurance groups, to establish a worldwide chain of Ella Miracle Care Centres. Because not every cure can come by prayer alone. We want to emphasise that. We want to work with the established sciences. We certainly would never recommend anyone to abandon a conventional course of medicine just because they had invested in the Ella Centre and begun praying with Ella. These things work hand in hand. The scientific and the mystical, the mundane and the miraculous. (I have to say that, I have to say it every interview – this is off the record, okay? – but it's very important to emphasise conventional medicine, otherwise, Christ knows, we are going to get sued by some sick gold-digger.)

'On to Power. Power for Peace. Ella says, "I want world

peace"; she just sounds so immature. I've tried to explain to her. I guess she understands really. This is what she wanted to say:

'Ella's high profile and her unique importance to so many people make her very desirable as a political element. World leaders want to be associated with her. I mean, I can pick up a phone and dial anyone. Literally anyone. And they'll talk to me. That's Power.

'People say power is responsibility. But I'll tell you what power really is – credibility. That's what we're striving for at the Ella Foundation. Credibility for psi power. People pray, Ella prays with them and they see their prayers answered. So they believe. But that's not enough. They have to believe before they pray. Before the result comes in. That's true belief. That's the credibility I'm demanding of every person on the planet. To have faith.

'No more laughing at psychic power. No more.

'So yes: I am courting world leaders. Because they bring credibility. We can get international enemies together at the table, talking, negotiating. That's credibility. Where the leaders go, the mass consensus follows. And the next time we do a Miracle in the Meadows, the American President will be there. I'm telling you – last time, the Vatican sent their number two, some cardinal. Next time it'll be the Pope. And the Queen. I mean it. They saw, this summer, what we could do. Now everyone's begging to get on board. That's credibility, that's power. The power to be a major influence on world events. We can be international players. We already are. And if we ever decide to launch a political party – well, least said about that for now. But you get my drift.'

'You want to be prime minister?' I suggested.

'I want to be the Director. Let's see how big that gets, shall we? It is already a little bigger than my father – he's chairman of his own construction company. His orders have doubled this year just because of who I am. He's international, but I think we're a little more international, don't you? Just a tad?

'Okay, that's enough. Doll it up, put it in Ella's language, show it to me when it's ready. I want approval on every word. Now, bedtime.'

He seized my hand and pulled me abruptly towards the stairs. I didn't fancy it much. I didn't fancy the Director much, suddenly. But with the real tape in my pocket and Ella's words etched on its magnetic reels, and the cold lump she had left in my stomach, I was feeling vulnerable. I followed him, wondering whether to claim I had my own period and demand an unmolested night. (I get my periods; nothing saintly about me.) I was still wondering at the door, when I saw his bed was already taken. Sweater girl, I mean scrambled-egg girl, the pug-faced one – Brooke was under the duvet. Or half in, half exposed.

The Director was grinning. Grinning at pug-face, then at me. He said, 'Let's have some fun.'

I told him to fuck off, and slept on the sofa. He kicked me out, made me ride past the attack dogs and through the gates in the delivery van, at eight the next morning. I still haven't had my mobile phone back.

Chapter Thirty-Eight

She heard him, through the closed door and the locked shutters and through the floorboards. Shouting.

She plunged her fingers into her ears and screwed up her eyes and gritted her teeth, but she could still hear him. Spitting and cursing and shouting.

Someone had made Peter very angry. Ella was scared it had been her. She would do anything to make him happy – she would bring any weight of unhappiness upon herself if Peter wanted it. But so what – it meant nothing. She was useless. She never seemed to please him, and now she had done something to anger him. She did not even know what. That's how stupid Ella was. She didn't even know. She wished he had believed her when she first told him she was useless and stupid and stupid and useless.

Any minute now he would come crashing up the stairs. Marching down the passage. Flinging open her door. Bellowing at her. She clamped her hands against her jaw. She didn't know if she could stand for Peter to shout at her.

Peter flung open her door.

He hurled something over her head.

It was dark in Ella's cell. The one window was barricaded, the light was off and the passage outside was unlit. Guntarson fumbled on the far side of the room for the lamp switch. Ella, hunched on the floor with her face on her knees, waited for a blow across her back or in her ribs, the way her father used to beat her.

When the blow did not come she squeezed open one eye. Guntarson, leaning back against the wall with his eyes upturned to the ceiling, was clutching a rag of newspaper in his hands. The rest of the paper was balled on Ella's bed. It was the *Observer*.

'Get up,' he ordered. 'Go on, get up.'

'I'm sorry,' she said.

'Sorry? What for?'

'It's my fault. Sorry.'

'You sound like your damned mother. It's nothing to do with you. It's me. If I have one besetting fault' – he slid down the wall till he was crouching opposite her – 'it's my inability to judge character. I seem to see the good points in everyone, and I'm blind to their bad sides until it's too late. You ought to be good at that, reading characters. You're much more intuitive – I rely too much on my intelligence. You tell me – what did you make of that journalist, a few weeks back? You were tired – do you remember?'

'Didn't like her.'

'Ah! Why not?'

''Cos you said she was special.'

'You knew she was bad news, just because I rated her? Is my judgment really that transparently abysmal? Or do you mean you saw how she'd ingratiated herself? Yes, I suppose I took her too much on trust.'

Ella said nothing. She remembered hating Aliss, just because she was scared Peter found the older woman attractive. The idea was sick. This journalist looked about thirty. It had been very wrong of Ella, of course, to accuse Peter secretly, because in the morning the woman had gone.

Ella had forced herself to talk and talk to the journalist as a punishment for being stupid. And she was so stupid, she said the wrong things to the journalist and her tape-recorder.

'That newspaper's really stitched us up.'

'I ain't going to read it.'

'Good. So long as they spell our names correctly, it's always good for us, eh? So you keep your thoughts pure for prayer. I'm not angry with you, Ella.'

'Honest?'

'Honest.'

He was generous, and forgiving, and kind. Ella didn't deserve a friend like him.

'I am angry. You're about the only person in the world I'm not angry with, and I'm trying not to take it out on you, Ella. I'm steamed up with that nerd, what does he call himself? Stewpot! What a name to give yourself. Stewed brains, more like. How can you make allowance for people like that – you leave them five minutes with a journalist and they start organising guided tours. I am so angry. I'm going to take it out on him. Stewpot! I'd like to drop him in the gorge.'

'I likes him.'

'You don't even know him. You can't like everyone, Ella.'

'He comes and looks at me. Like Frank used to. He don't say nothing, he's too scared.'

'And what right has he to disturb your prayers?'

'He don't disturb me, honest. I don't even see him. I just feel when he's come to the door.'

'He's going to suffer. How can I control what the world thinks about you if other people keep sticking their oars in? It's essential that there is only one viewpoint on you, Ella, a single global opinion. You do appreciate that? The idea of letting that ... that traitor ... the journalist, letting her meet you.' He was almost incoherent in his fury. 'She was supposed to tell our story positively. The trouble I went to, winning her round. I thought I'd won her round. I even dictated to her what she had to write. And she twisted it. Every fact presented in the worst possible light. The damage ... the damage. Thank God, people with any sense won't believe a word of it, they'll read between the lines. And it was so badly written – almost unreadable. The first week was awful, this second week is plain illiterate.

'But anyone who took it at face value – what are they going to think of me, for a start? That I'm some sleazy pervert? I am still single, I'd like to remind you!' Guntarson was jabbing both forefingers at Ella, across the little room. 'What I do in private, that's not a matter of public interest. Jesus! I think it would be a little more perverted, actually, if a man in my international position didn't have a healthy drive.'

He registered at last the frightened bewilderment on Ella's face. 'I don't have to justify myself to you, do I?' Guntarson asked more quietly. 'Ah well. Luckily for us, what people read today they don't remember tomorrow. It's chip wrappers.'

He grabbed the crumpled magazine and was about to hurl it harder into the corner when he paused, his eye snared by the bright colours of the back cover. He smoothed it over his knee and looked again. It was a tour company's ad – three kings on camels followed a burning star past the pyramids at Giza. Guntarson laid the page gently on the floor.

During the long silence that followed, Ella waited for him to go away.

'We need a fresh start,' he said. 'Realign the global viewpoint. A physical dislocation of sight-lines. We need to move, in other words. Where would you like to live, Ella, where in the world?'

She looked confused, but hopeful.

'Somewhere hot? Somewhere beautiful? By the sea? In the mountains? I suppose it doesn't matter much to you, since you're always going to be closed up, praying, out of the public eye. You just need your little shuttered room and you're happy then, eh? But I'm sure you get a sense of your surroundings. And I'm always going to be with you, and you'd like me to be living somewhere special, wouldn't you? So where do you say we should go?'

'With Frank. Frank and my mum and dad.'

'Your mother's in Florida. That's possible, I suppose, but it's a bit overcrowded for our purposes. Madonna lives there, Stallone, the BeeGees. Media-ridden. I suppose you mean you'd like the Florida climate. Or is it Disney World you want to see? You couldn't just visit, you know. There'd be riots. You wouldn't want anyone hurt on your account. But perhaps they'd open it up just for you, if we paid them enough – the way Michael Jackson goes shopping. I don't know . . . not Florida, I think.'

'I just want to live with my mum and dad.'

Guntarson laughed. 'Back in Nelson Road, you mean? Yeah, lovely. Seriously – we've got to make a new beginning.' He leapt to his feet, towering over her. 'Maybe you could do with some sunshine. We want you in the peak of health. Lovely shining skin. Otherwise you'll give more credence to this irresponsible nonsense about pallor and sadness and anorexia. Ella Wallis – anorexic! It just shows, these people know nothing about you. Nothing. And we must not let them colour the world's view of you. A fresh beginning. You have a think about it, and I will too.'

He shut the door briskly behind him, leaving Ella alone on the floor of her empty cell, then bobbed back into the room.

She glanced up, expectantly. 'Sorry,' he said, and flicked the lamp off. When he closed the door again the room was in utter darkness.

Where the borderline lay between prayer and sleep Ella no longer knew. She prayed herself into unconsciousness and, when she came round, the unfinished supplication was still on her lips.

When she was dreaming, she supposed, she must be asleep. She did not pray in her dreams. The dreams were vivid, an experience far more ferocious than the monotonous repetition of prayers in her shuttered room. But prayers were what she did when she was awake – prayers were the reality. The dreams weren't real. That was a comfort, at least.

The dream of drowning came and went like a tide. Sometimes it seemed to wash over her again and again, six or eight times before she woke. Sometimes it ebbed away, leaving her imagination exposed to other dreams.

When Peter switched off the light, the drowning dream began to lap at her. She never fought it – the struggle began only when she felt the hand clamped around her ankle and the fingers clawing into her tendons, ripping at her leg as the waves slopped over her face. She struggled to pull her foot from the inexorable clutch, and she struggled to reach the feeble hand of the child who could not rescue her. But she did not struggle to avoid the dream.

This time, though she could feel the iron claw at her ankle and the thin, weak hand round her wrist, Ella was not the one drowning. Ella was looking down on the scene.

Ella was the angel.

She saw the face of the blonde woman under the water, her hair flowing out around her. Ella had felt her terror so often, the shock of cold, dark water in her lungs and the agonising grip on her leg. But now she did not know if this drowning woman was really her. She did not look quite like Ella.

In her dream, Ella was hovering above the scene, the way she had heard a dead person's soul hovered above their body.

She could not make out the figure of the child, reaching down into the water, helpless to save the woman. The child was blond too, with a birthmark like a star glowing on the crown of his head.

Ella wanted to reach her, and strained down to touch the face beneath the muddy waves. A great shadow lay below the drowning figure.

Ella felt herself blazing with intensity, filled with the light she had seen so often.

This was how it felt. Being an angel.

Daily Express, Monday, December 20:

Ella Wallis is to quit Britain and transfer her global prayer mission to Israel, Director Peter Guntarson announced last night.

Her psychic powers were becoming blunted by 'negativity' left over from an often unhappy childhood, he said.

The decision sent shockwaves through government circles, as politicians assessed the implications of transplanting an international network into one of the world's most sensitive flashpoints.

In a terse statement, Director Guntarson said: 'Ella wishes me to inform her billions of devotees that she no longer feels she can make the greatest contribution to world prayer by remaining in Bristol, the city of her birth.

'This decision is hers and hers alone, and has not been reached without an intense degree of contemplation. Ella's acute psychic sensibilities are oppressed by the weight of a difficult upbringing and many unfortunate associations which cling to Bristol and to England in general.

'She wishes to assure all her friends that, in making a fresh beginning, she will not be casting aside all the warmth and love which has flooded upon her in Bristol, but simply sloughing off the negativity which has inevitably accrued.

'There can be no apter home for a holy child than the Holy Land. Israel, with its profound religious heritage, can provide a sounding-board for the quiet, invincible voice of Ella's prayers. It is from Israel that peace will flood over the globe, as her conflict with the Arab world is resolved. And it is in Israel that the Ella Foundation will put down roots which, as a sometimes cynical world will be forced to see, shall prove ever-lasting.

'It is Ella's avowed intent to remain above the factions of religion. Her presence in Israel will be in no way an endorsement for Judaism, Christianity or Islam, though she accepts and reveres the virtue of all major belief systems. She does devoutly hope that her presence in the Middle East will hasten the peace process which the world so urgently needs.'

Ella's decision comes after ten days of intense speculation, sparked by the first account of life inside the Ella Centre which revealed a regîme of secrecy and infighting.

Observers were nonplussed by the move, however. A switch to the United States or Guntarson's native Canada had been predicted in the past but, despite the Director's partly Jewish heritage, none had ever voiced suggestions of an Israeli connection.

One expert said last night: 'It seems a bizarre decision. Perhaps Ella's intention is to dislocate herself wholly from the past, to become a self-contained prayer unit.

'But she should beware of cutting herself off completely from the culture she knows. The recent descriptions of her suggest loneliness and home-sickness are already a source of depression for her, and a move away from Britain could exacerbate this factor.'

'I don't want to live in Israel.'
    'Why not? Israel's beautiful.'
    'I dunno.'
    'That's no answer.'
    'It ain't my home. I never been there.'
    'Ella, you've never been anywhere. And in a way it is your home, because it's the Holy Land. Wouldn't you like to see Bethlehem, where the baby Jesus was born?'
    'Don't want to go.'

'Why ever not?'

'It's cold.'

'Of course it isn't. It's the Middle East. Lovely and hot. Think what a tan you'll get.'

'There's no people.'

'Where do you get your ideas from? Did they teach you nothing at school? Of course there's people, Israel's full of people. My mother's family are there, you know.'

'My mum ain't there.'

'She can visit you. Let's face it, she doesn't visit you here. Okay, I'm sorry. I'll make sure she comes as often as you like. I'll pay for her tickets, first class, myself. And Frank. How about that?'

'I won't.'

'Ella. You've never refused to do anything for me.'

'So?'

'Don't you like me any more? Ella?'

'Yeah.'

'Yeah what?'

''Course I likes you.'

'So trust me. This is best for you. Okay?'

'Peter?'

'Hmm? What? What do you want to say? Don't be frightened. You know you can say whatever you like to me. Look, I'll just wait for you to say it, I'll just sit here and you tell me when you're ready . . . Oh come on Ella, I do have other things to do, you know. Okay. Sorry. I didn't mean to snap at you. I'll go downstairs and you tell me when I come back.'

'Peter?'

'Ye-es?'

'Is it next year yet?'

'What? No, it's still December.'

'I'm going to be sixteen next year.'

'Well, if you want a present or something, Christmas comes first.'

'Can't do it at Christmas.'

'Do what? Do what, Ella?'

'Get married.'

'Married? Who to? Oh Ella, I mean, come on . . . Ella that's very flattering and you're very sweet to be thinking it. Now look. I want you to put all thoughts of that out of your head for now. You're not sixteen, you're only fifteen, and quite a young fifteen at that. There are laws, you know that, and there's reasons for those laws. And if people thought we were acting like, you know, like an engaged couple when you're just fifteen, you could get me into a lot of trouble. A lot.'

'I don't want to cause no trouble.'

'Okay. So thank you for being brave enough to say that to me. And for thinking it in the first place. When we're in Israel, I expect we'll have a lot more time together. And we'll get to know each other more. And who knows? We'll wait and see when you're sixteen.'

'You going to be with me more? If we go to Israel?'

'I promise. And then when you're sixteen – who knows?'

'Honest?'

'Honest, honest, honest.'

'Give me your stone.'

'What?' he said.

'You know, your stone. What's always in your pocket. I'll keep it for you. For a pledge. Then you'll have to see me lots, 'cos I got your stone.'

'You mean this?' He reached inside his jacket and from the silk lining drew the long shaft of clear quartz. Ella held out her hand. 'This is mine,' he told her. 'It's very significant to me.'

'I wants it.'

Guntarson gazed into the rock. To his disappointed eyes it was, as it always was, lifeless. He handed it to Ella. 'I'm not giving it to you. I'm entrusting it. Do you understand?'

She stared at the sparkling crystal, nodding hard. Guntarson suspected she was not nodding an answer to him, but at something she saw on the faces of the stone.

She slipped the quartz under the folds of her bedding.

'Peter?'

'Uh-hmm?'

'What about Furbag, Peter?'

'Well, he can't come, he'd be too much trouble on the flight. And then there's quarantine and everything.' He knew this was a lie, that there was no quarantine in Israel, but it was a white lie. Whitish, surely. He just couldn't be bothered with a wretched dog. 'Much better to leave him.'

'I ain't going.'

'Oh Ella.'

'Furbag's mine, he's my dog, you give him me. I ain't never had him only a few months and he's just got to know me.'

'Ella, he prefers Ti . . . no he doesn't, you're right, he's your dog. But he's only a puppy, he'd soon make new friends.'

'This is his home. It ain't fair, just 'cos he's a dog. I ain't going.'

'Ella, there's lovely animals in Israel. You can have a rabbit or something.'

'I don't want no sodding rabbit.'

'Ella.'

'I ain't going to Israel! I hates it!'

'All right. All right. You want the dog – I'll see what I can do. I'll get round it. That's a promise.'

'Furbag can come?'

'I told you. I'll find a solution.'

They flew out the day before Christmas. Ella had not mentioned the date, and Guntarson suspected she was happier to ignore it. Christmas probably meant hours in a cold church, and her father's brother in front of the television, and her mother drunk before tea-time. Christmas was discouraged in the Ella Centre anyway. Relatives could not possibly be allowed to visit, and this would be the wrong time to give the staff home leave. Anyone who did not relish a new life in Israel might take the chance to decamp. And forget their sacred non-disclosure contract, and sell their story. So the Director had issued a stern little warning about the pagan origins of Christmas and the dangers of following the path to witchcraft.

Tim led Ella down the stairs. He had not brought Furbag to see her this morning. Tim was a youth with long curls and tiny pustules between the grains of stubble. His eyes were filmy, with sore rims, and this morning he stood over Ella, watching her swallow down her breakfast. When he brought her to the Director, she looked queasy and uncomfortable – he had not given her the privacy to vomit.

At the door she held back, one arm clasping the bag containing a change of clothes and the green teddy. Months ago, when Frank was only just cured, she had unpicked the back of the soft toy and hidden a photograph inside. A photo of Frank, when he was a baby, with their mother. It was something to hug.

Peter's arms were folded, with his shoulders hunched. His elbows jutted defensively. He did not step forward to greet her. 'I'm sorry about the dog, Ella,' he said.

Ella blinked. 'You said he can come. You promised. He's got to come.'

The Director's cold eyes locked on the long-haired youngster beside Ella. 'Haven't you told her?'

Tim tried to answer, but his voice choked him and the wet film welled over his eyelashes.

'I ordered you to tell her!'

Tim clasped despairingly at the air and turned away from Ella.

'Where's Furbag? Why ain't he coming?'

'Ella, Ella. Come on. I'll get you another one. Furbag got out last night.'

'He wouldn't run away.'

'Someone left the door open.'

'I ain't going nowhere till he comes back.'

'Ella, I'm sorry, he won't be back.'

'We can go look for him. He can't be lost – there's the wall. He's just hiding.'

'Ella, one of the big dogs saw him. It went for him.'

'That's why he's hiding.' She stared at Guntarson's face. 'He weren't hurt, was he?'

'He couldn't have suffered much.' The Director reached out his arms to comfort her, but for the first time she did not want to be held.

She clamped her suitcase to her chest instead.

'Poor Furbag, I was very upset.'

'He ain't dead! He's only a puppy. The big dogs, they wouldn't hurt him. It's some other dog.'

'Come on, Ella, how would another dog get in here?'

'So,' she said. 'He ain't going to Israel.'

'I wish he could.'

'You promised.'

'I couldn't know this would happen. It's tragic,' he added.

'No one's never left doors open before.'

'It was very unlucky.'

'And why'd he go out anyway?'

'Perhaps he saw a rabbit and wanted to chase it. See? At least he would have been happy.'

'There ain't no rabbits. They'd be got by the big dogs.'

'Ella, don't be cross with me. It wasn't me who let your dog out.'

'Who was it then?'

'I don't know. I'll find out.'

'Was it Tim? Is that why you wanted him to tell me?'

'Yes. I don't know. I promise I'll get you another.'

'You promised I could have Furbag.'

'Christ! Ella, it's a dog. You're standing here arguing with me about dogs when you could be saying prayers to save babies' lives. Little babies! Which is more important – dogs or babies? For God's sake. Act your age a bit. You're fifteen now. Look, the helicopter's out there. It's a lovely shining brand-new white R44, a four-seater. Isn't that great? We're going to have a nice exciting helicopter ride to the airport, and then we're going on an aeroplane. And I'm going to be sitting next to you all the way. I won't read or work, I'll talk to you all the time if you want. If you get scared, you can hold my hand. Does that sound good? Now come on, give me your bag.'

When Guntarson plucked the small suitcase from her arms, it came with a scream – a whine like a fingertip on the rim of a wet glass, going round and round, harder and faster. He ignored it. The noise hovered over him as he strode across the lawn and tossed the bag behind the pilot's cockpit.

When he pulled Ella across the grass by the wrist, she was looking around, searching for a sign of where her dog had died.

The pilot, a butch woman with cropped, henna'd hair, was twisting to find the source of the noise. 'There's something playing up,' she called out.

'Ignore it.'

'Have you got electrical items in that bag?'

'It's just an Ella thing,' insisted Guntarson, pulling the girl up into the passengers' compartment beside him. He reached across her to fasten the webbing belts.

The temperature gauge leapt as though a switch had been thrown. The pilot stared. The needle was stretched to maximum red and stayed straining and quivering before snapping to zero.

Guntarson followed her gaze. 'It's just Ella. It's not deliberate, she's just uptight.'

A packet of M+Ms flew between their shoulders and burst against the glass, scattering over the controls. The whine grew louder, pulsing.

'I don't care if it is deliberate.' The pilot tugged her headphones off. 'We're not taking off with her on board.'

'If you want to have a job tomorrow, we are.'

With a bang, the cockpit gave judder, as if a blast of air had hit it.

'No way, Mr Guntarson. You can't expect me to fly in these conditions.'

'Ella's your boss. You don't refuse.'

'For her safety, as well as mine. Yours too. I have to know the instruments are accurate.'

Guntarson raised his voice above the shifting tone. 'This is your last chance. I'm telling you.'

A fistful of stones rattled against the floor of the machine, and a small rock banged into the door. The cockpit was briefly silent, and another stone hit, hard enough to dent the metal.

'That's it. I've never seen anything like this. I'm getting out and I don't get back in till you two are off. Off my 'copter before you wreck it.'

'Right! I've warned you!' Guntarson almost pushed Ella through the door and leapt down after her. 'You'll never fly again! I'll have your licence. You'll be grounded – you think I can't do it? I can fix it like that!' He snapped his fingers above his head.

'Why doesn't she just fly away herself?' yelled the pilot, trying to rub a dent out of her helicopter.

'You'll see! I'll show you!' The Director strode towards the house, holding Ella's bag in his left hand and pointing at Stewpot with his right: 'You. Call a car! Now! We're driving out. Move!' Turning back to Ella, trailing across the lawn in the faint hope of spotting Furbag, he warned: 'This better not be deliberate.'

The shriek that hung over her suddenly leapt into the air, and switched like a whip's tip from the house, across the lawn, to the walls. It shattered window panes, showering glass at the foot of the house, and it cracked camera lenses and spectacles. The photographers on their ladders beyond the perimeter were suddenly as good as blind. Their cameras could see nothing. But that did not matter. They had their pictures of Ella, the first for months. They had pictures of Peter Guntarson pointing lividly at his little angel. Pictures like that would flash around the world. They were worth a year's wait – they were worth three years' salary.

There was no more waiting. The snappers were already on their mobiles to the agency picture desks, as they loaded equipment into the backs of their cars. No one was left to watch, by the time Guntarson and Ella slid through the gates and across the Suspension Bridge in a black-windowed Bentley.

Chapter Thirty-Nine

Two sounds troubled Peter Guntarson as he paced the floor. Broken glass crackled under his feet. And in the next room Ella sobbed.

She had broken the windows of the apartment, one by one. Not deliberately – none of her violence had been deliberate. If she had been shattering the panes with her fists, he might have stopped her. But the glass had blown out, frame by frame, showering jagged splinters across every brocaded chair, every four-poster bed, every embroidered rug and every mosaic floor, in all of the eight rooms, and she had seemed not to notice. Each window exploded with a boom like a grenade.

Crowds gathered to stare at the eighth-floor penthouse. The police, the ambulances and the bomb disposal unit came, thinking a terrorist bomb had detonated. They insisted on evacuating the building and marching into the apartment in bomb-proof body armour. Ella's huddled, whimpering body crouched on a chair.

The police were awed, and puzzled, and suspicious. They saw the glass had hurt no one. They saw that Ella was helplessly unhappy. They left, reluctantly.

With its dark, gaping windows and the horde of people gathered at the base of the building, this was Guntarson's anonymous hideaway.

Stewpot crouched, scooping glass into a bucket. He had been chosen to accompany the Director and Ella to Israel. The other disciples were to remain in Bristol while the new Ella Centre was constructed. Stewpot had been chosen, partly because the Director felt he might be trusted by Ella, but mostly because he happened to cross Guntarson's line of sight at the moment of decision. Plus, his passport was up to date.

From the moment the Bentley drove out of the grounds, new phenomena were flinging themselves around Ella in uncontrollable tantrums. It was as if little demons were climbing out of her undersized suitcase and throwing themselves into the air. The Director had ordered Ella over and over to get a grip on them, and she kept whispering that she wanted to. She was cowed and scared, sitting almost motionless in the back of the limousine, but the outbursts became more explosive.

Objects appeared and were hurled around their heads and disappeared. Stewpot clutched his seat, eyes closed and praying hard, while the car was filled with noises – cloth ripping and meaningless voices and chinaware smashing. The TV flicked on, off, on, off. Walnut fascia was ripped from the dashboard. The driver refused to look around or speak; at Heathrow he got out of the £250,000 car and walked away, abandoning it to the short-stay car-park.

The whine was unending. It swelled furiously when Guntarson tried to hypnotise Ella. It throbbed as he led her through security, into the VIP area, and onto their executive chartered DC-9. It rose to a head-splitting whistle when the two jet engines started up. Ella hunched, Stewpot sitting silently beside her. With her chin on her knees and her fingers in her ears, Ella stared miserably at the ceiling. She had never travelled in an aeroplane before.

A steady beating began on the aircraft's shell once they were over the continent, like a fist drumming against the door. But the instrument panels were calm, and Guntarson tried to assure the captain and first officer that these noises were quite normal: 'Providing I can hear that racket, I know Ella's powers are tip-top. Honestly.'

A Waterford jug split in two and ice-cubes went spinning across the floor.

A drawer of cutlery at the stewardess's elbow emptied itself so violently that dinner knives, all of them bent, were embedded in seats six rows away.

'It looks worse than it is. You take these things for granted after a while. No one ever gets hurt,' he reassured the speechless air hostess. She ran to report to the captain.

At Ben-Gurion airport they were met by a benefactor whose grey Mercedes ferried them away from the terminal's King David first class lounge. They rode discreetly and circuitously through Tel Aviv. The benefactor, at first delighted to see Ella, was quickly panicked by the unremitting whine, by the sudden flashes and smashes in the air round his head, by Ella's skeletal frailty and by her constant, mumbled pleas to see Frank and Juliette.

The benefactor, a nervous man, carried Valium with him. In the car he offered the box to Guntarson. Between them, they tried to administer the tranquillizer to Ella. Stewpot held her shoulders, gently, while the benefactor proffered the pills and Guntarson attempted to prise open her mouth. She seemed not to resist, but whenever the pill touched her lips they were sealed.

They arrived at a luxurious penthouse on the top floor of a Tel Aviv apartment block, seven curved, panoramic windows like vast eyes staring across the Mediterranean. The benefactor was very glad to abandon his home to Ella and seek refuge with friends.

Before he had left the lobby, his windows began to blow in. He did not turn back.

Crash. 'Jesus, Ella!' Fragments of glass scattered like rice-grains across the floor. 'Please Ella, that is too much.' *Crash*. 'Ella, I know you can stop this if you want.' Guntarson shied as each pane detonated. Ella just stood, in the centre of the sitting-room, mumbling, with her hands clasped.

Stewpot faced her, staring horror-struck at her upturned eyes.

'Ella, are you praying?' the Director demanded. 'Ella, I can't stand this. There's no control. There must be control.' *Crash*. 'Psi power isn't meaningless. It has intelligence. This isn't intelligent. If you're praying, pray for this to stop. What's she saying?' He shouted the last words to Stewpot.

'The same.'

Peter, still flinching at the blasts which Ella seemed not to hear, put his ear close to her lips.

'I wants my mum. I wants my mum. Where's my mum? I wants her. Where's Frank? I wants him. Where's my mum?'

'Ella, you know that's just not possible.'

Crash.

'If your mum wanted to be here, she would.'

Crash.

'All right. Jesus Christ, all right. I'll do what I can.'

Crash.

'I said I'd do . . . Okay okay okay she can come. You can see her. I'll bring her here.'

Ella sighed. The sudden respite from shattering glass made Peter realise how intense the invisible whine had become, shrieking like radio feedback.

'Ella please, calm down.'

'You get her now?'

'I can't get her now, but soon.'

Crash. The last curved expanse of glass blew in.

'Yes, yes, now then. If that's what it takes.'

'And Frank too.'

'Of course Frank, you don't think I'd forget him, do you? Is that better?' The whine started to die back. 'God, I wish I thought of that a long time ago. Start clearing this up, can't you?' he told Stewpot. 'No, put her in a chair first. Get her sitting down. We can't stay here now. Look at it.' He went to one of the torn windows. Approaching sirens wailed in the streets below. 'God, look out there. Half Tel Aviv's come to look. We can't stay here. And it was perfect, so right. It's ruined. Destroyed.'

He stared across the street, at the Arabian estate which occupied the block opposite – a shuttered, grey stone villa set in one corner, mosque-like with its arches and verandahs. It had been left almost untouched since the days of Palestine. A high, rusted fence sealed off the grounds.

The police arrived. When they had gone and Guntarson had tried briefly to settle Ella, he stared again at the deserted Arab house. It sparked a brainwave. He would place Ella in the monastery of St Catherine in Sinai. It would be close to the site of the Foundation's new head-quarters, it would be remote, it would be secure and it would convey the proper image of sanctity and devotion. Much better than hiding out in some business-man's penthouse. In the meantime, they would just have to lodge at a hotel.

Guntarson looked at Ella. Her knees were drawn up to her eyes and her body trembled with tears.

But she would like St Catherine's. She was bound to.

Coming to Israel had not been a horrible mistake at all. It was the only way to keep control. Guntarson was certain of it.

The Monastery of St Catherine was honoured to offer refuge to Ella. She was provided with a prayer cell and, as she now seemed oblivious to whatever room sheltered her, it was as good a place as any to keep her.

But before she was taken to St Catherine's, she saw her family again.

CHAPTER FORTY

Everyone in the world Ella knew had dropped away from her as she floated higher and higher. Parents, schoolfriends, teachers, brother. Home, neighbours. Now she had even left her country behind.

Guntarson could not regret it, of course. It was her destiny, and his. Something that mattered much more than her happiness. And after all, she had hardly been happy to start with.

On the sofa in their double suite at the Tel Aviv Hilton, he reached over and took her hand. It lay between his fingers, like cold dough.

'Juliette will be here soon,' he promised. 'Here it is, Christmas Day, I've hired these rooms especially and I booked the tickets myself to bring her here. It isn't easy to get tickets for December 25th on twenty-four hours' notice, but I did it for you. Because I promised. Isn't that a great Christmas present?'

Ella began to cry. The sobs began as hard, sudden breaths. He thought she was going to sneeze, and wondered if she might be allergic to something, when tears ran over her cheeks and onto her hair, so quickly that some strands gathered eight or nine drops like pearls on a string. 'I wants to go away.'

'Before your mother comes?'

'With her.'

Guntarson did not contradict her. He was beginning to be afraid of contradicting Ella.

They waited. The whine which had never ceased since the plane touched down at Ben-Gurion was more distant now, as though it had wandered away and become lost and separated from Ella.

Ella's sobs faded too. She muttered once, 'If it's Christmas morning, we got to be in church.'

'We should pray,' agreed Guntarson.

They prayed. It helped to pass the time. Guntarson did not dare leave her side. He felt an impending catastrophe.

At eleven minutes to eleven, there came a tap at the door. 'Here we go,' whispered Guntarson.

He unbolted the door.

The gleaming head of Dr José Dóla peeped round. 'The right room,' he exclaimed.

Guntarson slipped out into the corridor and slammed the door behind him. Though he disliked to abandon Ella for a moment, he was more reluctant still to allow Dóla back into her presence.

Beside Dóla stood Juliette. No Frank.

Movement caught his eye and Guntarson glanced up the dim passageway. Frank stood with his father, Ken, and his Uncle Robert.

'No,' said Guntarson. 'No, no, no.'

'My dear Director.' Dóla seized his hand. 'Perhaps it would be better if we stepped into your suite?'

Guntarson shook off Joe Dóla and took hold of Juliette's arm.

'Mrs Wallis may come in. Frank too, if he likes. The rest of you can piss off now.'

'You can let go of my wife, pal.' Ken came striding towards him. 'I bet you ain't forgotten last time you crossed my path. Want some more, do you?'

'And big brother's here this time,' growled Uncle Robert.

'Boys, boys.' Dóla threw up his hands. 'You did promise.'

'I am sorry,' Juliette was murmuring, 'you know he is still my husband.'

'No one invited them,' Guntarson told Dóla. 'Or you.'

'I invited them,' the doctor protested. 'And Mrs Wallis invited me. Really, must we bicker in the corridor? Is Ella on her own behind this door? Are you not concerned? What do you suppose she is thinking?'

Frank had wriggled past his family and had his eye pressed to the keyhole. 'I can't see her,' he announced.

Guntarson was twitching. To leave the girl alone in her present mood, with windows unguarded and all the bolts on her side of the door – it was dangerous. And to let this rabble back into her life – it was madness.

'Mrs Wallis, Frank, yes. The rest of you – Ella hasn't asked for you. She is not your client, Dóla, and Ken Wallis, she is no longer your daughter.'

'Bollocks,' snarled Ken. 'And whatever she is to you, pal, you ought to be in nick for it.'

'Get him away from here,' hissed Guntarson.

'I really don't think,' the doctor said with mild venom, 'that he wants to go away.'

'Okay. I'm calling the police.' The Director had his mobile in his hand.

'Ella might not be so pleased,' suggested Dóla. 'Her whole family here for Christmas, and you have them arrested. And again, think of the publicity.'

'Which you have already tied up, I imagine?'

'You should be pleased, Director. I'm sure you will be. The most famous fractured family in the world, Ella's own family, healed by prayer on Christmas Day. I'm surprised at you, Peter. I hadn't imagined that your timing was accidental.'

'I chose Christmas,' said Guntarson, still blocking the door with his back, 'because Ella asked at Christmas. She asked for her mother and her brother. She hasn't asked before, and she has never asked to see her father. Or the exorcist.'

'She's still not there,' Frank called from the keyhole.

Guntarson wanted to crack the boy's head against the handle. The sofa ought to be visible to him – why was Ella not there?

'You go in,' he conceded, 'and if Ella asks any of you to leave, you leave at once. Is that understood?'

'Open the door,' said Ken and, shoving his son aside, he did it himself.

Ella stood at the window, staring seventeen storeys down. All that lay above her was the roof and the Hilton sign and the blue sky. She had not been in so high a building before. To the people in the gardens below, under parasols and drinking coffee at round, white tables, and to the bathers and rowers in white boats bobbing on gold-tipped waves, Ella would be as tiny as they appeared to her. But they were not aware of her presence. She could see them. She was praying for them.

Frank squealed, 'Ella,' and launched himself across the room at her.

She let him hold her hands. He stared at her, his eyes almost level with hers and his bones much stronger, and she whispered, 'You grown.'

Juliette, rooted in the doorway, said: 'Oh my God. My God.'

With the light of the window behind her, Ella was almost transparent. Her skin, hanging on her face like the papery wrinkles of a seventy-year-old, was without colour or substance. It was as if Juliette could have pressed a fingertip through it, onto her daughter's bones. Her skull seemed swollen, a rough globe which was nothing more than a stand for Ella's always magnificent, apparently endless, silver hair.

Against the glare of the sunlight, Ella's thin frame was merely a blurred line.

'You are not well,' breathed Juliette.

'You been starving her?' demanded Ken.

'Now I understand your reluctance,' remarked Dóla. 'In your position, I should not be anxious to let people see her. You might find yourself answering questions about child abuse.'

Ella said, 'I'm okay.'

'I'm sorry, but you do not look okay.'

'I been praying. It drains me. Peter says.'

'Then you are to stop praying,' declared her mother. Ella faced her across the room.

Juliette, tentatively, held out her hands.

Ella walked gratefully into the embrace.

'I have been working not to drink so much,' whispered Juliette. 'But without my daughter, there is not so much point to be good. Now you are back, I will not have drinks any more. That's a promise.'

Ella looked up. 'You always had Frank.'

'Thank you for Frank,' said Juliette, and gave her daughter a hug. She meant that hug more than she had ever meant anything she felt for Ella. Without Ella, Frank would be dead.

Dr Dóla's camera flashed.

Guntarson made a lunge, and missed. 'Film,' he snapped.

'I don't think so,' smiled Dóla. 'I mean, the first embrace. Reunited, mother and daughter. Could you really ask to obliterate the memory of such a joyous moment?'

'Give it here,' repeated Guntarson.

A knock sounded, and at the same time the door, which Guntarson had not bolted, began to open. He jammed his foot against it.

'It's Stewpot,' pleaded a voice in the corridor.

Guntarson checked, and let him in. 'Yes?' he asked.

Stewpot stared around. 'They all came,' he said.

'Quite. Did you want something?'

'Reception's ringing to ask if we want Christmas dinner. I said yes for me, is that okay?'

'Tell 'em yes for all of us,' Ken butted in. 'There's six of us. Make it seven 'cos your precious Ella needs double portions.'

Stewpot looked dubiously at him. He had heard stories of Ella's father.

'Go and ring,' ordered Guntarson. 'They can eat, and when they've eaten they can leave.' But Stewpot did not go back to his own suite. He slipped into the adjoining bedroom and used the phone there.

'Photo-opportunity,' yelped Dóla. 'Come on, gather round. All the family on this grand sofa. Ella, you must sit in the middle. The centre-piece. And Juliette, you will look charming beside her. Now you could be sisters – who would suppose you were mother and daughter?'

Guntarson watched with his lip curling. But Ella still clutched her mother's hand. She seemed truly glad of her presence.

'Frank, it's best if you take Ella's other hand. You started it, in a way, all this prayer business.'

'Brave lad,' approved his father.

'Ken and Robert, you're the guardians at either end. You'll squeeze in. Ah, Robert, your posterior is a trifle broad, isn't it? You won't quite fit.'

'Frankie,' suggested Uncle Robert, 'can sit on my lap.'

'Not necessary,' Dóla said hastily, 'not at all. You should sit on the sofa arm, to emphasise your stature.'

At the other end of the chair Ken, to be sure of equal stature with his brother, raised himself on the arm too.

'I shall stand behind the group,' declared Guntarson.

'No you won't,' said Ken.

'This is a family portrait, now smile please,' Dóla said, raising the camera. 'Director,' he exclaimed, 'you have ruined this shot.'

Guntarson had walked into the frame as the doctor pressed the shutter.

'Get out of it,' growled Uncle Robert, seizing Guntarson's lapel and pushing him back. Guntarson raised his fists and thought better of it.

'On Christmas Day!' he mocked, but kept his distance. Uncle Robert scowled.

'Please, let us have our family picture,' asked Juliette.

'Ella's family is the world now,' answered Guntarson, 'and I am the head representative of that family.'

'You're a fuckin' crackpot, that's what you are,' said Ken.

'Please, I am sorry but please language, really,' said Juliette, gesturing at her son.

'Someone's got to tell him,' nodded Uncle Robert.

'And it's going to be me,' said Ken, rising up.

Guntarson's mobile was out again. 'One step and I'm calling the police.

'You'll be dead meat, crack-pot, before they get here.'

'You think so. I'm ready for you this time,' answered Guntarson, curling his fists like a university boxer. 'And whatever the outcome, you're heading for an Israeli prison.'

'I'd be doing the world a favour, putting you out of everybody's misery.'

Ella whispered, 'Stop fighting. Stop fighting.' Nobody listened.

Uncle Robert was mimicking Guntarson's stance, feet apart, forearms up. 'Reckon he'd last long on a Saturday night up North Street, Kennie?'

'Ooh yeah, he'd look lovely strung up on a lamppost.'

'Strung up,' agreed Uncle Robert, 'that's what the dirty little pervie ought to be.'

'Right,' said Guntarson, and started to dial. Ken Wallis took two swift steps, locked his hand over Guntarson's and twisted. The phone dropped and Ken glanced down to crush it under his heel.

Guntarson's fist came up, a neat schoolboy uppercut that drew a spurt of blood from Ken's nose.

Ken roared and swung forward, but Guntarson had moved. Uncle Robert lunged too, and Dóla, who had been hovering, leapt forward, palms outstretched on the big men's chests. The crown of his head barely came up to their throats, but his gesture was enough to slow them.

'That is enough.'

'If we don't kill you today,' shouted Ken, 'we're taking Ella. And I'm coming back another time to rip your guts out and choke you on them.'

Guntarson had his back to the corner. He was eight feet from the door and barely out of Ken's reach. 'Give me your phone,' he ordered Dóla.

'I don't think this is really working out,' said Dóla, trying to force the Wallis men back. Juliette pushed between them and Frank edged to his father's side. The boy's face was contorted in fear and anger.

'You give us my sister back!'

Guntarson could not see past Ella's family to the sofa where she crouched.

'You are not looking after her,' accused Juliette.

'You milked her enough! You made money enough out of my girl! Now we come to take her home safe.'

'No,' protested Dóla, 'that isn't why we came. We came for a nice Christmas reunion and I'm sorry to say – Robert, please don't spit at him, remember your position in the community – I'm sorry but we just don't have one usable photo yet.'

'I'm going to make you sorry you ever laid a finger on my girl.'

'You beat her!' Guntarson yelled back. 'You struck her and punched her and belted her. And I have turned her into an object of international love and veneration. So who do you think treated her better?'

'Is she thriving?' asked Juliette. Her blood was up, to see the men fighting. Her voice was unnaturally loud. 'Does she look well? At least when we have her, she looks like she eats.'

'He don't feed her, Julie. He starves her. He's evil.'

'This is not,' shouted Dóla, flapping his arms between them, 'why we came. But since you all seem to want to make a fight of it, why don't we ask the girl herself?'

'She'll do what I tells her,' Ken snapped back.

'I swear to God,' roared Guntarson, his eyes blazing blue in his ashen face, 'after today none of you is going to see her again.'

'Let. Us. Ask. Her.' Dóla was stamping his foot. 'Does she want to remain a prisoner? In a strange country? Or would she rather be with her mother?' He looked around for her. 'Where's she gone?'

'Ella? Ella?'

Guntarson seized the moment to escape from his corner. He dived past the empty sofa. 'She's in the bathroom.'

But she wasn't. Ella was nowhere.

CHAPTER FORTY-ONE

'She can't have just gone,' said Uncle Robert, marching back from the bedroom. He had checked under the mattress and in the cupboards for his niece.

'Yes she can,' said Juliette.

'Where?' demanded Ken. 'If she's done this deliberate . . .'

'She doesn't dematerialise deliberately,' Guntarson snapped.

'That's what you call it, is it? She ain't just done a runner?'

'Last time she comes to me,' wailed Juliette. 'Now where is she gone?'

'Back to Bristol, maybe? Ring Auntie Sylvie, Mum, ring Auntie Sylvie,' yelled Frank.

'Yes. Yes. That is it. José, phone, if you please.'

'She can't just have gone into thin air,' Uncle Robert repeated.

'I'm not sure it would not be for the best if that were exactly what the dear girl did do,' murmured Dóla. 'To have her atoms scattered through the ether – at least for people to think that – would be a very satisfying solution for both the girl and her admirers.'

Guntarson said, 'I'm getting her back.'

'Only if you can find her, Director.'

Stewpot edged into the room. 'Director. Urgently, Director. The phone. Now.'

The Wallises, searching the cushions for Ella, barely noticed as Guntarson walked from the room. Dóla watched, doubtfully, but did not follow.

'She's upstairs, Director,' Stewpot told him in the corridor. 'I saw you were all fighting, and it was upsetting Ella. She was starting to go into herself, you know what I mean? So I grabbed her. I took her out while they were all crowded round you.'

'Ella let you take her? Was she in a trance? I don't believe she even knows who you are.'

'Actually Director,' admitted Stewpot, his dark skin helping to hide his blush, 'I think I'm starting to get a bit of a rapport with Ella.'

'You leave the rapport to me, my lad. Where have you left her?'

'On the roof.'

'You *what?*'

Ella, when they reached her, was standing still as a pillar, with the humming scarlet of the Hilton's neon sign beside her and the electric blue of the sea flowing over the horizon.

Daily Post, Tuesday, December 28

By Monty Bell, Paranormal Correspondent

Sun-seeking psychic Ella Wallis checked into the holiest hotel in the world last night – with monks for her chambermaids – while she waits for her brand new Prayer Centre to be built in the middle of the desert.

Guru Peter Guntarson has chosen the world-renowned Monastery of St Catherine as the temporary lodging for his miracle-worker.

The mountain community, one of the oldest in the Christian world, is cradled spectacularly by Mount Sinai – reputed to be the spot where God handed down the Ten Commandments to Moses.

Last night Director Guntarson handed the world a stern Eleventh Commandment: 'Thou Shalt Not Pry.'

Ella-watcher fervour reached a peak last week with the revelation that the prayer-power priestess was quitting Britain for good to make her home in the Holy Land.

And as pictures emerged yesterday of Ella's Christmas Day reunion with her family, the worldwide mania for fresh news of her health and state of mind reached a new pitch.

Speculation has been out of control since the alarming portrait of a sad, underweight and confused Ella in the run-up to the festive season.

Director Guntarson insisted last night that his pocket-sized angel was in top shape and eager to resume her rota of international prayers. She was hungrily reading the thousands of pleas for holy help which had arrived by eMail and post since her departure by chartered jet from Heathrow.

But he added: 'There is no question that this ghoulish interest in her figure is very upsetting to her. I think it is a very poor way for the world to repay a young girl whose goodness has done so much for so many – to criticise her physique. I can't think of anything crueller.'

Experts had little doubt that the monks would be on holy orders to fatten their guest up. Nutrition expert Dr Hillary Stoop said last night: 'That degree of asceticism, even in a saint, cannot be healthy. Jesus himself tucked into loaves and fishes from time to time.'

St Catherine's is officially in Egypt, though it lies on the Middle Eastern side of the Suez. Early indications are that the Prayer Centre too will be in Egypt, deep in the Sinai desert at the base of Moses' mountain.

Trucks and jeeps laden with construction materials and fencing drove in long convoy into the desert in the early hours of Boxing Day, prompting speculation that Director Guntarson had come to a swift agreement over the siting of his new project with Egypt's President Mubarak.

One rumour circulating at political altitudes last night suggested the President, in exchange for his permits, had been promised an international airport to be built wholly at the Ella Foundation's expense.

Coupled with a 125,000-seater Astrodome project, so that pilgrims can come en masse to be physically close to Ella as they pray, the airport could rejuvenate Egypt's tourist trade, currently laid low by terrorist attacks on buses and the Valley of the Queens massacre near Luxor.

If this plan were enacted, a tourism complex of hotels, hostels, restaurants and entertainment centres could see a spiritual version of Las Vegas springing from the arid desert sands within five years.

The centre itself is likely to be a focus for a wide range of psychic investigation, and not merely the prayer factory which many accused the British centre of being.

The Director, a former *Daily Post* reporter, has hinted at plans to help more psychically gifted youngsters to develop. 'Psi-power, the positive power for making the world a better place, is about enabling,' he claimed yesterday, 'and I am a supreme enabler.'

· Ella's father, print worker Ken Wallis, flew in from Tel Aviv last night and claimed: 'Guntarson has got my daughter captive.'

The angry evangelical preacher declared: 'She looks half-starved and, until Guntarson had her spirited away by his minions, she couldn't stop clinging to her mother. She ought to be back in the bosom of the family that loves her, and I'm prepared to fight through the courts to get her.'

Full story: Pages 4–5.

CHAPTER FORTY-TWO

Guntarson stood back, surveying the string of wooden huts that was Ella's new home. The landscape was crowded with crouching shadows, hemming the buildings like boulders slowly rolling into a circle. Guntarson thrust his hands into the cuffs of his sheepskin jacket. He had not expected Sinai to be cold, and the drop in temperature was giving him a headache. It was dusk now, and he could feel the heat flowing away like water running into the rocks.

The temporary Centre had the look of a construction site, with planks stacked against the walls and red-tipped girders on the ground, pointing randomly. But for all its rough and splintery edges, the new Centre was a bit of a miracle itself. Six days from conception to habitation, a little universe which Guntarson would rule.

From the moment he had seized the conception, his imagination had not rested. He had won over the President, leased the land for 111 years, hired the constructors and assembled the materials in what seemed a matter of hours. It wanted running water, but the stockroom was stacked with kegs of the bottled stuff. It urgently needed electricity, but for now there were candles and blankets.

Wood cost a fortune in Sinai – there were no forests – and labour charges were high as well. Teams of Bedouin, replete with camels, had been drafted in, for only they could withstand the back-breaking work under an intense sun. In a way, he was sorry his eye had not fallen on a tour ad for south-east Asia or central America, but then – why should his whims be miserly? Money was very easy to get. And with money, and ingenuity, and determination, he had brought Ella to the holiest of wildernesses. Only God could know what she might accomplish here.

In a day or two, the disciples would join her and, in the New Year, the equipment would arrive. Air-conditioning units, satellite dishes, VCRs, decoders, TV screens, receptors and radio aerials, boosters, generators, unlimited supplies of videotape, PCs with transferable storage discs, 56 Kbps modems running Java-enhanced versions of Netscape to access every search engine on the World Wide Web – all this supplied the power to examine every link on the Internet, to archive every TV news item and every documentary, to listen to every word spoken on radio about Ella. He wanted the clippings service to scan every article into a database, and he wanted that database maintained and backed up. Daily.

Every word that was spoken about her. He wanted to control it.

He would need more staff. If the technicians who set up the hardware were any good, he would pay them well enough to make them stay. Otherwise – disciples were easy to find. And better, too, on balance – not professional, not always well-educated, not even half-witted some of the time, but indebted. They owed him everything, just because he let them be near Ella.

'I wants to go back.'

It was the litany of her St Catherine's cell. She repeated it over and over. Guntarson had visited her every morning for the past five days. The monks kept her comfortably. They spoke to her kindly. Guntarson knew he could trust them to be discreet, and he had impressed upon them the vital importance that she should not be permitted other visitors. Especially her family. She was too frail.

'I wants to go back.'

He had been content to abandon her to their care for a few days, and was pained to bring her away with him to the rough-hewn remoteness of the new Ella Centre. That eternal refrain got on his wick.

The monastery at the foot of Mount Sinai, which the monks called Jebel Musa or Mount Moses, was steeped in symbolism. Guntarson had revelled in it, pleading with Ella to take the mystic history of her temporary home and nourish herself upon it. He told her the Emperor Junstinian had ordered it built, fifteen centuries ago, around the spot where God manifested Himself to Moses as a burning bush. The bones of St Catherine, whose disciples believed she had been carried to heaven by angels, were stored in a marble reliquary in the Basilica. The spot was sacred to three religions, for there was a mosque there, and the Prophet Mohammed's horse Boraq had ascended to heaven from Mount Moses.

Ella had shown a flicker of interest when he mentioned the horse.

New people, that was what the Ella centre needed. Fresh ones, young ones, eager for his Sinai challenge. He needed this stage of the mission to run smoothly. As soon as New Year was over he would track down some quality disciples. Not just bodies off the street, but people who reflected a little of his own talent. Just a little, mind – not enough to make them a threat.

'I wants to go back.'

She droned it through tears. How could she be praying, if that was all she had to say?

The huts were just bare shelves and bunks. For now, just eight of them, and in the last some sort of kitchen. The Director pushed open the door and checked the cupboards. Shelves were neatly stacked with gigantic packets of powdered food, thousands of cans and hundreds of vitamin bottles, as he had ordered it. Until pilgrims could be properly accommodated, there was no point in having daily deliveries of fresh food – it just encouraged sightseers.

The perimeter fences would keep most of the photographers and mad pilgrims at a distance. If there were infiltrators, the spy videos with their infra-red sensors and motion detectors were already perched on posts. Observation towers were to be manned by mixed units of Israeli and Egyptian commandos – the first time their two armies had co-operated.

The Ella Centre monitors would see intruders long before they caught sight of Ella. And surely, there couldn't be many people who would trek across the Sinai, just to stare at a row of huts.

It was a nice irony, one he had not considered till now – taking this girl who never saw a scrap of news, for fear of seeing something about herself, and hiding her in a nest of television screens collected to catch every story ever aired about her.

'I wants to go back.' She was probably muttering it in her bunk now. Stewpot and the Director had collected her from her cell that afternoon. She went with them meekly and without enthusiasm, even when Guntarson told her she would have a whole hut to herself, with a bedroom and a sitting-room and her own little kitchen.

She was carrying the green teddy that always sat with her when she prayed. Nothing else. No clothes, no possessions. Her little suitcase had been abandoned in the glass-strewn apartment in Tel Aviv. Ella relied on others to give her laundry. She did not care what she wore.

'Where's my crystal?' he asked, and she showed him the ripped back of the teddy. In the stuffing was her crumpled photo of Frank and Juliette, her comb and the rock quartz.

Now it was getting dark, and the Director had taken Ella to her hut. She would need feeding, and he did not suppose she would begin unravelling the mysteries of her little kitchen right away.

Guntarson fingered a packet of turkey-and-stuffing soup. He certainly had not ordered this gunge for his own consumption. His helicopter would be bringing better fare soon from a five-star hotel beside the Gulf of Aqaba. But for now, he had to eat. It would be a good gesture to take something to Ella too. He would tell her it was almost New Year. She might be encouraged to pray again. The Director splashed water from a flagon into the tin kettle and lit a Bleu burner beneath it.

'Soup,' he called out to her, and then asked: 'Why aren't you in your room?'

She was squatting on the hard ground, a dozen paces from her door. For some reason she reminded his aching head of a chess piece. The patches of gritty sand and the black rock beneath her had a chequered look, like a chessboard. 'Let's move you then,' he thought.

'Come on, it's too cold out here,' the Director said.

He glanced through the door of her hut.

Her bunk was burning.

The fluffy, red blanket was alight and the flames were already on the bed posts.

'God, Ella!' he shouted, 'what have you done?'

She did not move. Her green teddy lay beside her. As Guntarson ran into the hut, Ella repeated: 'I wants to go back.'

He tried to beat the fire out with his shoe, and in desperation emptied the water flagon over the bed, but there was no way to stop the flames from devouring the hut. The expensive, imported wood fell away from the twisted girders like flakes of flesh from a carcass. Ella sat with her back to the heat, not feeling it.

'Come on, Ella,' he pleaded with her, 'give me the matches. You can't burn the whole place to the ground.'

'Weren't me,' she said.

At first, naturally, he did not believe her. But hours later, as he sat at a window and stared at the faint smudge in the darkness that was Ella, he understood she never had lied to him. The fire was not deliberate. This was not the first time conflagrations had begun around her, after all. And it was he who had brought her to the Holy Land, to the desert battery which could re-energise her miracles.

Side-effects were bound to occur at first. She would naturally be seized by random psychic convulsions. Maybe it was better she remained outside. Until things settled down. Anyhow, she did not seem to feel the cold. And she refused to let him drag her indoors. So he draped a blanket over her thin shoulders and he left her, squatting on the ground, whispering the same words. He left her all night.

In the morning she was gone.

CHAPTER FORTY-THREE

Peter Guntarson stared panic-stricken all around for Ella, yelling into the dim light for her. His shouts woke Stewpot, who stumbled out of his hut. They ran to the dirt track that led towards the mountain. Could they chase after her on foot? Could she really have set out to walk to St Catherine's? Or home? Or had she vanished, the way she vanished in Oxford?

It was not until he turned to run back for his mobile phone that he thought to look up.

She had been lifted above the rooftops, still hunched and clutching her teddy in her lap. It was hard to see how far away she was – she appeared simply as a small, black mark against the grey sun. But Guntarson soon realised she had done nothing but rise vertically from her post in front of the ashes of her hut. Perhaps it had happened when she fell asleep. She had certainly ceased that irritating refrain.

He shouted, and she could not hear him. He had no way of ascending to her level, so he had to wait.

Maybe the wind would set her drifting. Or maybe she'd start to droop, or maybe she'd fall like a stone. Maybe she wouldn't come down at all. Ever. It would have been amusing if it weren't such a pointless bloody waste of time.

He began to worry that the miracles would dry up. Her power was evidently very strong here, but what if it grew too overwhelming to be harnessed? She was losing control of her strength. Was it bursting out of its channels? The Director sat almost directly underneath Ella – just a little to one side, for safety, in case she fell – and he fretted. He had a new mobile, but whom could he phone? Whom could he ask, 'Are the prayers still working?' Journalists? Hardly. Disciples? Impossible. Politicians? Madness. Friends? Name one.

At the moment the levitation ended Ella did not seem to fall. She was transferred in a flicker from air to earth.

When the disciples were ferried in by Stewpot at dawn on January 3 they found Ella tethered to the ground, like a sacrificial victim set out for crows to peck. Guntarson had sat all night beside her, reading

aloud from letters. He had harnessed a loop of rope about her waist
and fastened it to a girder. Two lighter guy-ropes were knotted round
her ankles. The tethers seemed to work. Ella was in levitation, by six
or eight inches, which was the greatest extent the ropes allowed.

She looked ridiculous, but not uncomfortable. Guntarson, in contrast, was pale and shivering. His fingers and lips were tinged blue.
'She won't go inside,' he hissed at the approaching party. 'She won't
have a blanket over her, she won't eat. And she won't bloody speak to
me.'

Tim and Stewpot untied Ella, while the others led the Director
indoors to boil him mugs of reviving soup. The boys gently led Ella to
a hut. She stood up and walked outside. They led her back and she
did not resist but, as soon as they set her down, she made to leave.
There was no way to stop her, except for barring the doorway. To be
kept in the hut she would have to be tied down. And she might as well
be tethered to the spot she chose for herself, so they let her outside.

She would not speak to them, nor eat for them. They set up a
canopy over her, for a roasting sun had risen quickly. And they lit
candles about her. She seemed to like that, and the flames began to
blaze angrily, with spirals of waxy smoke. A good deal of heat and
smoke was generated about Ella this way, but the candles had to be
replaced only once a day and did not blow out even when the winds
were strong.

A fence was thrown around her, steel posts in concrete feet with
tungsten sheets of chainmail strung eight feet high. Ella's restraints
kept her below this level. The single gate was doubly padlocked. The
second fence, around the camp's perimeter, was already complete.

On Ella's face nothing could be read. Her lips were still, and her
eyes were open most of the time, staring between the flames into the
flaming desert. The heat made her white face red and her silver hair
gold. The disciples who brought bowls of lumpy, wet powder could
not tell whether she was praying. Sometimes she was. Her prayers
were joyless, dutifully gritted out, and she did not know whether
anyone wanted them. She saw very few of the thousands of pleas and
thanks addressed each week to her from the mothers of sick children
and the children of dying parents. Ella just prayed, because she knew
that as long as she stayed existing there might as well be some point
to it.

She refused to eat. She did not seem to drink anything, except for
water which sometimes Stewpot poured on her lips. The very fact of
her continuing life became a miracle to the disciples.

Brooke and Xenia tried pushing vitamin and protein tablets
between Ella's teeth, but the pills evaporated on her tongue. The
Director decided at last to force her to eat. But the tube they screwed

between her lips became fused and blocked, and nothing would go through.

On many days, she showed no sign of anything. She did not move, tremble – she scarcely breathed. Only the unpredictable phenomena acted as a barometer of her strength. After cold nights, the reactions were weak. On the hottest days, sudden havoc would explode, as psychic charges built up on her and then sparked away. Flames appeared in the sky. Sounds shrieked around the camp. Deep notes sounded, like whales swimming far underground. Many of the Bedouin fled. Those who remained would sit motionless for hours, studying her.

Ella, agonisingly thin already, grew thinner. The cameras which prowled beyond the perimeter could glimpse her at the very end of the day, when the heat haze subsided. Pictures appeared around the world which made many believe Ella was actually starving.

The Director was forced to announce she was fasting for world peace. Her psychic energy was undiminished. The candles blazed constantly, sometimes with answering flares around the huts or in the wilderness. Two more of the buildings were burned down by March. The disciples despaired of running all their electronics on 'snow days' – days when Ella's energy swamped the airwaves.

At first the disciples were afraid of the Director, the way they had been afraid in England, and they would do nothing wrong. But then it became apparent he was not fully in control, and never could be, and the knowledge weakened him.

Ella's weakness was echoed by the Director's incontinence of purpose. Her complete withdrawal seemed to shut down the strongest part of his mind. His willpower was sapped, and the resolve which had forced them out into the desert was suddenly dissipated.

He pursued schemes in fits and starts. His plan to discover new Ellas was in action for only a few days – teenagers with supposed psychic powers were brought to the Centre and then abandoned, left to roam around and wander away as they liked. He issued press releases in spurts, always referring to himself as the ultimate psychic enabler, but as a catalyst he had never seemed to work for anyone but Ella. Now, he was not even her catalyst – merely her mirror. When her barometer climbed, he bounced around the camp issuing edicts, planning spectacular demonstrations, phoning the offices of world leaders. He talked of himself as a peace-maker in the mould of Mandela, of Gandhi. He would summon his helicopter and soar away on spontaneous missions.

When her barometer dipped, lethargy paralysed the Director. He would not emerge from his hut. He slept for days on end. He did not want to see reports and, when he did read them, he was plunged into despair. A heavy-duty paper shredder was brought, and he stood for days at a time feeding it with newspapers.

The world was beginning to absorb Ella. She was more remarkable for her reclusiveness than her mystical powers. Guntarson, sitting for hours beside Ella's always-airborne form, begged her to pray for better media coverage. Her influence was waning as people took prayer power for themselves. She had to re-establish herself, reinvent herself. Pray for that. But she did not respond.

For the disciples, who had been permitted only limited access to the media for a year, the surprise was that much of the coverage was hostile to Ella and, particularly, to The Ella Foundation. Reporters regarded the charity as a blood-sucker, the Director as a thief and Ella as a fraud. A fraud who could levitate, but a fraud all the same. Where were the hospitals Guntarson had promised? Some commentators called him a manipulator, a Svengali. Others said he was a puppet of the ruthless, power-hungry, reclusive Ella.

The Ella Centre continued to respond to all applicants with a format letter and a dubious autograph. In April, however, the policy changed: every correspondent now received a format letter, a large photograph of the Director with the US president, and a small picture of Ella, autographed by machine.

There were persistent rumours that Ella had died. The figure that had distantly been spied by photographers, behind the fences and circled by candles, was in fact a mannequin. Ella had killed herself, wasted away, been abducted by a UFO, died from an alien disease or escaped to live a new, fabulously wealthy life in Indonesia. Depending on which rumour you heard, and depending on whether you listened – there would always be millions whose devotion to Ella outweighed anything that could be said.

But as the photographers crept closer and the disciples became more lax, new proofs of her existence emerged. Spy satellite pictures were published, and then photos taken at close hand with a hidden camera – the first for eighteen months. They showed a girl with skin like wax, eyes blindly turned up and locks that clung to her head like hair on the skull of a corpse. There was none of her luminescence now. Light from the roaring flames of her candles seemed to be sucked into her skin. She never ate – it was as though she lived on this light.

Whenever Guntarson was away, the disciples rebelled. In return for gifts – fresh food, alcohol, a ride into Tel Aviv or Cairo and back – the disciples would allow visitors through the gates to be pictured with Ella. They could crouch or stand beside her floating body, though they were supposed to touch her only if they had come to seek a cure. Some clipped lengths of her hair, as souvenirs, so when Stewpot was on duty he would insist on scanning visitors with a metal detector – a relic of Ella's tests at Christ Church, Oxford. Visitors whose intentions were detected would sometimes return with undetectable plastic scissors. One strand of Ella's hair would fetch £10,000, though the market had been debased by fakes.

In Internet conferences the disciples boasted of their lifestyles. They gave interviews. Brooke talked so candidly that she was signed up by a television company, and flown to Houston, Texas, to present a chat show. Nick met a Jerusalem girl and moved in with her. The rest kept leaving but coming back. Stewpot loyally made sure he was there each night and morning, to leave hot food for Ella which she did not eat and to shoo away visitors who became too inquisitive. He was still not sure that Ella would know his face.

Nothing seemed to register with Ella, but the barometer ran particularly high when the disciples told her of miraculous new cures. Stewpot began to make notes of the best prayer stories listed on Websites, and kept the more touching letters. He went out at night to read them to her by candle-light. He hoped it was helping to sustain her.

One morning in December, he found her more alert than usual. Her pupils were visible, and her shoulders moved as she breathed. She turned her head a little as he trudged across the compound to her.

'Hello, Ella,' said Stewpot. 'I've come to see you before breakfast.' It was what he always said. 'I've brought your water.' And he squeezed a few drops from a sponge onto her dry lips.

Ella's lips pursed, as though she was sipping one or two droplets in.

'Good,' said Stewpot, 'that's good. Would you like some more?'

She nodded. It was her first communication during the whole of that year.

Stewpot carefully administered the sponge, trying not to upset her with sudden movements. He backed away, saying: 'I'll be back now, don't go away.' She was tethered to three girders.

It took all Stewpot's self-control not to run shouting into Guntarson's hut, but he reached the door with a clear idea of what to say. He was not panicking as he rapped on the frame. He served Ella best by remaining calm.

'Enter!' called the Director, up and shaving at his mirror. Four days' growth of golden beard sparkled on his face. 'Morning, Stewpot! It's a good day today. A day for new beginnings. I feel confident – better than I've felt for a long time.'

That made sense – Ella revived and the Director's spirits lifted with her, as if they were different parts of one organism.

'Ella's awake,' said Stewpot carefully.

'What do you mean, awake?'

'She's drunk a little water and she seems conscious. She hasn't spoken but I have the feeling . . .' His cautiously rehearsed words began to falter.

'Yes? What feeling?'

'She might want to see you.'

'Of course she wants to see me. And she won't,' the Director added, rubbing the electric razor around his jowls, 'want to see me half-shaven. Okay. Let's see what planet she's on.'

He strode into the sun. 'Ella! Ella, can you hear me?'

The whole camp could hear him. The disciples hung out of windows to see Guntarson sit down beneath Ella's canopy.

'Stewpot says you're awake,' he said more quietly. The sight of her always shocked him now. She was brittle, like a twig. Her eyes were sunken and loose skin hung in thin flaps under her chin. 'Can you hear me?'

She was floating, a fact so commonplace that Guntarson no longer registered it. She always floated. It was no longer miraculous or interesting or comical. This morning she was at the highest reach of her stays, which was probably a good sign.

She turned her hollow, distant eyes on him.

'I wants to ask you a question,' she whispered.

CHAPTER FORTY-FOUR

Her voice was dry and distorted, issuing from a mouth which had not spoken in almost eleven months, from a swollen throat and a cracked tongue.

Guntarson said seriously, 'I'll try to answer.'

'Is it next year yet?'

'Next year? What do you mean? It's this year. You know Ella, it's always this year, like it's always today.'

'Have we,' she asked slowly, 'had Christmas yet?'

'No. It's the beginning of December. Why?'

'How old am I?'

'You're . . . I'll work it out . . . you're fifteen.'

'Not sixteen yet?'

'Does it matter?'

'I don't know.'

There was a silence, while Guntarson calculated how to seize the advantage.

'I do understand, Ella,' he said at last. 'You're not happy here. It isn't the right environment. I feel it myself. It should have been wonderful here, we were going to be at the centre of a spiritual revolution. People coming from all over the world to be taught by me, guided in the evolution of their energies. And to be inspired by you. But I promise you – it still can be like that.'

Ella whispered, 'When I'm sixteen . . .'

'What? What when you're sixteen? It's only a few days off.'

'Nothing.'

'Do you want a party or something?'

'No.'

'The whole planet ought to be throwing you a party. Global. But the world is very ungrateful. It took our miracle and used it and got back on with its life as if hardly anything had happened. I can't believe it. Our names ought to be on everyone's lips every minute of every day. We should be the indelible wonder of the universe. We've proved the psychic power of prayer, and absolutely no one can deny that, but are they amazed? Not any more. They've become used to us. Prayer, it's a familiar thing now. They all do it for themselves. Everyone's praying and curing each other, Ella. So ungrateful.' He fell silent.

The candles around them were flaring loudly. Guntarson stared into the jet of one for a long while. His fingers tapped on his boots. Ella gazed past the candles, into the desert.

'Ella, we have to do something wonderful. Something to open the world's eyes. We woke the planet up, Ella. It's drifting away again now, but we did it once. We can do it again. We've got to think of something, Ella. Dream something up. Yes. Shake everyone awake. Shock their senses. We can't let the miracle peter out, Ella. I won't permit it.'

Ella said: 'Will you marry me?'

'Wow. That would get some coverage. You mean, big wedding, world leaders for guests, massive bidding for photo rights? Maybe – this is good – maybe we could have a mass pray-in, instead of a honeymoon.'

'When I'm sixteen, you can marry me then, can't you?'

'I suppose, in theory.' Guntarson was suddenly doubtful. 'It's not really paranormal, though, is it? A wedding. Big news, but not psychic.'

'Will you marry me?'

'You're really asking? Why? Do you want that?'

'I been waiting for it,' said Ella. 'Sixteen. That's what I'm waiting for.'

Guntarson rested a hand on one of the girders. It was humming with energy. 'It's like you've been hibernating, isn't it,' he said. 'Restoring your energy. Waiting for your sixteenth birthday. Which is, what, five days away now.' He stared at her, trying to strip away contemptible layers of familiarity that obscured his vision and to see her, truly and really, as if for the first time. 'You could do anything, couldn't you? It's beyond my imagination. I have to, I must force myself to imagine it.

'You could ... you could perform a resurrection. Bring someone back to life. Pray the life back into their body. You could do that, couldn't you? No one except Jesus ever did that. None of the saints, never anyone. But you could. Could you?'

'Then you'd marry me?'

'Marry you ... come on, let's separate out the strands here. Marriage is a big thing, we're both still very young. You know I love you, I'm sure you love me, but that doesn't mean necessarily marriage.'

The candles suddenly flickered, as if in a strong breeze.

'I'm not saying no,' Guntarson said hastily. 'That wasn't a refusal. Let's just talk it all through.' The flames gradually crept back up. 'There's two issues. You'll be sixteen, okay. But first we need to amaze the world. Listen to me. A resurrection – are you truly that strong? Can your prayers reverse death? I think they are – look at the cures you've produced. Cancers evaporate, hearts become strong again, brain tissue regenerates. So is it such a big step to restart a heart? Maybe in a case where there isn't massive physical damage? No bullet wounds or car crash victims – something like a lethal injection. Maybe we could get hold of the corpse of a murderer, someone executed by the state, and prayer him back to life.

'Or perhaps that wouldn't be right. The murderer has been executed for a reason. Too controversial. And people wouldn't want to pray for him. Plus, he lives again and he's a double celebrity, because he's a murderer and he has been resurrected. No, it's got to be the right person. Sympathy. The body must command sympathy.

'A child. A dead child. But again there's the celebrity question. That child would carry its miracle status around for the rest of its life. More importantly, the focus would be on the resurrected child and not us. On the miracle and not the miracle workers. We can't afford to cede centre-stage here. This is our one big roll.'

He fell silent. An idea had crept into his head which he did not want to voice.

Ella heard the idea. She said, 'I think I could.'

'You mean . . .?'

'If we was going to get married.'

'That's the price? I mean, you're making a deal.'

Ella said, 'Yes.'

'You'll perform the most wondrous psychic experiment ever conducted. By resurrecting *my* body.' This was the idea which he had not dared speak. 'You are going to bring me back to life. And when you've given me life, you'll claim me as your husband.'

Ella said, 'Yes.'

Peter sat nodding and nodding. 'I'm not . . .' he said. 'I'm not . . . you know . . . dead. I'm still alive. First of all I should have to – die.

'And then marriage. I can't tell you, you're not even sixteen, but as you grow up, you'll realise. Marriage is a massive commitment. You think you want it now, but . . . My mother made a mistake. When she married my father. They both were wrong. Too young, married the wrong people, and regretted it.'

He reached out and took her dusty teddy from the desert stones. 'My rock quartz is still here?' He pulled the crystal from the stuffing. 'Will you look into it? I never see anything. Maybe you'll find an answer in there.'

Ella reached down and took it from him. 'I can see a leg,' she whispered slowly. 'It's a leg and it's underwater and there's a hand holding it.'

'Oh Jesus. Jesus, oh Jesus.'

She handed the crystal back to him but he did not want to touch it and let it fall among the stones.

'I should tell you,' Guntarson said, 'how I got that stone.'

CHAPTER FORTY-FIVE

'I was thirteen. My mother and I lived in a cabin by the lake, and I used to watch the ships come down. Motor yachts, mostly, thirty or forty feet, but some working ships too, with lumber and skins. Fishing boats too. They all had to pass close to our house, because the lake is at its narrowest there. Narrow and rocky and shallow. Plenty of boats used to wind up aground, and that's how my mother's boyfriend made his living, fixing up these boats in the Straits of Reykjavik.'

Guntarson spoke evenly, not looking at Ella or the stone on the ground. The desert heat was growing fiercer.

'One time, a fishing party came down from Toutes Aides at the top of the lake, and they ran aground. I watched them. They tried to steer her off the rocks, holed her and she capsized. She went over very fast. The fishermen dived overboard, but instead of making for shore they were hanging back, treading water near the wreck. Very dangerous.

'At first I thought they were mad. And then I heard the shouting. Shouting in my head. I was about a mile off, but I heard the drowning man shout as if he were no further from me than those huts. Telepathic, you see. Psychic shouts.

'He must have known he was psychic – he knew how to transmit. Whether he knew I was there and I was receiving, I couldn't tell. But these cries were beaming into me – "Trapped! Trapped! Rescue! Get help! Man trapped!" he was locked in the upturned hold, with the water rushing in.

'I knew I was a telepathic receiver. My mother experimented all the time. But I wasn't such a good sender in those days. My mind was less disciplined. I tried to transmit back to him, "Help coming," and then I ran to find my Uncle Clarence.

'Clarence's motor-launch was first to the wreck, and I was in the bows. But when we had still half a mile to cover, I sensed the trapped man's last thoughts. There was a message for his children, a word of love for his wife – and a promise for me. Something was in his hold-all. Something valuable. "Get the bag. Save it. The key is inside. Save it and it's yours." They were the last words he sent to me. "*It's yours.*"

I can hear them in my head now. I've never forgotten them.

'They pulled his body out of the hull, but not his hold-all. And it preyed on my mind. Years later I traced his family through his ID bracelet, and they told me this man's great-great-grandfather was an Egyptian immigrant who worked on Brunel's bridge in Bristol – he dug this key, whatever it was, out of the cliffs, and that was how it came into their family. But when the boat sank, I had no idea of this. I just had this message. Beamed into my mind.

'I begged Clarence to take me back to the wreck, but he wouldn't. It had to lie until the salvage crew came, he said. So I begged my mother. And to whet her appetite, I asked her to imagine what was in this dead sailor's hold-all. What was so valuable.

'Something gem-like, she said. That was what she sensed. A gemstone, wrapped in wool. That got both of us excited. And my mother never could deny me anything.

'We went in Clarence's launch, and we picked a bad afternoon for it. The rain had been coming down steadily all morning, and after lunch it turned to lashing torrents. The level of the lake started to rise. We went very carefully in the straits, because of the currents, and two or three times our bottom scraped on rocks. It was a mad thing to do, in that foul weather.

'My mother moored at the prow of the wreck and stripped to her swimming costume. We knew there was a hole in the upturned hull, because we'd been there when Clarence and the rescuers cut their way into the hold. So my mother eased herself over the side of our launch.

'The water was bitterly cold, and the rain was hurting us, it came down so hard. There were swirling, muddy currents in the water. My mother took one, deep breath and disappeared below the surface.

'After a minute, she had not reappeared. There was no hope of trying to see her through the dark waters. My mind was searching for her, trying to sense her in the hull. She was a strong swimmer, but she should not have been down that long. What if she were trapped? Could she find her way back to the opening in the lightless hull? She could have knocked herself unconscious.

'I wasn't getting any telepathic guidance. If she were unconscious, that would explain it, why I wasn't receiving anything. I tried to transmit, "Are you okay, are you okay?" but what I really wanted to do was plunge into that water and find her.

'Almost two minutes ticked by.

'Then she bobbed up, with a yell of joy and a blue, sodden mass in her hands. "I got it, I got it," she was screaming, and waving this dripping bundle over her head as she thrashed back down the hull.

'Five yards from me she shrieked, the most, awful sound, and lurched under the surface. When her face came back up, it was screaming and distorted. She was yelling, "My foot, my foot". She had stepped straight through the metal, and the torn edges were biting into her ankle. The metal was trapping her.

She had her head above water, but the blue bundle was pulling her down. I paddled the launch towards her and took the thing from her hands. I flung it beneath my seat. That gave her some freedom, and I reached out for her hands. But as she twisted to grab hold of me, the metal of the wreck gave way some more, and she was pulled under.

'She was back, fighting for the surface, right away, but her lips and nose could barely reach the air. She was shouting and swallowing water.

'I was panicking. I dived in fully clothed, and had to waste half a minute stripping off in the water, or I would have drowned too. Then I ducked under to try and pull her leg free. I just drove the metal teeth in deeper. I couldn't see anything, I had to do it all by feel. Through five feet of water, I could hear my mother screaming.

'I broke the surface. The rain was coming down more densely than ever, making it hard for her to breathe even when she could get her face to the air through the swell. And the lake was rising – you could see by the hull of the wreck how fast it was rising. The water was getting deeper, making it more and more difficult for her to reach the air. She managed to get one good breath in her, held it and ducked down. When she came up, she was gasping, "Bend the metal, with your mind. Bend it. Get me out."

'I dived again, and I could feel where some of the metal edges had loosened slightly. She'd done this with her willpower, with psi strength. She couldn't have done it with her hands. The metal was too thick, and it was biting too deep into her leg.

'I tried. Ella, Christ knows I tried. I focused on this metal, and I said, "Bend! Bend! Bend!" My mother's life was hanging on this. I had never managed to bend even a teaspoon before, but I had to prise off this iron hand.

'And I couldn't do it. I just couldn't do it. I dived and dived, until my mother was not struggling in the water any more, and I still kept on diving and pushing at this metal, going: "Bend! Bend, fuck you! Bend!" I was totally focused, in a panic I suppose but focusing through it. Oblivious to anything else I could be doing. And then I realised she wasn't moving now because she was dead.

'I tried to blow air into her. I knew people could seem to be drowned but come back very quickly if you got oxygen into their lungs. So I gulped air down me and forced my mother's mouth open, and water poured in because the lake was rising all the time and she was completely submerged now. I blew air into her mouth and it bubbled straight out. And that kiss of life, if you can call it that, was the last time I kissed my mother.

'I got my arm round her waist, and the other hand on the boat and I pulled and pulled. Just trying to get her face above the surface, so I could blow air into it. If I could have lifted her and the wreck out of the water, I would have. But I was only thirteen.

'I kept that up, I don't know how long. It was dark when I gave up. And her blank, white face was shining at me from under the water, and her blonde hair drifted around her face like a halo.

'I flung the blue bundle over the side, back into the lake, before I steered Clarence's boat back to the shore. The men collected her body that same night. But a week later, I went back. I shouldn't have thrown the bundle away, you see. That made her death even more pointless. I was meant to have whatever was in that bag.

'The rains had washed a lot of silt into the straits, and it had settled, and the water was a little shallower and a lot clearer. It wasn't hard to dive to the wreck and find the bundle on the lake floor. And as I turned to swim back to the surface, I saw something like a post, marking the spot where my mother had drowned.

'Her leg. It was her leg, hacked off below the knee by the men who came for her body. Her leg was still trapped in the hull.

'Beside that awful thing lay the blue bundle. It turned out to be a jumper, tied around itself. And in the middle was this lump of rock quartz. The key that was to be mine. But he never told me the key to what, did he? The key to what?'

Guntarson picked the crystal off the desert stones. It had lain glinting in the sun while he talked, and was blisteringly hot in his hand. He thrust it back into the stuffing of Ella's teddy.

Chapter Forty-Six

Ella knew she would not have the dream again. She knew now that no part of Peter's mind was closed to her. In her dreams she had gone beyond the high, sheer wall which she could not breach when she was conscious, and she had seen his secret. There never had been a secret between them. Not really.

And now, she could see all of his mind at once. It made less sense than ever to her. She thought that perhaps it no longer made sense to Peter either.

If he would marry her, she might change that. She was not sure how she could help him. But she might soothe him. Possibly.

Ella did not know that anything good would happen if Peter married her. But she had wanted it for a long time. She had been in love with him ever since she saw him, she thought. And now, now that she was so close, now she had endured until she was so nearly sixteen – she would not give up her ambition now. She would give him anything, but he would have to marry her.

Ella did not sleep that night. She cradled her teddy and watched the candles flaring in the darkness, listening to sounds of the desert which she had been too weak to notice until now.

She concentrated on drawing each breath. She did not pray. Her energy was needed for herself now, to give strength back to herself. She had prayed herself, almost literally, to a shadow. There were four days to go till her sixteenth birthday. The world could do without her prayers that long.

When she saw a man crouching by a flame, Ella knew she was not dreaming but she also knew what she saw was not quite real. Real, but not physical.

His body seemed to be hunched a long way off, though it was within the ring of the fence. Ella was not aware at first that she was watching him. He swayed by the candle, and she realised she wanted him to get warmth from the flame. She willed him closer.

The figure was almost naked. The December night was freezing, but he wore only a filthy sheet knotted round his middle. His arms and chest were smeared with black dirt. His hair fell over his shoulders and his beard masked his throat.

There was a sweet scent drifting from his dirty body, like the smell of trees in summer.

Ella strained at her ropes and reached a hand out to the figure. He did not look up, but his face was vivid in the flame. It was a lined, brown face with wide eyes and a straight nose. She had seen it thousands of times, but now she did not know where.

'Have you come to see me?' asked Ella.

'I've been here with you a long while,' he answered.

'What's your name?'

He looked at her and smiled, and Ella felt such affection for this man that a sob burst in her throat. She loved him for smiling at her, loved him gratefully, without wanting anything more. Her passion for Peter was greedy love, love always pleading, love that lusted for attention, love that would not be satisfied.

The sudden wave of love she experienced as *this* stranger smiled was not lustful. It washed over her, engulfing her.

It was a love she had once prayed for, before she had forgotten to hope for it. An unconditional love. The way she imagined a dog would love her.

'You're Him, ain't you?' she said.

The figure in the candle's flame twisted to face her. She saw that the black dirt on his body was congealed blood, spreading from ancient wounds in his hands and side.

'You are Ella,' said the man. 'Do not be afraid to speak my name.'

'You're Jesus.'

'And I love you, Ella. Soon your bonds will be loosened.'

She stared for a long time at the figure. His knees bulged on bone-thin shins, drawn up to his chin. His wrists were like bolts driven through the spindles of his arms. She wondered if he had the strength to stand up.

'Why're you here?'

'I'm always here if you want me. I think you wanted me.'

'Why?'

'You must ask yourself.'

His answers were kind. She felt the confidence to ask herself the questions she had asked him.

'I'm not dead, am I?' she said.

'No.'

'But I will be, one day. Will I go to Hell, then? I ain't been good.'

'Do you love me, Ella?'

'I wants to love you, really, loads.'

'Then you won't go to Hell.' He was smiling, but not mocking. It was not like Peter's smile.

'Can I be an angel?'

'The angels already think of you as one of their own.'

'Honest, no kidding?'

'You should ask them.'

'I've never seen no angels.'

'When angels speak, Ella, not everyone hears alike. It is no good listening with your ears. Angels talk nonsense to the ears. Listen within. Listen in your heart.'

'I don't know how.'

'For you, Ella, it's the only way you've ever known.'

She thought about that for a long while.

'I wants you to have this. It's all I got, but you're s'posed to give everything. Ain't you?'

Clutching the teddy which contained Guntarson's crystal, she stretched out her hand to him. He stretched his hand to her. As he took the toy, his fingers brushed hers.

'Them lights. Them three lights, spinning. Is that angels too?'

'The three lights are in all your prayers, Ella. Think of the words which complete your prayers.'

'I always says, "In the name of the Father, the Son and the Holy Ghost".'

'The Father, the Son and the Holy Ghost. The three lights.'

Ella watched the figure hunched at the flame for a long time, until her consciousness ebbed away. She was not aware of a moment when she could no longer see him, but after a time all that remained of her vision was the candle, and three lights spinning at its base.

In the morning Peter came to her. He did not see that the teddy was gone. Ella said: 'Anything you wants me to do, I'll try and do it. But you got to promise we'll get married, soon as we can after my birthday.'

'Anything?'

'Anything. And you got to promise.'

'All right,' Peter said. 'I'll marry you. Right after you resurrect me.'

CHAPTER FORTY-SEVEN

The Times, Friday, December 8

A media caravan was struggling across the Sinai desert last night in a race to record the most bizarre publicity stunt ever devised.

Despite international condemnation, outcry from the Vatican and a pervasive suspicion that this will turn out to be a colossal joke at the world's expense, camera crews and reporters were streaming in four-wheel-drive convoys from every direction to converge on the Ella Foundation's Prayer Centre in the foothills of Mount Sinai.

Overhead, Sea King helicopters were transporting a bewildering collection of hardware which suggested that, if Director Guntarson is enjoying a convoluted private joke, the laughter is not to be had for free.

The Director's extraordinary announcement to CNN via satellite from the Prayer Centre yesterday spoke more of uncontrolled megalomania than a well-developed sense of humour.

He declared himself ready to be drowned – to be submerged in a tank and left there till dead – in order for his protegée, Ella Wallis, to resurrect him by prayer.

Drowning was apparently chosen as suicidally suitable in preference to more common – and less drawn-out – methods of execution, such as death by hanging, injection, electrocution or firing squad.

His promise that, once he had been brought back to life, there would be a further, world-shaking announcement to be made jointly by himself and Ella, seemed to many nothing but another good yolk in an over-egged pudding.

TV medic Dr Hillaire Stoop warned last night that, even if

Ella possesses strength enough to attempt the miracle, she is unlikely to be able to reverse the profound chemical changes which a body undergoes immediately after brain death, even for a victim of a demise so apparently 'harmless' as drowning.

And he added his warning to the general alarm surrounding Ella's emaciated appearance: 'If anyone needs resurrecting, it's her. Months of fasting, or starvation, will have destroyed her internal organs, with her body actually feeding on itself to remain alive. Even in her obvious state of trance, as attested by her levitations, she will have consumed far more energy than a healthy body could supply.

'I believe she may have only weeks to live.'

Seasoned Ella-observers believe Guntarson could be serious in his intention. Journalist Aliss Holmes, who interviewed the Director with Ella twelve months ago, said: 'Frankly, he's quite mad enough for this. He has already proved himself insatiable in his morbid quest to deify this poor girl. Her cult dwarfs the Evita phenomenon, it easily outdoes the Kennedy grave-robbing obsession. What I want to know is, what's the point?

'We all know Ella's prayers can move mountains. She has unleashed the God-botherer in all of us. So what is she trying to prove? That we're all going to live forever? Ella conquers death?

'To look at her now, I'd have to say she was ill when I met her and she looks a damn sight iller now. I'd be surprised if she has the strength to raise an eyebrow, never mind raise the dead.'

Miss Holmes's voice was not the only one to chime a note of cynicism yesterday. Students of international politics believe a private agreement must have been reached between Guntarson and Eygpt's President Mubarak for the demonstration to go ahead.

With senior figures from all major faiths clamouring to condemn the Director, and self-drowning being an apparent contravention of Egyptian law, it is difficult to conceive that the event as billed has the President's blessing.

One possible explanation is that Guntarson will in fact only appear to die. To be suspended in a tank of water for anything up to half an hour is an unpleasant but not necessarily fatal experience, as Houdini was proving eighty years ago.

The tank has been designed and constructed at almost

superhuman speed by a firm of Tel Aviv plumbers. Four sheets of strengthened plate glass in copper frames are to be set on a marble base.

The base features two iron anklets and a ring of pipe, with four outlets, which will be plumbed to a five-hundred-gallon reservoir. All the water is being flown in by helicopter, since connecting the Prayer Centre to a main pipeline has always proved too costly even for the Foundation's considerable reserves.

The four base-points supplys water to each of the hollow frames. Nozzles midway and at the top of the walls will spray water from the pressurised reservoir into the container at fifty gallons a minute. For its three-hundred-gallon capacity to be reached will take six minutes – six long, slow minutes if the Director really is intending to breathe his last when the water reaches his chin.

His feet will be securely fastened to the marble base, to prevent damage to his body by floating rather than to make escape more difficult. The water will be released by an automated timer at 8pm tonight Middle Eastern time – 6pm in London, and 1pm in New York.

Unlike Houdini, who used a prearranged signal for an accomplice to get him out of the water if his trick went wrong, Guntarson says he has made no provision for his escape should he change his mind while drowning.

But if trickery is involved, Guntarson will surely be found out, and it is hard to see how Ella's reputation could survive the ensuing scandal. Her levitations, always notorious for taking place in Guntarson's presence, were for many the only real proof of her psychic powers – since the extraordinary phenomena which accompanied her television appearances were generally of a spontaneous, unscientific nature which was hard to quantify.

And since the undeniable miracles which flowed from her exhortations to prayer are now held to be manifestations of mass mental energy, and not attributable to Ella Wallis alone, her once-unassailable position as the world's most wondrous psychic would be severely undermined if Guntarson were caught cheating.

In other words: If by tonight Director Peter Guntarson is not dead, Ella Wallis's reputation is.

The Independent, **Friday December 8:**

Director Guntarson's announcement has unleashed a worldwide wave of rumour. One claim, by a right-wing cult calling itself The Children Of Dorcas, was sent to every e-Mail address on the Internet, in a process called 'spamming', and contained a prediction that the world would end within days.

The group's apocalyptic vision will terrify many, though its logic might impress few. They argue that the Old Testament prophet, Elijah, performed a resurrection, bringing a widow's son back to life. And Elijah himself, so the Bible says, will have to live again before the Day of Judgement can come. And isn't Ella almost the same word as Elijah?

The Mirror, **Friday December 8:**

American shock jock Boris Kalmanovich drew more than two million complaints last night after making outrageous comments about Ella Wallis.

Kalmanovich refused to apologise but admitted he had been forced to triple his security in the face of fifty death threats, after stating on air: "There's nothing wrong with that girl a good f*** wouldn't fix."

They came from Cairo, from Tel Aviv, from Port Said, from Suez, from Aqaba, from Larnaca, from every port and city in the Near East that gave them a fighting chance of making Sinai in time. Their LandCruisers and LandRovers came hammering down the roads from Eilat and Port Taufiq, laden with water and petrol and satellite transmitters and journalists. Their first, lofty intentions to ignore what could only be called a sick, sad stunt were abandoned when CNN made it clear that they were covering the whole event. The whole event, live – not only the attempt at resurrection but the drowning itself. On screen, from the moment the taps went on to the moment the bedraggled body was fished out.

If CNN covered it, they all covered it. At 13.00 EST on December 8, who would be watching anything else?

In Bristol, Ken and Robert Wallis would be watching. Auntie Sylvie would be watching.

And from her enclosure, Ella would be watching. She sat where she always sat, ringed by a fence of tungsten chainmail and a dozen bright candles, with a ragged canopy above her and a disciple at her side. Almost at her side – Stewpot sat on the ground, and Ella floated in the air, her tethers hanging slackly from the girders.

The glass tank, ten feet high on its black marble plinth, stood beyond her fence. Designed by Josef Kiriaty an Eilati architect specialising in underwater observatories, it had been constructed by a team of aquarium experts and plumbers. The compound was dazzlingly arc-lit, the lights of three hundred camera crews a mere flicker beside the stadium arrays and runway landing lights which Guntarson had suspended over the arena. Their glow in the night sky was visible from 150 miles away.

Beside the tank stood a single microphone. Circling the tank, seven deep and ten yards back, were a thousand journalists. A joke was passed around – who had seen Steven Spielberg's Close Encounters? And didn't this look like the set where a UFO landed in front of the world's press? And who wanted to bet a UFO was going to zoom out of the sky now, scoop Ella up and carry her back to the planet she came from?

They edged forward – one hundred security guards with Dobermanns and German shepherd dogs ushered them back.

Guntarson strutted the fifty yards from his hut to the tank at three minutes to eight. He wore a blue towelling robe with the hood up, like a boxer. At its breast the Golden Ella Centre monogram shone. The compound had the air of a sports stadium, as though it was about to witness a big match and not a spiritual mystery. There should have been rock music as the Director strode to the microphone with a nod to the cameras and a wave to Ella – but the only soundtrack was the murmuring of reporters and the barking of dogs, the overhead clatter of 'copters and the flickering buzz and rattle of cameras.

He stared about him, imperiously, as the muttering died. Relishing the silence, Guntarson gripped the microphone stand for a few seconds and then began: 'You are gathered here today to witness the union between the known and the unknown. I am about to enter that unknown. When I return, I shall be proud to reveal what secrets of it I have learned.

'My actions today are rooted in faith. Faith in miracles, and in one miracle-worker. Ella, frail but burning with an unquenchable inner fire, will see me step onto that mysterious plane we call the afterlife. And Ella, with her passionate prayer, will bring me back.

'I ask all of you to help her. You who are here today, you who are watching around the globe. Add your prayers to Ella's prayers. I ask you to pray for my safe return. But do not fear for me. Do not fear, for my soul is with Ella.'

He turned, slipped his robe off his shoulders and flung it to the desert floor. The camera crews jostled forward, elbowing through the ranks, and the dog handlers let slip their beasts a link or two so that the journalists at the inside of the ring had to lean back.

Naked, the arc lights bleaching the muscular lines of his body, Peter Guntarson climbed the aluminum rungs to the top of the tank and swung one leg across to the other side. Finding a foothold with care, he began his descent, into the tank.

He stood, facing Ella, his feet straddling the chains on the marble floor, and he knelt to fasten each steel hoop around his ankles. The bracelets were secured by three links to bolts in the floor.

Guntarson stood and clasped his hands at chest height. There were three or four silent seconds in which he stared ahead at a point in the sky high above Ella. Then the jets opened.

The water was warm. Standing in an open vat, under the Sinai sun, it had become pleasantly tepid. Four powerful streams soaked his sides and four more hosed down onto his head. His hair was instantly drenched, and he blew the running water away from his lips and turned his face up into the spray.

Already he felt the water lapping over his feet. He closed his eyes.

The heat of the lights was less uncomfortable now that the water was sluicing his bare skin. He resisted an urge to massage his scalp with his fingertips, as he did in the shower.

The banal image of his morning shower sent a shudder through him. Was he risking such small pleasures, as well as the grand delights of life? Not only the magnificence of a life lived on the international stage, but the minor splendour of soap lathering on his skin? And a blast on his Kawasaki 1100? A decent cup of coffee?

Were these things truly valuable and, if so, why had he not thought of them till now?

They were valuable. And he must trust to Ella to restore them to him. She must realise that she would be praying for both the exalted Director Guntarson and for young, talented, life-loving Peter.

The water was at his knees. He shuffled his feet. The lights hurt his eyes and he looked down, where the lamps were reflected in the rippling tank. Rooted to his thighs in the water, he suddenly saw himself as totally, vulnerably bare. The water would reach his penis soon. It would be buoyed up, ridiculously and uncontrollably, and then it would be submerged.

Had Ella, virginal and unimaginative and uneducated and sheltered, had she any conception of what he, Peter Guntarson, was willing to sacrifice? He was laying at her feet his sexual energy, his psychic energy, his life-lust. Could he make her understand? Could he reach her?

He clenched his eyes shut and shouted in his mind, 'I am alive. I am alive. Ella, life.' His thoughts could not form the notions coherently. How could he tell her? He was beginning to panic.

He had felt this chaotic surge before. When his mother drowned, and he was diving to free her foot from the metal jaws. She had gone through this, and he had felt its echoes. And now he was experiencing it for himself.

The water touched his hips. The jets in the centre of the frames were underwater now, pumping gallons in a current into the centre of the tank.

He had to make Ella feel it too. The value of life. She had to know what she was praying for. She had to know how badly he needed his life back.

Guntarson breathed hard, hunting for words. He wanted to tell her, 'Save me! Rescue me! Turn it off! Get me out!' But the panic had not reached that frenzy yet. He would not be deflected from his purpose. He was going to die, to live again.

There was a word for it – Resurgam. I shall rise again. And she wouldn't understand that. Who would understand it? Of all the dull and witless minds that could be sacrificed, why should his brilliant, original brain be the victim? It was pointless. Did the world know what it was risking, letting him do this?

The water was at his chest. It seemed to be rising faster than ever.

Were they going to let him go through with it? The macabre circus of drooling voyeurs with their cameras and mikes and lights, closing in like a pack of wild dogs? Were they callous enough to stand and watch this, every one of them? Would not someone leap forward and shut off the taps?

The water, pitted by the power of the jets, splashed choppily at his shoulders.

No. He could not do this. No one could expect this of him.

He was getting out.

The water supported his weight as he leant back and seized the rungs of the ladder, but he had to submerge his face almost to the eyebrows in reaching it. The ankles chains held him fast.

He had to free himself. He had to get out. He was going to drown. He had to pull his feet from the steel loops.

The loops were on a ratchet. When he tugged, they tightened.

Guntarson pushed himself away from the ladder, swam upright and heaved two, lung-splitting breaths. Then he doubled up, clutching for his ankles. His frantic fingers scrabbled at the ratchets.

The hoops were biting into his flesh. There was no gap into which he could slide a fingertip, no way to prise them open. The bracelets were drawing blood – little trickles that diffused invisibly around his feet.

Brilliant light blazed in from all sides. It was like bathing in a prism. Could they see him clearly, outside? Couldn't they tell he was trying to free himself? Were they not going to rescue him now?

Guntarson plucked at the anklets till his lungs were blazing and bursting, and then he turned his efforts to the bolts. He should have tried these earlier. How secure could they be? Surely one good heave would pull them free.

He placed his feet flat on the marble, wrapped both hands round the three links at his right ankle and heaved.

He felt it give. Was the bolt loose or were the links stretching? Guntarson heaved again.

Images from his life, like flickering pictures on a broken movie reel, flashed in his mind. He saw himself at thirteen, submerged and crouching at his drowning mother's feet, tearing at the metal that held her. Screaming, 'Bend!' in his mind, 'Bend! Bend!'

And then kissing her lifeless face.

His lungs were fit to explode. He needed more air. Straightening his legs he launched himself at the surface.

The surface was no longer in his reach.

He felt the drumming water on his forehead, so the air could not be more than millimetres away. If he arched back his head, then the tip of his nose would . . .

No.

He was underwater. If he breathed out now, he would have to breathe in. And if he breathed in, he would drown.

He had to free his feet.

Guntarson doubled over again, wrapped both hands around the weakened chain and pulled to save his life.

The bolt burst out. One foot danced wildly in the water.

Now for the other. He gripped the chain and strained every muscle.

The bolt held fast.

He strained again.

The air rolled from his mouth in a great, silver bubble. His emptied lungs shrieked for air.

He must not breathe in, he must not breathe in. Dizzily, he fumbled for the chain again. His grip was much weaker now. There was not a fraction of give as he tugged fitfully.

The vacuum in his lungs overrode his mind. His mouth, angry and unwilling, gulped in water.

The water choked him, and he gasped again and again, water bursting into his nose and throat and stomach. A pain like a sword-cut sliced above his eyes.

In his panic, his hands could not even reach the bolt that held him. They found a nozzle instead, one of the four that was pumping water in under the water, and desperately his hands pushed against that, blocking the flow.

Peter Guntarson, hands, face and shoulder pressed against the side of the tank, and left foot chained to the floor, blacked out and died.

CHAPTER FORTY-EIGHT

The first face that appeared at Ella's fence as the security cordon broke was Dr Dóla's. 'Ella,' he was hissing through the links, 'Ella, your mother and Frank are here.'

Stewpot struggled to his feet. He heard Dóla's voice but he was unable to shake his eyes from the twisted, submerged corpse of Peter Guntarson. The Director would not be lifted out now. He had left instructions that he must not be touched for twelve hours, to make absolutely certain of his death.

'Ella!' shouted Dóla, for he was not alone now. The crews were with him.

There was yelling all around. 'Ella, do you think you can save him? What's your emotional state right now, Ella? Are you confident? Were you able to watch? Do you think he was trying to get free in those final seconds? Did he change his mind? Did he send you any final messages?'

Ella ignored them. They were swarming all around, shining their lights at her, blocking her sight of the Director's tank.

'Ella, can prayer really beat death? Are you certain of success? What's your state of health right now? Ella, you're no longer levitating, why's that?'

Stewpot looked around in surprise. The reporter was right. Ella was on the ground. She had not been on the ground since they brought her to Sinai.

'Ella, you're staring into space – tell us, what is it you can see? Is it heaven? Can you see heaven, Ella?'

'I'm watching his soul rise,' said Ella quietly.

'What? What was that please? Do you mind repeating that, for the benefit of viewers who might not have heard you?'

They were clawing at the chain fence now, shaking its links, making the girders rattle.

Ella said nothing more.

Stewpot leapt up. 'Can you get back, can you back off please? It's frightening in here, I don't want you scaring Ella.' He saw Dóla's face. 'Make these people give her some room,' ordered Stewpot.

'Okay, people, okay, let's relax now,' shouted Dóla, his voice high and penetrating. 'Let's remember we're in a *circle* here. We're all filming each other. All over the world, viewers are watching us, and I think we can make a better impression than this. Let's have a little discipline here. No one's going to lose out if we just cool it now. Everybody, everybody, three steps back. And another three. Yo. Well done people. Now, I'm going to call names and it'll be one question at a time.'

'What are you, Joe, Ella's agent now?'

'Okay, no, I'm not, but someone's got to take charge here. I'm Ella's mother's agent, and I think the first question we should be asking is: Ella, do you want your mother with you now?'

Ella said, 'Okay.'

'Is there a key?' Dóla muttered to Stewpot.

'If I open this gate, you don't come in,' Stewpot warned. 'Nobody comes in. Only Ella's mother. Agreed?' He waited till Juliette was close to the gate, then turned the padlock. She pushed Frank through the gap and squeezed in after him before the gate slammed shut.

Juliette knelt beside her daughter. 'Do you feel okay?'

'I feels . . . yeah. It's better.'

'Better, how?'

'Dunno. It don't feel so much pressure. In my head.'

'The pressure is gone, when?'

'Just now. When Peter . . . when his soul went up to Heaven. That's a good thing, ain't it, Mum?'

'Of course.'

Frank laid a hand on Ella's shoulder.

'He wants me to bring him back.'

'I don't think you should be doing that.'

'He wants me to say really strong prayers for him.'

'Maybe it is better where he is, Ella.'

'When's my birthday, Mum?'

'God, Ella, I don't know. Tomorrow, I think. Yes, in the morning.'

'And how old will I be?'

'Come on, Ella, you must know these things. How do I know? Sixteen. Yes, sixteen.'

'When Peter comes back, he's going to marry me.'

'Ella, he is not coming back.'

'He can come back if I prays hard enough. And we're getting married.'

'God, Ella, as if we do not already have enough problems.'

Dóla let the journalists call out a couple of questions but, when Ella ignored them, he raised his hands for hush. Most of the microphones were straining to hear the girl's conversation with her mother.

'Ella, do you want to go away?'

'No. I live here. Peter's here.'

'Not really here. Peter's in . . . Heaven now. Or wherever.'

'I'm going to bring him back here.'

'Okay, so do you want to go inside?'

'No. Like I said. I live here.'

'Not outside. It is too cold.'

Ella did not answer. Stewpot edged over. 'Ella, can we untie you? Is it safe now?'

She shrugged: 'Yeah.' Stewpot's fingers worked at the year-old knots around her waist, a waist no thicker than his wrist. Frank helped, and then he reached up and kissed his sister's face.

'Ella,' asked Juliette, 'Do you want food? Because I am hungry now.'

'You eat, Mum.'

'But you, you are so thin, you must eat.'

Frank unzipped a bag at his waist and pulled out a soft, misshapen Mars bar. It had travelled with him every stage from Florida, and secretly his hopes for Ella had been all tied up with bringing this favourite treat for her.

She took it, but she did not open it.

'I don't eat, Mum. I worked it out. If I don't eat, I don't have to throw up. It's easier.'

'You will die if you don't eat.'

'I offer her food every day, Mrs Wallis,' said Stewpot. 'Four times every day. Sometimes she drinks some water, just lately.'

Juliette ignored him. She did not like this boy taking so close an interest in her daughter.

'Ella,' called a reporter, 'would you like to talk about what's happened tonight – put it in some kind of perspective for us?'

'No,' said Ella. 'I don't want to talk about nothing.'

'Okay people, I think that's final,' called José Dóla. 'That's the first public statement you've had from this young person, I think, for almost two years, and it's time to give it a rest. Let's pay Ella the respect of taking her words at face value. She doesn't want to talk tonight.'

A bed was brought for Juliette and she tried to sleep outside, shivering, beside her daughter. Stewpot lay awake on the ground, under a blanket. He had done it many times before, under billions of glittering stars on ice-clear Arabian nights. His eyes had long learned to trace the constellations of the zodiac but this night he gazed at Ella's symbol, Ophiuchus, the thirteenth birthsign. She had been born outside the realm of conventional astrology. Stewpot had whispered to Ella sometimes, 'You're Ophiuchus, the sign of positive thinking. You can do anything if you will it.' But he had never received a flicker of recognition from her, and as months passed he had grown to accept that Ella could not respond to ideas. Only to feelings.

Stewpot stared at her constellation until it seemed the stars were linked in chains of light, and the snake-charmer Ophiuchus was moving in the heavens.

In the morning the Director's corpse was hauled from the tank. Rigor mortis had come and gone, and the body was slumped like a drunk in one corner. Tim dived down, naked but for a Speedo costume, and the cameras watched as the contours of his torso were magnified by the tank. He looped a rope under the Director's arms, so that he and Stewpot could fish the corpse out. This inglorious surfacing was broadcast live in three hundred ways, with camera crews watching the tank, watching Ella, watching Juliette and watching each other.

No provision had been made for drainage, so the disciples set up a siphon to remove the water before dismantling the glass plates.

An altar had been prepared under the December sun, so that the Director could be laid out amid purple linen and flowers. The disciples straightened his limbs and covered his loins with a fold of cloth. Flowers, flown from Cairo and arranged to form religious and mystical symbols, were placed around him. The crews were driven back, and back further, by men with dogs and the Egyptian border police.

The gate to Ella's enclosure was unlocked.

Stewpot and Juliette led her out, supporting each arm as she walked, with Frank at her back. Ella had not walked for a long time. Her legs shook. She kept her eyes on Guntarson's naked, wet, white flesh.

Four doctors stepped forward – Guntarson's own, one each from CNN and the BBC, and one a veteran of the Walls Unit in Texas, where one hundred and seven death-row executions had been carried out. Each in turn checked the corpse for a pulse, for breathing, for pupil response and for body heat. Peter Guntarson's temperature was 79.4°F. Peter Guntarson was dead.

The announcement was made: Director Guntarson was clinically dead. What now remained to be seen was whether prayers could raise the dead.

Ella stepped forward very slowly. On camera her paces were cloaked in a solemn symbolism generating tension around the globe. She did not intend this. She was simply walking towards Peter's body, and at the same time holding back. She was scared to touch him. The cold, white thing on the altar was nothing like her living Peter.

She stopped and stared intently. Her gaze was reproduced on a billion television screens. In every country there were countless believers who knew that her gaze had the power to conquer death. The world watched Ella, and believed she was willing the Director back to life.

She touched Guntarson's hand. She touched his forehead.

Peter Guntarson began to rise from his marble slab, two inches and then three.

Ella's little gasp was lost in the shrieks and yells from the throng of journalists. The guards let their dogs lunge to the longest extent of the chains, and as the animals barked and the humans roared the sound of Hell seemed suddenly to have been unleashed in the desert.

Guntarson's body sank back down, cold and white and motionless again. His doctor leapt forward and now repeated his tests – no pulse, no pupil reaction, and a foetid odour over the corpse. The doctor turned, crossing and uncrossing his arms before him until the sound subsided.

'Just air,' he called out. 'Just wind, I'm afraid. Very common in drowning victims. Air trapped in the stomach escapes and causes physical contortions easily confused with voluntary movement. Mr Guntarson is quite dead, I am afraid. Whether Miss Wallis wishes to begin her prayers now . . .'

Juliette was praying silently, a few paces away: 'God, our maker, our redeemer . . .'

Ella knelt before the altar. She still gazed at Peter's body. She could pray. She scarcely knew how to do anything else. She could pray and pray, for the rest of her life if she had to. Just kneeling here. Peter had told her, Pray and the whole of the world prays with you. She did not believe this could be true for her and only her. It must be true for everyone. When one person prayed, God heard it like the whole world was praying.

But if Peter came back to life – what then? He had promised to marry her. She knew he wouldn't want to, but she could make him want to, by keeping on and on and on. She knew she could – she had been trying, on and on, for so long now. She could do it, if she really wanted it. But then, would she have the energy to change his heart, once she had spent so much to make it beat again?

The hum of cameras had become part of the desert silence, like the hum of heat. The whole desert and the whole world saw Ella pray, without knowing she was praying for guidance – not a prayer for superhuman power over death, but a simple, human prayer of weakness, for divine help.

Ella looked at Peter, and envied him. He did not have to try at all, lying there. No questions in his head. No journalists screaming at him. No one pleading with him to eat, to pray, to talk. No need to tie him down to iron bars.

If she could have brought him back to life by trading places with him, she would. Peter living, Ella dead.

And that would be so selfish. Wasn't it wrong to envy? Worst of all to envy someone she loved. How could she love him, and wish that he had her life, just so that she could have his death?

She did love him.

She wanted to show him how deeply she loved him.

There was one way, one good way.

Not to pray.

Not to pray, not to bring him back, not to raise him up. Leave him where he was. In Heaven.

All this went through Ella's heart as she knelt, with her head bowed, for all the world a child deep in prayer.

This was an answer, an answer she heard in her heart. Maybe, she felt, it was an answer from the angels. An answer from the man who had touched her fingers as she gave him her teddy.

Ella raised her head and looked around. Mount Sinai loomed on the horizon. She whispered to her mother, 'I wants to go up there.'

The camera crews' confusion was a frenzy, and when Ella was helped into one of the Centre's LandRovers, crouched between Juliette, Frank and Stewpot, and the car had scrambled away across the desert in a plume of dust, the frenzy focussed on Joe Dóla. Where was Ella going, why was she going, what was the problem, did the Director have a chance now, had it all gone terribly wrong, had Ella ever believed she could raise the dead, was it blasphemous, was it impossible, was it planned, would she return, would she live with her mother now, were her powers gone without Guntarson, was that why she'd stopped levitating, had Guntarson failed to realise in time, had he guessed at the last minute, had Ella tricked him, what now? What now?

And Joe Dóla simply didn't know. But he thought time would tell, and he was sure Ella would be living with Juliette, who was of course his client, and he was quite sure that at some later date he would be able to organise some interviews which would put the whole thing straight. And in the meantime, perhaps they should be following that LandRover.

Tim had driven the LandRover along the track onto the mountain as high as he could, but the ascent beyond the monastery could only be achieved on foot. Generations of monks had hewn 3,750 steps into the Sinai stone, from St Catherine's to an ampitheatre known as the Seven Elders of Israel. From the Seven Elders 750 steps rise further, to the Chapel of the Holy Trinity on the very peak of the mountain. This was the path Ella wanted to climb.

Stewpot, looping a video camera around his neck, said, 'Shall I carry you?'

'I can walk,' Ella said. 'I'm all right. Honest. Let me go, on my own. Ahead a bit.' And she did, with a strength and litheness in her legs that astonished Stewpot. He had never seen her move faster than a hobble – and for a year she had not walked at all. But now she surged ahead of him and Tim, and left Juliette wheezing behind them. Her light step was filled with life, and only Frank could keep up with her.

Stewpot was obeying an impulse when he switched on the camera. There was a purpose in her rapid steps which he could not divine, but the mystery of it thrilled him. Here was Ella, doing her own thing. Ella, taking control. He had to record this, though he struggled to keep his footing with one eye against the view-finder.

Folds of brown rock hung down to the desert floor like a curtain that hid the next world as they climbed higher, two thousand feet, then four. On this mountain, through a crack in the rocks, God had permitted Moses to snatch a glimpse of His back.

Juliette toiled far behind, Tim at her side. The sun was no less fierce at this altitude, and the air was much sparser. Two or three camera crews, scuffling dangerously for the straightest shot, were close on Juliette's paces, but Ella was almost too far ahead to be seen. Her brisk, feather-weight figure all but flew from step to stone step, and with each one the distance between her and her pursuers increased.

Two arches straddled the path, the Gate of St Stephen and the Gate of the Law. And at the second of these pairs of high pillars, Ella stopped and reached out to her brother. The light around their hands sparked and burned as their fingers entwined for a moment.

Frank broke the grip and stepped back, tears glistening on his face. And Ella turned suddenly and began to climb up from the path.

Stewpot, though he was nearly running, had lagged twenty yards behind. He tried to keep the video on her as she scrambled up the ragged rocks above the steps. Her grip was strong and her footholds were certain. This weakling mountaineer seemed to have no fear that she might slip.

Stewpot called after her, 'Where are you going? Ella! What's up there? Am I supposed to follow?'

Ella motioned him with a wave of her arm to stay on the path. She stretched out one leg onto the flat top of the Gate of the Law, pulled herself across, and drew herself upright on its peak. The mountain lunged downwards around her.

And quite suddenly, she stepped out. Into the air.

Juliette in the distance screamed, and screamed. But Ella fell without a sound.

Her body was not recovered. It was never found. There was some conjecture that it might be wedged into the cliffs, invisible behind a tongue of rock. Or that, light as a feather, it had been borne away by the air currents, drawn into a secret, unknown cavern. Many said her body, like St Catherine's two millennia before, had been carried up to Heaven by messengers from God. Or that her bones had simply been so delicate that the wind and dust had disintegrated and dissolved them.

One camera had glimpsed her fall. For an instant of video, she did not seem to be falling but flying forwards. Ella soared out of shot in less than a second, one second which was pinpointed on the computerised clock of the camera. The digits were burned into the upper right corner of the image – 11:11:11.

Each frame was analysed in laboratories on every continent. The last frame was different to those before it. Ella seemed to be encased in a crystal of light. Fine golden bars described five clear walls around her, tapering to a point at her head and her feet. Some scientists tried to demonstrate how sunlight refracting on the video lens could create the effect. Others called the crystal a key, a key that fitted the locks of heaven.

Some cynics said she must have levitated to safety. Many devout admirers believed her body had ceased to exist in this world, that it had dematerialised, flickering into another dimension, and that one day she would return when the world needed her most.

Stewpot had seen her fall. And ever after, he always said that at the instant Ella Wallis walked off the path, she grew wings and flew into the void as an angel.

'For with the Lord there is mercy, and with him is plenteous redemption.'

                                                              Psalms, 130, v. 7

'Now faith is the substance of things hoped for, the evidence of things not seen.'

                                                              Hebrews, 11, v. 1

AUTHOR'S NOTE

Where I could not draw on personal experience for my descriptions of paranormal phenomena, I investigated detailed sources.

- One of the most absorbing was the Jesuit priest Herbert Thurston's collection of monographs, *The Physical Phenomena Of Mysticism* (Burns Oates, 1951). Beginning with dozens of accounts of levitation, he proceeds to describe all sorts of weird and very wonderful things in detail. Each chapter is more incredible than the last, and all are based on reliable evidence from first-rate witnesses. The phenomenon of Ella's halo is developed from here.
- The best, and quite convincing, descriptions of levitation are recorded in Madame Home's rose-tinted biography of her husband: *DD Home, His Life And Mission*, edited by Sir Arthur Conan Doyle (Kegan Paul, Trench, Trubner and Co, 1921).
- Another fine reference work is Nandor Fodor's *An Encyclopaedia of Psychic Science* (first published 1934; my copy was reprinted by Citadel Press, Secaucus, New Jersey, 1966). And there is a story with this book which you might find hard to believe, because I can scarcely believe it myself.

On the night I finished writing *Ella*, I sat back in my chair and reached out for something to read. My hand fell on Fodor's encyclopedia. Perhaps because I had just completed my own book, I turned to the last page and for the first time I read Fodor's final entry. It concerned a pubescent girl in Rumania after the Great War, who became the centre of a poltergeist phenomenon. Objects moved and flew around her, and stigmata appeared – her hands, feet and face bled, as though she were suffering the same wounds Christ suffered at His crucifixion.

Her family and neighbours believed she was possessed by the devil, and incarcerated her in an asylum. When her first menstrual period occurred, the psychic phenomena vanished completely.

And her name? Her name was Ella – to be precise, Eleonore Zügun.

- The power of prayer is finally attracting serious scientific interest, with clinical trials currently being conducted in the USA to determine whether patients heal more quickly when prayers are said for them. In a CNN report on September 11, 1997, Dr Herbert Benson of Harvard Medical School in Boston, USA, voiced his opinion that belief itself could heal.

- In the October 1997 issue of The International Journal of Psychiatry In Medicine, Dr Harold Koenig revealed a link between good church-going and good health. His study of more than 1,700 people in North Carolina showed sixty per cent went to church at least once a week – and they were twice as likely to have strong immune systems as their less Godly neighbours. Dr Koenig concluded: 'There's a lot of negative stuff said about religion, but there may be a lot of benefits to it in terms of mental and physical health.'

- Psychokinesis tests on random number generators carried out at Princeton University, New Jersey, by Professor Robert Jahn in 1997, proved conclusively that ordinary people could cause certain numbers to recur – simply by concentrating their thoughts on the computer. Thousands of the mindpower experiments using hundreds of subjects were monitored. 'It seems to be a common ability,' said Professor Jahn. The chances against achieving Jahn's results by fluke were calculated at one in 1,000 billion.

- Psalm 130, the De Profundis, an extract from which closes Ella's story, is one of the most beautiful and resonating passages in the entire Bible. The Book of Psalms is a collection of prayers, holy to Jews and Christians alike. My encyclopedia describes Psalm 130 as an appeal for divine mercy and purity of heart, very movingly inspired in the certainty that God will hear and answer. Nothing could more succinctly describe the spirit of Ella, yet I chose the quotation without forethought: my Bible fell open at that page and my eye lit upon that verse.

- Some of my books and lots of other incredibly interesting information and pictures are available on my two Internet web-sites. One is at **http:www.tcom.co.uk/hpnet/** where you will find my biography and more personal items relating to me and my work. For more fascinating information and games, visit also **http:www.urigeller.com**

- If you experienced any extraordinary psychic, paranormal, synchronous, deja vu-type or just plain strange event while you were reading this book, I want to know about it. Write to me, c/o Headline, 338 Euston Road, London NW1 3BH, United Kingdom.

- And lastly, after reading Ella, the number eleven could come up many times in your life in different forms. Your attention will be drawn to clocks and watches at exactly 11:11, 11:01, 10:11, 10:10,

10:01 and 1:01. The whole world will be looking at 11.11 am Greenwich Mean Time on August 11, 1999 – that is the moment of a total solar eclipse. It is my opinion and feeling that the endless recurrence of the number eleven represents some kind of a positive connection or a gateway to the mysteries of the universe. And beyond . . .